image® comics presents

SKULL KICKERS

SIX SHOOTER on the SEVEN SEAS

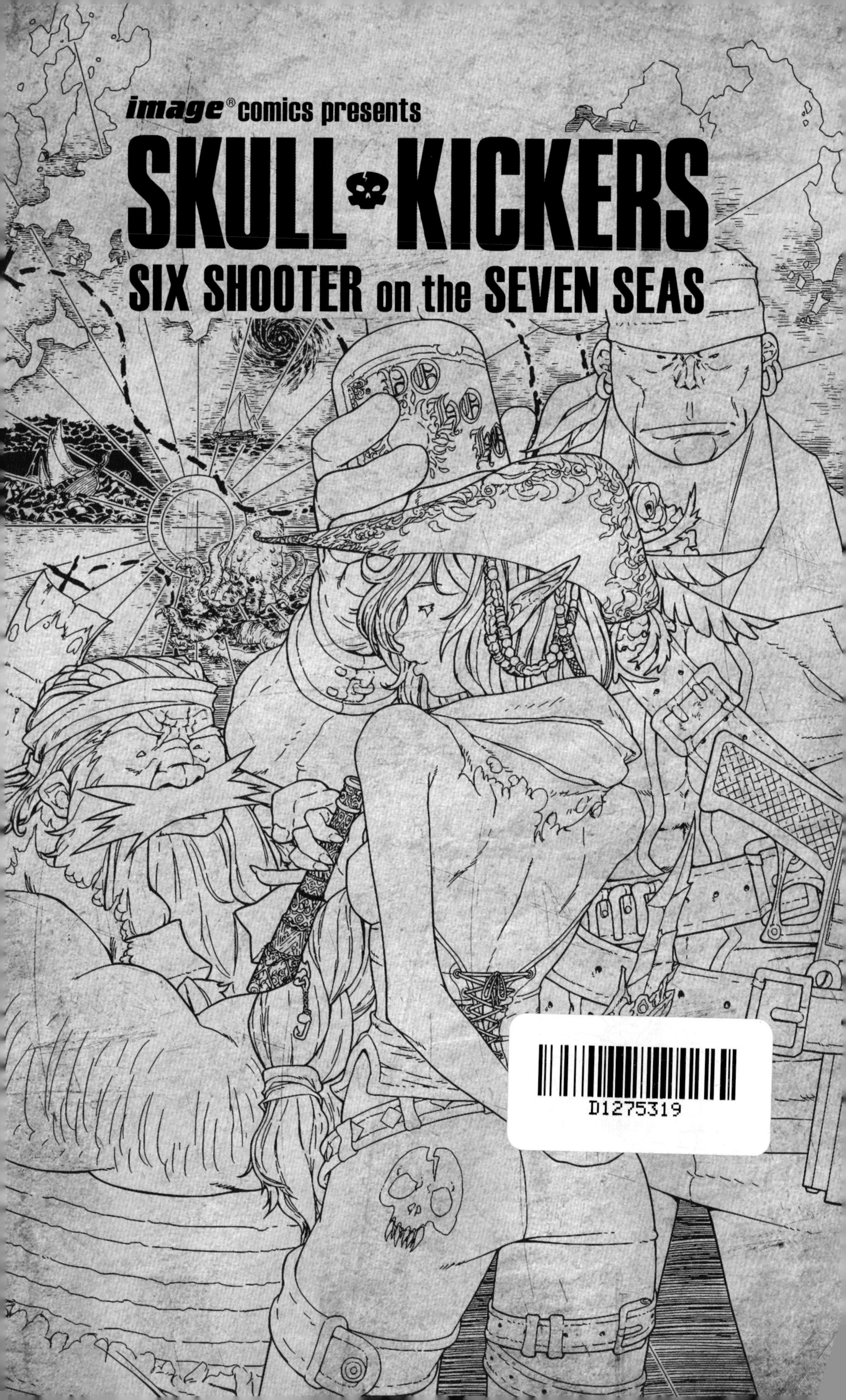

IMAGE COMICS, INC.

Robert Kirkman - chief operating officer
Erik Larsen - chief financial officer
Todd McFarlane - president
Marc Silvestri - chief executive officer
Jim Valentino - vice-president

Eric Stephenson - publisher
Ron Richards - director of business development
Jennifer de Guzman - pr & marketing director
Branwyn Bigglestone - accounts manager
Emily Miller - accounting assistant
Jamie Parreno - marketing assistant
Emilio Bautista - sales assistant
Susie Giroux - administrative assistant
Kevin Yuen - digital rights coordinator
Tyler Shainline - events coordinator
David Brothers - content manager
Jonathan Chan - production manager
Drew Gill - art director
Jana Cook - print manager
Monica Garcia - senior production artist
Vincent Kukua - production artist
Jenna Savage - production artist
www.imagecomics.com

SKULLKICKERS VOLUME 3
ISBN: 978-1-60706-612-5
Second Printing

Published by Image Comics, Inc. Office of publication: 2134 Allston Way, 2nd Floor, Berkeley, California 94704. Copyright © 2013 JIM ZUBKAVICH. Originally published in single magazine form as SKULLKICKERS #12-17. All rights reserved. SKULLKICKERS™ (including all prominent characters featured herein), its logo and all character likenesses are trademarks of JIM ZUBKAVICH, unless otherwise noted. Image Comics® and its logos are registered trademarks and copyrights of Image Comics, Inc. All rights reserved. No part of this publication may be reproduced or transmitted, in any form or by any means (except for short excerpts for review purposes) without the express written permission of Image Comics, Inc. All names, characters, events and locales in this publication are entirely fictional. Any resemblance to actual persons (living or dead), events or places, without satiric intent, is coincidental.

International Rights Representative:
foreignlicensing@imagecomics.com

PRINTED IN SOUTH KOREA.

Writer
JIM ZUB

Pencils
EDWIN HUANG

Inks
EDWIN HUANG
KEVIN RAGANIT

Colors
MISTY COATS
ROSS A. CAMPBELL
MIKE LUCKAS

Color Flatting
LUDWIG OLIMBA

Lettering
MARSHALL DILLON

"Tavern Tales" Writers
JIM DEMONAKOS
KYLE STEVENS
HOWARD TAYLER
ZACH WEINER
JIM ZUB

"Tavern Tales" Artists
JOE NG
ESPEN GRUNDETJERN
MIKE LUCKAS
BEN McSWEENEY
JIM ZUB

Issue Covers
SAEJIN OH

Trade Cover
EDWIN HUANG
ESPEN GRUNDETJERN

Graphic Design
VINCENT KUKUA
JIM ZUB

Skullkickers Logo
STEVEN FINCH

Skullkickers
Created by
JIM ZUB
CHRIS STEVENS

check us out online
www.skullkickers.com

Special Thanks
STEVE JACKSON
STACY KING
SCOTT KURTZ
PHIL REED
STRONGBOW

Skullkickers as a Creative Business

I really like **Skullkickers**. But clearly so do you, or you wouldn't be reading the third collection, let alone the intro to the third collection. So I'm not going to talk about the story. You probably know the story by now. Well, you think you do. Nothing you know now will prepare you for this book. And I'm not giving any spoilers. Arrrrrr!

Instead, I'm going to talk about the business of creativity, with Jim Zub as my example.

Note that word **business**. If you think that means "selling out to the Man," quit reading now, because I'm only going to make you cry. I mean business as in "Follow your passion so awesomely that people **pay** you to keep doing it, and so well that you can **keep** doing it on what they pay you."

Jim did things right. And if your own passion is any kind of writing, or any kind of art, or any kind of media at all... even non-geeky media... pay attention!

To start with, Jim didn't try to do it all himself. He built a team. (Pretend I wrote another 300 words explaining how smart that is.) And he published with Image and retained the creative rights. (Pretend another 300 words, maybe 3,000.)

So **Skullkickers** was launched. The critics said it was smart and the fans said it was fun. Then Jim asked a good question. "Does this property have a future outside comics?"

He did another good business thing. He got an agent. I'd worked with Surge Licensing on Axe Cop and I respect them (in fact, they represent me now on **Illuminati**, but that's a different story). Surge pitched **Skullkickers** to me for **Munchkin,** our million-plus-selling card game parody of dungeon-crawling RPGs.

I read the comic, and I looked at a proposal that I otherwise wouldn't have. This is what an agent can do for you.

Still... I didn't quite get it. The theme was perfect for Munchkin, the art was great... but for whatever reason, it wasn't quite hitting my A-list.

Meanwhile, Jim was doing the smartest thing of all. He was working his butt off, going to conventions, meeting fans, meeting other pros. Trading ideas, learning how to make a business work, networking. Making connections. Including Howard Tayler, who writes and draws **Schlock Mercenary**, which I read daily, usually as soon as it posts.

And Howard, with no idea that I had a **Skullkickers** proposal on my desk, invited me and Jim to lunch at GenCon. It was a good lunch. I know "Be a nice guy" is easier said than done, but trust me, it makes deals. It made this one. Jim seemed like the kind of guy I wanted to work with. Simple as that.

In one afternoon, I went from "Well, it's a possible," to "I want to do this." At that point, card ideas started falling into place, like the running gag with the panicked villagers. And we did it, and the **Skullkickers** property moved beyond comics.

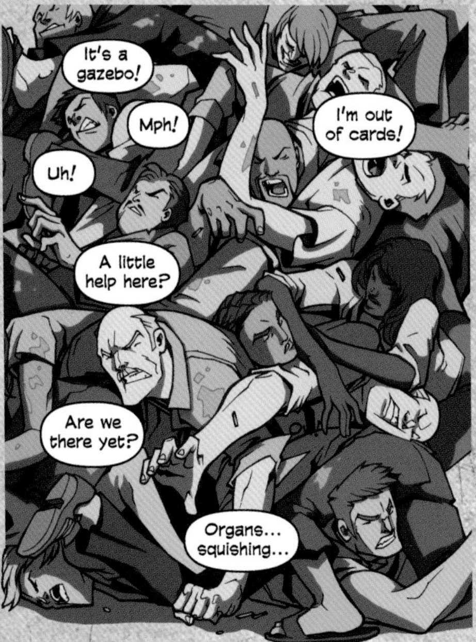
It's a gazebo!
Mph!
I'm out of cards!
Uh!
A little help here?
Are we there yet?
Organs... squishing...

So... as you enjoy the comic, be happy the creator works hard at the business of creation and is good at it. That gives Shorty and Baldy better odds of kicking monster skulls for years to come.

– Steve Jackson
August 2012

Steve Jackson has been designing games for more than 30 years and has no plans to stop. His creations include Munchkin, Illuminati, the GURPS roleplaying system, Ogre, and Zombie Dice. He is a citizen of the Internet, or a Texan, depending on who's asking.

CHAPTER ONE

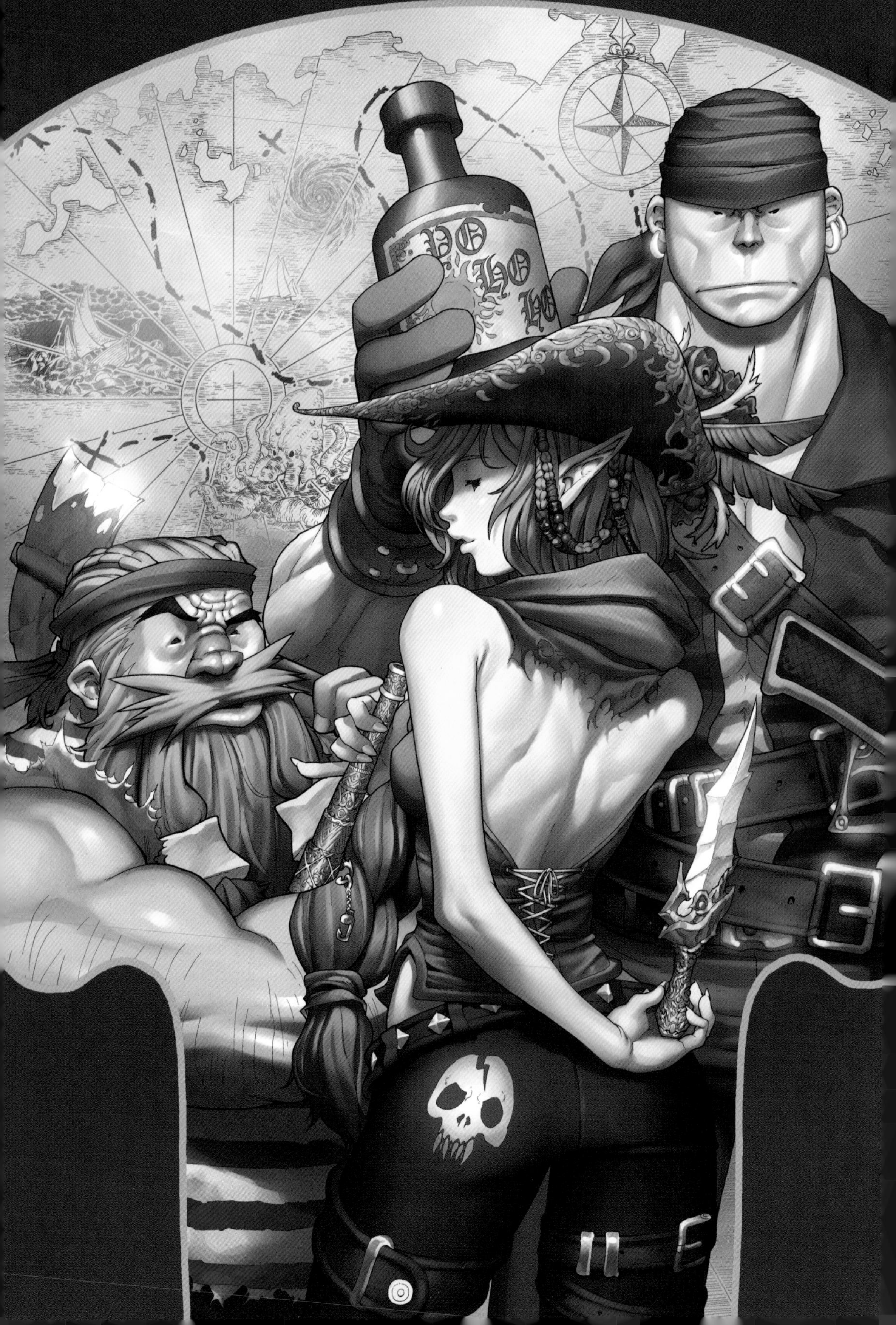
YO HO HO

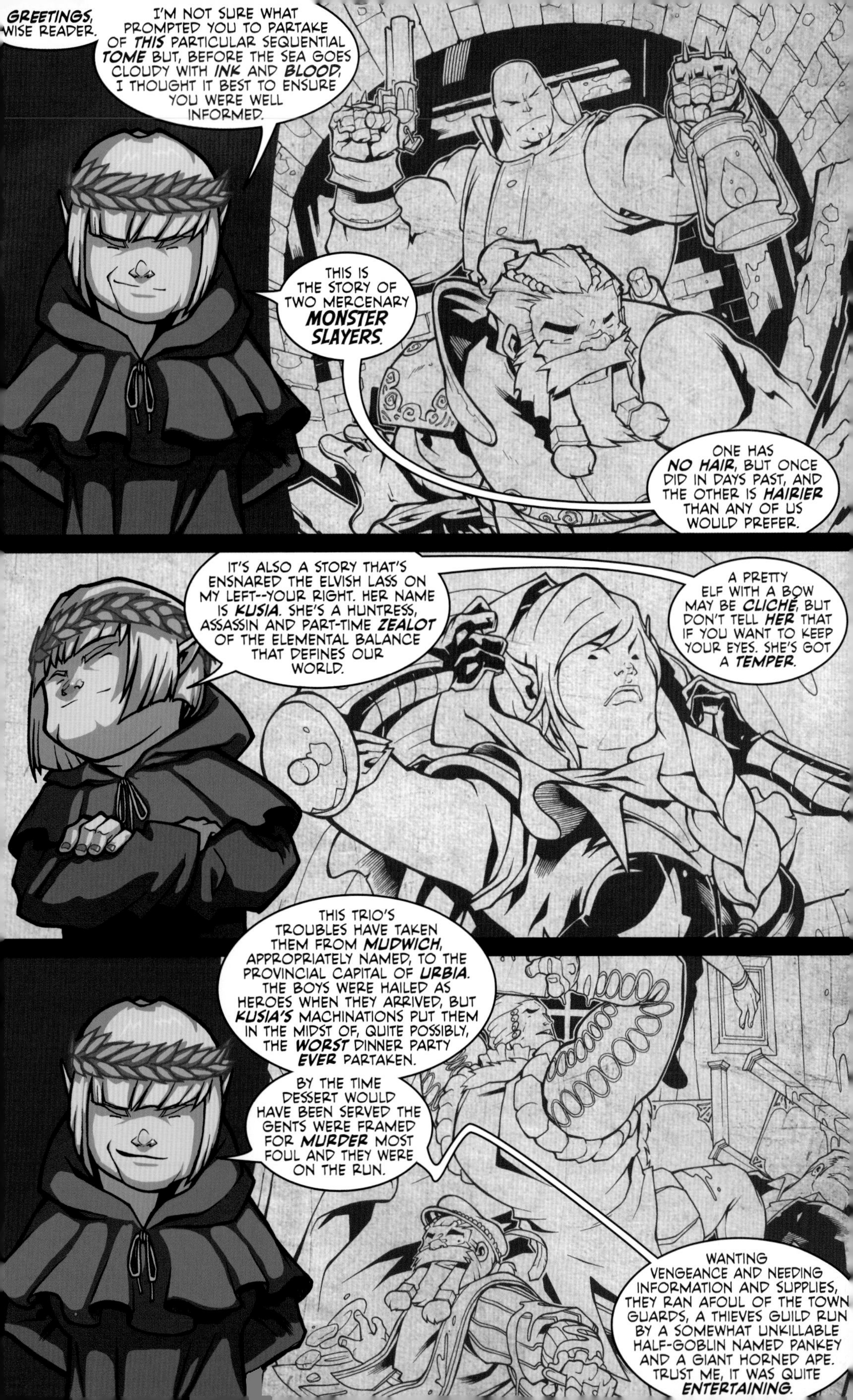
GREETINGS, WISE READER.
I'M NOT SURE WHAT PROMPTED YOU TO PARTAKE OF THIS PARTICULAR SEQUENTIAL TOME BUT, BEFORE THE SEA GOES CLOUDY WITH INK AND BLOOD, I THOUGHT IT BEST TO ENSURE YOU WERE WELL INFORMED.
THIS IS THE STORY OF TWO MERCENARY MONSTER SLAYERS.
ONE HAS NO HAIR, BUT ONCE DID IN DAYS PAST, AND THE OTHER IS HAIRIER THAN ANY OF US WOULD PREFER.
IT'S ALSO A STORY THAT'S ENSNARED THE ELVISH LASS ON MY LEFT--YOUR RIGHT. HER NAME IS KUSIA. SHE'S A HUNTRESS, ASSASSIN AND PART-TIME ZEALOT OF THE ELEMENTAL BALANCE THAT DEFINES OUR WORLD.
A PRETTY ELF WITH A BOW MAY BE CLICHÉ, BUT DON'T TELL HER THAT IF YOU WANT TO KEEP YOUR EYES. SHE'S GOT A TEMPER.
THIS TRIO'S TROUBLES HAVE TAKEN THEM FROM MUDWICH, APPROPRIATELY NAMED, TO THE PROVINCIAL CAPITAL OF URBIA. THE BOYS WERE HAILED AS HEROES WHEN THEY ARRIVED, BUT KUSIA'S MACHINATIONS PUT THEM IN THE MIDST OF, QUITE POSSIBLY, THE WORST DINNER PARTY EVER PARTAKEN.
BY THE TIME DESSERT WOULD HAVE BEEN SERVED THE GENTS WERE FRAMED FOR MURDER MOST FOUL AND THEY WERE ON THE RUN.
WANTING VENGEANCE AND NEEDING INFORMATION AND SUPPLIES, THEY RAN AFOUL OF THE TOWN GUARDS, A THIEVES GUILD RUN BY A SOMEWHAT UNKILLABLE HALF-GOBLIN NAMED PANKEY AND A GIANT HORNED APE. TRUST ME, IT WAS QUITE ENTERTAINING.

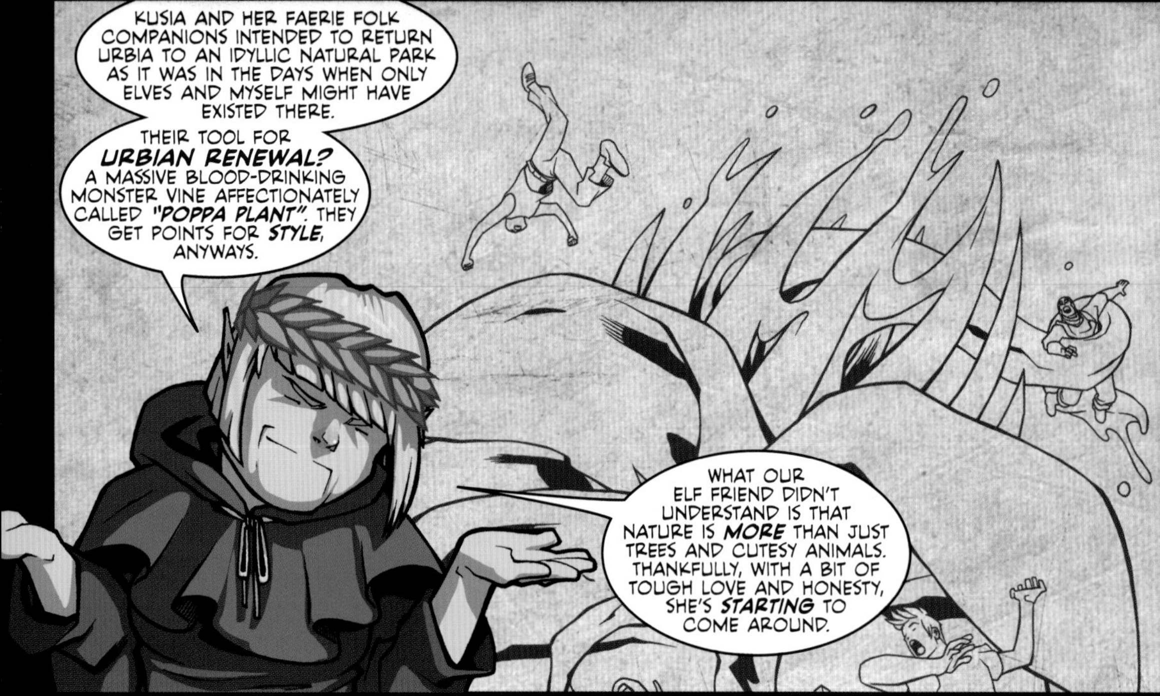
KUSIA AND HER FAERIE FOLK COMPANIONS INTENDED TO RETURN URBIA TO AN IDYLLIC NATURAL PARK AS IT WAS IN THE DAYS WHEN ONLY ELVES AND MYSELF MIGHT HAVE EXISTED THERE.
THEIR TOOL FOR ***URBIAN RENEWAL?*** A MASSIVE BLOOD-DRINKING MONSTER VINE AFFECTIONATELY CALLED ***"POPPA PLANT"***. THEY GET POINTS FOR ***STYLE***, ANYWAYS.
WHAT OUR ELF FRIEND DIDN'T UNDERSTAND IS THAT NATURE IS ***MORE*** THAN JUST TREES AND CUTESY ANIMALS. THANKFULLY, WITH A BIT OF TOUGH LOVE AND HONESTY, SHE'S ***STARTING*** TO COME AROUND.

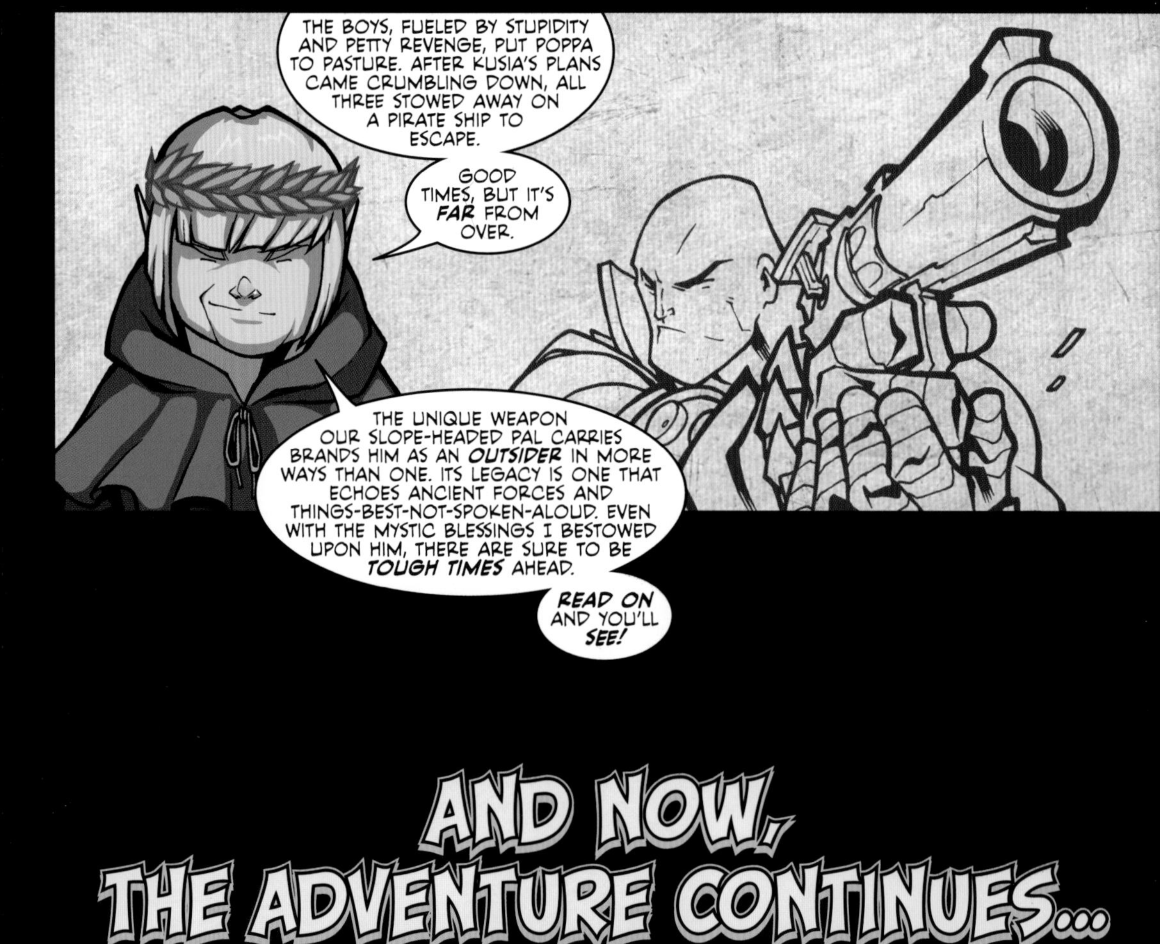
THE BOYS, FUELED BY STUPIDITY AND PETTY REVENGE, PUT POPPA TO PASTURE. AFTER KUSIA'S PLANS CAME CRUMBLING DOWN, ALL THREE STOWED AWAY ON A PIRATE SHIP TO ESCAPE.
GOOD TIMES, BUT IT'S ***FAR*** FROM OVER.
THE UNIQUE WEAPON OUR SLOPE-HEADED PAL CARRIES BRANDS HIM AS AN ***OUTSIDER*** IN MORE WAYS THAN ONE. ITS LEGACY IS ONE THAT ECHOES ANCIENT FORCES AND THINGS-BEST-NOT-SPOKEN-ALOUD. EVEN WITH THE MYSTIC BLESSINGS I BESTOWED UPON HIM, THERE ARE SURE TO BE ***TOUGH TIMES*** AHEAD.
READ ON AND YOU'LL ***SEE!***

AND NOW, THE ADVENTURE CONTINUES...

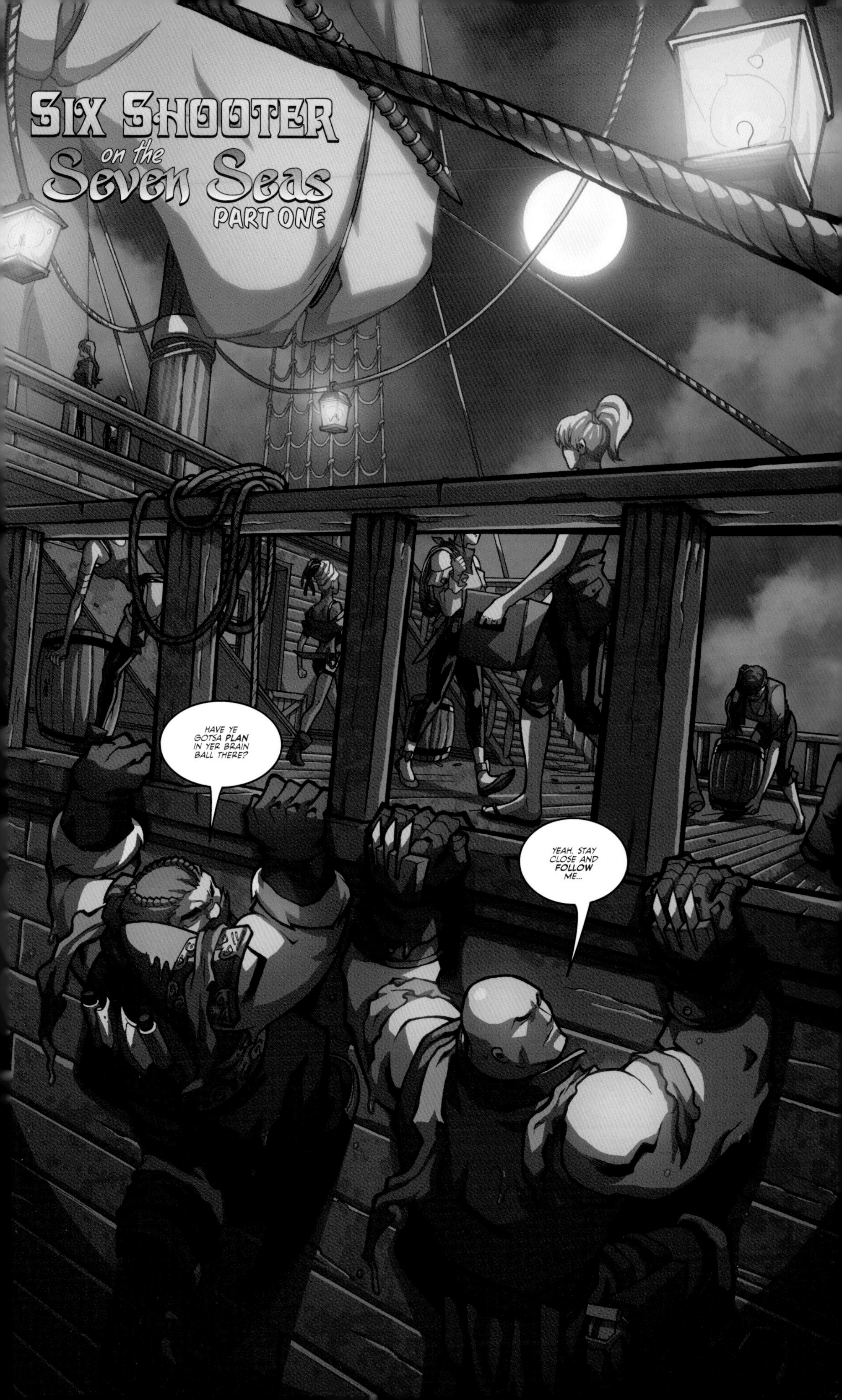
SIX SHOOTER on the Seven Seas
PART ONE
HAVE YE GOTSA PLAN IN YER BRAIN BALL THERE?
YEAH. STAY CLOSE AND FOLLOW ME...

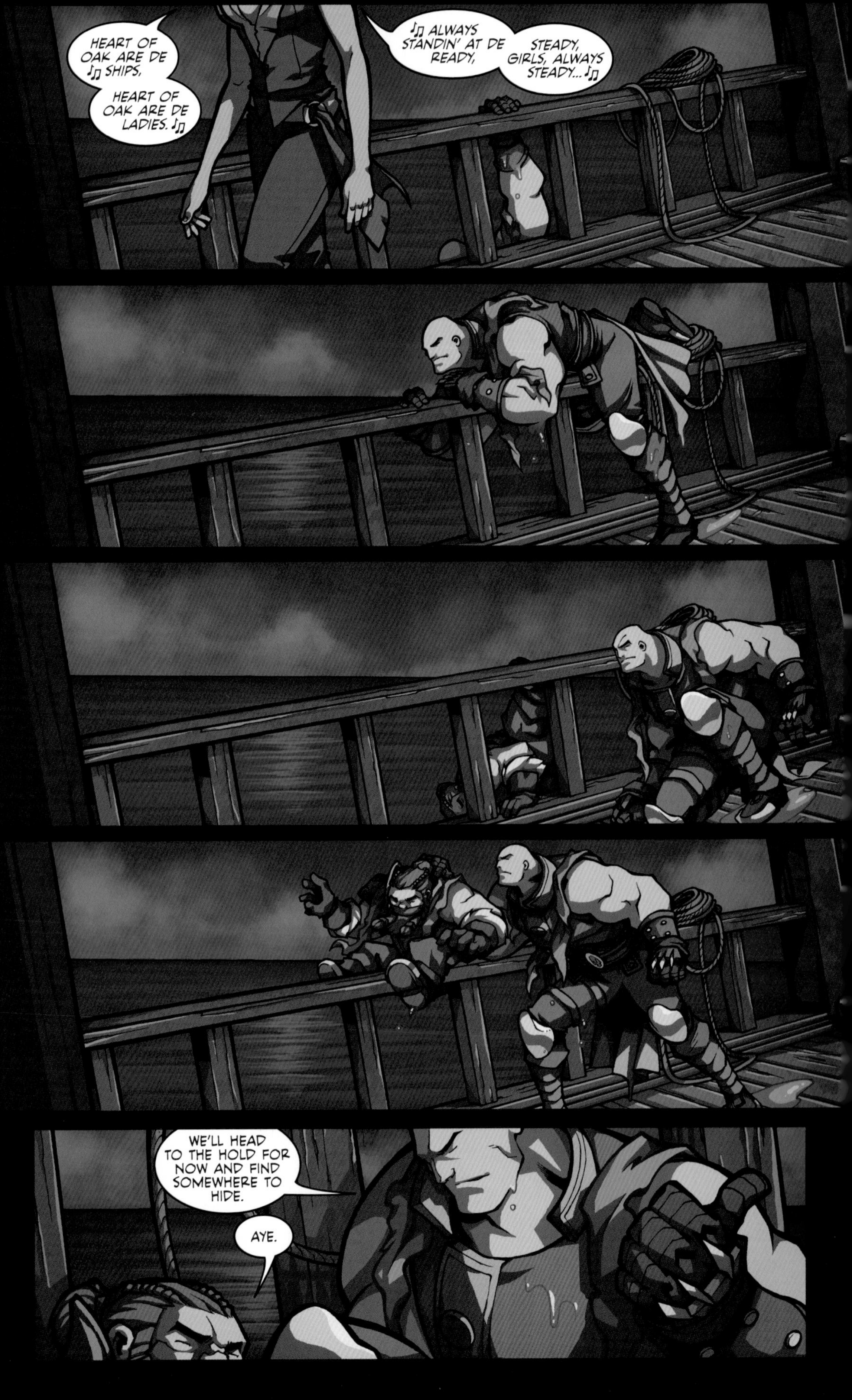
HEART OF OAK ARE DE ♪♫ SHIPS,
HEART OF OAK ARE DE LADIES. ♪♫
♪♫ ALWAYS STANDIN' AT DE READY,
STEADY, GIRLS, ALWAYS STEADY... ♪♫
WE'LL HEAD TO THE HOLD FOR NOW AND FIND SOMEWHERE TO HIDE.
AYE.

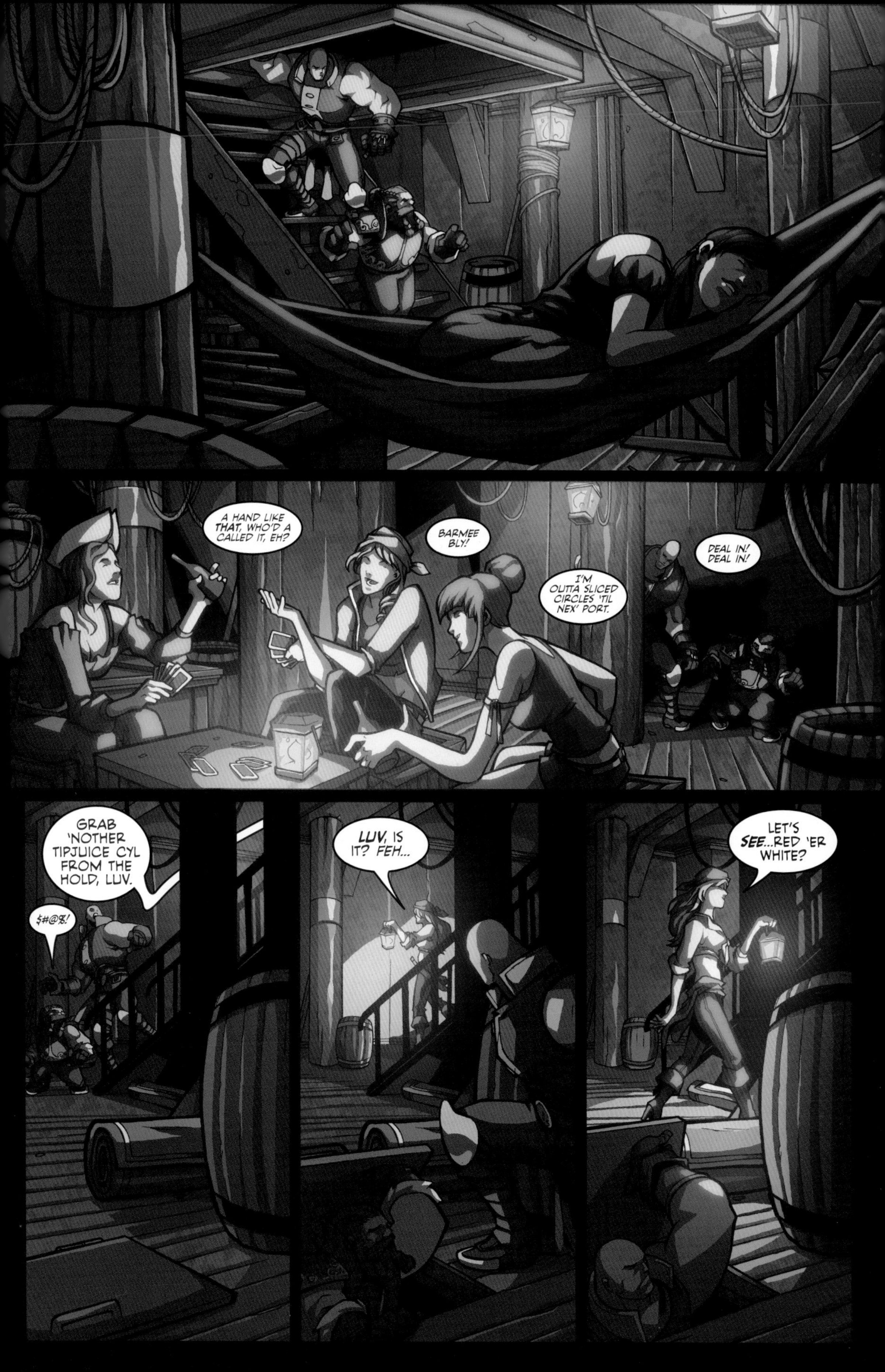
A HAND LIKE THAT, WHO'D A CALLED IT, EH?
BARMEE BLY!
I'M OUTTA SLICED CIRCLES 'TIL NEX' PORT.
DEAL IN! DEAL IN!
GRAB 'NOTHER TIPJUICE CYL FROM THE HOLD, LUV.
$#@%!
LUV, IS IT? FEH...
LET'S SEE...RED 'ER WHITE?

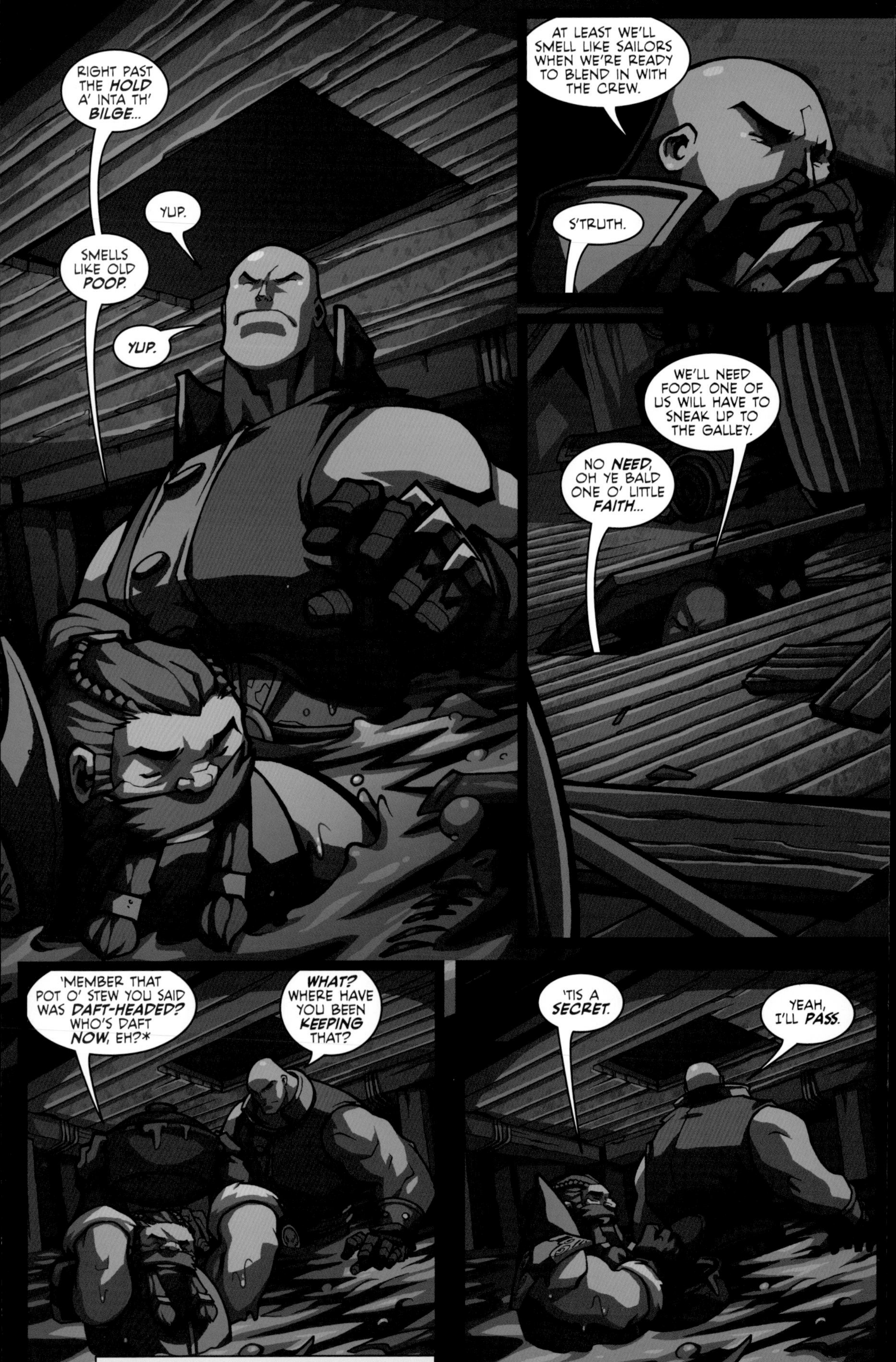
RIGHT PAST THE HOLD A' INTA TH' BILGE...
YUP.
SMELLS LIKE OLD POOP.
YUP.
AT LEAST WE'LL SMELL LIKE SAILORS WHEN WE'RE READY TO BLEND IN WITH THE CREW.
S'TRUTH.
WE'LL NEED FOOD. ONE OF US WILL HAVE TO SNEAK UP TO THE GALLEY.
NO NEED, OH YE BALD ONE O' LITTLE FAITH...
'MEMBER THAT POT O' STEW YOU SAID WAS DAFT-HEADED? WHO'S DAFT NOW, EH?*
WHAT? WHERE HAVE YOU BEEN KEEPING THAT?
'TIS A SECRET.
YEAH, I'LL PASS.

*IN THE SHIPYARD MARKET FROM SKULLKICKERS VOL. 2

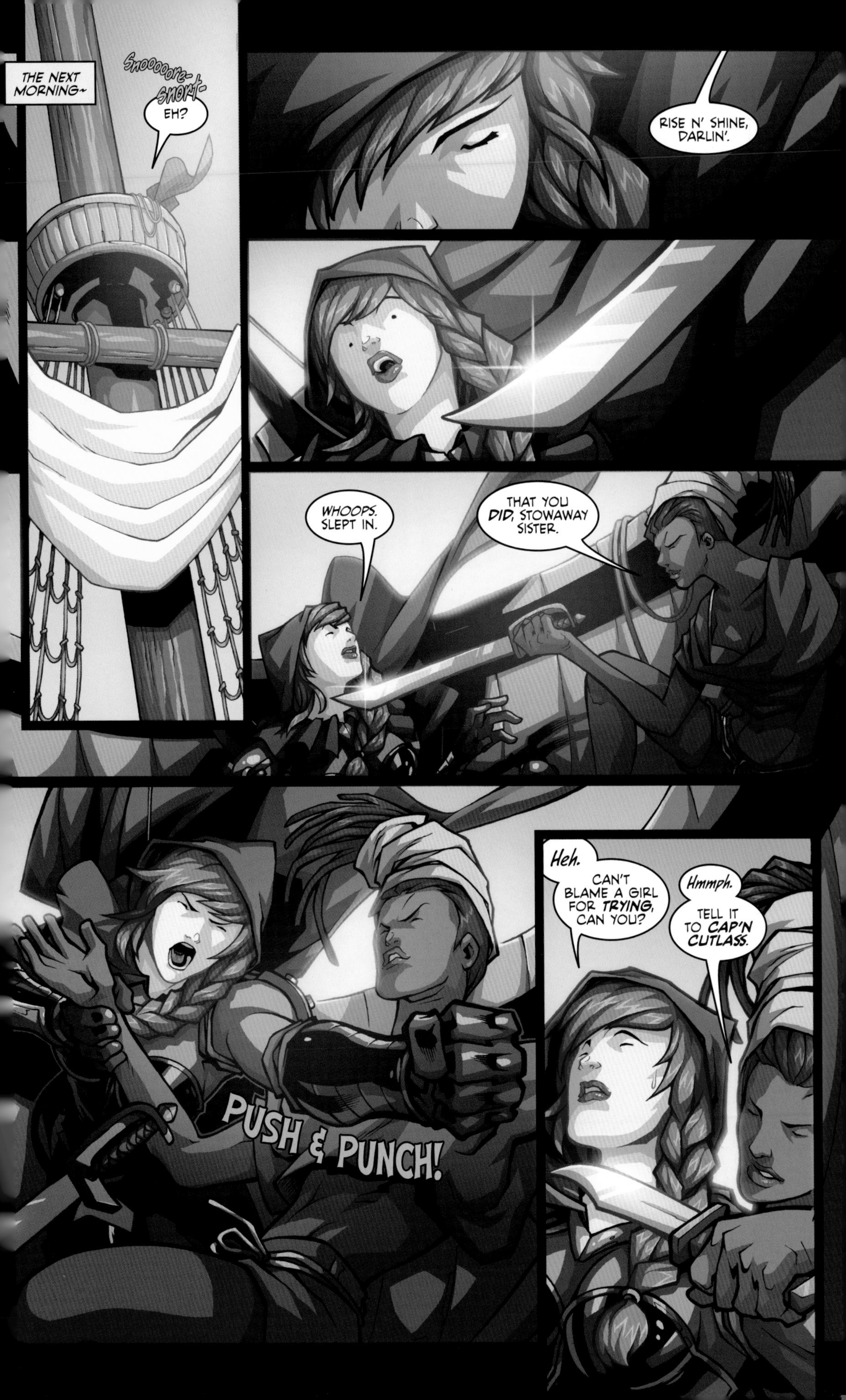
THE NEXT MORNING~
Snoooore-snort-
EH?
RISE N' SHINE, DARLIN'.
WHOOPS. SLEPT IN.
THAT YOU DID, STOWAWAY SISTER.
PUSH & PUNCH!
Heh.
CAN'T BLAME A GIRL FOR TRYING, CAN YOU?
Hmmph.
TELL IT TO CAP'N CUTLASS.

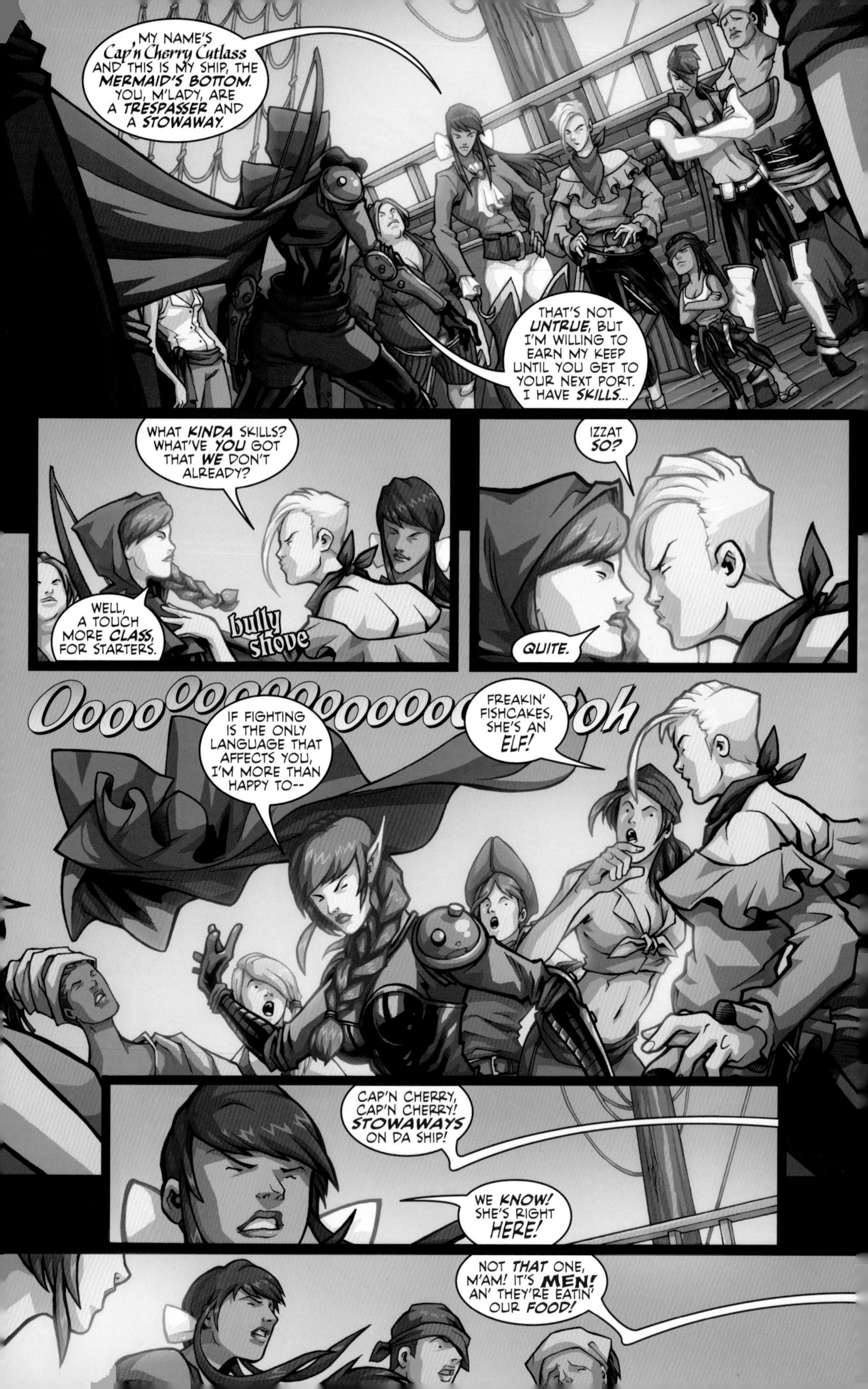
MY NAME'S Cap'n Cherry Cutlass AND THIS IS MY SHIP, THE MERMAID'S BOTTOM. YOU, M'LADY, ARE A TRESPASSER AND A STOWAWAY.
THAT'S NOT UNTRUE, BUT I'M WILLING TO EARN MY KEEP UNTIL YOU GET TO YOUR NEXT PORT. I HAVE SKILLS...
WHAT KINDA SKILLS? WHAT'VE YOU GOT THAT WE DON'T ALREADY?
WELL, A TOUCH MORE CLASS, FOR STARTERS.
bully shove
IZZAT SO?
QUITE.
Oooooooooooooooooooh
IF FIGHTING IS THE ONLY LANGUAGE THAT AFFECTS YOU, I'M MORE THAN HAPPY TO--
FREAKIN' FISHCAKES, SHE'S AN ELF!
CAP'N CHERRY, CAP'N CHERRY! STOWAWAYS ON DA SHIP!
WE KNOW! SHE'S RIGHT HERE!
NOT THAT ONE, M'AM! IT'S MEN! AN' THEY'RE EATIN' OUR FOOD!

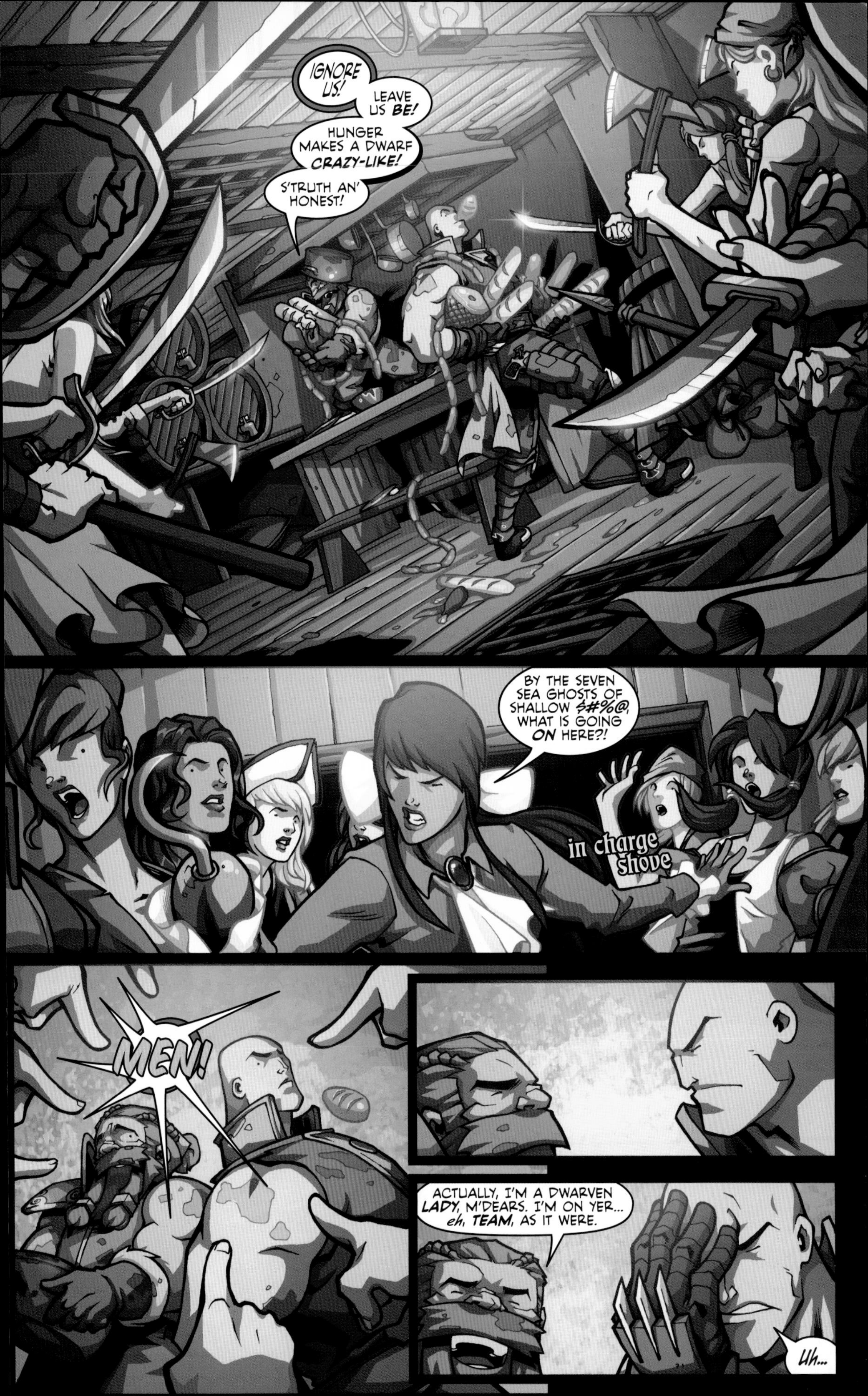
IGNORE US!
LEAVE US BE!
HUNGER MAKES A DWARF CRAZY-LIKE!
S'TRUTH AN' HONEST!
BY THE SEVEN SEA GHOSTS OF SHALLOW $#%@, WHAT IS GOING ON HERE?!
in charge shove
MEN!
ACTUALLY, I'M A DWARVEN LADY, M'DEARS. I'M ON YER... eh, TEAM, AS IT WERE.
Uh...

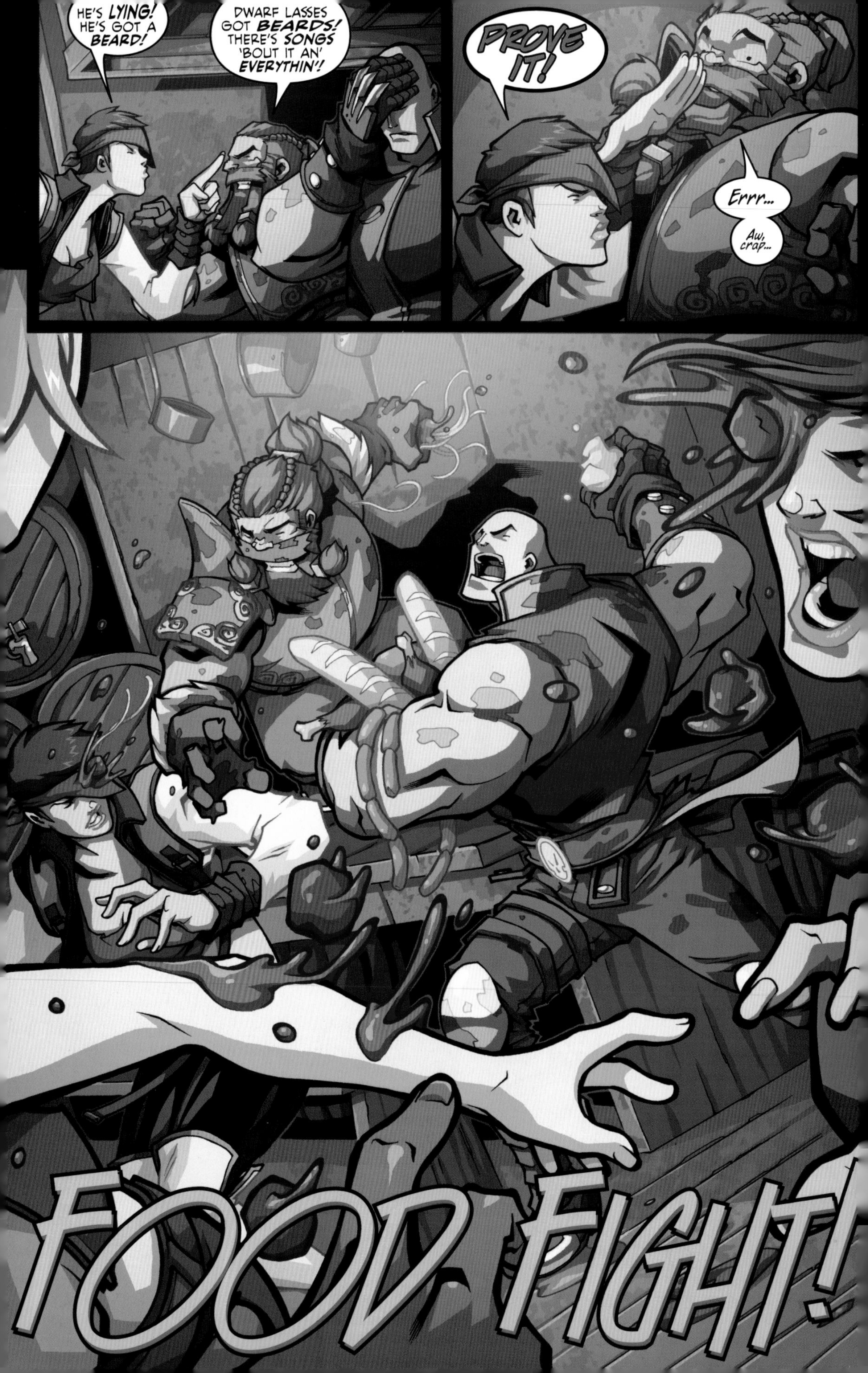
HE'S LYING! HE'S GOT A BEARD!
DWARF LASSES GOT BEARDS! THERE'S SONGS 'BOUT IT AN' EVERYTHIN'!
PROVE IT!
Errr...
Aw, crap...
FOOD FIGHT!

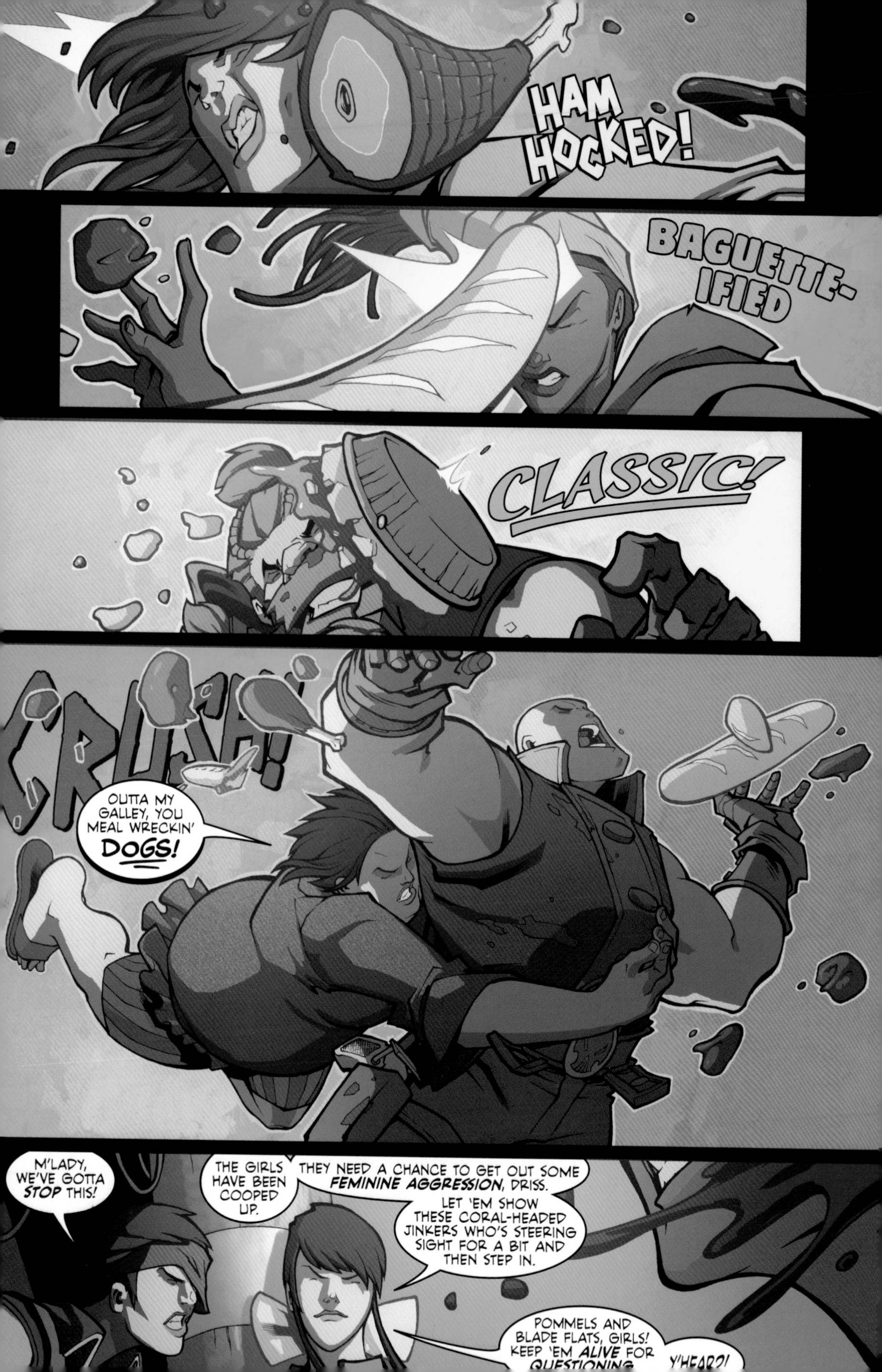
HAM HOCKED!
BAGUETTE-IFIED
CLASSIC!
OUTTA MY GALLEY, YOU MEAL WRECKIN' DOGS!
M'LADY, WE'VE GOTTA STOP THIS!
THE GIRLS HAVE BEEN COOPED UP.
THEY NEED A CHANCE TO GET OUT SOME FEMININE AGGRESSION, DRISS.
LET 'EM SHOW THESE CORAL-HEADED JINKERS WHO'S STEERING SIGHT FOR A BIT AND THEN STEP IN.
POMMELS AND BLADE FLATS, GIRLS! KEEP 'EM ALIVE FOR QUESTIONING
Y'HEAR?!

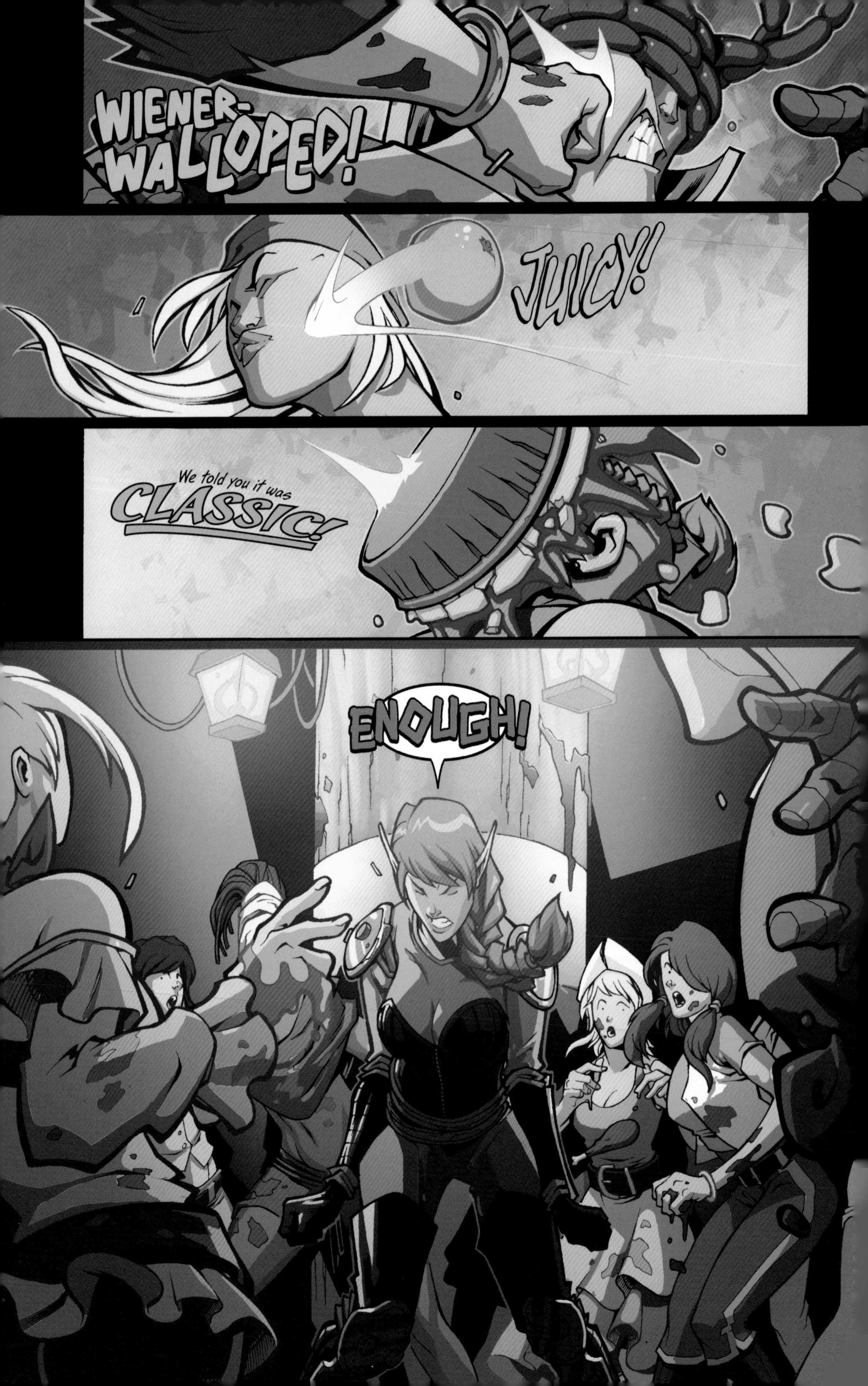
WIENER-WALLOPED!
JUICY!
We told you it was CLASSIC!
ENOUGH!

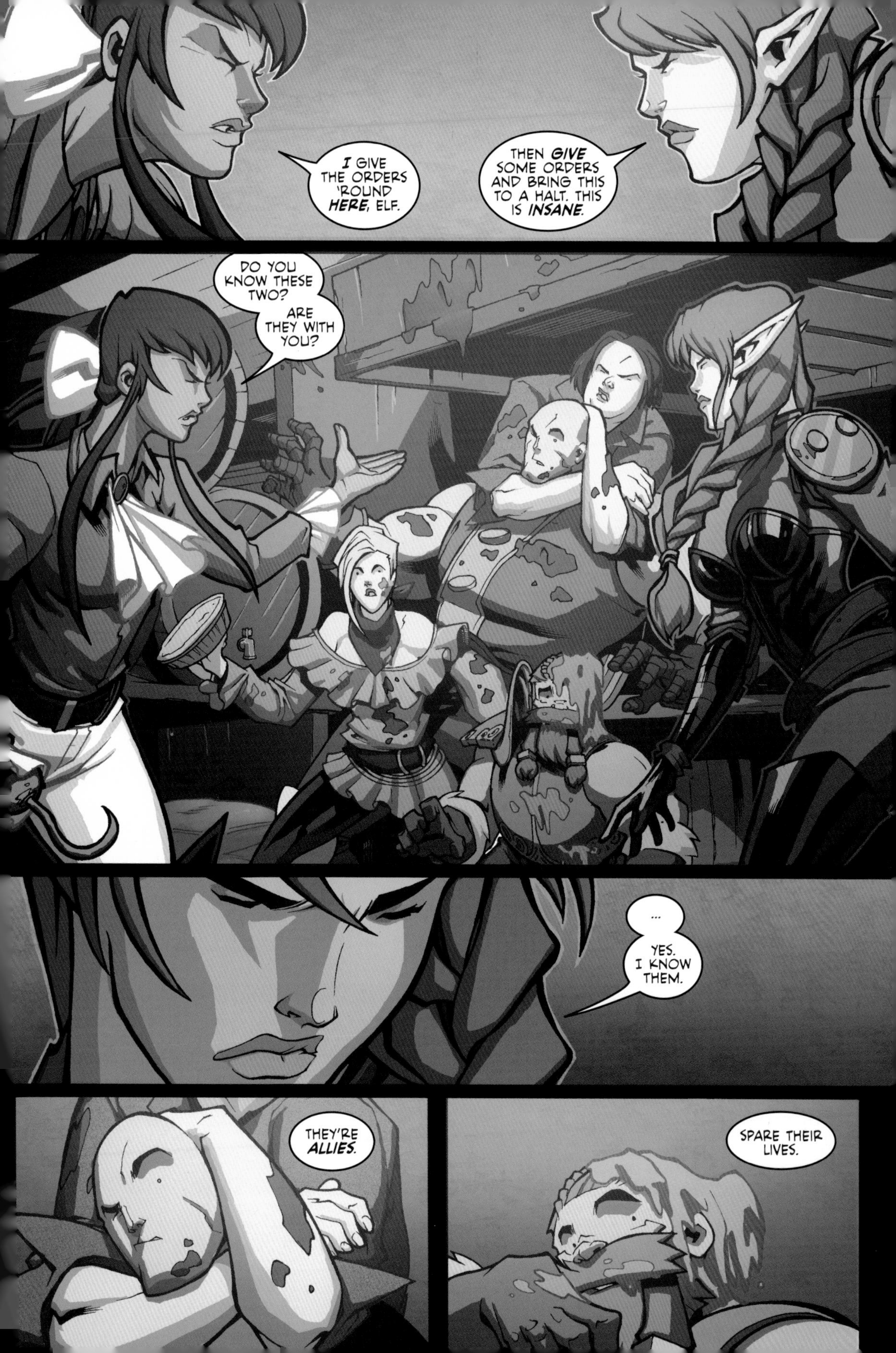
I GIVE THE ORDERS 'ROUND HERE, ELF.
THEN GIVE SOME ORDERS AND BRING THIS TO A HALT. THIS IS INSANE.
DO YOU KNOW THESE TWO?
ARE THEY WITH YOU?
...
YES. I KNOW THEM.
THEY'RE ALLIES.
SPARE THEIR LIVES.

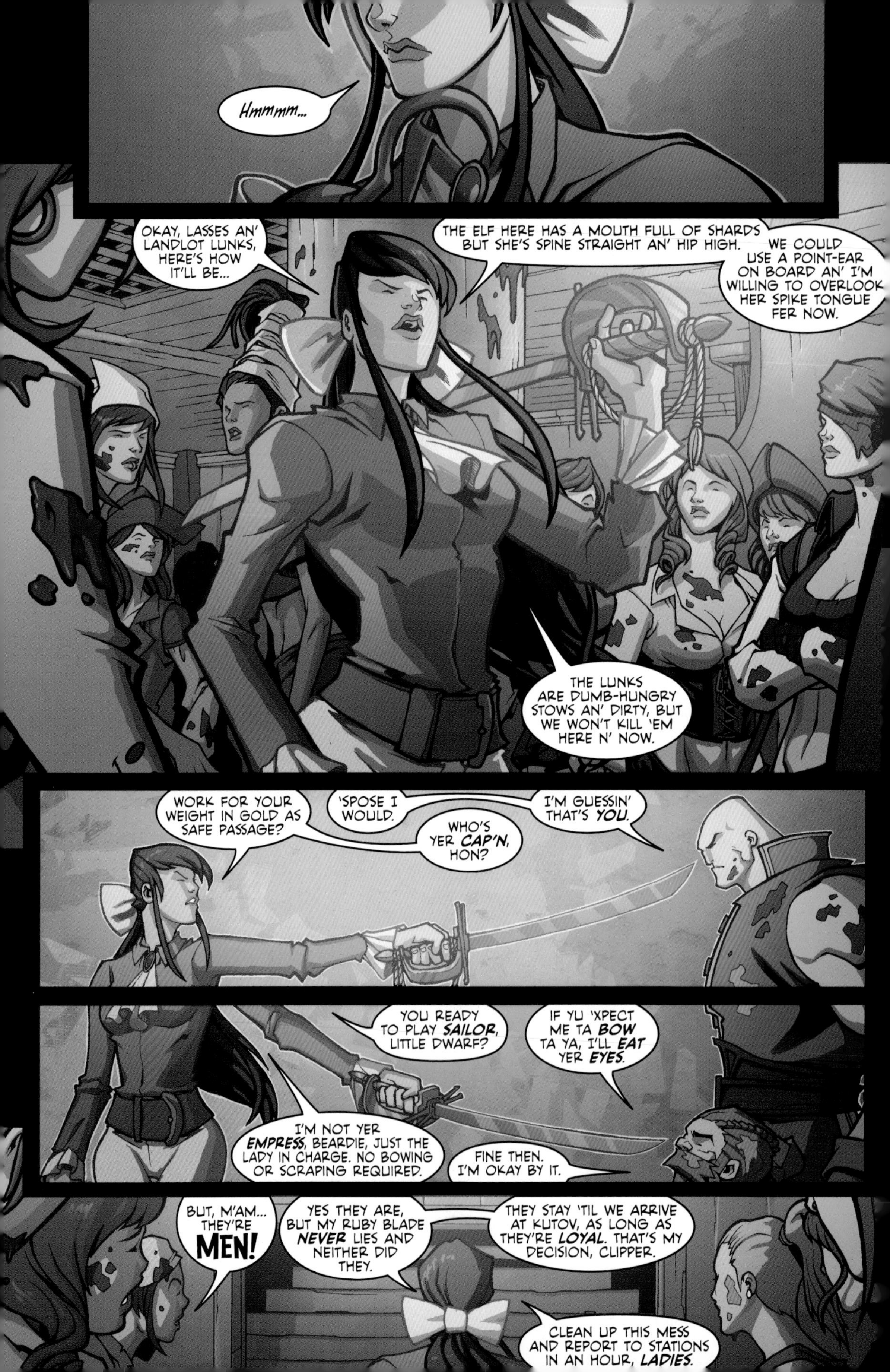
Hmmmm...
OKAY, LASSES AN' LANDLOT LUNKS, HERE'S HOW IT'LL BE...
THE ELF HERE HAS A MOUTH FULL OF SHARDS BUT SHE'S SPINE STRAIGHT AN' HIP HIGH.
WE COULD USE A POINT-EAR ON BOARD AN' I'M WILLING TO OVERLOOK HER SPIKE TONGUE FER NOW.
THE LUNKS ARE DUMB-HUNGRY STOWS AN' DIRTY, BUT WE WON'T KILL 'EM HERE N' NOW.
WORK FOR YOUR WEIGHT IN GOLD AS SAFE PASSAGE?
'SPOSE I WOULD.
WHO'S YER CAP'N, HON?
I'M GUESSIN' THAT'S YOU.
YOU READY TO PLAY SAILOR, LITTLE DWARF?
IF YU 'XPECT ME TA BOW TA YA, I'LL EAT YER EYES.
I'M NOT YER EMPRESS, BEARDIE, JUST THE LADY IN CHARGE. NO BOWING OR SCRAPING REQUIRED.
FINE THEN. I'M OKAY BY IT.
BUT, M'AM... THEY'RE MEN!
YES THEY ARE, BUT MY RUBY BLADE NEVER LIES AND NEITHER DID THEY.
THEY STAY 'TIL WE ARRIVE AT KUTOV, AS LONG AS THEY'RE LOYAL. THAT'S MY DECISION, CLIPPER.
CLEAN UP THIS MESS AND REPORT TO STATIONS IN AN HOUR, LADIES.

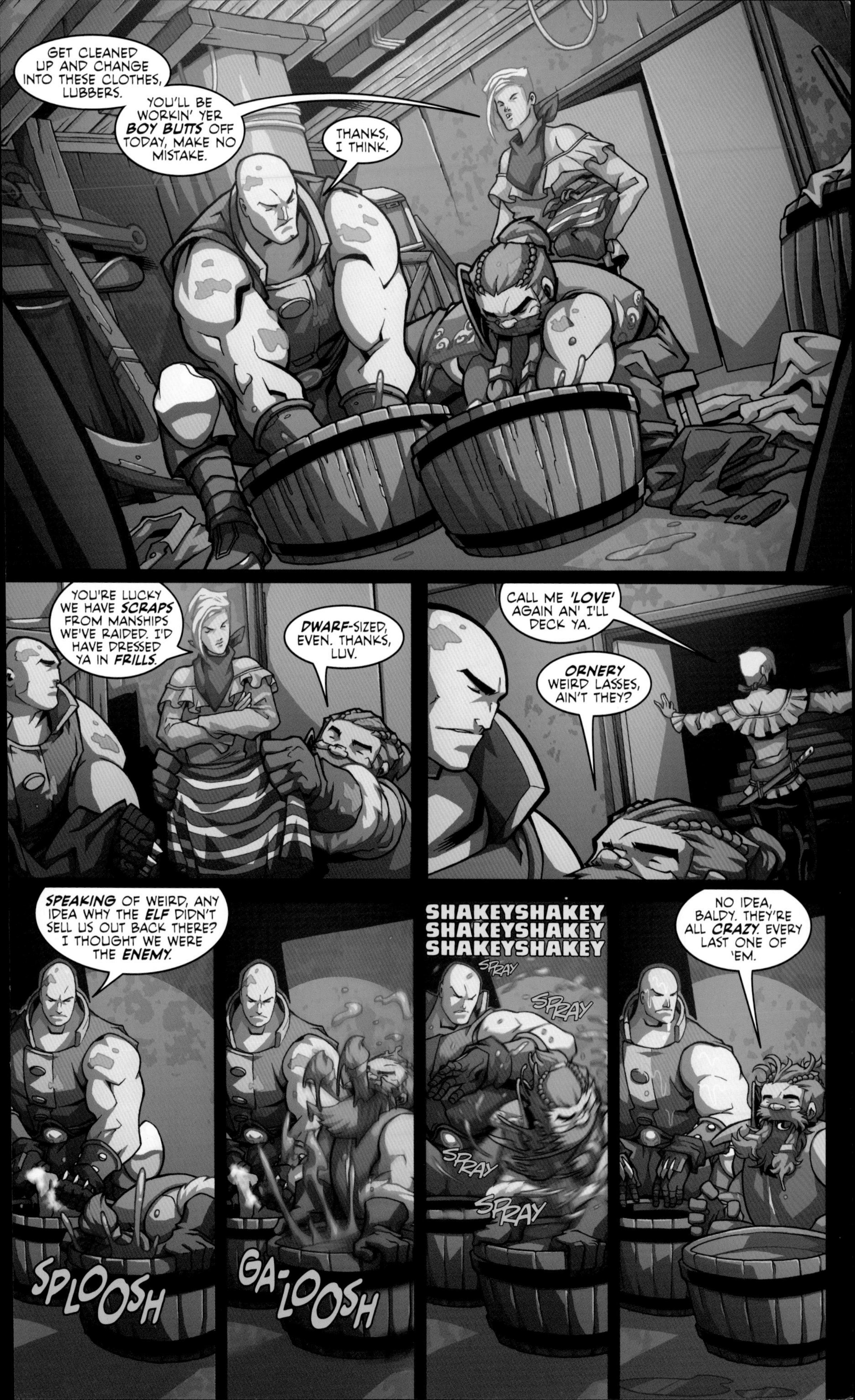
GET CLEANED UP AND CHANGE INTO THESE CLOTHES, LUBBERS.
YOU'LL BE WORKIN' YER BOY BUTTS OFF TODAY, MAKE NO MISTAKE.
THANKS, I THINK.
YOU'RE LUCKY WE HAVE SCRAPS FROM MANSHIPS WE'VE RAIDED. I'D HAVE DRESSED YA IN FRILLS.
DWARF-SIZED, EVEN. THANKS, LUV.
CALL ME 'LOVE' AGAIN AN' I'LL DECK YA.
ORNERY WEIRD LASSES, AIN'T THEY?
SPEAKING OF WEIRD, ANY IDEA WHY THE ELF DIDN'T SELL US OUT BACK THERE? I THOUGHT WE WERE THE ENEMY.
SPLOOSH
GA-LOOSH
SHAKEYSHAKEY SHAKEYSHAKEY SHAKEYSHAKEY
SPRAY
SPRAY
SPRAY
SPRAY
NO IDEA, BALDY. THEY'RE ALL CRAZY. EVERY LAST ONE OF 'EM.

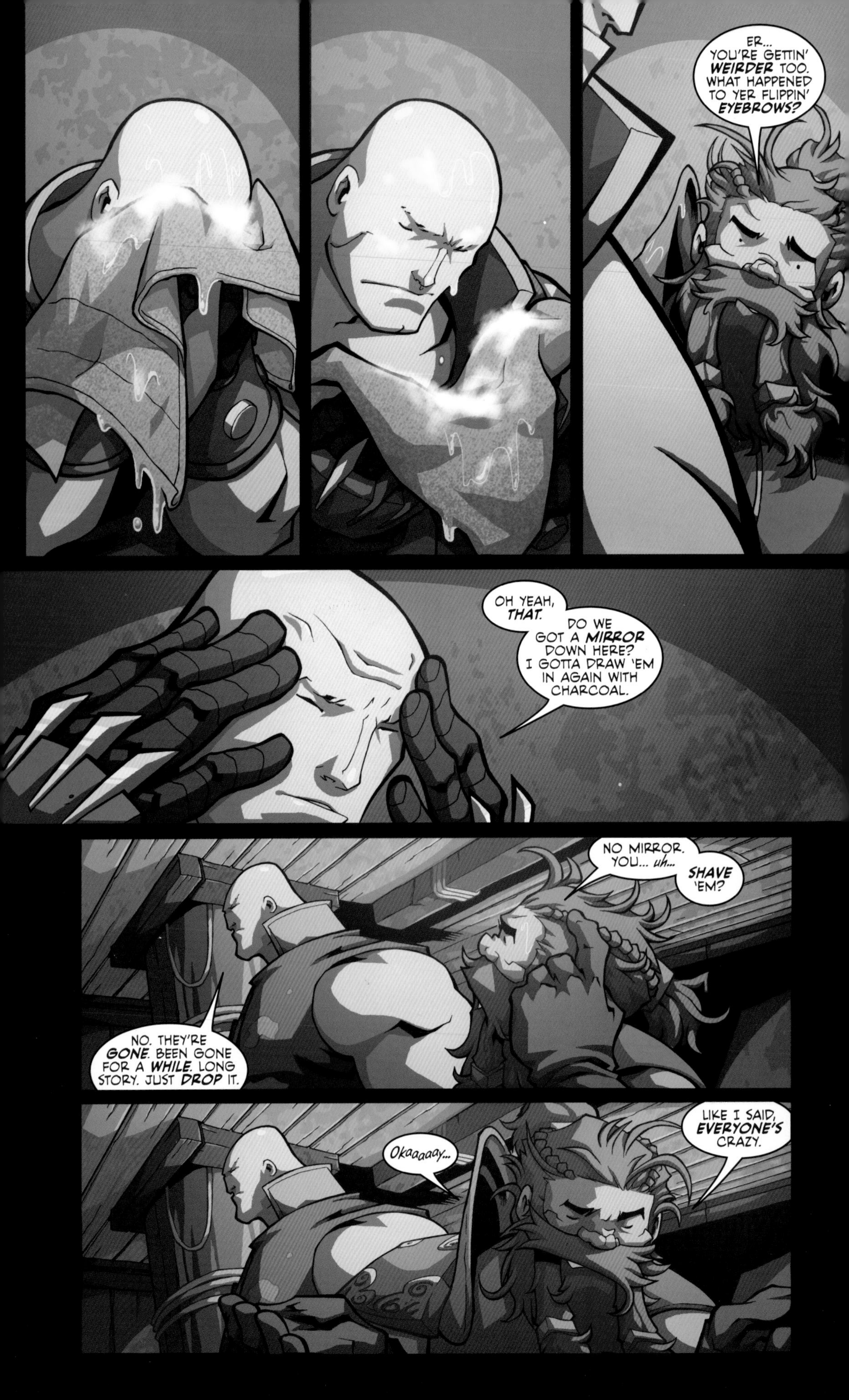
ER... YOU'RE GETTIN' WEIRDER TOO. WHAT HAPPENED TO YER FLIPPIN' EYEBROWS?
OH YEAH, THAT.
DO WE GOT A MIRROR DOWN HERE? I GOTTA DRAW 'EM IN AGAIN WITH CHARCOAL.
NO MIRROR. YOU... uh... SHAVE 'EM?
NO. THEY'RE GONE. BEEN GONE FOR A WHILE. LONG STORY. JUST DROP IT.
Okaaaaay...
LIKE I SAID, EVERYONE'S CRAZY.

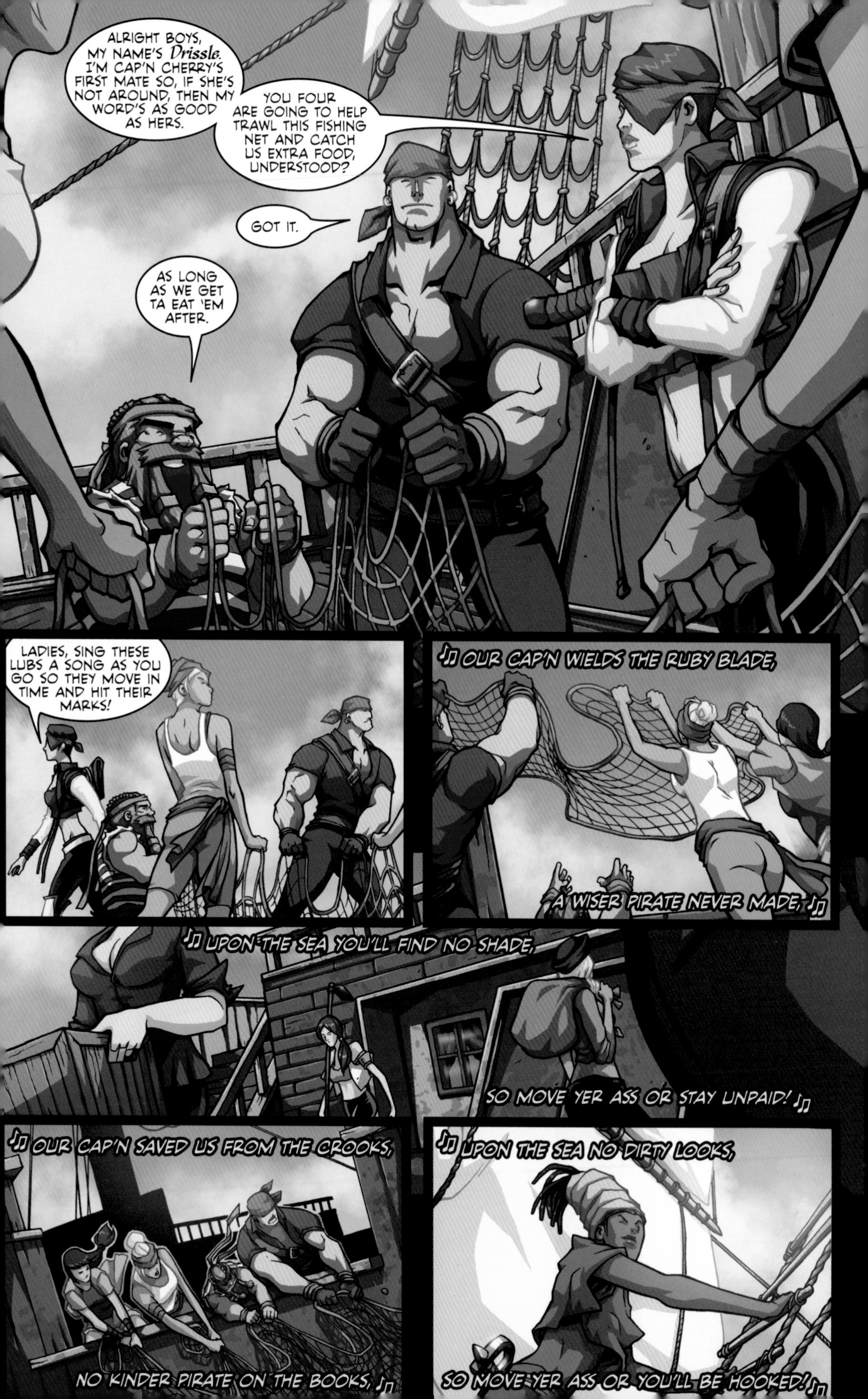
ALRIGHT BOYS, MY NAME'S *Drissle.* I'M CAP'N CHERRY'S FIRST MATE SO, IF SHE'S NOT AROUND, THEN MY WORD'S AS GOOD AS HERS.
YOU FOUR ARE GOING TO HELP TRAWL THIS FISHING NET AND CATCH US EXTRA FOOD, UNDERSTOOD?
GOT IT.
AS LONG AS WE GET TA EAT 'EM AFTER.
LADIES, SING THESE LUBS A SONG AS YOU GO SO THEY MOVE IN TIME AND HIT THEIR MARKS!
♫ OUR CAP'N WIELDS THE RUBY BLADE,
A WISER PIRATE NEVER MADE, ♫
♫ UPON THE SEA YOU'LL FIND NO SHADE,
SO MOVE YER ASS OR STAY UNPAID! ♫
♫ OUR CAP'N SAVED US FROM THE CROOKS,
NO KINDER PIRATE ON THE BOOKS, ♫
♫ UPON THE SEA NO DIRTY LOOKS,
SO MOVE YER ASS OR YOU'LL BE HOOKED! ♫

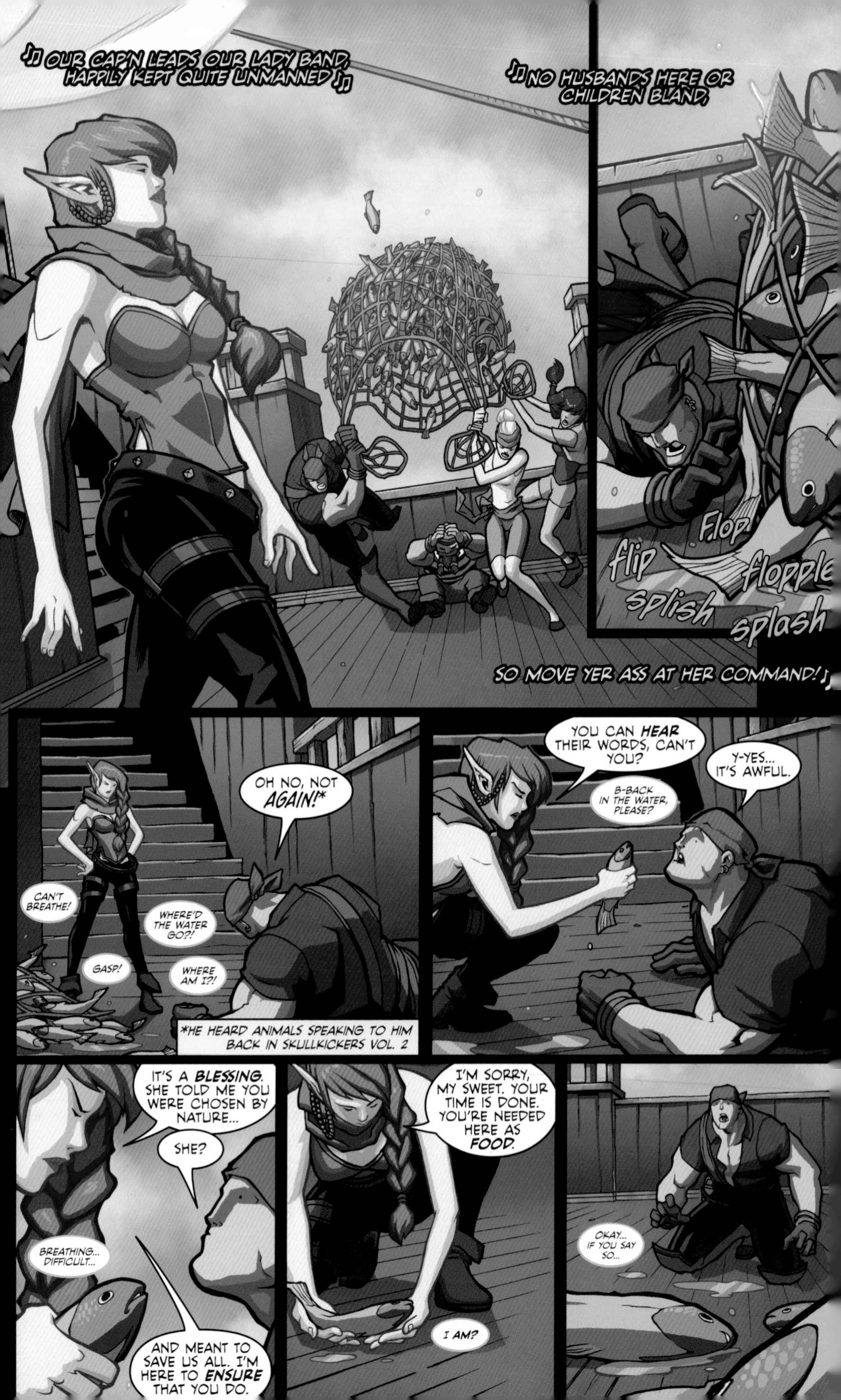

♫ OUR CAP'N LEADS OUR LADY BAND, HAPPILY KEPT QUITE UNMANNED ♫
♫ NO HUSBANDS HERE OR CHILDREN BLAND,
Flop
flip
flopple
splish
splash
SO MOVE YER ASS AT HER COMMAND! ♪
OH NO, NOT AGAIN!*
CAN'T BREATHE!
WHERE'D THE WATER GO?!
GASP!
WHERE AM I?!
*HE HEARD ANIMALS SPEAKING TO HIM BACK IN SKULLKICKERS VOL. 2
YOU CAN HEAR THEIR WORDS, CAN'T YOU?
B-BACK IN THE WATER, PLEASE?
Y-YES... IT'S AWFUL.
IT'S A BLESSING. SHE TOLD ME YOU WERE CHOSEN BY NATURE...
SHE?
BREATHING... DIFFICULT...
AND MEANT TO SAVE US ALL. I'M HERE TO ENSURE THAT YOU DO.
I'M SORRY, MY SWEET. YOUR TIME IS DONE. YOU'RE NEEDED HERE AS FOOD.
I AM?
OKAY... IF YOU SAY SO...

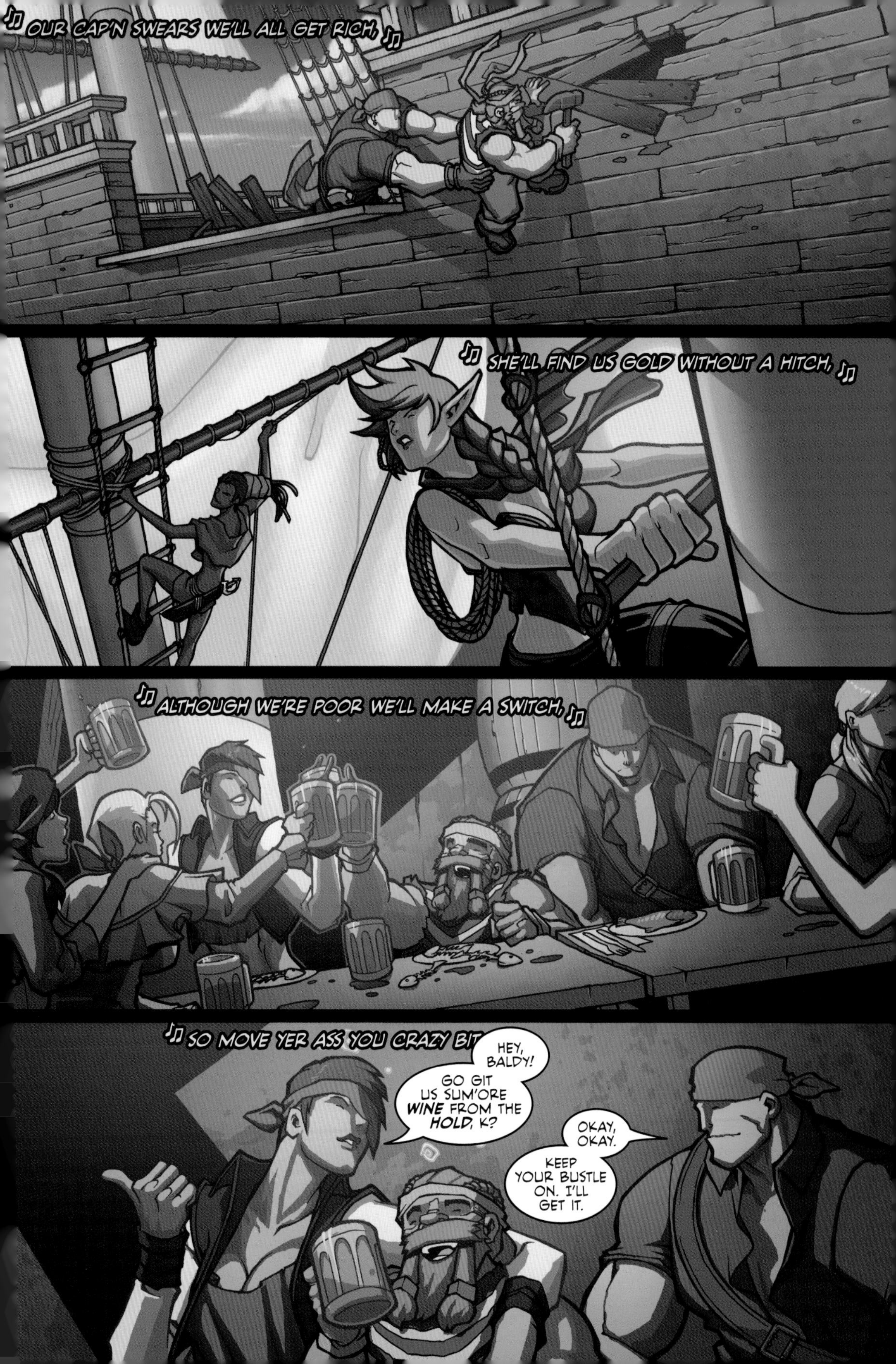
♫ OUR CAP'N SWEARS WE'LL ALL GET RICH, ♫
♫ SHE'LL FIND US GOLD WITHOUT A HITCH, ♫
♫ ALTHOUGH WE'RE POOR WE'LL MAKE A SWITCH, ♫
♫ SO MOVE YER ASS YOU CRAZY BIT
HEY, BALDY!
GO GIT US SUM'ORE WINE FROM THE HOLD, K?
OKAY, OKAY.
KEEP YOUR BUSTLE ON. I'LL GET IT.

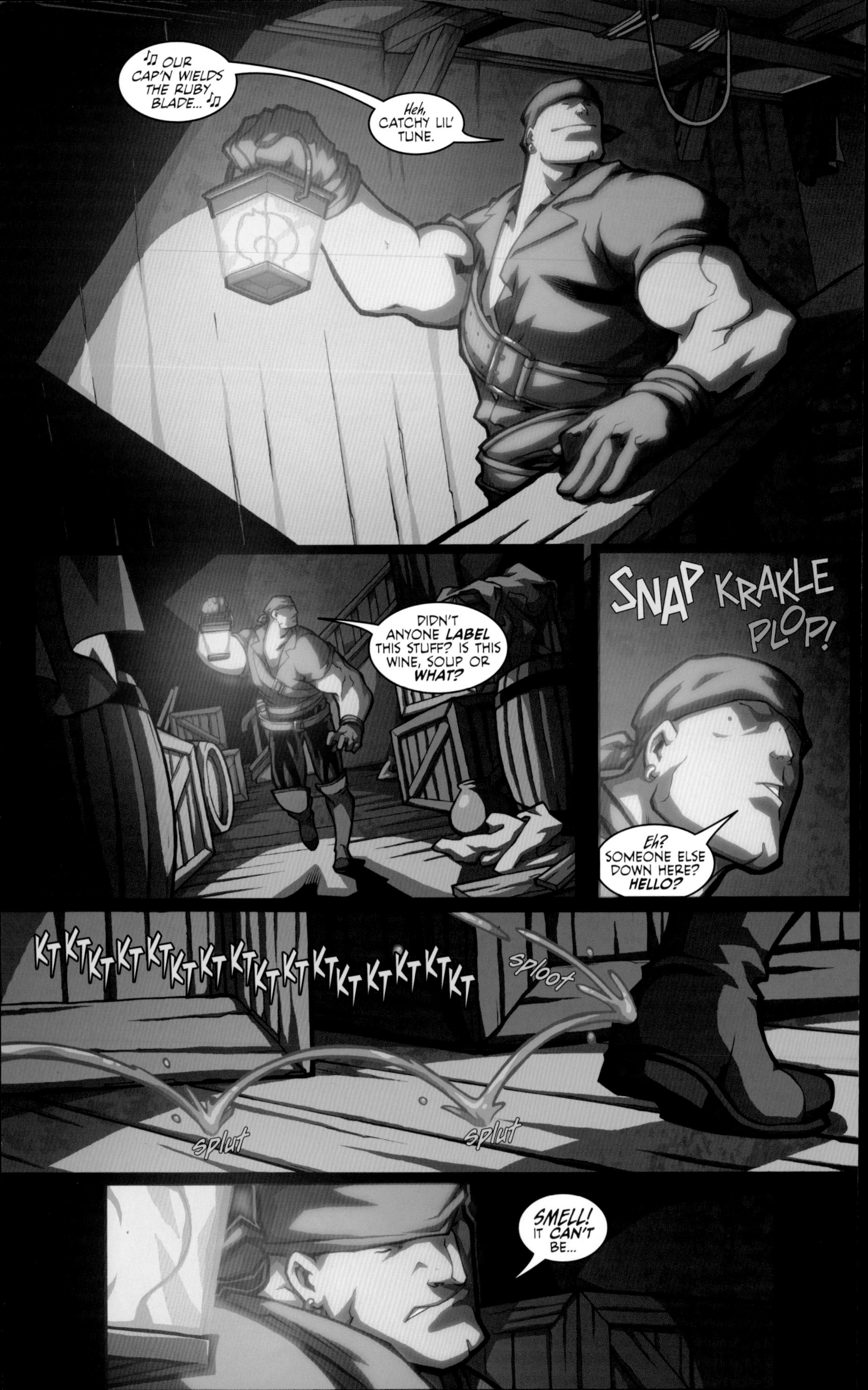
♫ OUR CAP'N WIELDS THE RUBY BLADE... ♫
Heh, CATCHY LIL' TUNE.
DIDN'T ANYONE LABEL THIS STUFF? IS THIS WINE, SOUP OR WHAT?
SNAP KRAKLE PLOP!
Eh? SOMEONE ELSE DOWN HERE? HELLO?
KT KT KT KT KT KT KT KT KT KT KT KT KT KT KT KT KT
sploot
splut
splut
SMELL! IT CAN'T BE...

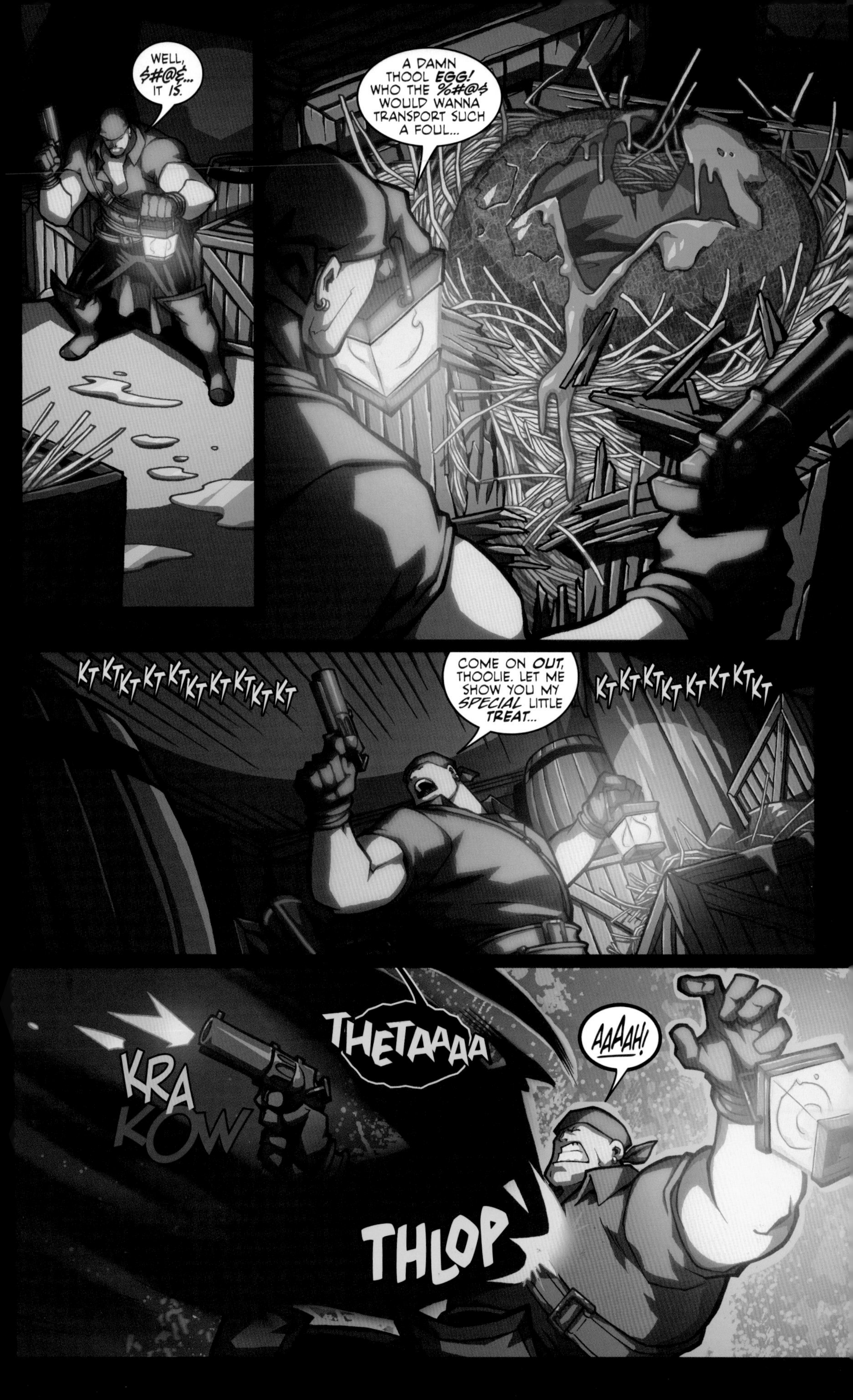
WELL, $#@&... IT IS.
A DAMN THOOL EGG! WHO THE %#@$ WOULD WANNA TRANSPORT SUCH A FOUL...
KT KT KT KT KT KT KT KT KT KT KT KT KT
COME ON OUT, THOOLIE. LET ME SHOW YOU MY SPECIAL LITTLE TREAT...
KT KT KT KT KT KT KT KT
KRA KOW
THETAAAA
AAAAH!
THLOP

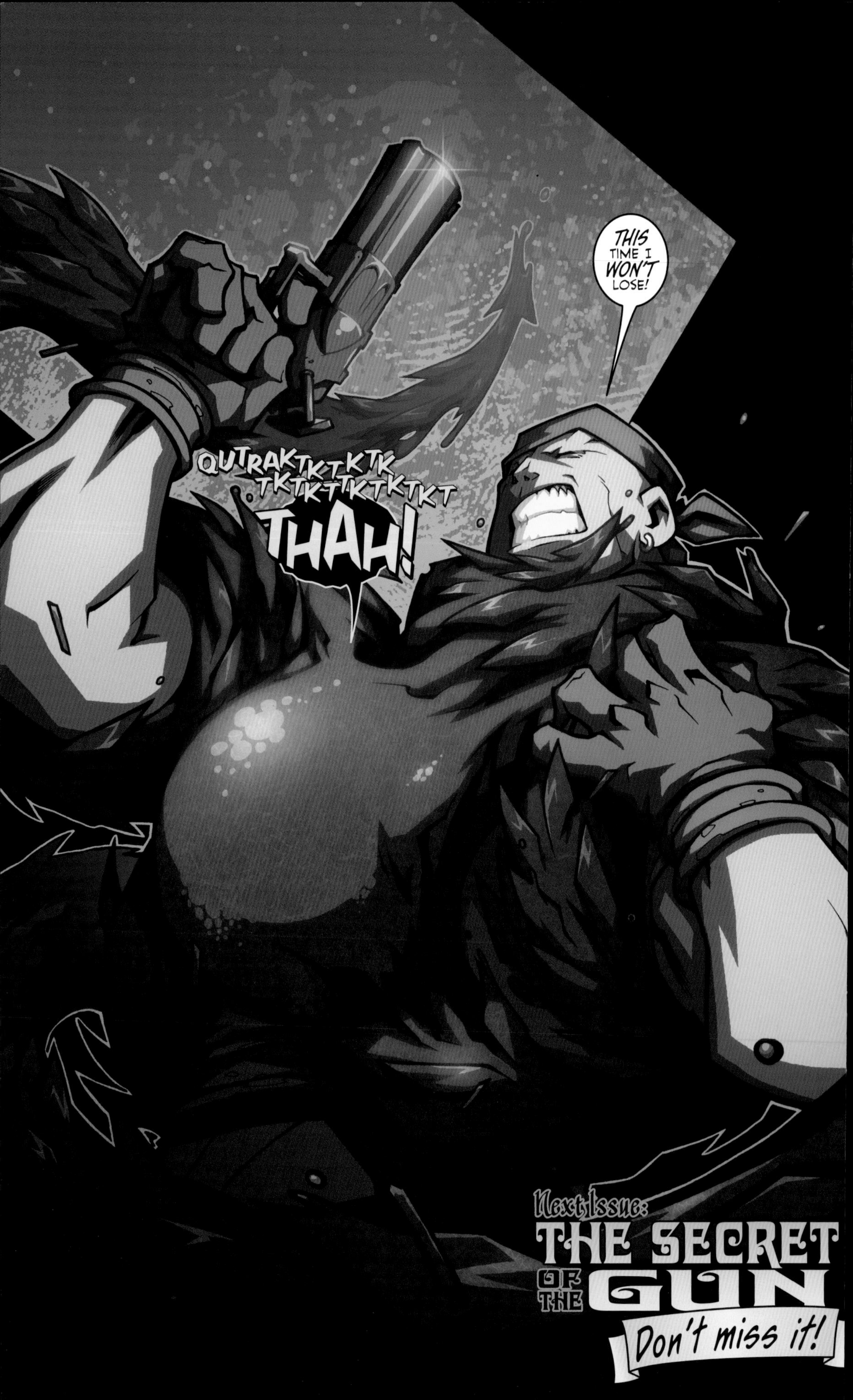
THIS TIME I WON'T LOSE!
QUTRAKTKTKTK TKTKTTKTKTKT THAH!
Next Issue:
THE SECRET OF THE GUN
Don't miss it!

CHAPTER TWO

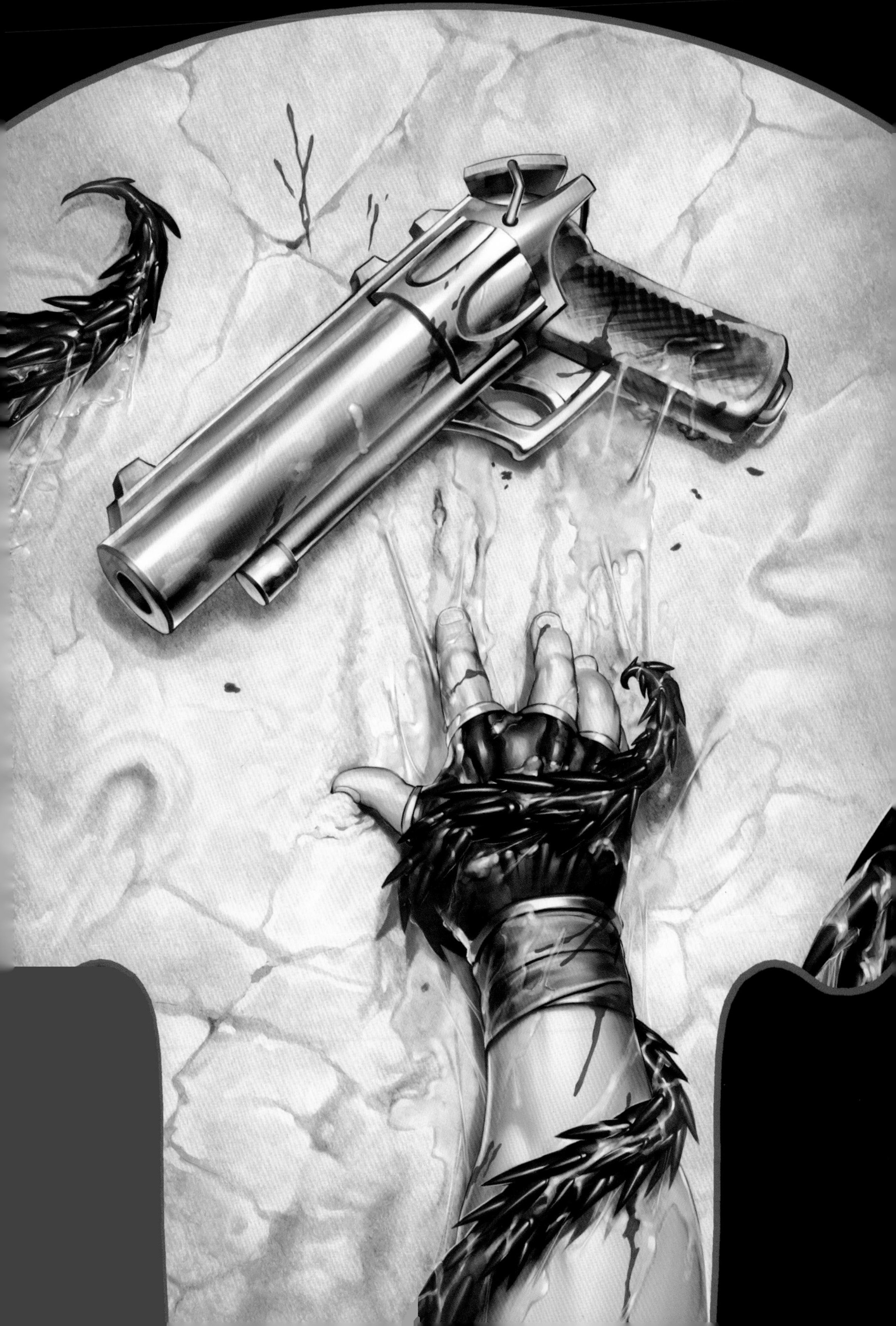

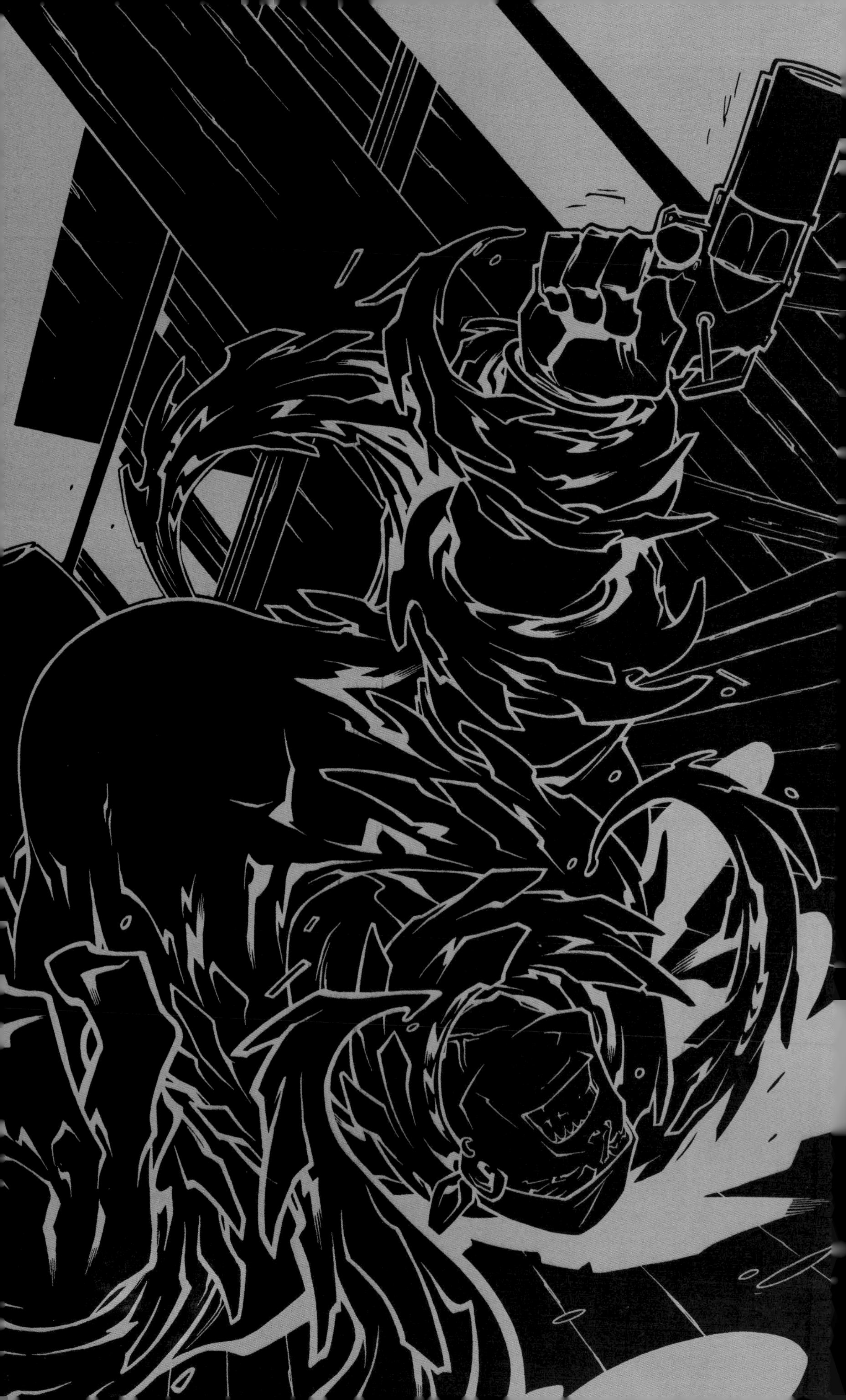

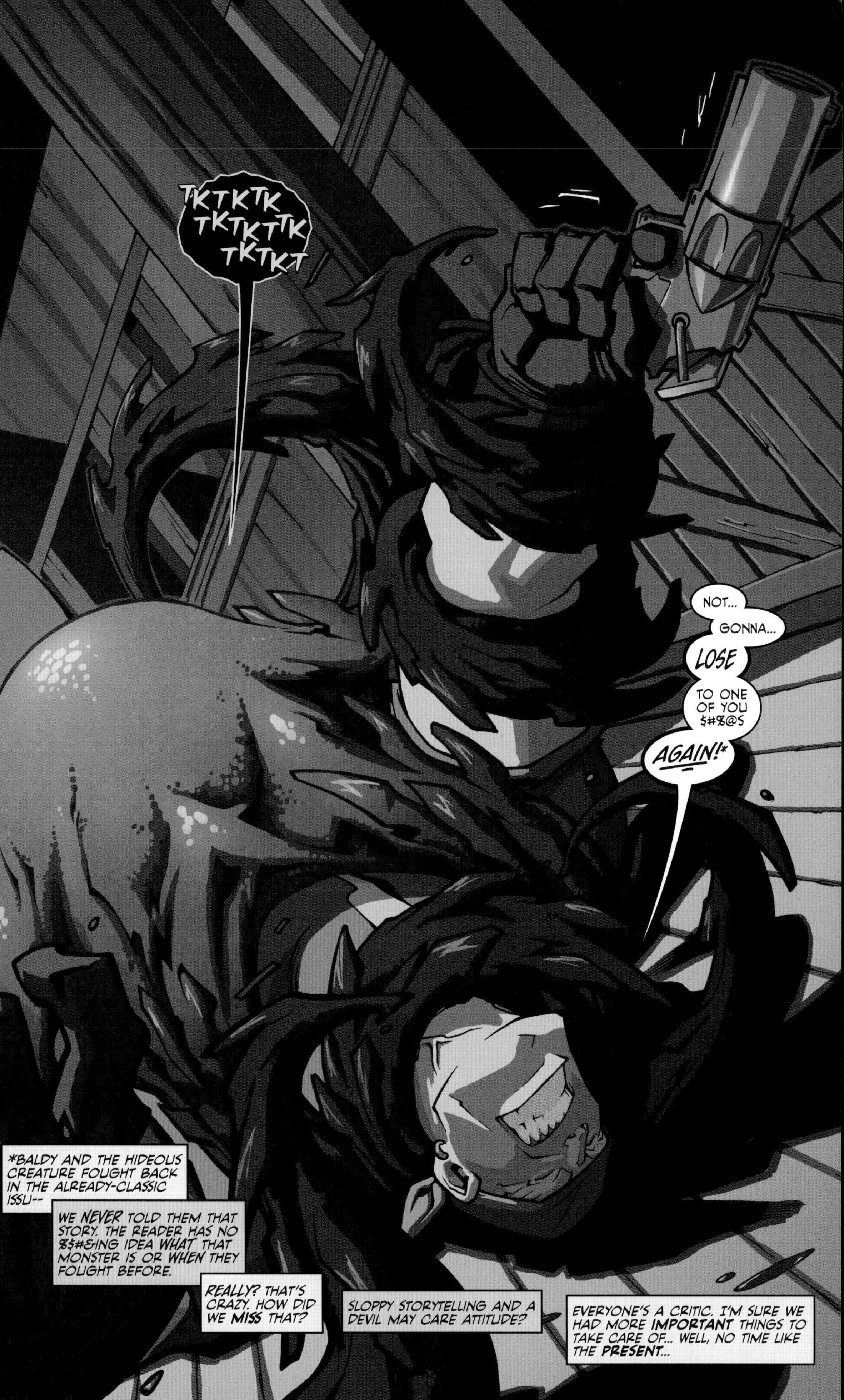
TKTKTK TKTKTTK TKTKT
NOT...
GONNA...
LOSE
TO ONE OF YOU $#%@S
AGAIN!*
*BALDY AND THE HIDEOUS CREATURE FOUGHT BACK IN THE ALREADY-CLASSIC ISSU--
WE NEVER TOLD THEM THAT STORY. THE READER HAS NO %$#&ING IDEA WHAT THAT MONSTER IS OR WHEN THEY FOUGHT BEFORE.
REALLY? THAT'S CRAZY. HOW DID WE MISS THAT?
SLOPPY STORYTELLING AND A DEVIL MAY CARE ATTITUDE?
EVERYONE'S A CRITIC. I'M SURE WE HAD MORE IMPORTANT THINGS TO TAKE CARE OF... WELL, NO TIME LIKE THE PRESENT...

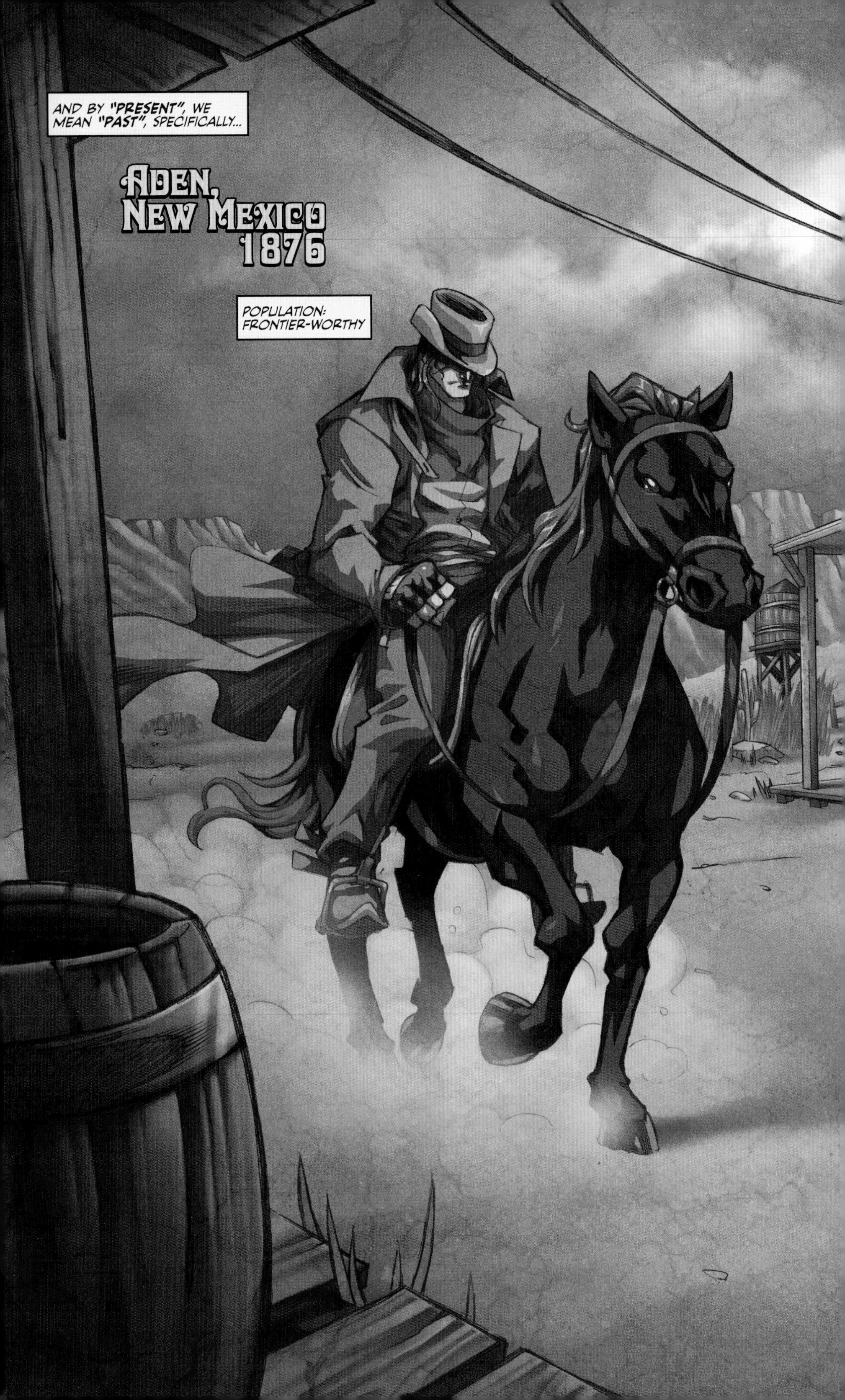
AND BY "PRESENT", WE MEAN "PAST", SPECIFICALLY...
ADEN, NEW MEXICO 1876
POPULATION: FRONTIER-WORTHY

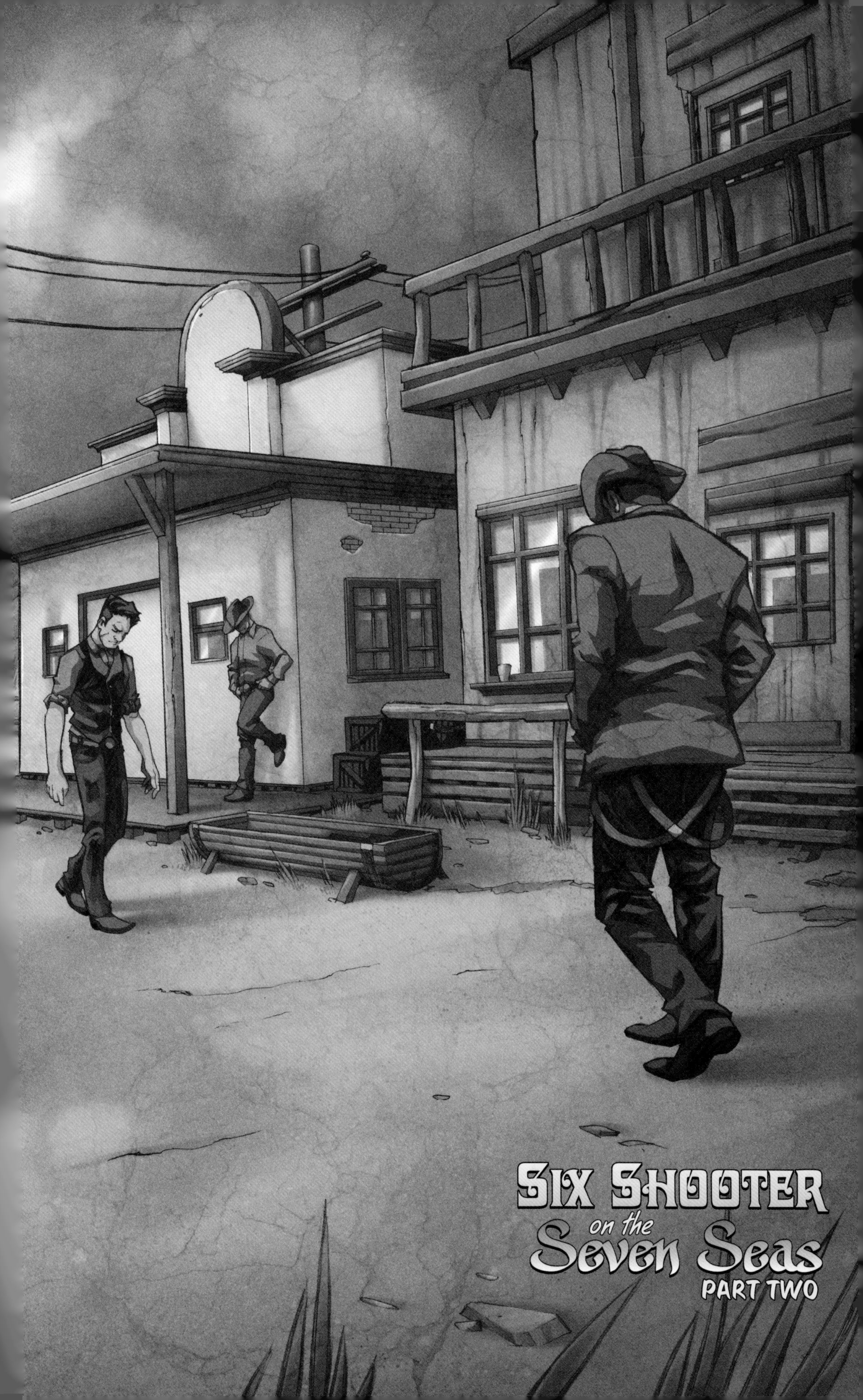
SIX SHOOTER
on the
Seven Seas
PART TWO

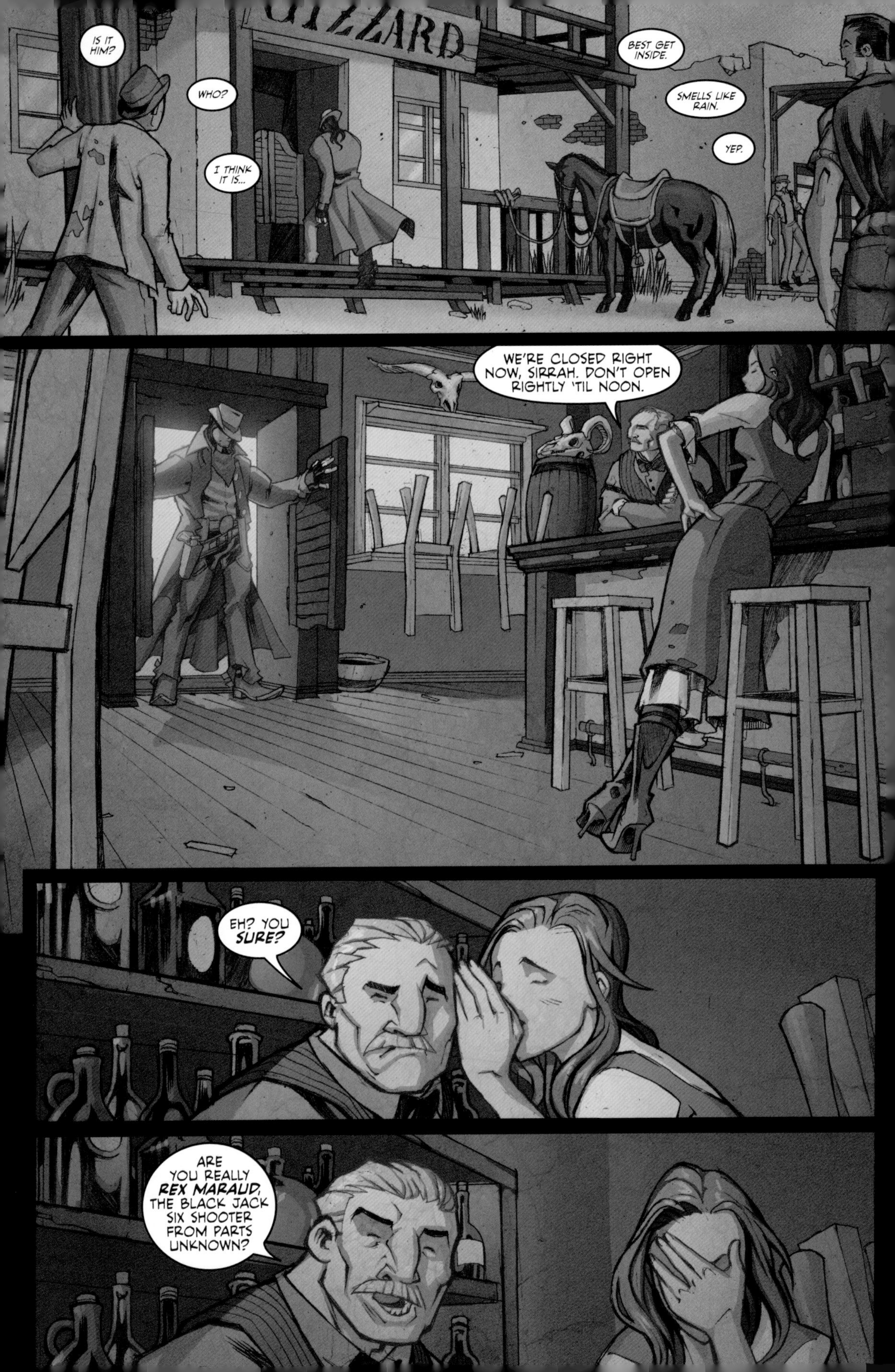
GIZZARD
IS IT HIM?
WHO?
I THINK IT IS...
BEST GET INSIDE.
SMELLS LIKE RAIN.
YEP.
WE'RE CLOSED RIGHT NOW, SIRRAH. DON'T OPEN RIGHTLY 'TIL NOON.
EH? YOU **SURE?**
ARE YOU REALLY **REX MARAUD,** THE BLACK JACK SIX SHOOTER FROM PARTS UNKNOWN?

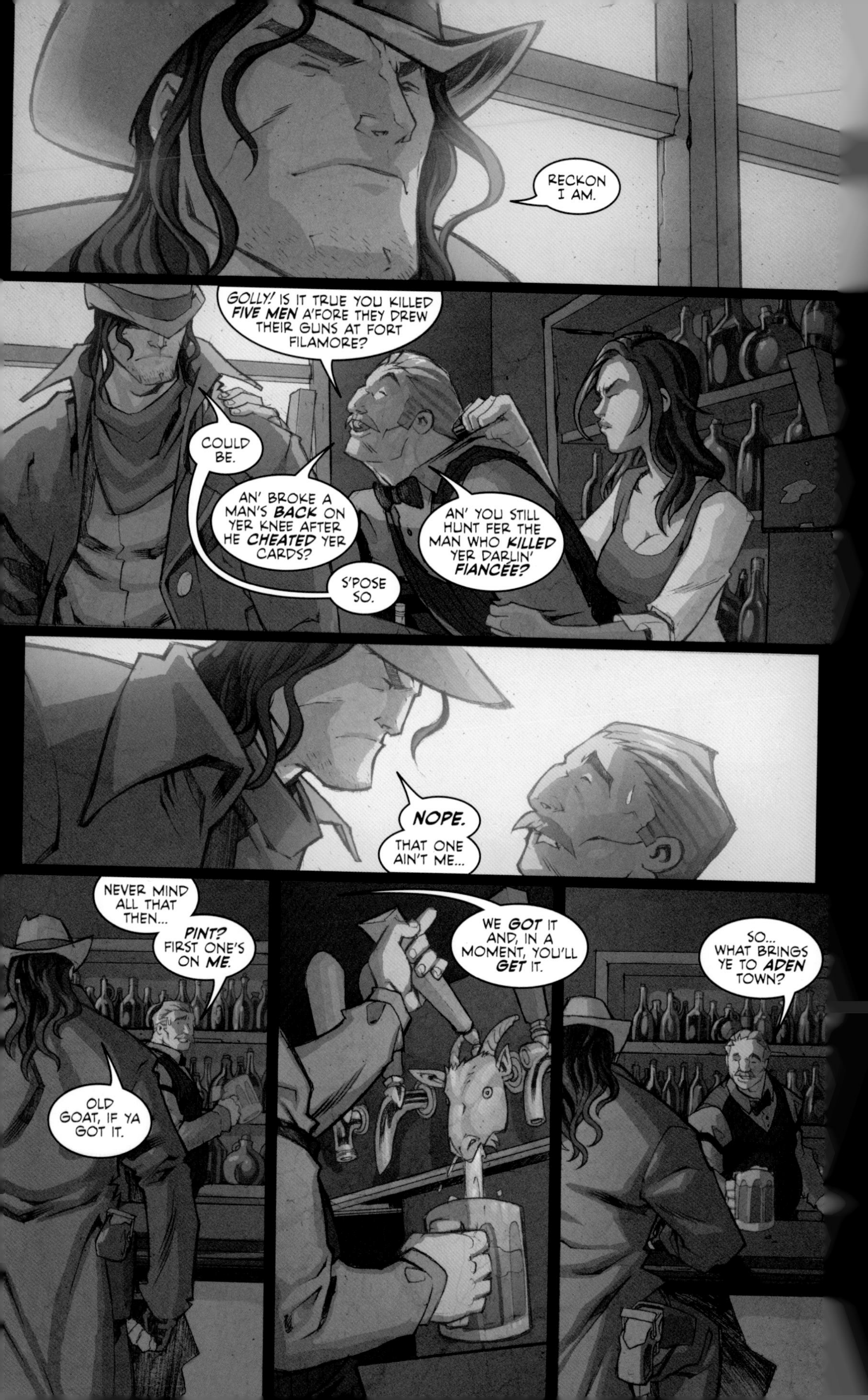
RECKON I AM.
GOLLY! IS IT TRUE YOU KILLED FIVE MEN A'FORE THEY DREW THEIR GUNS AT FORT FILAMORE?
COULD BE.
AN' BROKE A MAN'S BACK ON YER KNEE AFTER HE CHEATED YER CARDS?
S'POSE SO.
AN' YOU STILL HUNT FER THE MAN WHO KILLED YER DARLIN' FIANCÉE?
NOPE.
THAT ONE AIN'T ME...
NEVER MIND ALL THAT THEN...
PINT? FIRST ONE'S ON ME.
OLD GOAT, IF YA GOT IT.
WE GOT IT AND, IN A MOMENT, YOU'LL GET IT.
SO... WHAT BRINGS YE TO ADEN TOWN?

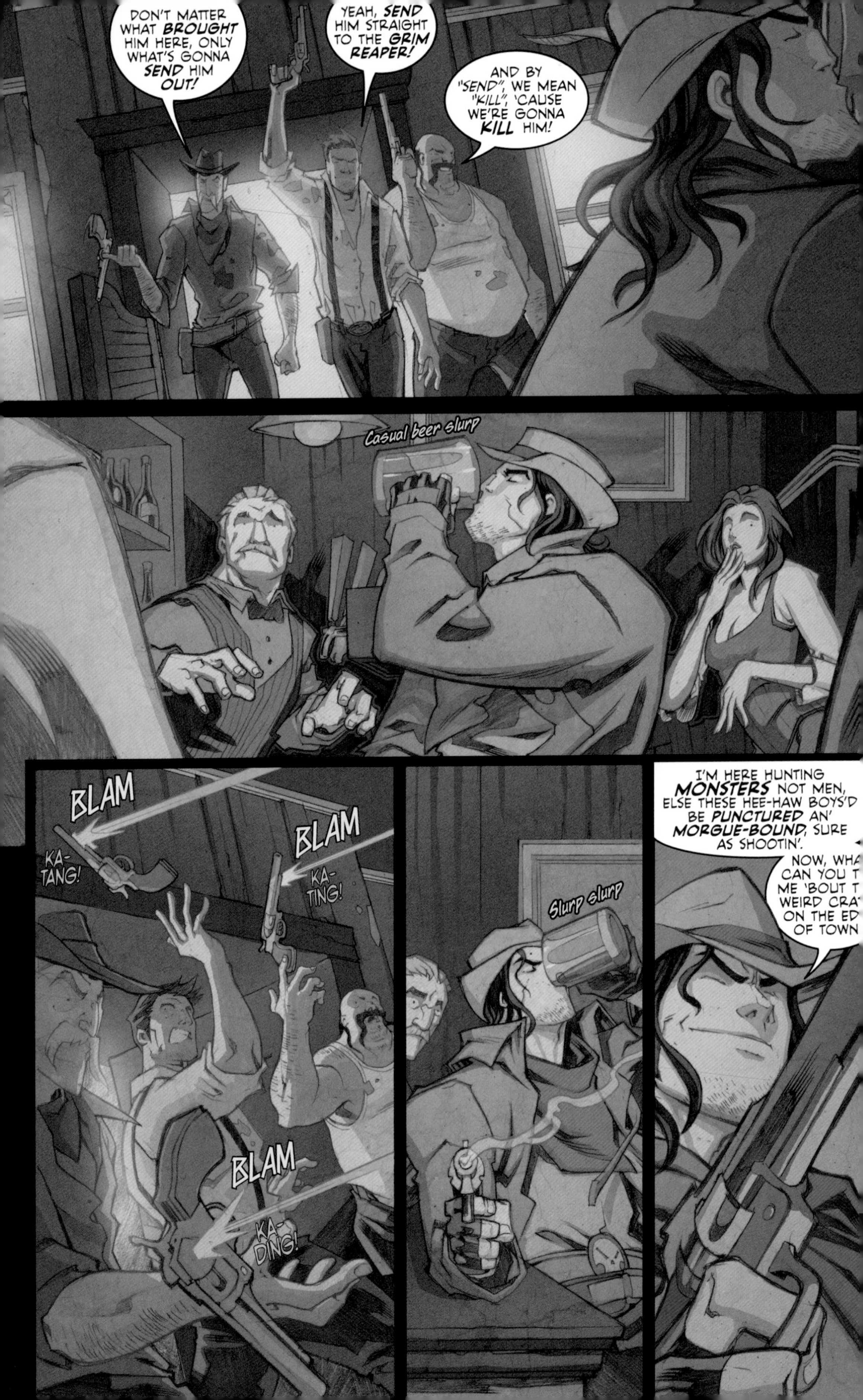
DON'T MATTER WHAT BROUGHT HIM HERE, ONLY WHAT'S GONNA SEND HIM OUT!
YEAH, SEND HIM STRAIGHT TO THE GRIM REAPER!
AND BY "SEND", WE MEAN "KILL", 'CAUSE WE'RE GONNA KILL HIM!
Casual beer slurp
BLAM
KA-TANG!
BLAM
KA-TING!
BLAM
KA-DING!
Slurp slurp
I'M HERE HUNTING MONSTERS NOT MEN, ELSE THESE HEE-HAW BOYS'D BE PUNCTURED AN' MORGUE-BOUND, SURE AS SHOOTIN'.
NOW, WHA CAN YOU T ME 'BOUT T WEIRD CRA ON THE ED OF TOWN

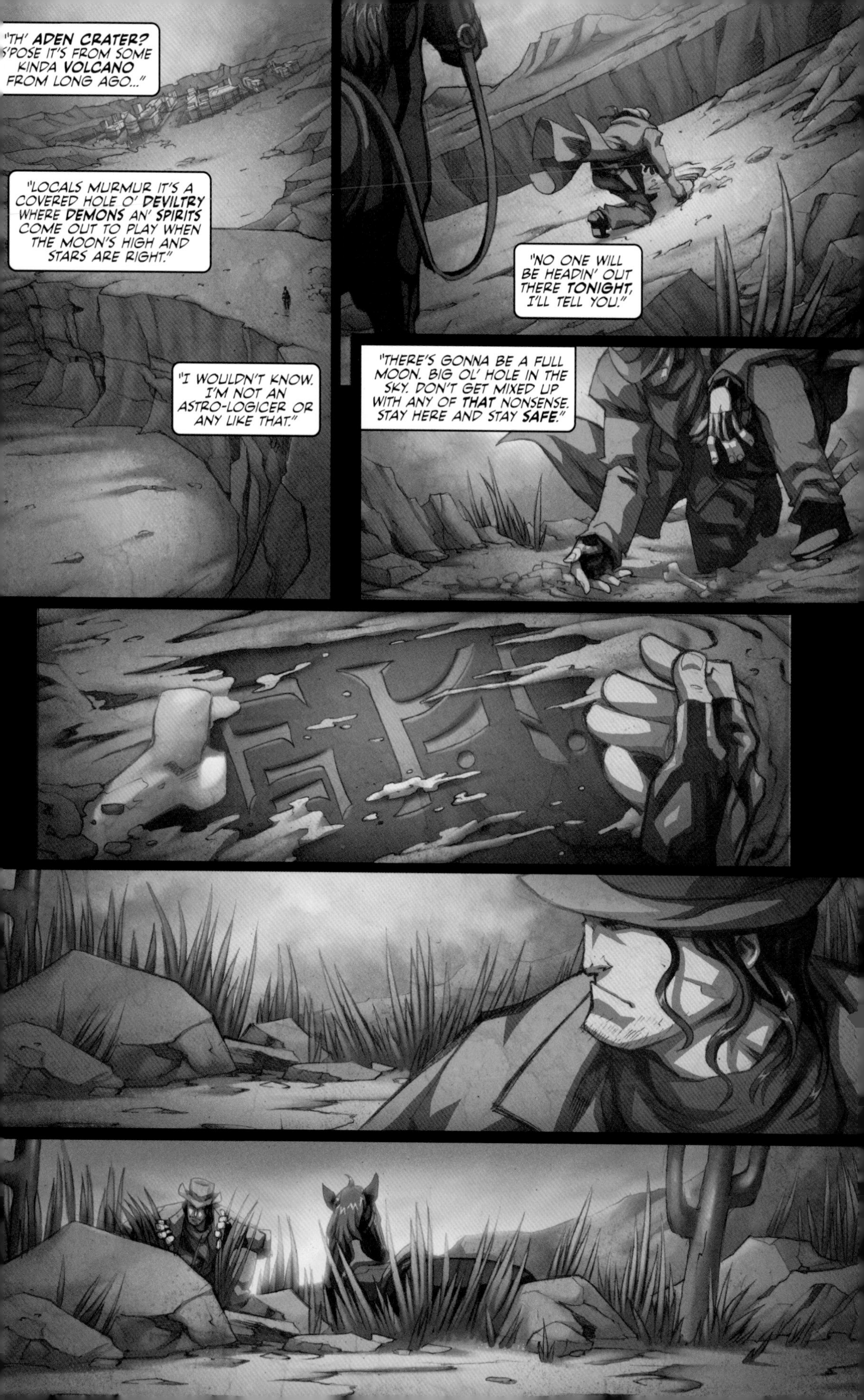
"TH' ADEN CRATER? S'POSE IT'S FROM SOME KINDA VOLCANO FROM LONG AGO..."
"LOCALS MURMUR IT'S A COVERED HOLE O' DEVILTRY WHERE DEMONS AN' SPIRITS COME OUT TO PLAY WHEN THE MOON'S HIGH AND STARS ARE RIGHT."
"I WOULDN'T KNOW. I'M NOT AN ASTRO-LOGICER OR ANY LIKE THAT."
"NO ONE WILL BE HEADIN' OUT THERE TONIGHT, I'LL TELL YOU."
"THERE'S GONNA BE A FULL MOON. BIG OL' HOLE IN THE SKY. DON'T GET MIXED UP WITH ANY OF THAT NONSENSE. STAY HERE AND STAY SAFE."

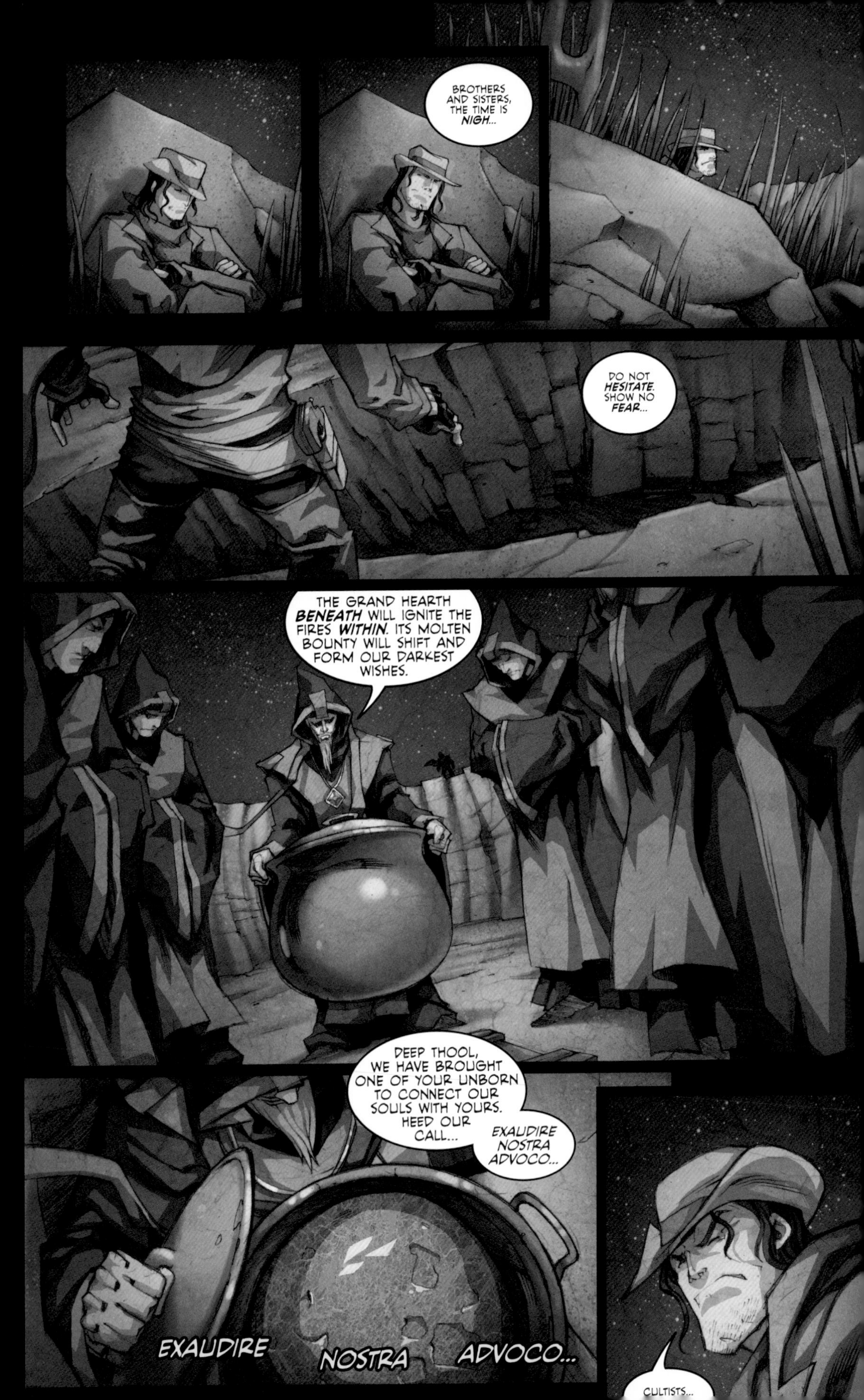
BROTHERS AND SISTERS, THE TIME IS NIGH...
DO NOT HESITATE. SHOW NO FEAR...
THE GRAND HEARTH BENEATH WILL IGNITE THE FIRES WITHIN. ITS MOLTEN BOUNTY WILL SHIFT AND FORM OUR DARKEST WISHES.
DEEP THOOL, WE HAVE BROUGHT ONE OF YOUR UNBORN TO CONNECT OUR SOULS WITH YOURS. HEED OUR CALL...
EXAUDIRE NOSTRA ADVOCO...
EXAUDIRE
NOSTRA
ADVOCO...
CULTISTS...

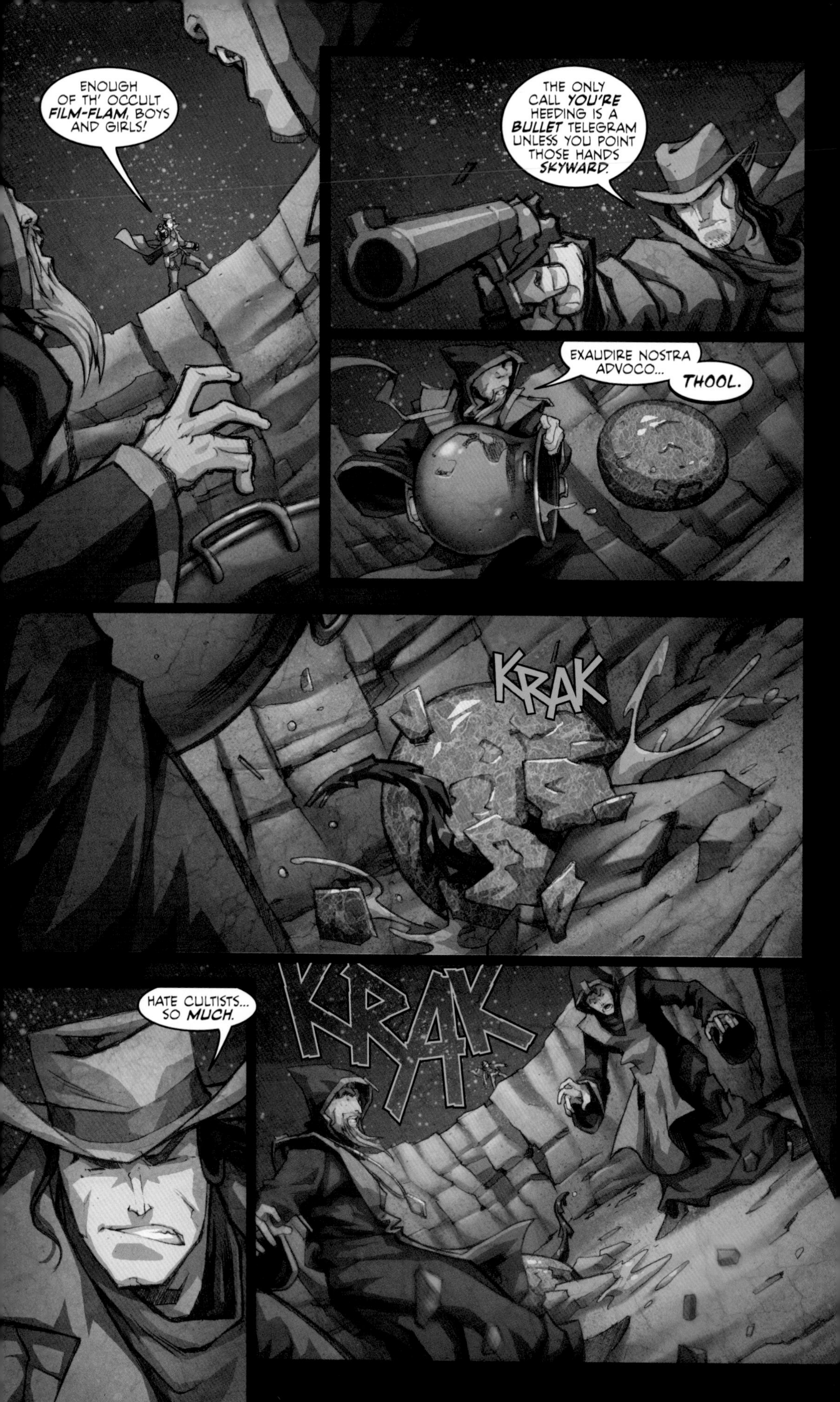
ENOUGH OF TH' OCCULT *FILM-FLAM*, BOYS AND GIRLS!
THE ONLY CALL *YOU'RE* HEEDING IS A *BULLET* TELEGRAM UNLESS YOU POINT THOSE HANDS *SKYWARD*.
EXAUDIRE NOSTRA ADVOCO... *THOOL.*
KRAK
HATE CULTISTS... SO *MUCH*.
KRAK

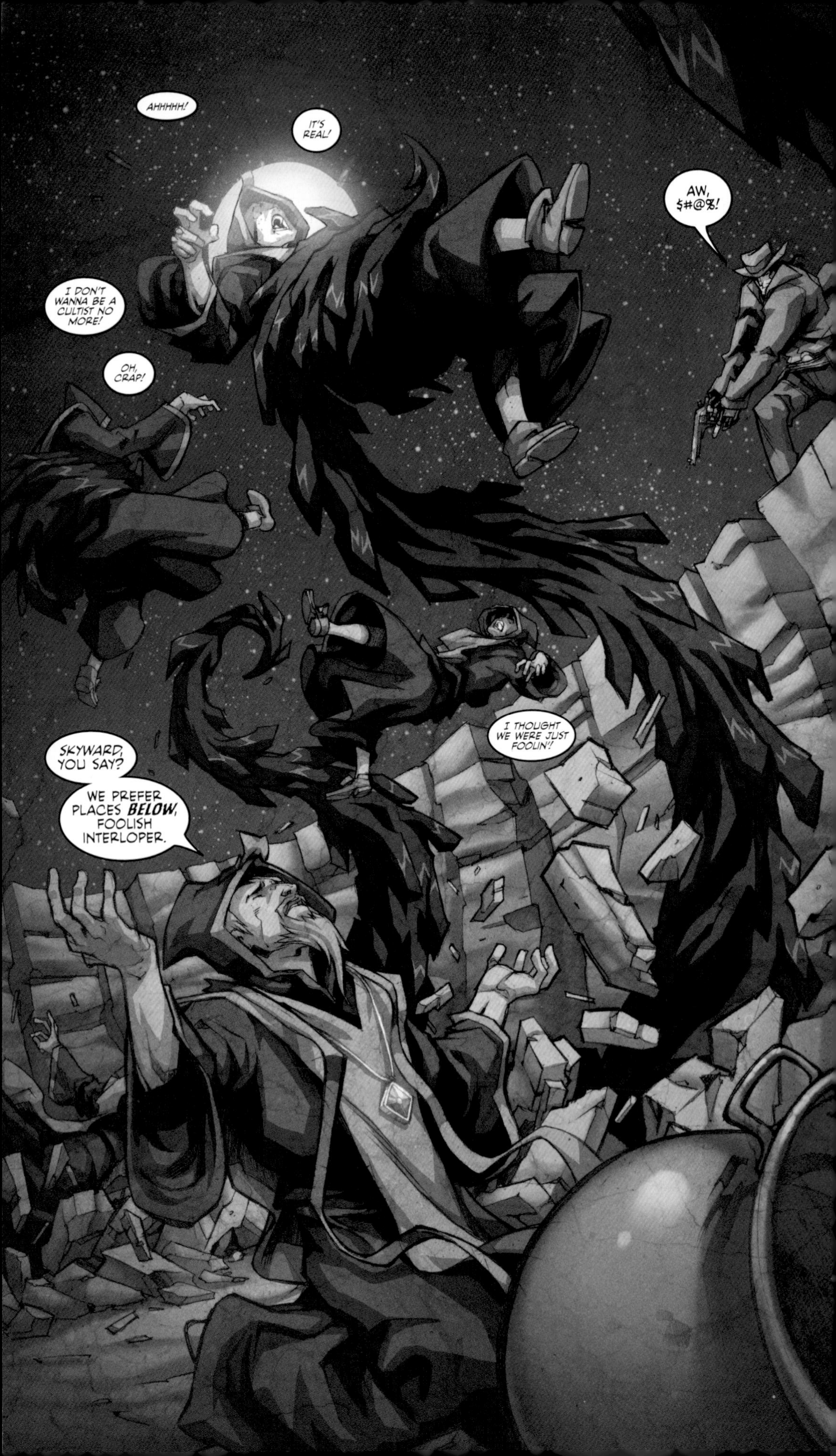
AHHHHH!
IT'S REAL!
I DON'T WANNA BE A CULTIST NO MORE!
OH, CRAP!
AW, $#@%!
I THOUGHT WE WERE JUST FOOLIN'!
SKYWARD, YOU SAY?
WE PREFER PLACES **BELOW**, FOOLISH INTERLOPER.

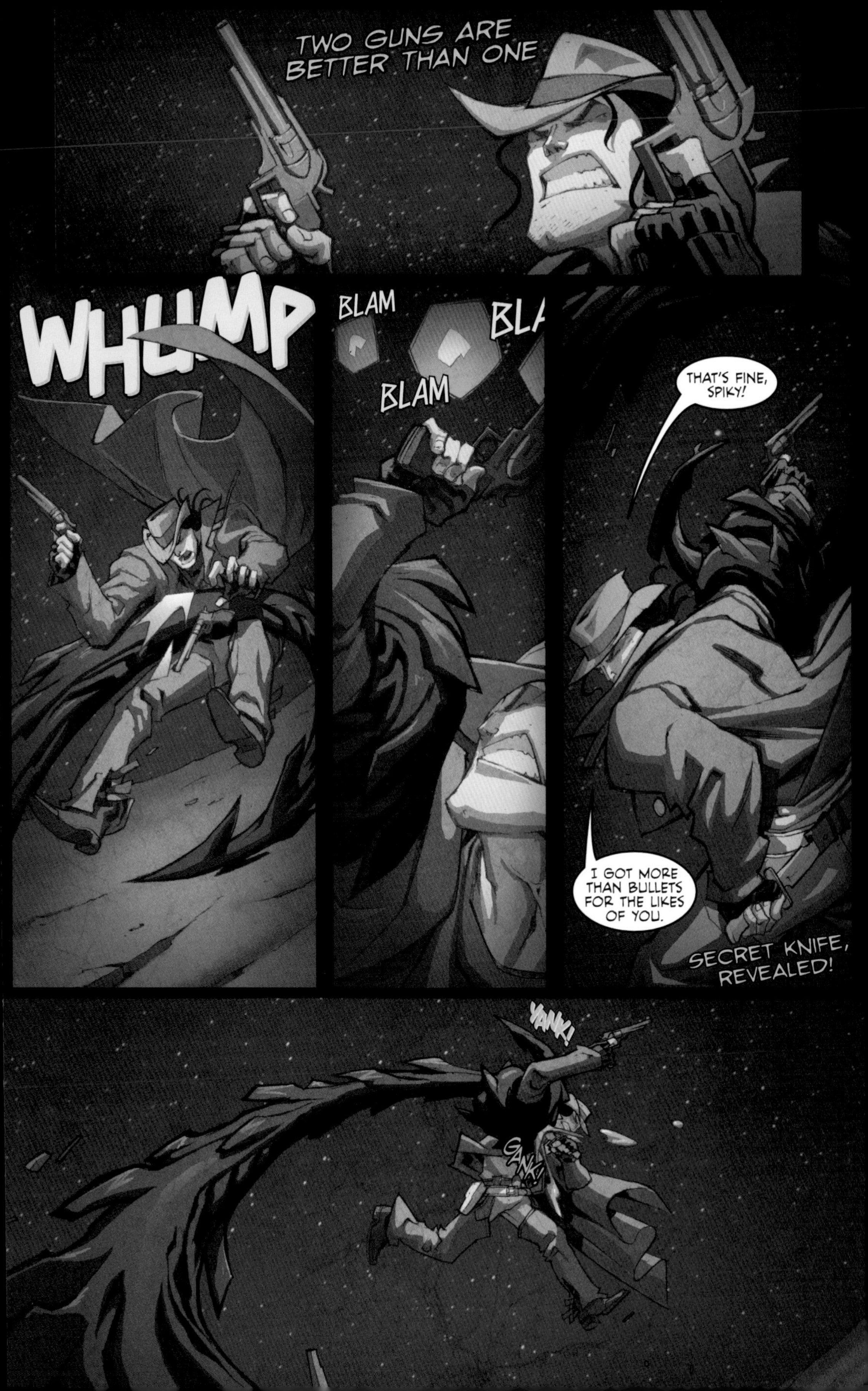
TWO GUNS ARE BETTER THAN ONE
WHUMP
BLAM
BLAM
THAT'S FINE, SPIKY!
I GOT MORE THAN BULLETS FOR THE LIKES OF YOU.
SECRET KNIFE, REVEALED!
YANK!
GANK!

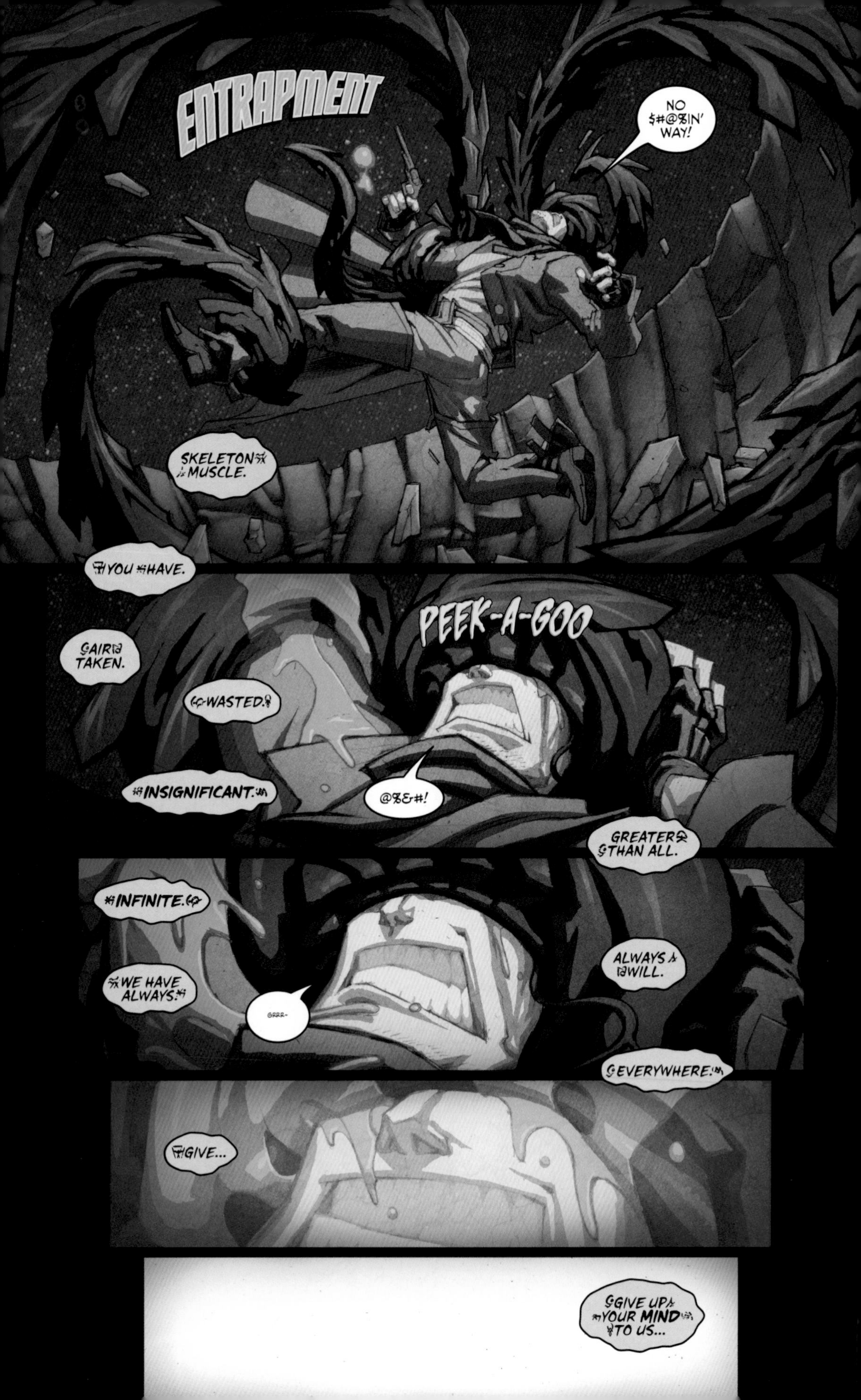
ENTRAPMENT
NO $#@%IN' WAY!
SKELETON MUSCLE.
YOU HAVE.
PEEK-A-GOO
AIR TAKEN.
WASTED.
INSIGNIFICANT.
@%&#!
GREATER THAN ALL.
INFINITE.
WE HAVE ALWAYS.
GRRR-
ALWAYS WILL.
EVERYWHERE.
GIVE...
GIVE UP YOUR MIND TO US...

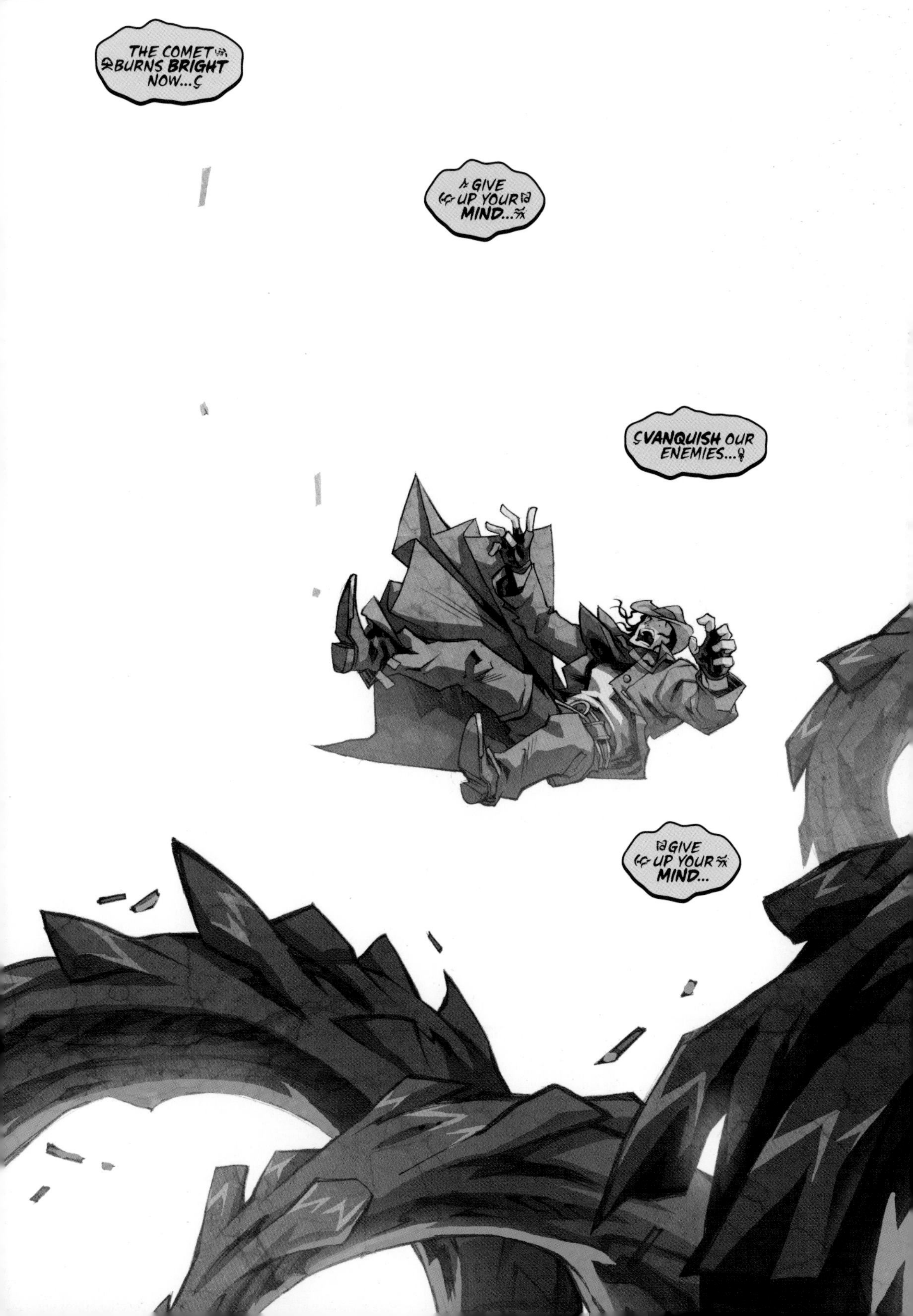
THE COMET BURNS BRIGHT NOW...
GIVE UP YOUR MIND...
VANQUISH OUR ENEMIES...
GIVE UP YOUR MIND...

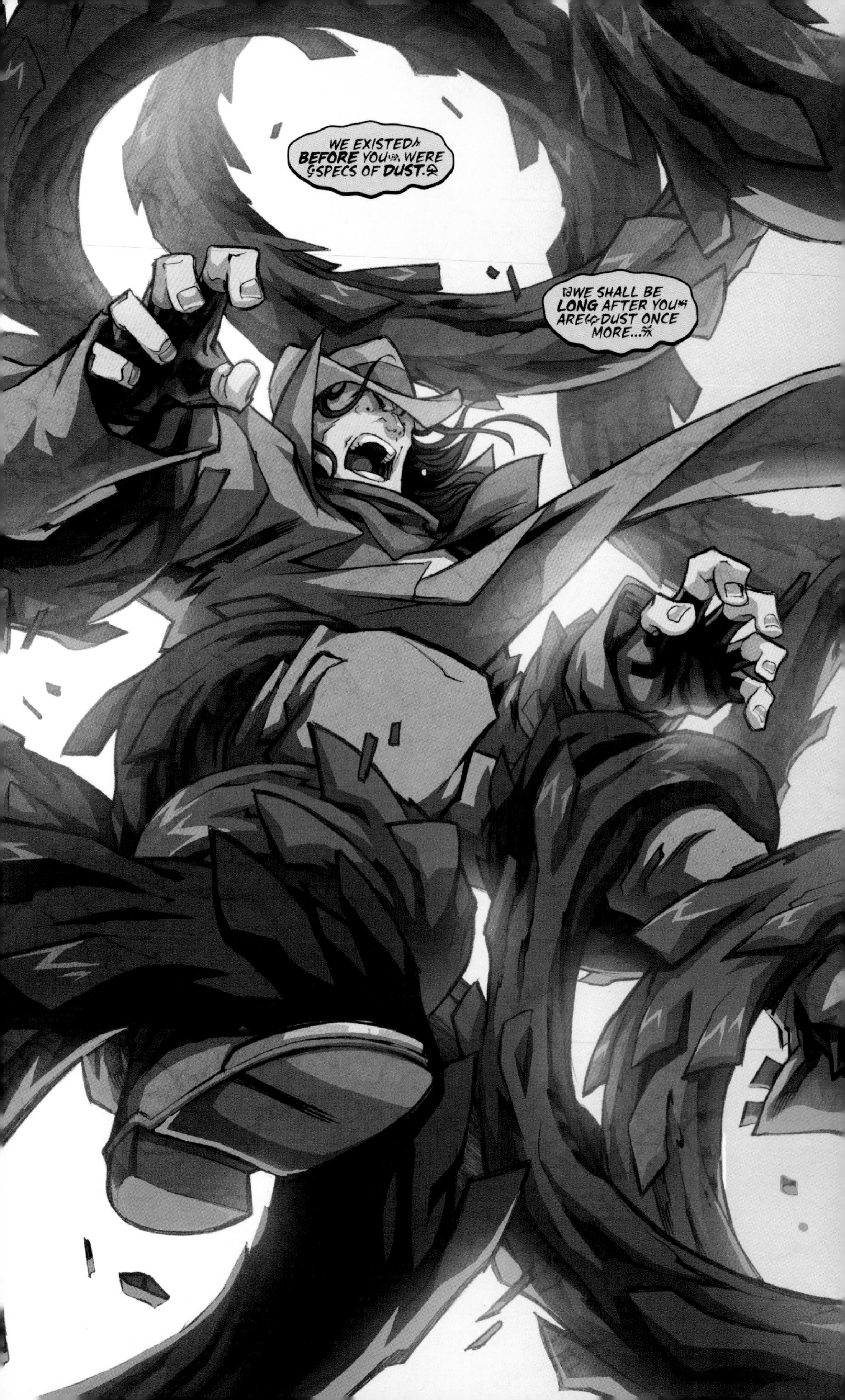
WE EXISTED BEFORE YOU WERE SPECS OF DUST.
WE SHALL BE LONG AFTER YOU ARE DUST ONCE MORE...

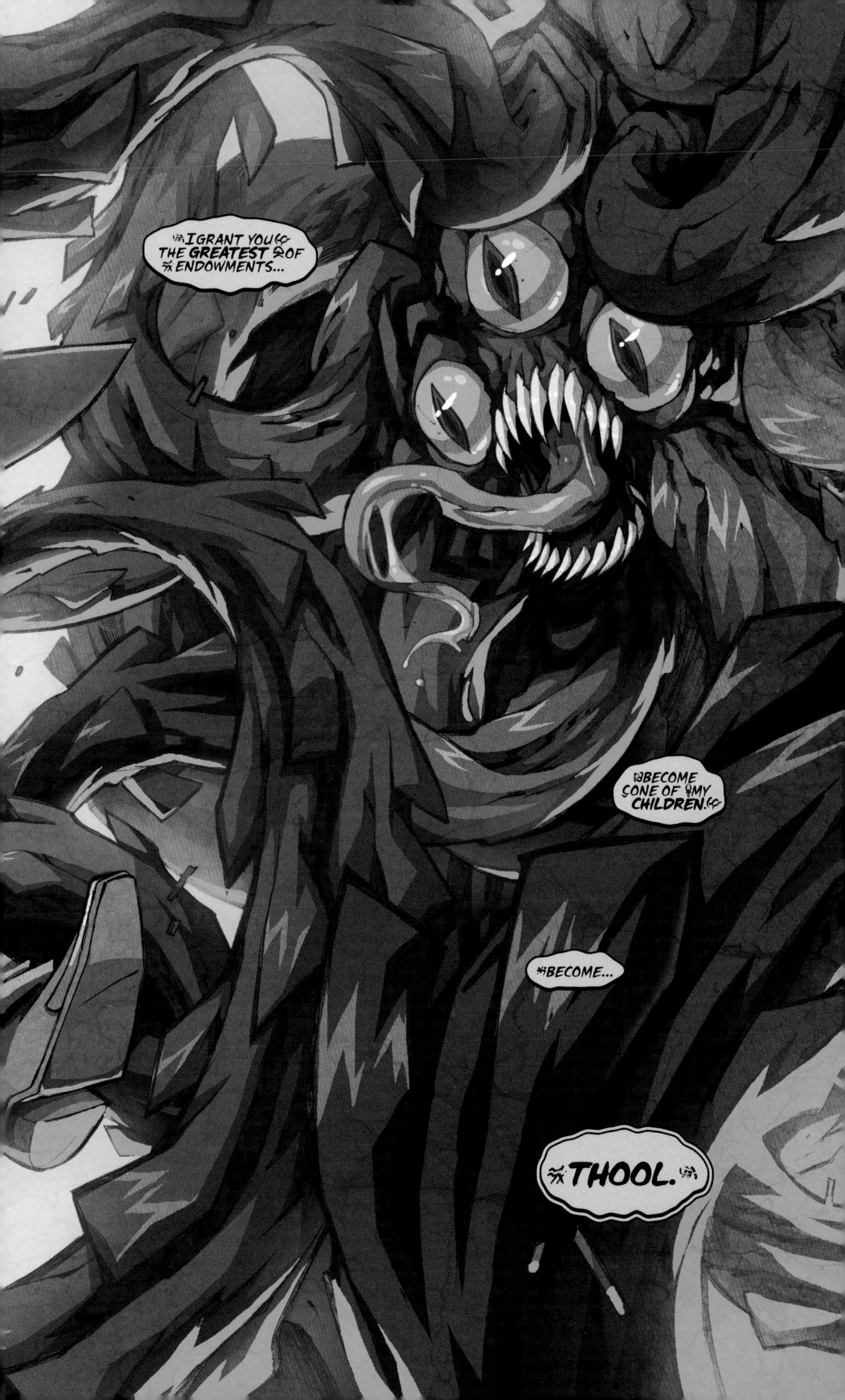
I GRANT YOU THE GREATEST OF ENDOWMENTS...
BECOME ONE OF MY CHILDREN.
BECOME...
THOOL.

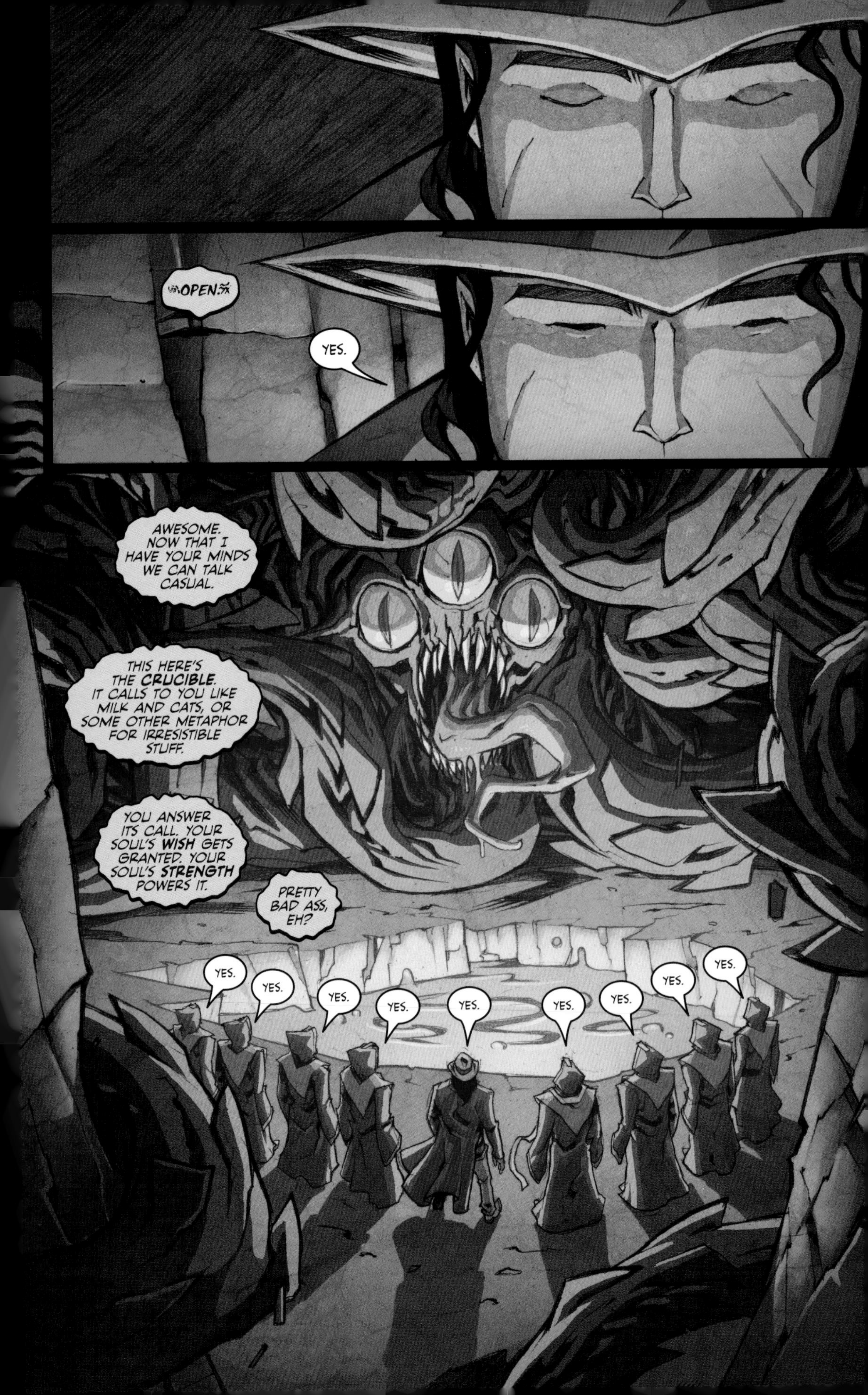
OPEN.
YES.
AWESOME. NOW THAT I HAVE YOUR MINDS WE CAN TALK CASUAL.
THIS HERE'S THE CRUCIBLE. IT CALLS TO YOU LIKE MILK AND CATS, OR SOME OTHER METAPHOR FOR IRRESISTIBLE STUFF.
YOU ANSWER ITS CALL. YOUR SOUL'S WISH GETS GRANTED. YOUR SOUL'S STRENGTH POWERS IT.
PRETTY BAD ASS, EH?
YES.
YES.
YES.
YES.
YES.
YES.
YES.
YES.
YES.

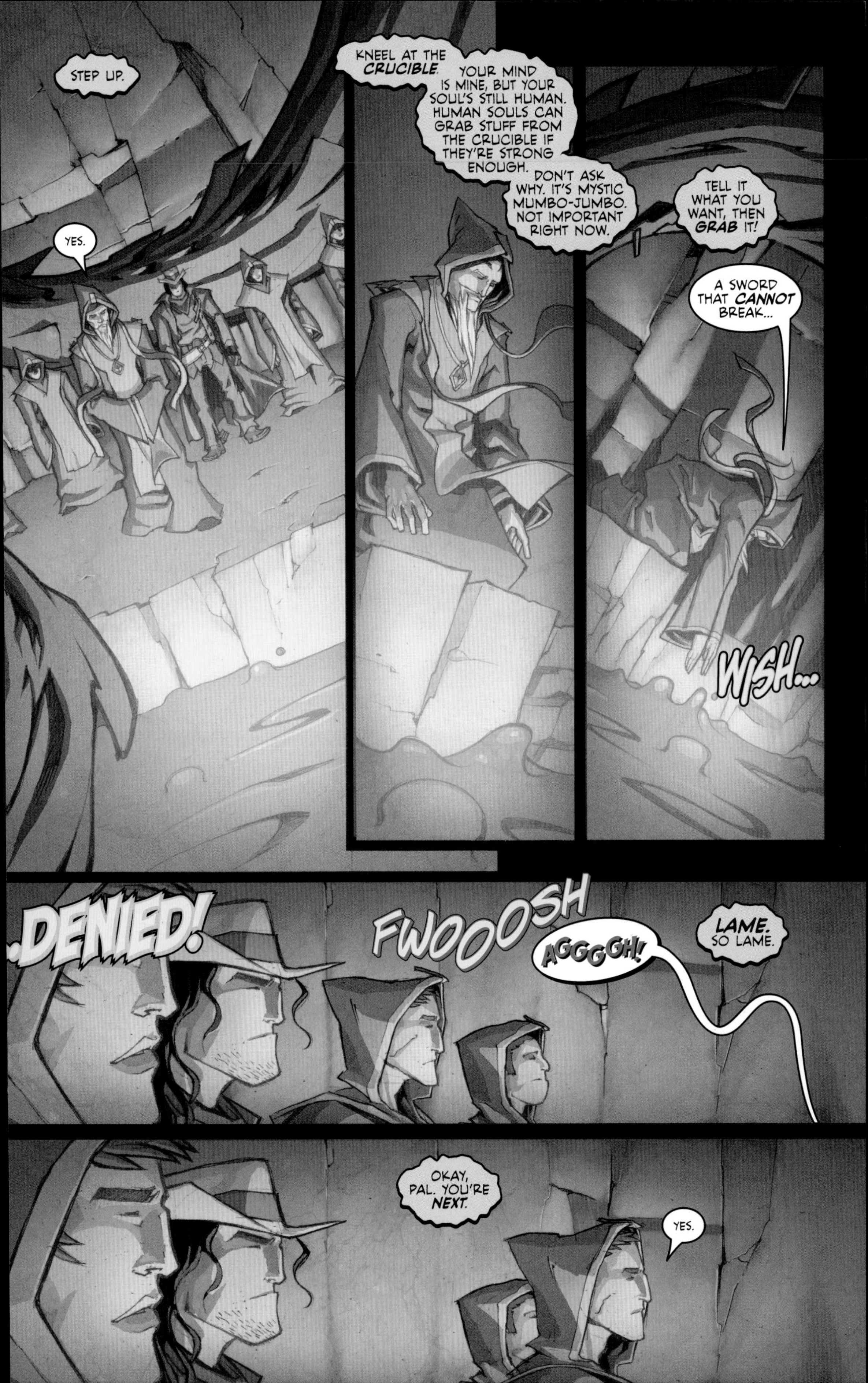
STEP UP.
YES.
KNEEL AT THE CRUCIBLE. YOUR MIND IS MINE, BUT YOUR SOUL'S STILL HUMAN. HUMAN SOULS CAN GRAB STUFF FROM THE CRUCIBLE IF THEY'RE STRONG ENOUGH.
DON'T ASK WHY. IT'S MYSTIC MUMBO-JUMBO. NOT IMPORTANT RIGHT NOW.
TELL IT WHAT YOU WANT, THEN GRAB IT!
A SWORD THAT CANNOT BREAK...
WISH...
..DENIED!
FWOOOOSH
AGGGGH!
LAME. SO LAME.
OKAY, PAL. YOU'RE NEXT.
YES.

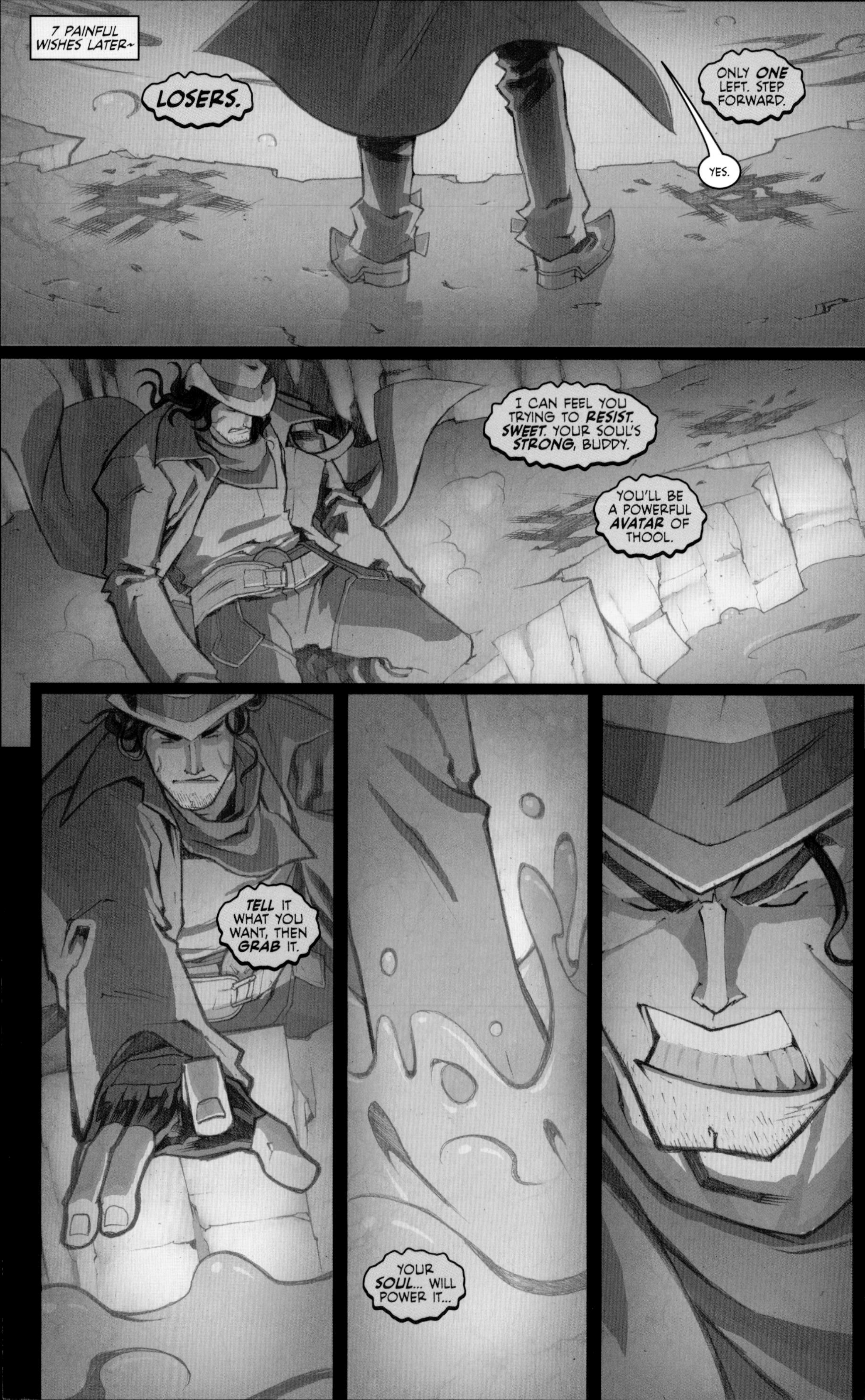
7 PAINFUL WISHES LATER~
LOSERS.
ONLY ONE LEFT. STEP FORWARD.
YES.
I CAN FEEL YOU TRYING TO RESIST. SWEET. YOUR SOUL'S STRONG, BUDDY.
YOU'LL BE A POWERFUL AVATAR OF THOOL.
TELL IT WHAT YOU WANT, THEN GRAB IT.
YOUR SOUL... WILL POWER IT...

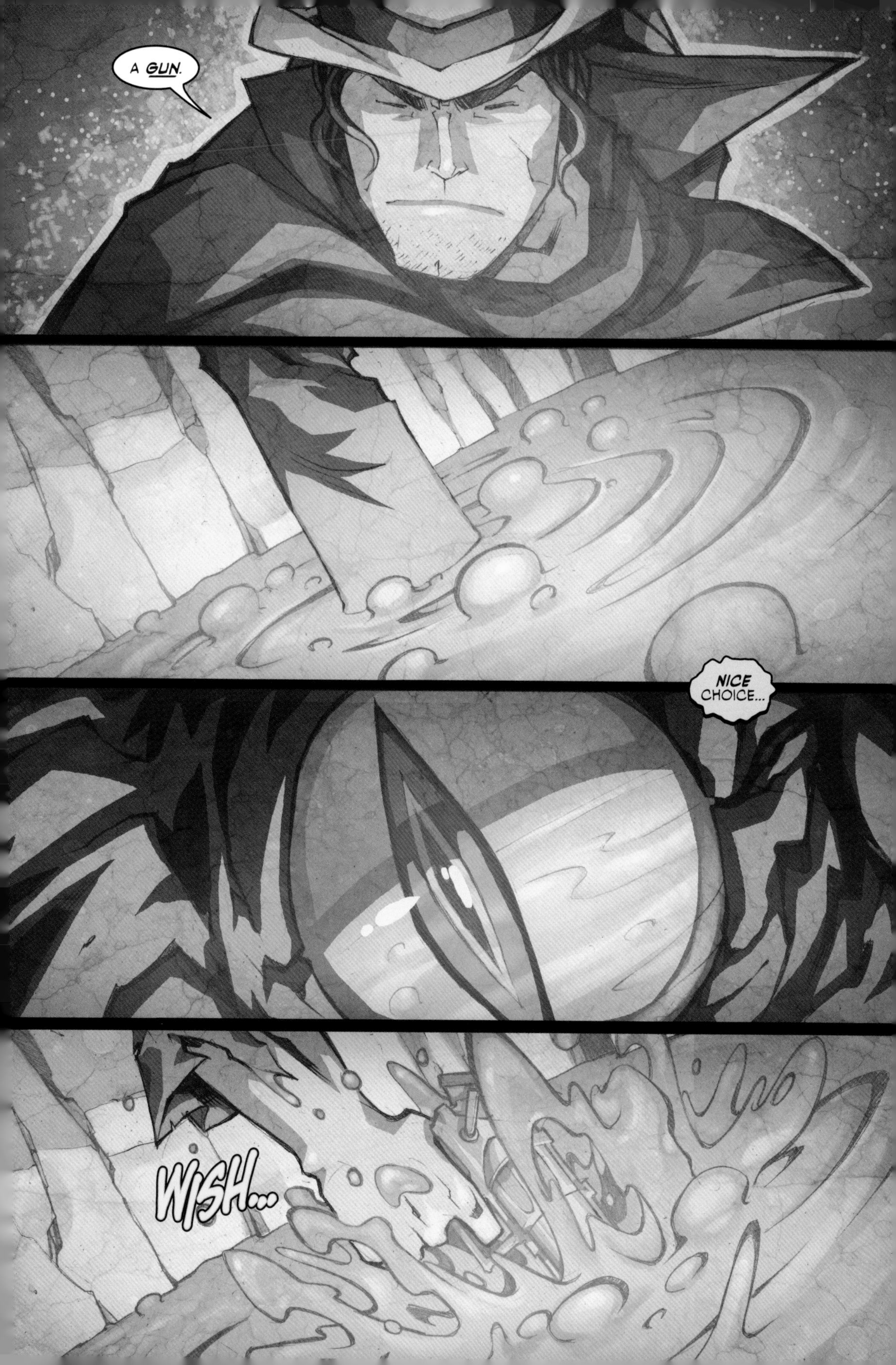
A GUN.
NICE CHOICE...
WISH...

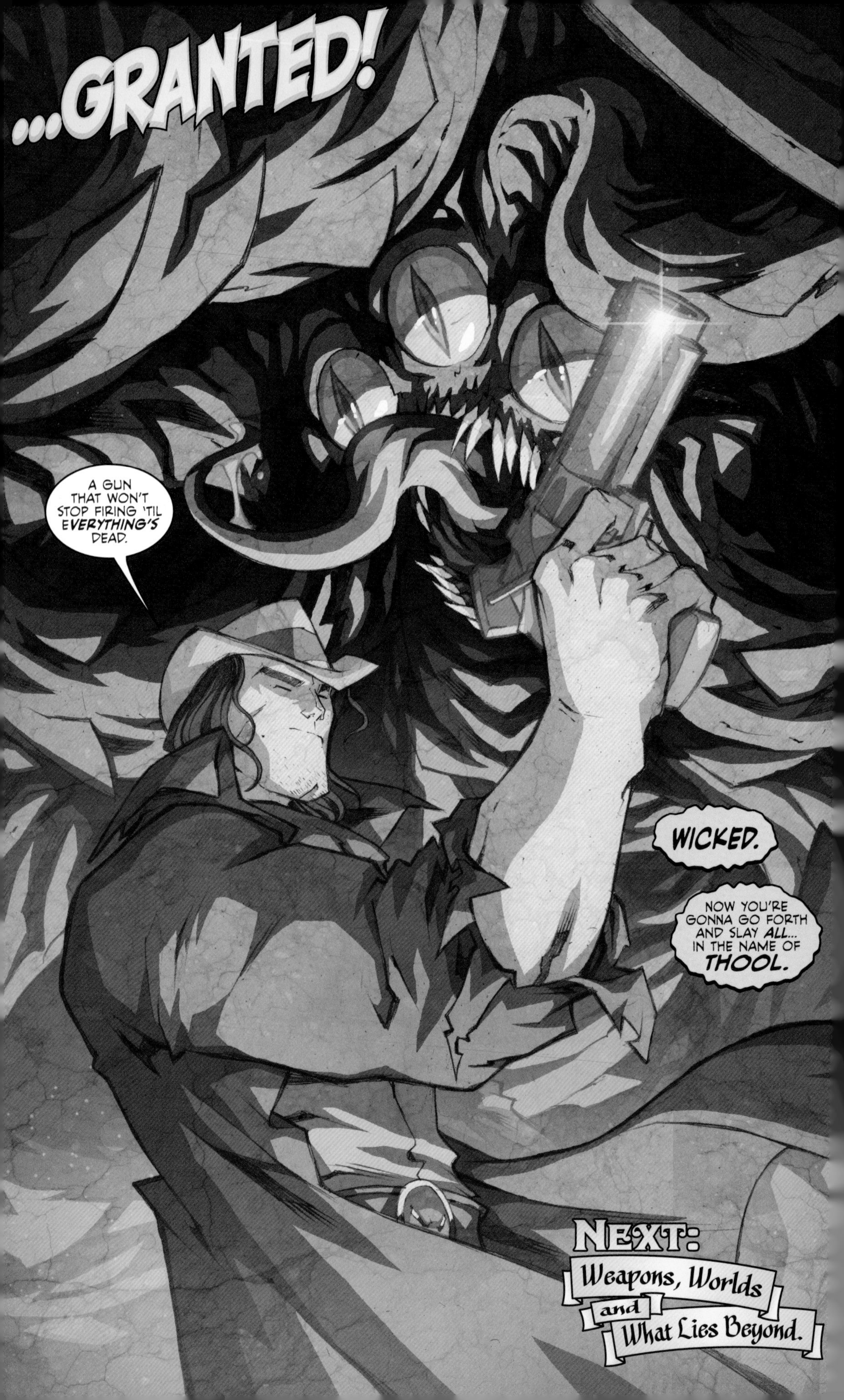
...GRANTED!
A GUN THAT WON'T STOP FIRING 'TIL EVERYTHING'S DEAD.
WICKED.
NOW YOU'RE GONNA GO FORTH AND SLAY ALL... IN THE NAME OF THOOL.
NEXT:
Weapons, Worlds and What Lies Beyond.

CHAPTER THREE

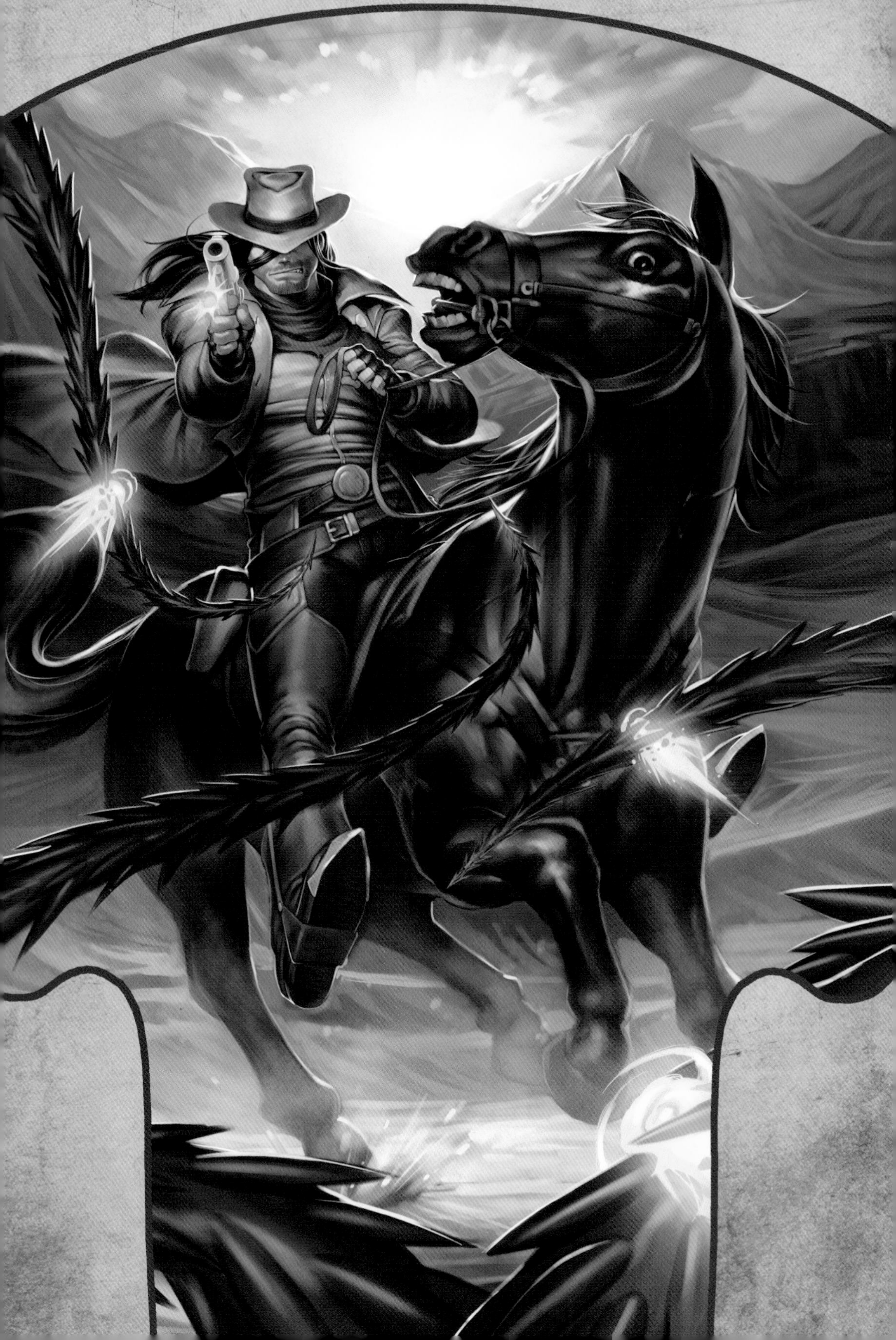

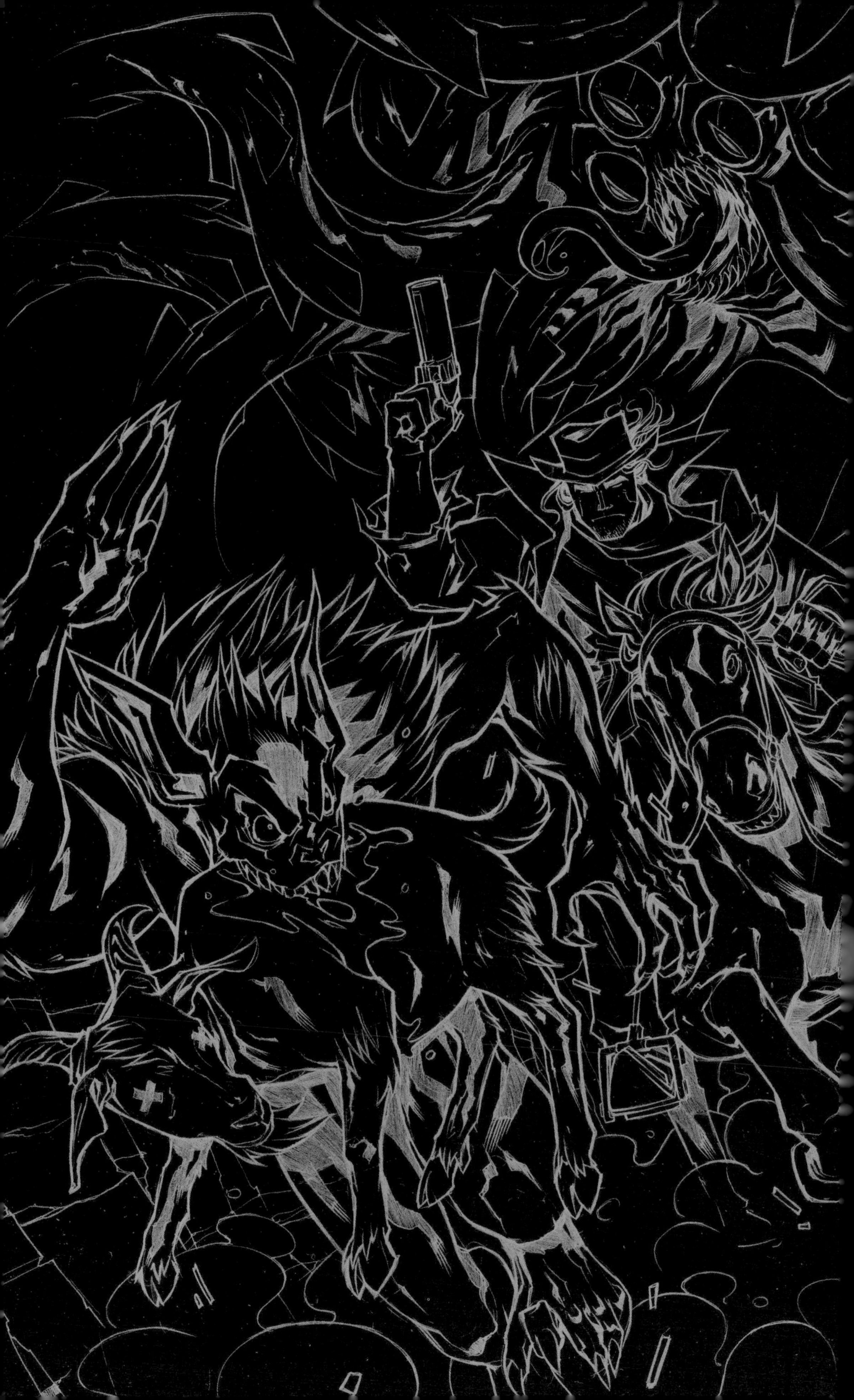

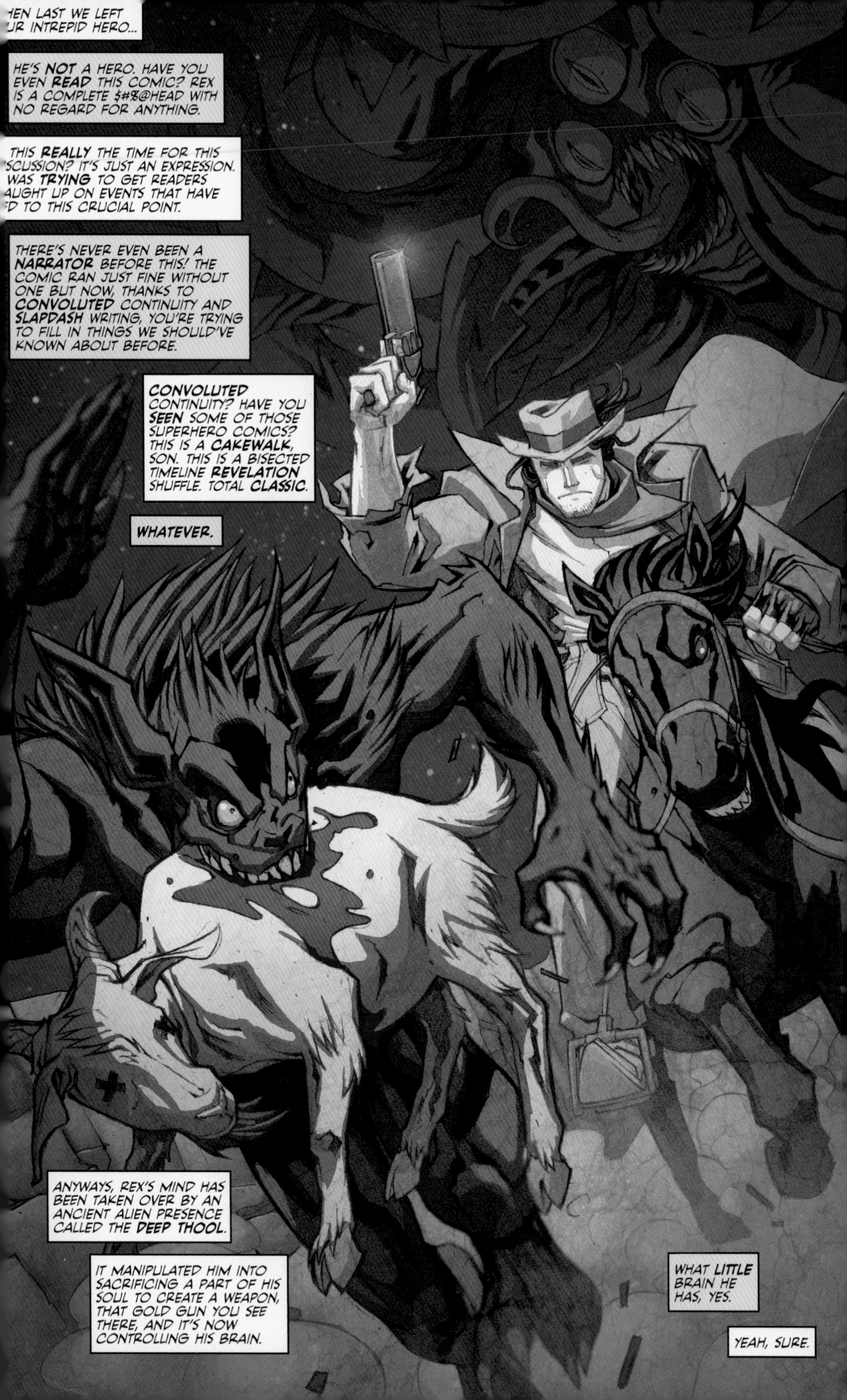
HEN LAST WE LEFT UR INTREPID HERO...
HE'S NOT A HERO. HAVE YOU EVEN READ THIS COMIC? REX IS A COMPLETE $#%@HEAD WITH NO REGARD FOR ANYTHING.
THIS REALLY THE TIME FOR THIS SCUSSION? IT'S JUST AN EXPRESSION. WAS TRYING TO GET READERS AUGHT UP ON EVENTS THAT HAVE D TO THIS CRUCIAL POINT.
THERE'S NEVER EVEN BEEN A NARRATOR BEFORE THIS! THE COMIC RAN JUST FINE WITHOUT ONE BUT NOW, THANKS TO CONVOLUTED CONTINUITY AND SLAPDASH WRITING, YOU'RE TRYING TO FILL IN THINGS WE SHOULD'VE KNOWN ABOUT BEFORE.
CONVOLUTED CONTINUITY? HAVE YOU SEEN SOME OF THOSE SUPERHERO COMICS? THIS IS A CAKEWALK, SON. THIS IS A BISECTED TIMELINE REVELATION SHUFFLE. TOTAL CLASSIC.
WHATEVER.
ANYWAYS, REX'S MIND HAS BEEN TAKEN OVER BY AN ANCIENT ALIEN PRESENCE CALLED THE DEEP THOOL.
IT MANIPULATED HIM INTO SACRIFICING A PART OF HIS SOUL TO CREATE A WEAPON, THAT GOLD GUN YOU SEE THERE, AND IT'S NOW CONTROLLING HIS BRAIN.
WHAT LITTLE BRAIN HE HAS, YES.
YEAH, SURE.

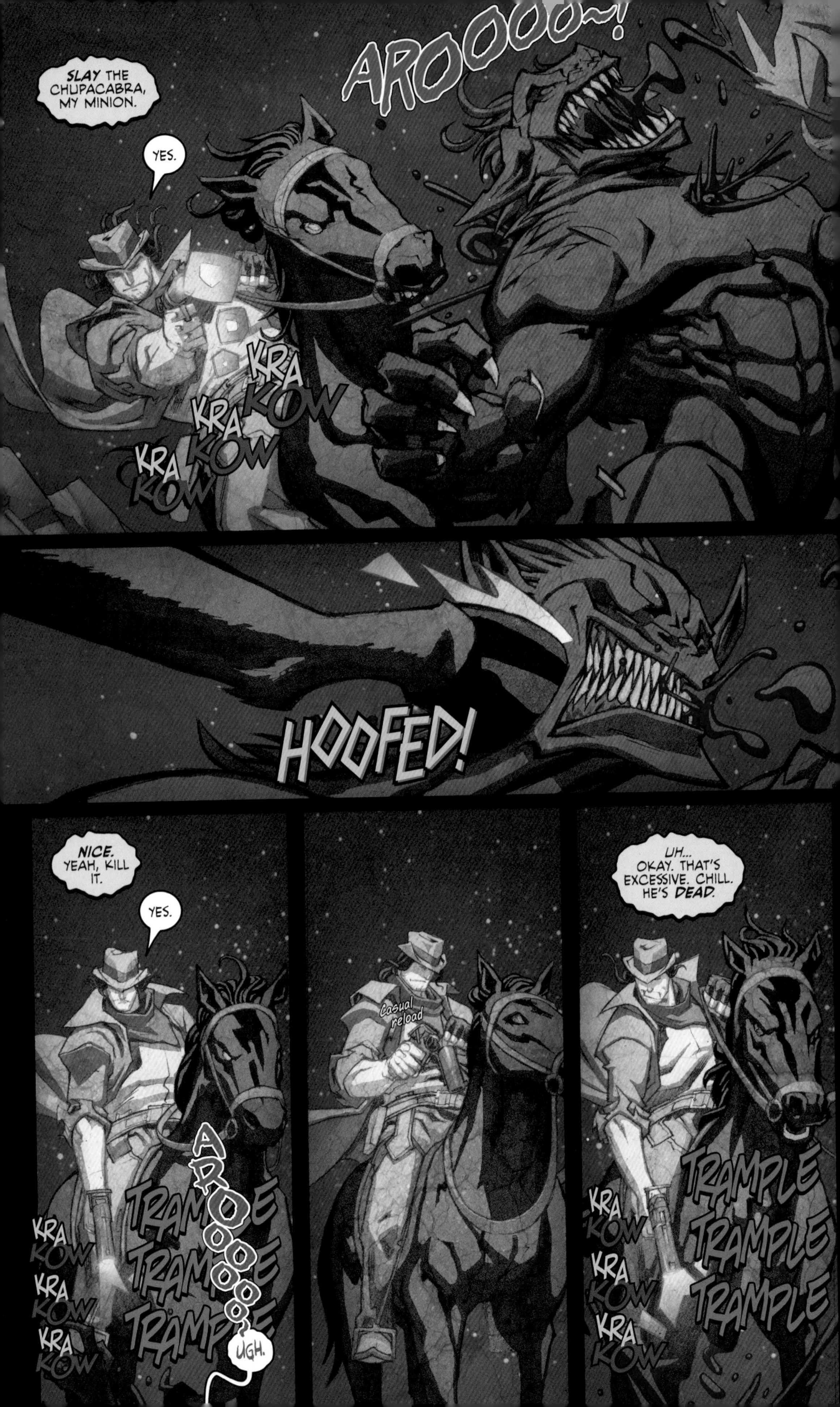

SLAY THE CHUPACABRA, MY MINION.
AROOOOO~!
YES.
KRA KOW
KRA KOW
KRA KOW
HOOFED!
NICE. YEAH, KILL IT.
YES.
KRA KOW
KRA KOW
KRA KOW
TRAMPLE TRAMPLE TRAMPLE
AROOOOOO~
UGH.
Casual reload
UH... OKAY. THAT'S EXCESSIVE. CHILL. HE'S DEAD.
KRA KOW
KRA KOW
KRA KOW
TRAMPLE TRAMPLE TRAMPLE

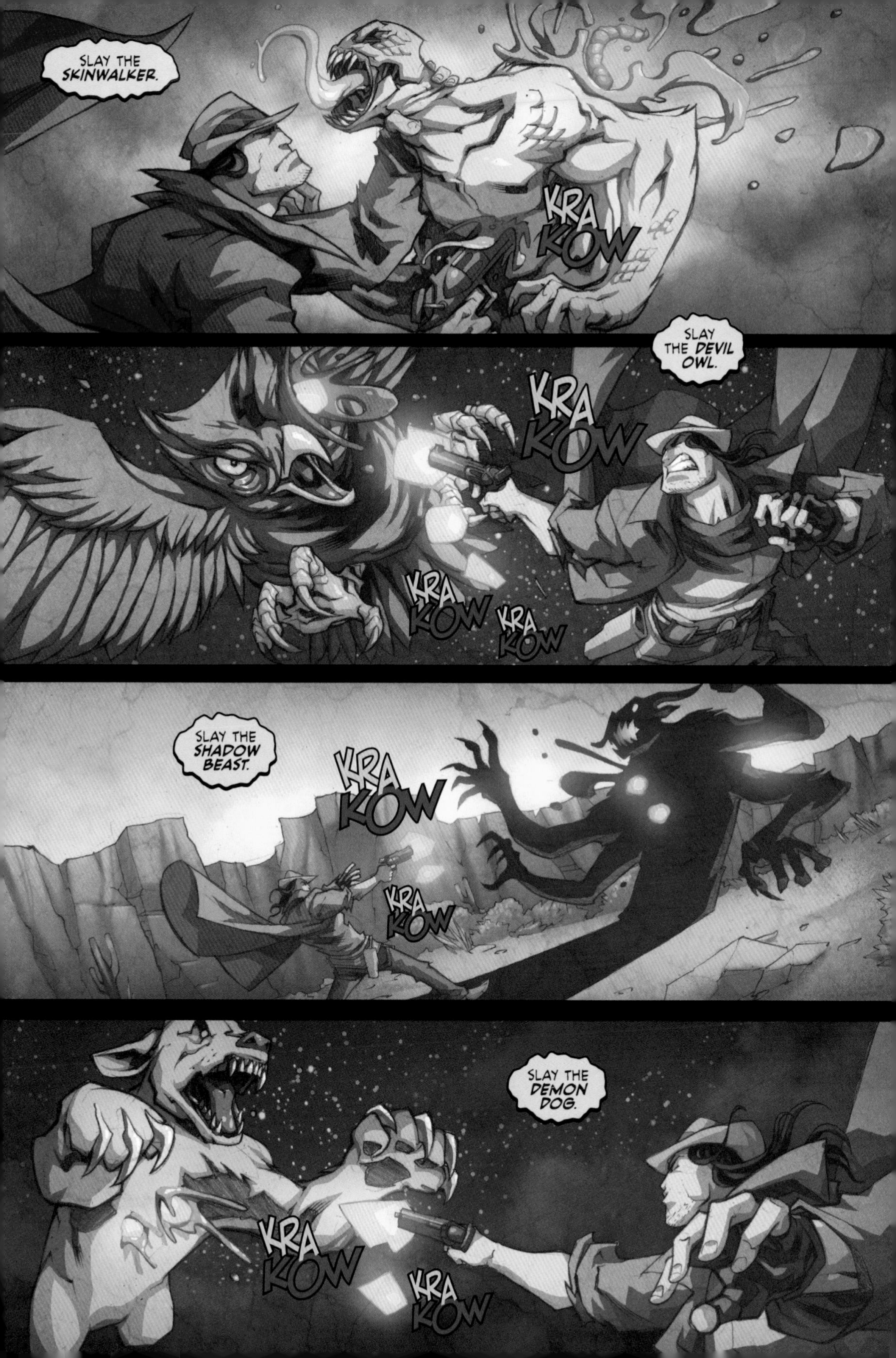
SLAY THE SKINWALKER.
KRA KOW
SLAY THE DEVIL OWL.
KRA KOW
KRA KOW
KRA KOW
SLAY THE SHADOW BEAST.
KRA KOW
KRA KOW
SLAY THE DEMON DOG.
KRA KOW
KRA KOW

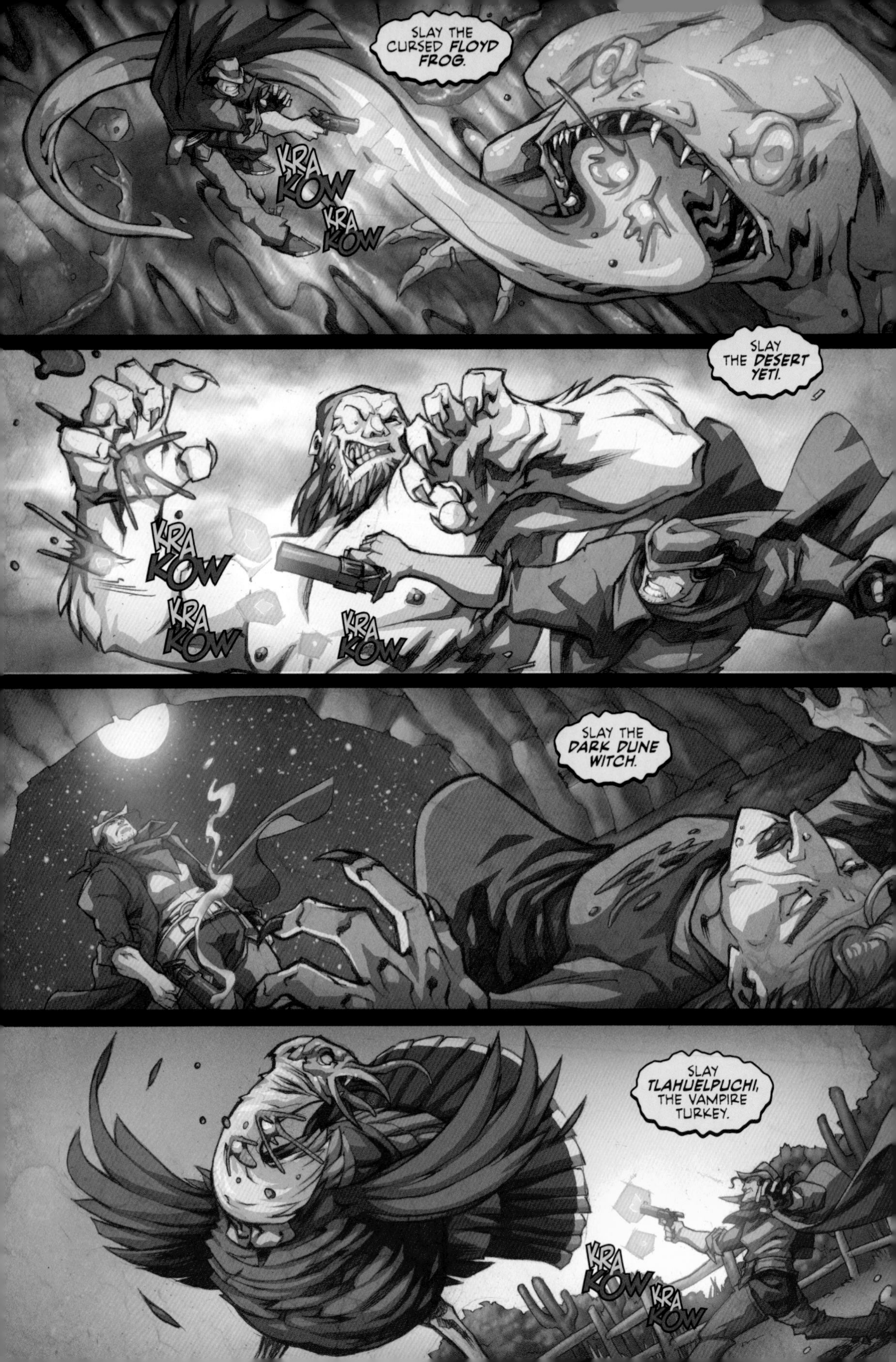

SLAY THE CURSED FLOYD FROG.
KRA KOW
KRA KOW
SLAY THE DESERT YETI.
KRA KOW
KRA KOW
KRA KOW
SLAY THE DARK DUNE WITCH.
SLAY TLAHUELPUCHI, THE VAMPIRE TURKEY.
KRA KOW
KRA KOW

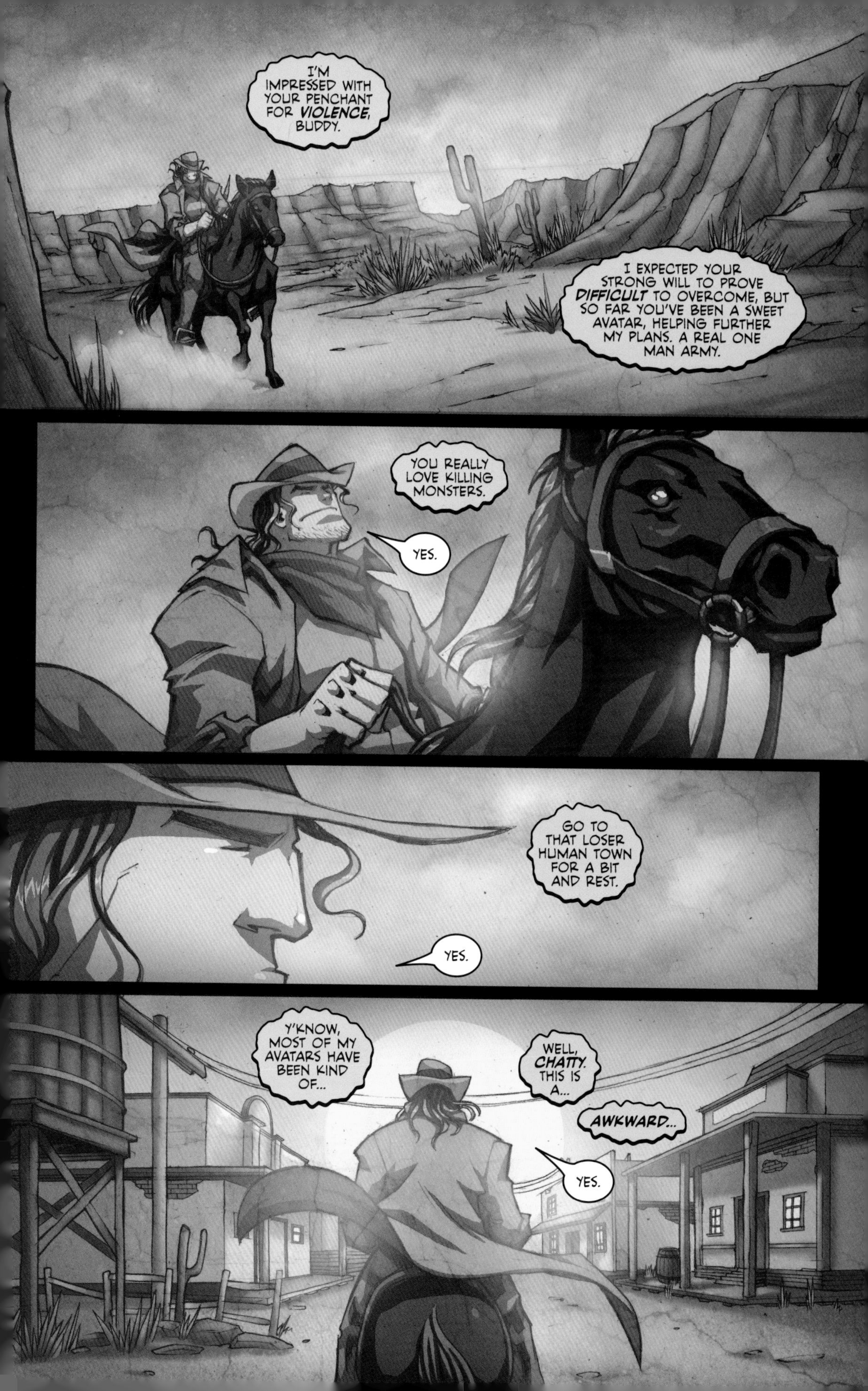
I'M IMPRESSED WITH YOUR PENCHANT FOR VIOLENCE, BUDDY.
I EXPECTED YOUR STRONG WILL TO PROVE DIFFICULT TO OVERCOME, BUT SO FAR YOU'VE BEEN A SWEET AVATAR, HELPING FURTHER MY PLANS. A REAL ONE MAN ARMY.
YOU REALLY LOVE KILLING MONSTERS.
YES.
GO TO THAT LOSER HUMAN TOWN FOR A BIT AND REST.
YES.
Y'KNOW, MOST OF MY AVATARS HAVE BEEN KIND OF...
WELL, CHATTY. THIS IS A...
AWKWARD...
YES.

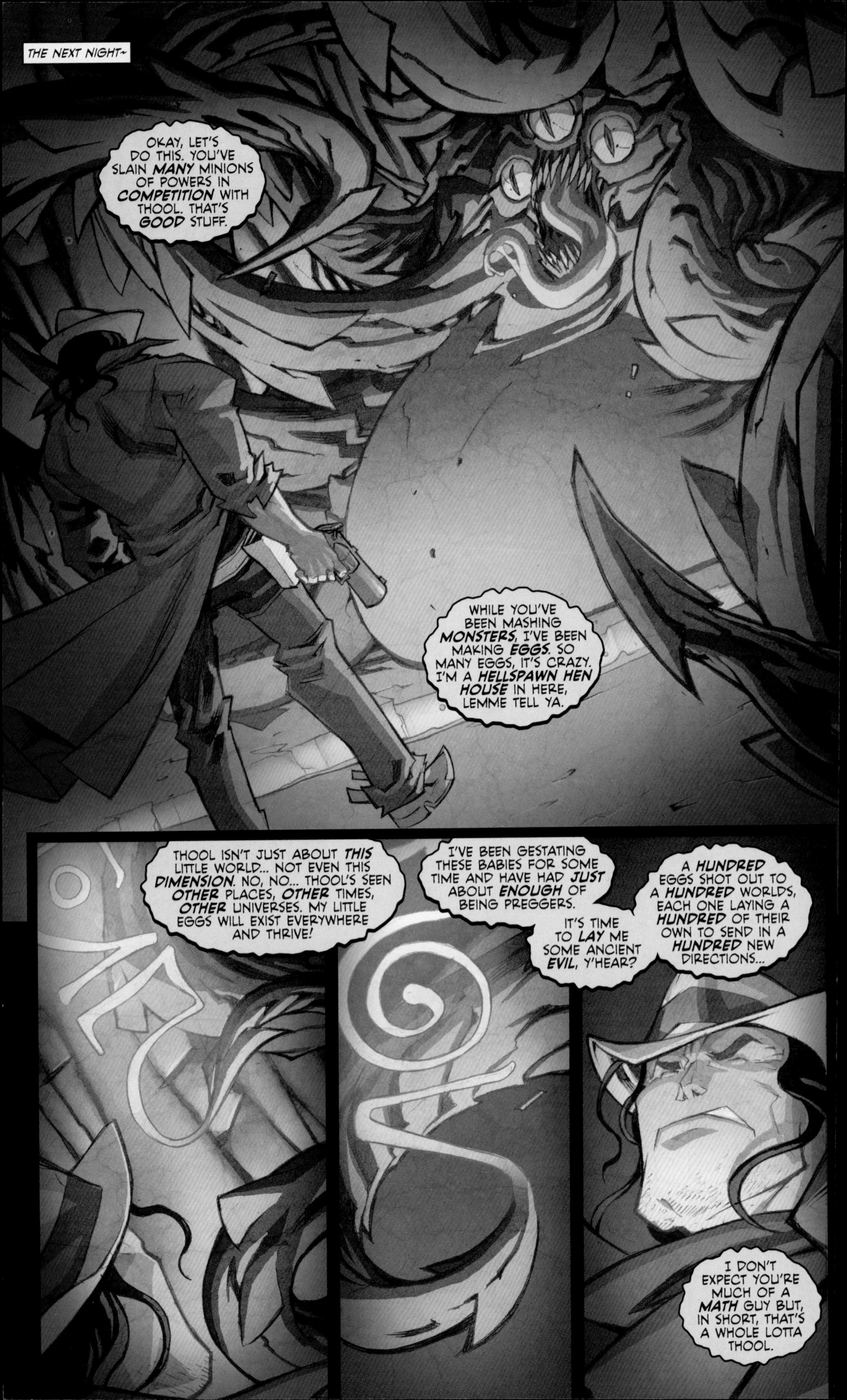
THE NEXT NIGHT~
OKAY, LET'S DO THIS. YOU'VE SLAIN MANY MINIONS OF POWERS IN COMPETITION WITH THOOL. THAT'S GOOD STUFF.
!
WHILE YOU'VE BEEN MASHING MONSTERS, I'VE BEEN MAKING EGGS. SO MANY EGGS, IT'S CRAZY. I'M A HELLSPAWN HEN HOUSE IN HERE, LEMME TELL YA.
THOOL ISN'T JUST ABOUT THIS LITTLE WORLD... NOT EVEN THIS DIMENSION. NO, NO... THOOL'S SEEN OTHER PLACES, OTHER TIMES, OTHER UNIVERSES. MY LITTLE EGGS WILL EXIST EVERYWHERE AND THRIVE!
I'VE BEEN GESTATING THESE BABIES FOR SOME TIME AND HAVE HAD JUST ABOUT ENOUGH OF BEING PREGGERS.
IT'S TIME TO LAY ME SOME ANCIENT EVIL, Y'HEAR?
A HUNDRED EGGS SHOT OUT TO A HUNDRED WORLDS, EACH ONE LAYING A HUNDRED OF THEIR OWN TO SEND IN A HUNDRED NEW DIRECTIONS...
I DON'T EXPECT YOU'RE MUCH OF A MATH GUY BUT, IN SHORT, THAT'S A WHOLE LOTTA THOOL.

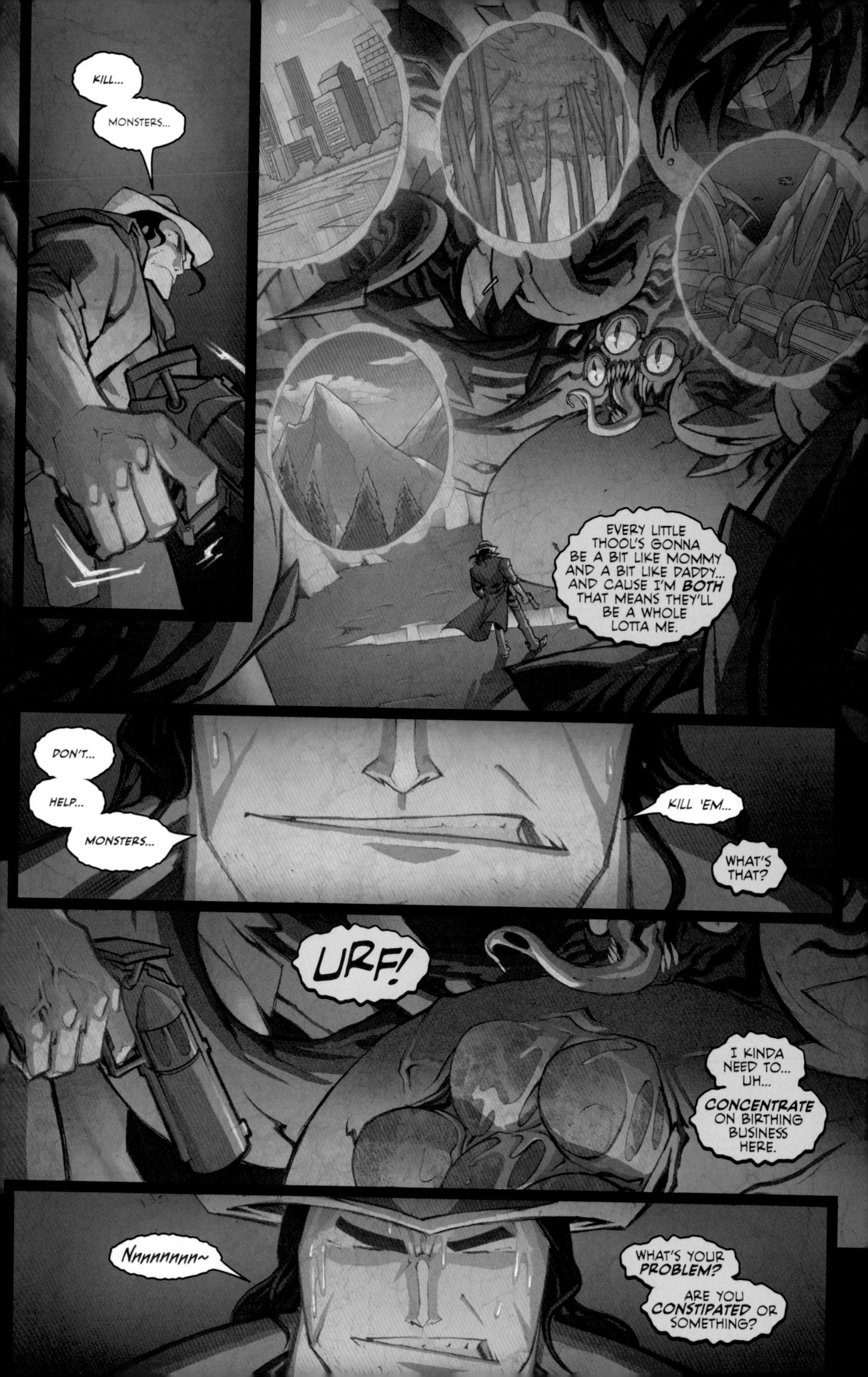
KILL...
MONSTERS...
EVERY LITTLE THOOL'S GONNA BE A BIT LIKE MOMMY AND A BIT LIKE DADDY... AND CAUSE I'M **BOTH** THAT MEANS THEY'LL BE A WHOLE LOTTA ME.
DON'T...
HELP...
MONSTERS...
KILL 'EM...
WHAT'S THAT?
URF!
I KINDA NEED TO... UH... **CONCENTRATE** ON BIRTHING BUSINESS HERE.
Nnnnnnnn~
WHAT'S YOUR **PROBLEM?**
ARE YOU **CONSTIPATED** OR SOMETHING?

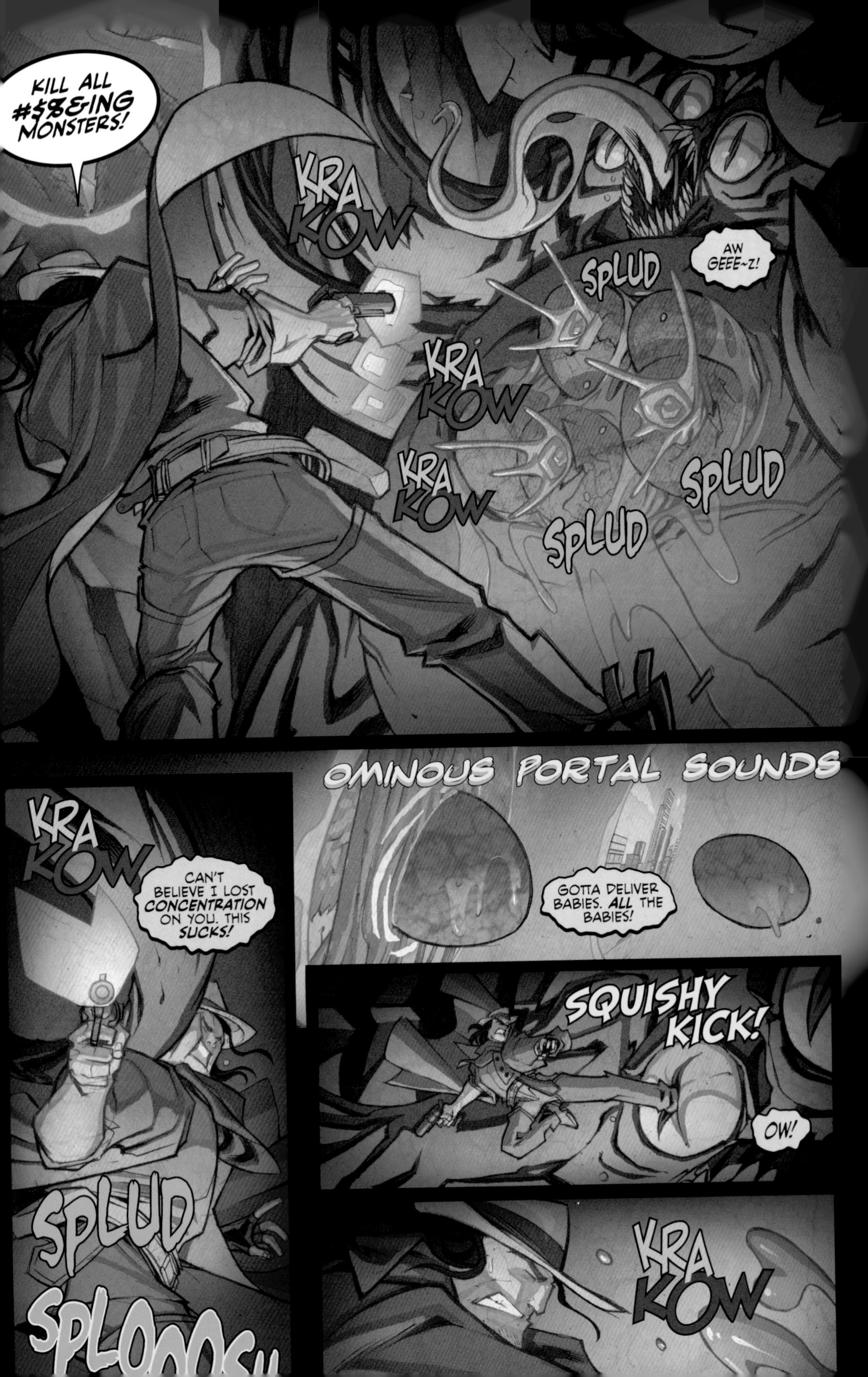
KILL ALL #$%&ING MONSTERS!
KRA KOW
SPLUD
AW GEEE~Z!
KRA KOW
KRA KOW
SPLUD
SPLUD
OMINOUS PORTAL SOUNDS
KRA KOW
CAN'T BELIEVE I LOST CONCENTRATION ON YOU. THIS SUCKS!
GOTTA DELIVER BABIES. ALL THE BABIES!
SQUISHY KICK!
OW!
SPLUD
SPLOOOSH
KRA KOW

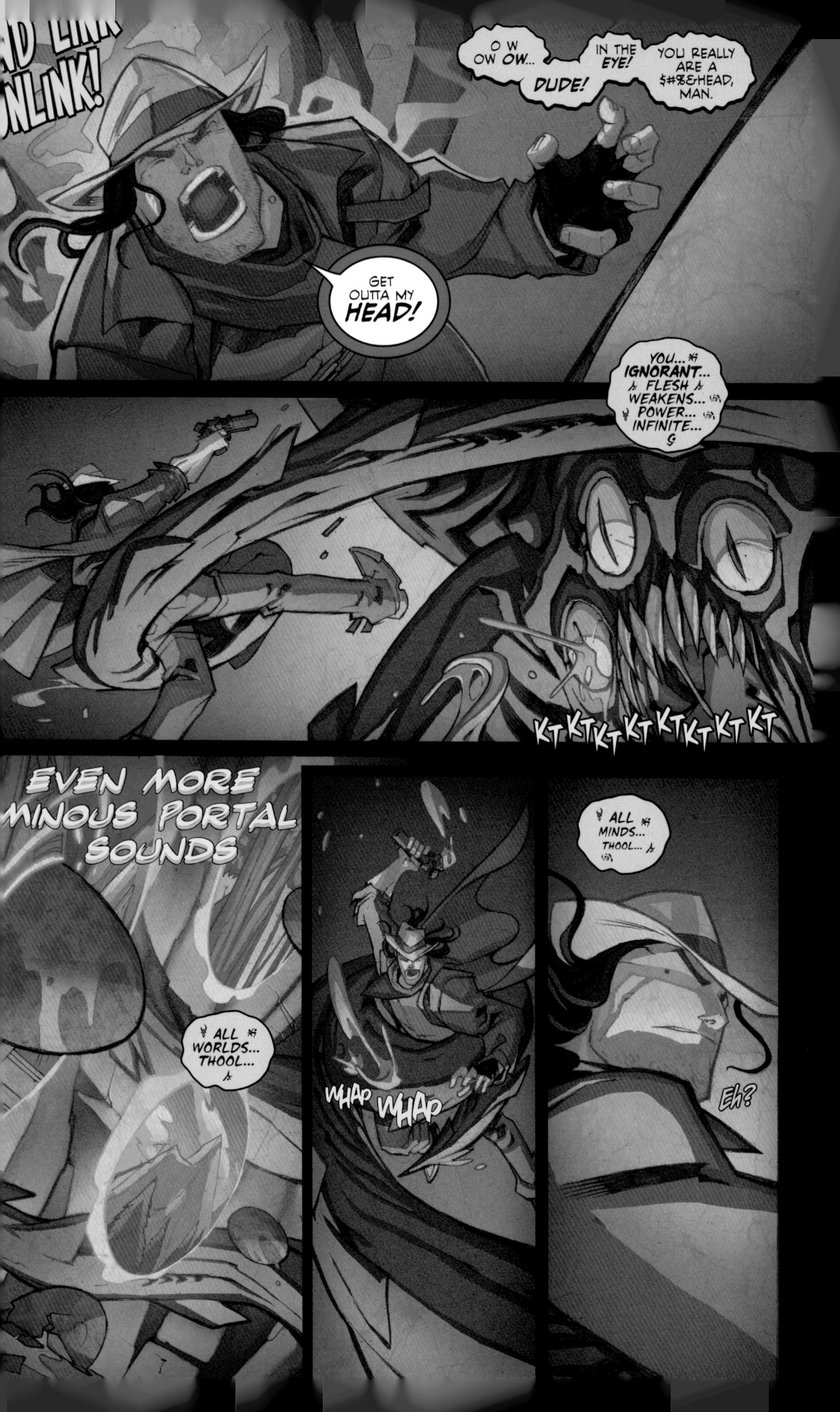

O W OW OW...
DUDE!
IN THE EYE!
YOU REALLY ARE A $#%&HEAD, MAN.
GET OUTTA MY HEAD!
YOU... IGNORANT... FLESH WEAKENS... POWER... INFINITE...
KT KT KT KT KT KT KT KT KT
EVEN MORE MINOUS PORTAL SOUNDS
ALL WORLDS... THOOL...
WHAP WHAP
ALL MINDS... THOOL...
Eh?

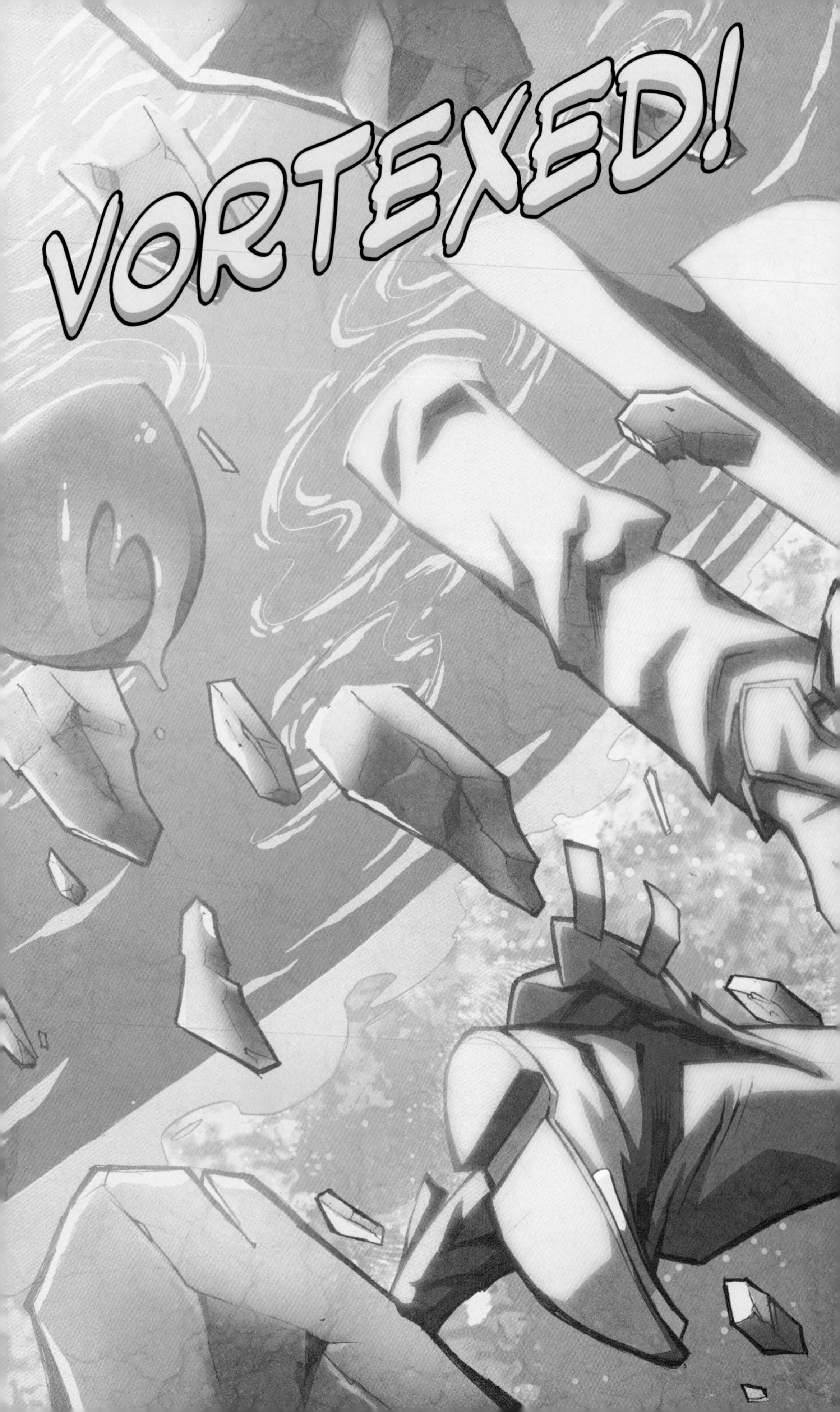
VORTEXED!

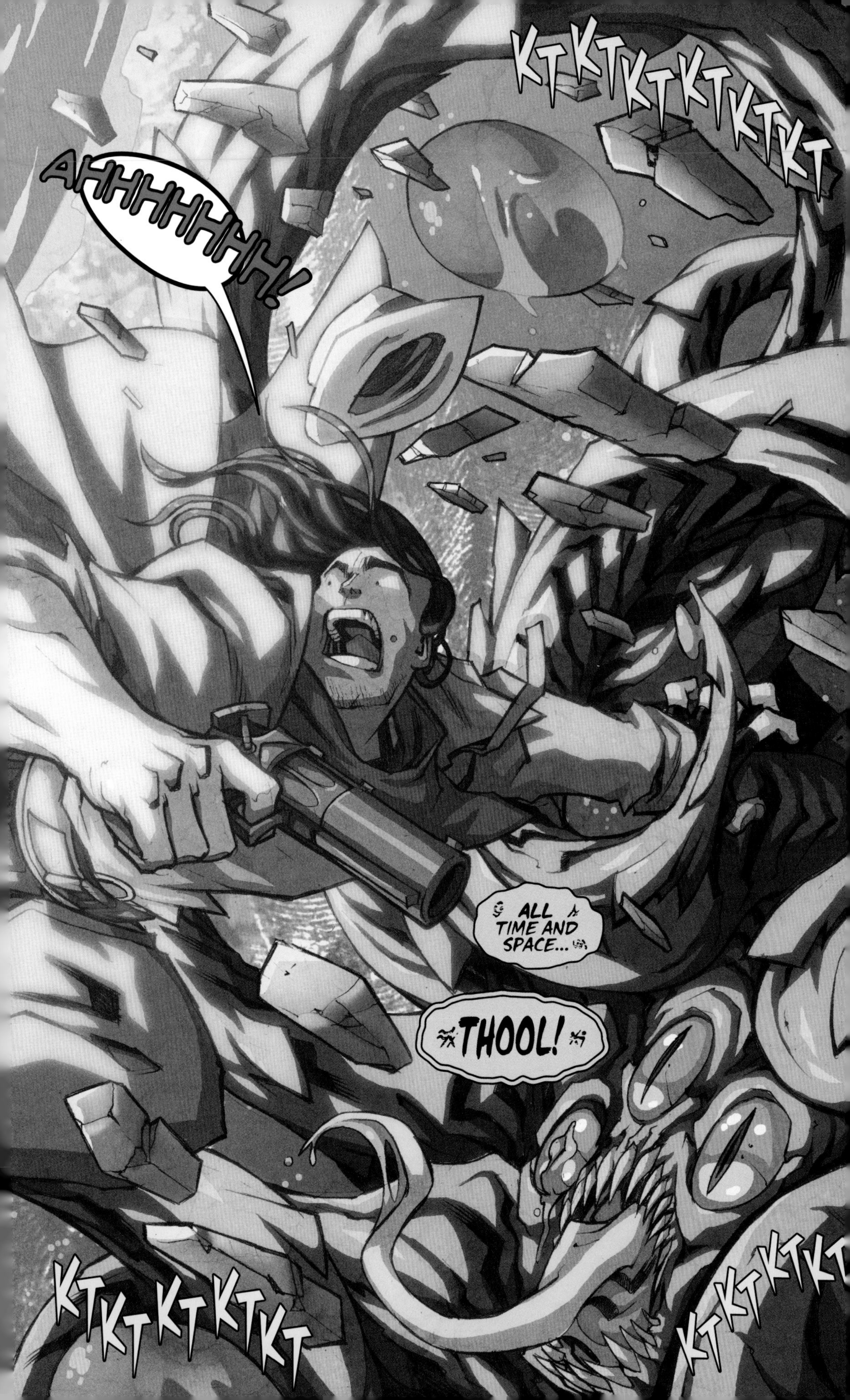

KTKTKTKTKTKTKT
AHHHHHHH!
ALL TIME AND SPACE...
THOOL!
KTKTKTKTKTKT
KTKTKTKTKT

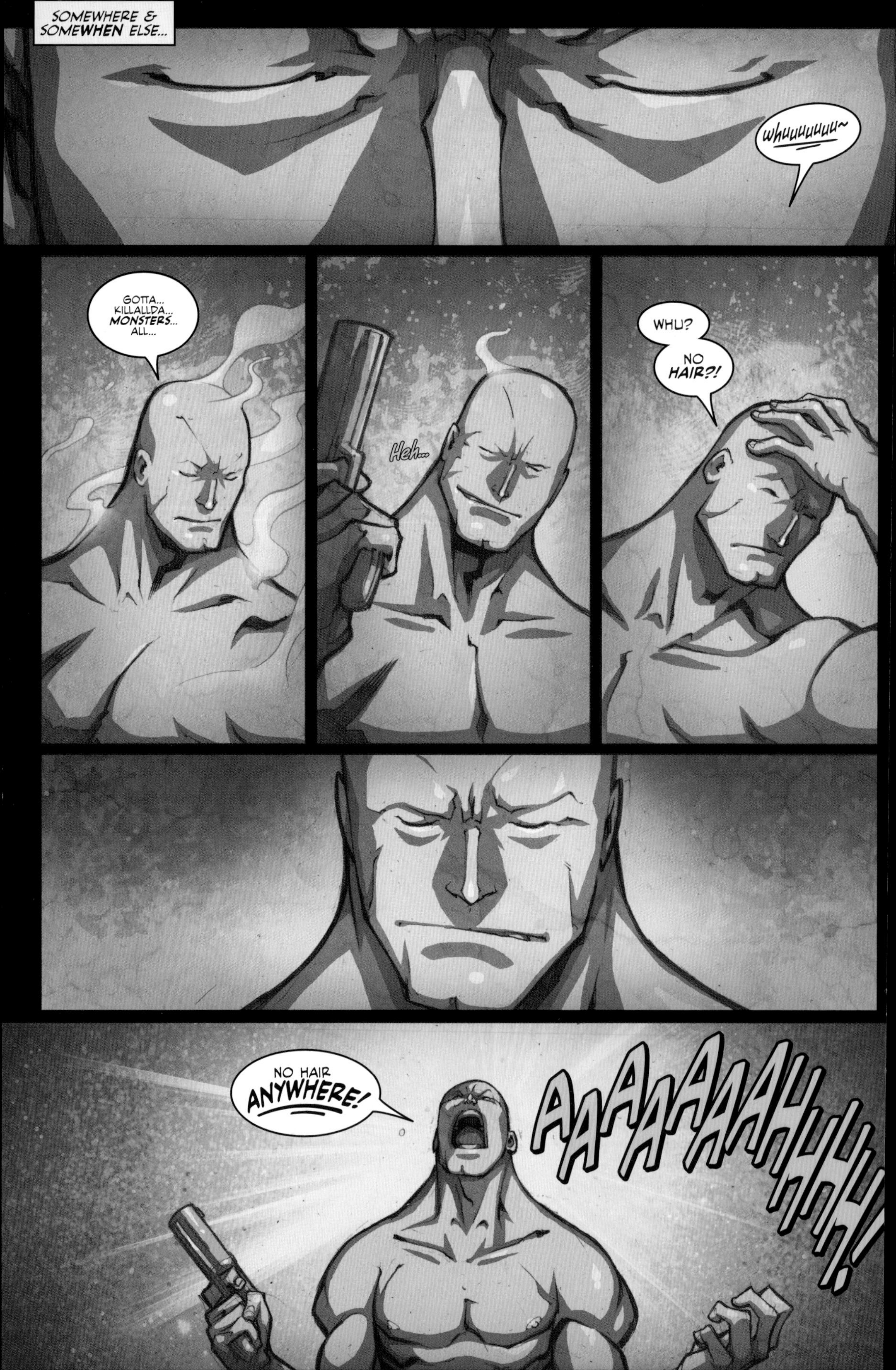
SOMEWHERE & SOMEWHEN ELSE...
whuuuuuuu~
GOTTA... KILLALLDA... MONSTERS... ALL...
Heh...
WHU?
NO HAIR?!
NO HAIR ANYWHERE!
AAAAAAAHHHHH!

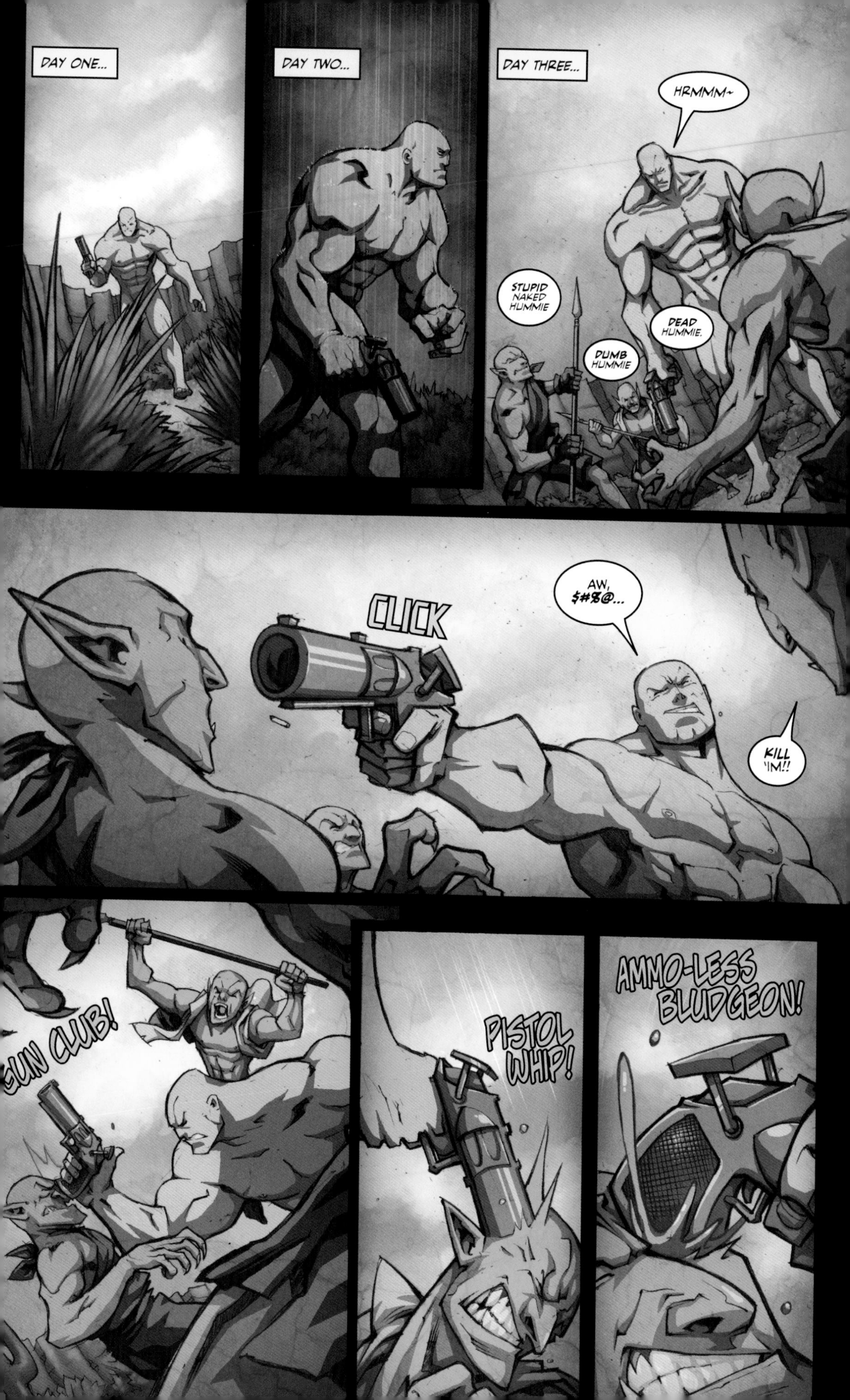
DAY ONE...
DAY TWO...
DAY THREE...
HRMMM~
STUPID NAKED HUMMIE
DEAD HUMMIE.
DUMB HUMMIE
CLICK
AW, $#%@...
KILL 'IM!!
GUN CLUB!
PISTOL WHIP!
AMMO-LESS BLUDGEON!

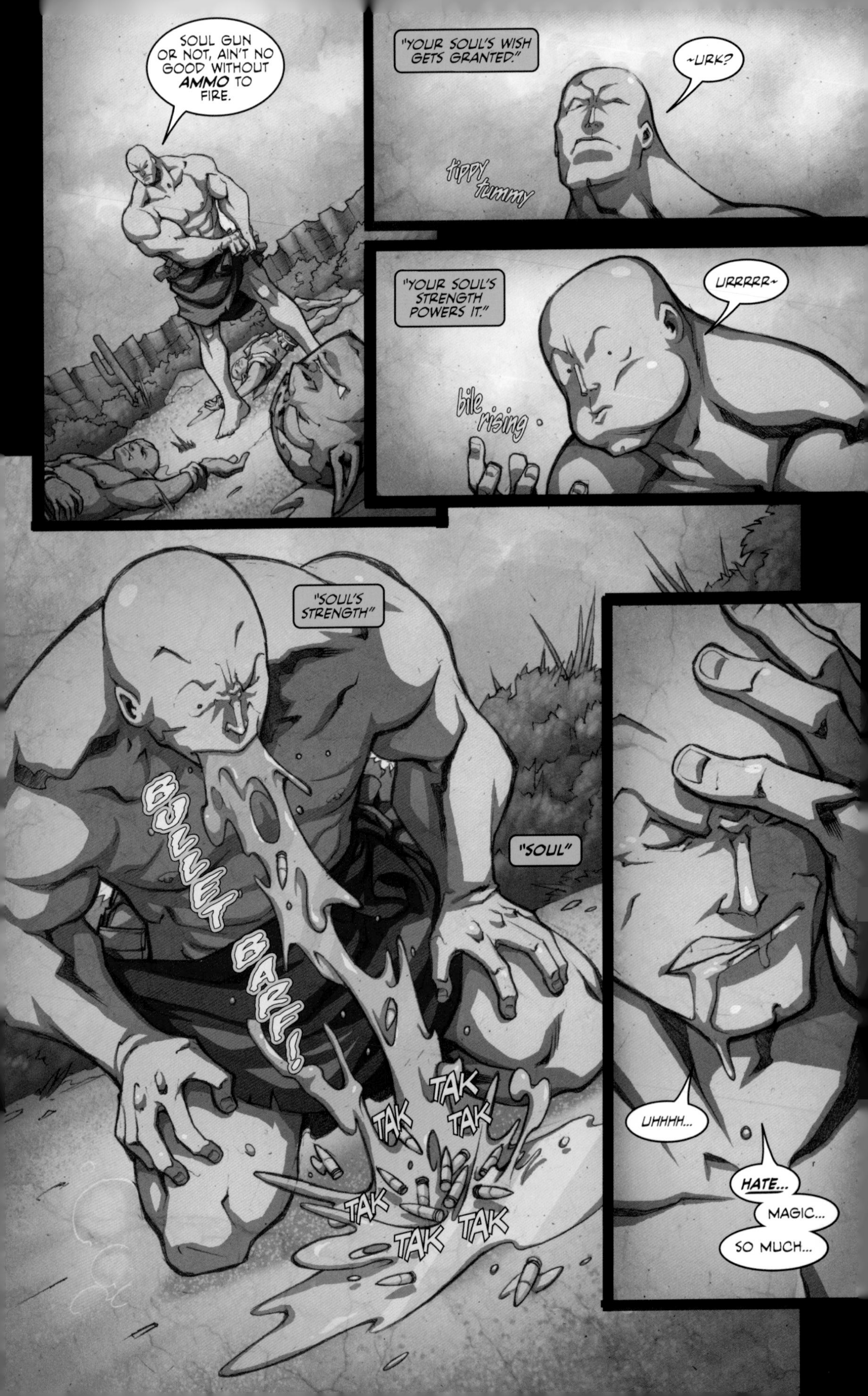
SOUL GUN OR NOT, AIN'T NO GOOD WITHOUT AMMO TO FIRE.
"YOUR SOUL'S WISH GETS GRANTED."
~URK?
tippy tummy
"YOUR SOUL'S STRENGTH POWERS IT."
URRRRR~
bile rising
"SOUL'S STRENGTH"
BLUUEK
BARF!
"SOUL"
TAK
TAK
TAK
TAK
TAK
TAK
UHHHH...
HATE...
MAGIC...
SO MUCH...

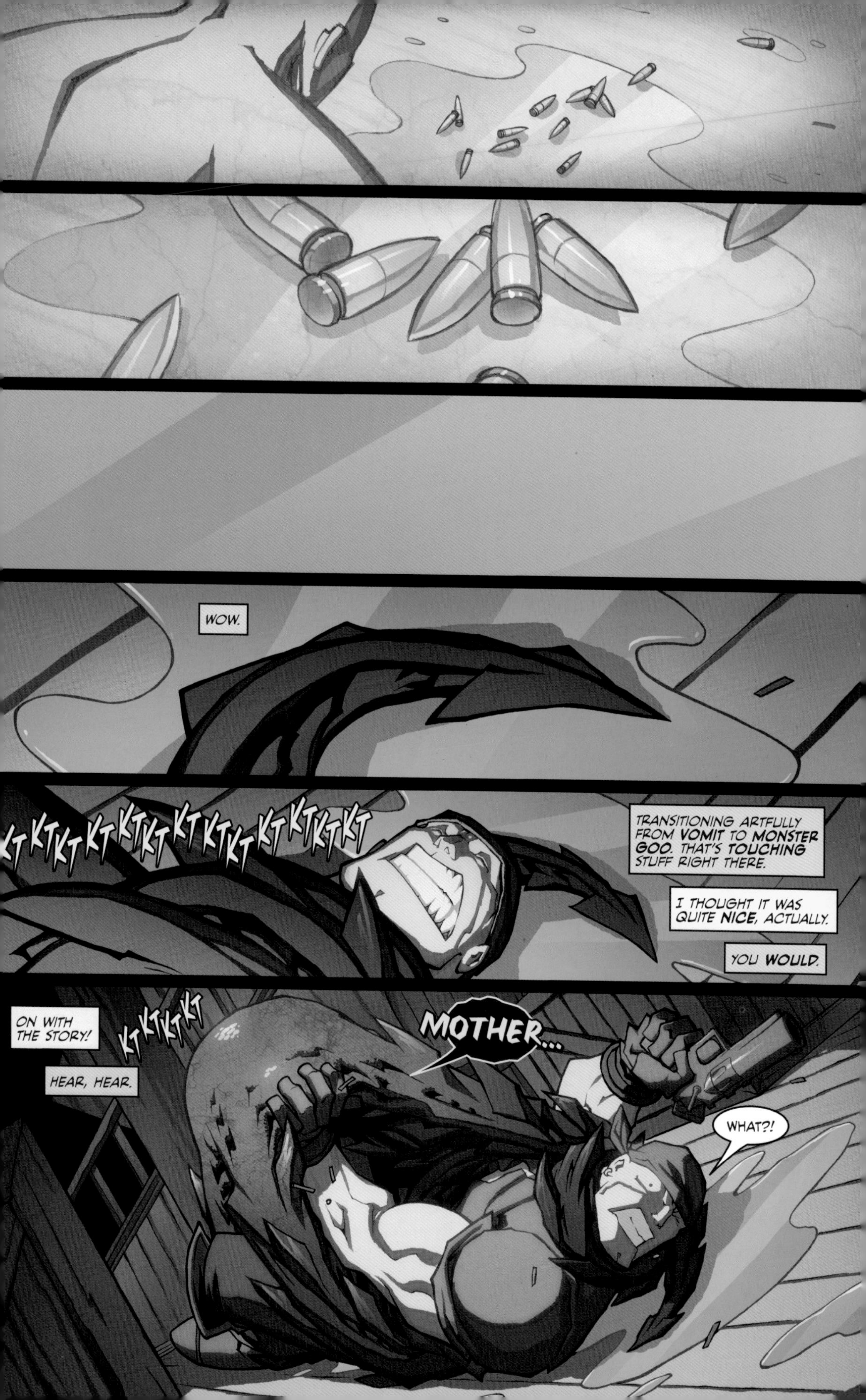
WOW.
KT KT KT KT KT KT KT KT KT KT KT KT KT KT KT
TRANSITIONING ARTFULLY FROM VOMIT TO MONSTER GOO. THAT'S TOUCHING STUFF RIGHT THERE.
I THOUGHT IT WAS QUITE NICE, ACTUALLY.
YOU WOULD.
ON WITH THE STORY!
HEAR, HEAR.
KT KT KT KT KT
MOTHER...
WHAT?!

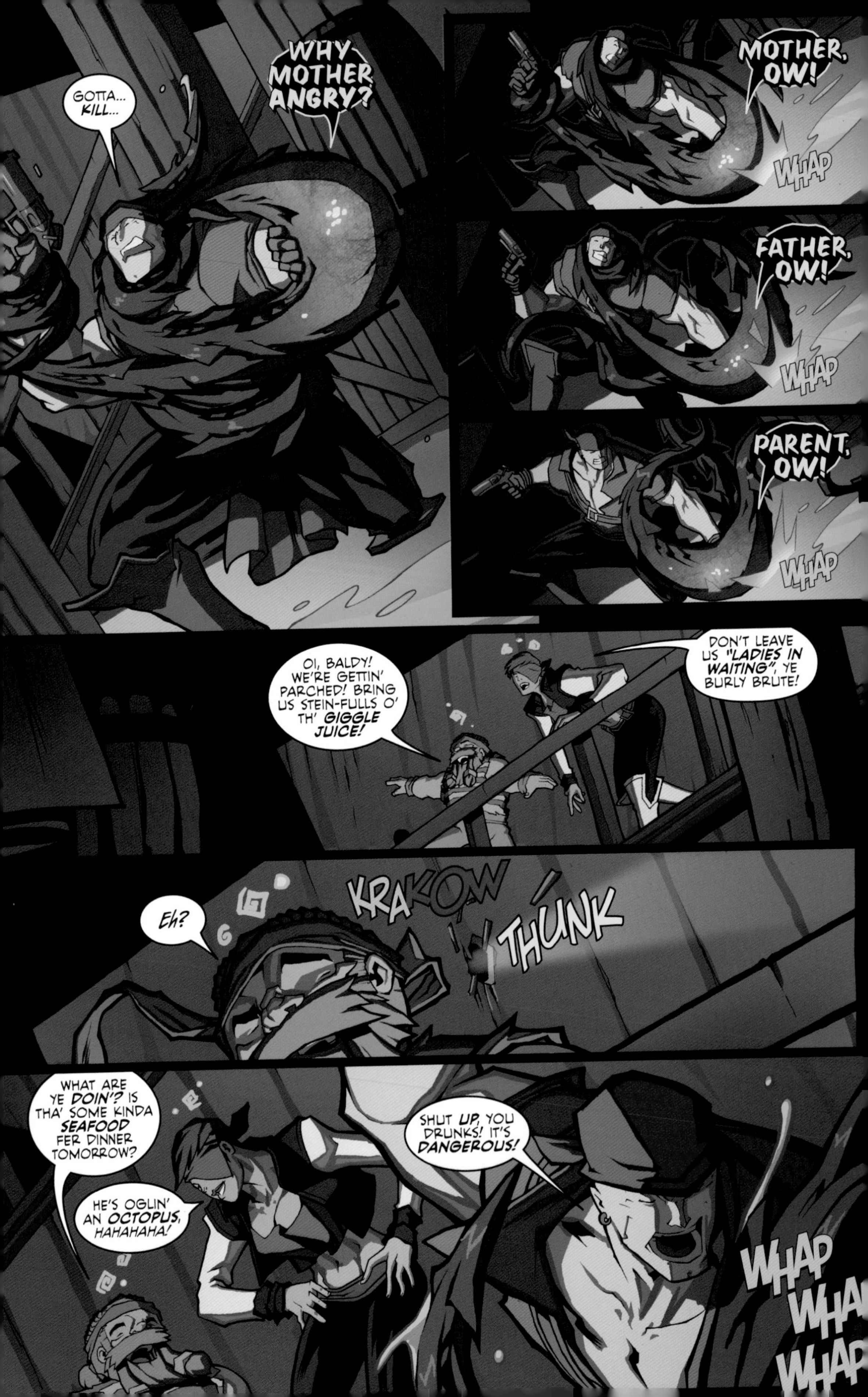

GOTTA... KILL...
WHY MOTHER ANGRY?
MOTHER, OW!
WHAP
FATHER, OW!
WHAP
PARENT, OW!
WHAP
OI, BALDY! WE'RE GETTIN' PARCHED! BRING US STEIN-FULLS O' TH' GIGGLE JUICE!
DON'T LEAVE US "LADIES IN WAITING", YE BURLY BRUTE!
KRAKOW
THUNK
Eh?
WHAT ARE YE DOIN'? IS THA' SOME KINDA SEAFOOD FER DINNER TOMORROW?
HE'S OGLIN' AN OCTOPUS, HAHAHAHA!
SHUT UP, YOU DRUNKS! IT'S DANGEROUS!
WHAP
WHAP
WHAP

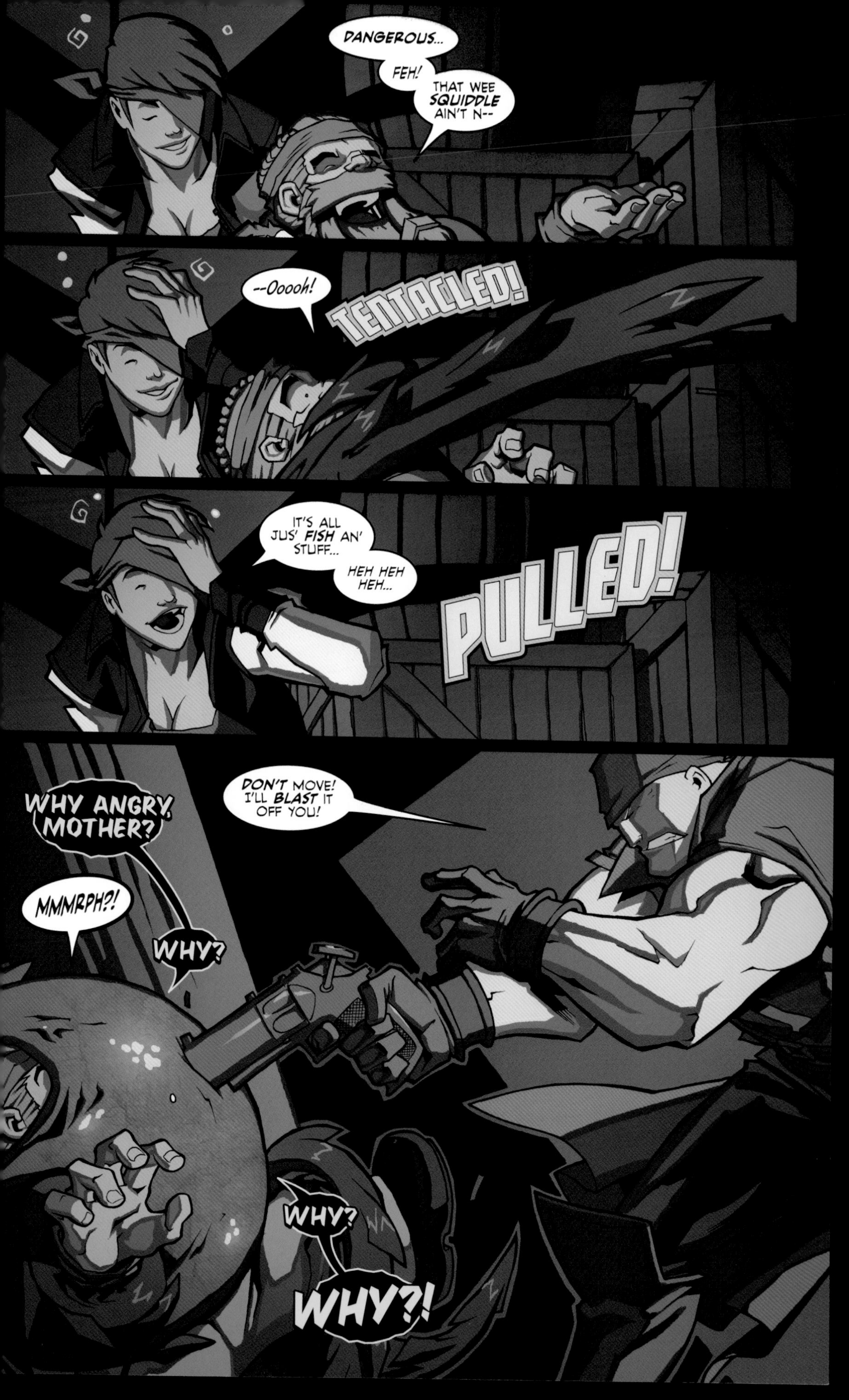
DANGEROUS...
FEH!
THAT WEE SQUIDDLE AIN'T N--
--Ooooh!
TENTACLED!
IT'S ALL JUS' FISH AN' STUFF...
HEH HEH HEH...
PULLED!
WHY ANGRY, MOTHER?
DON'T MOVE! I'LL BLAST IT OFF YOU!
MMMRPH?!
WHY?
WHY?
WHY?!

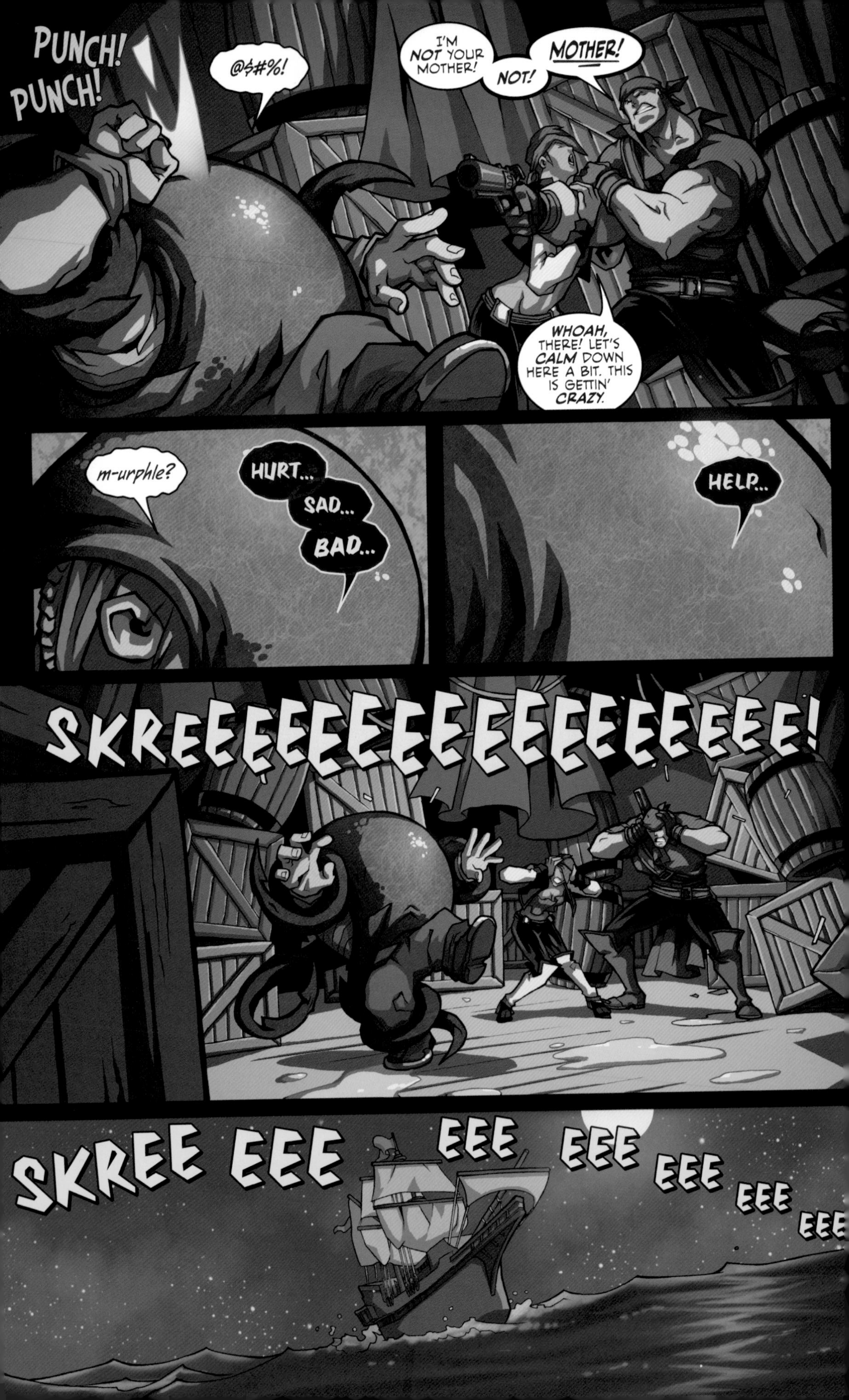
PUNCH!
PUNCH!
@$#%!
I'M NOT YOUR MOTHER!
NOT!
MOTHER!
WHOAH, THERE! LET'S CALM DOWN HERE A BIT. THIS IS GETTIN' CRAZY.
m-urphle?
HURT...
SAD...
BAD...
HELP...
SKREEEEEEEEEEEEEEEEEEE!
SKREE EEE EEE EEE EEE EEE EEE

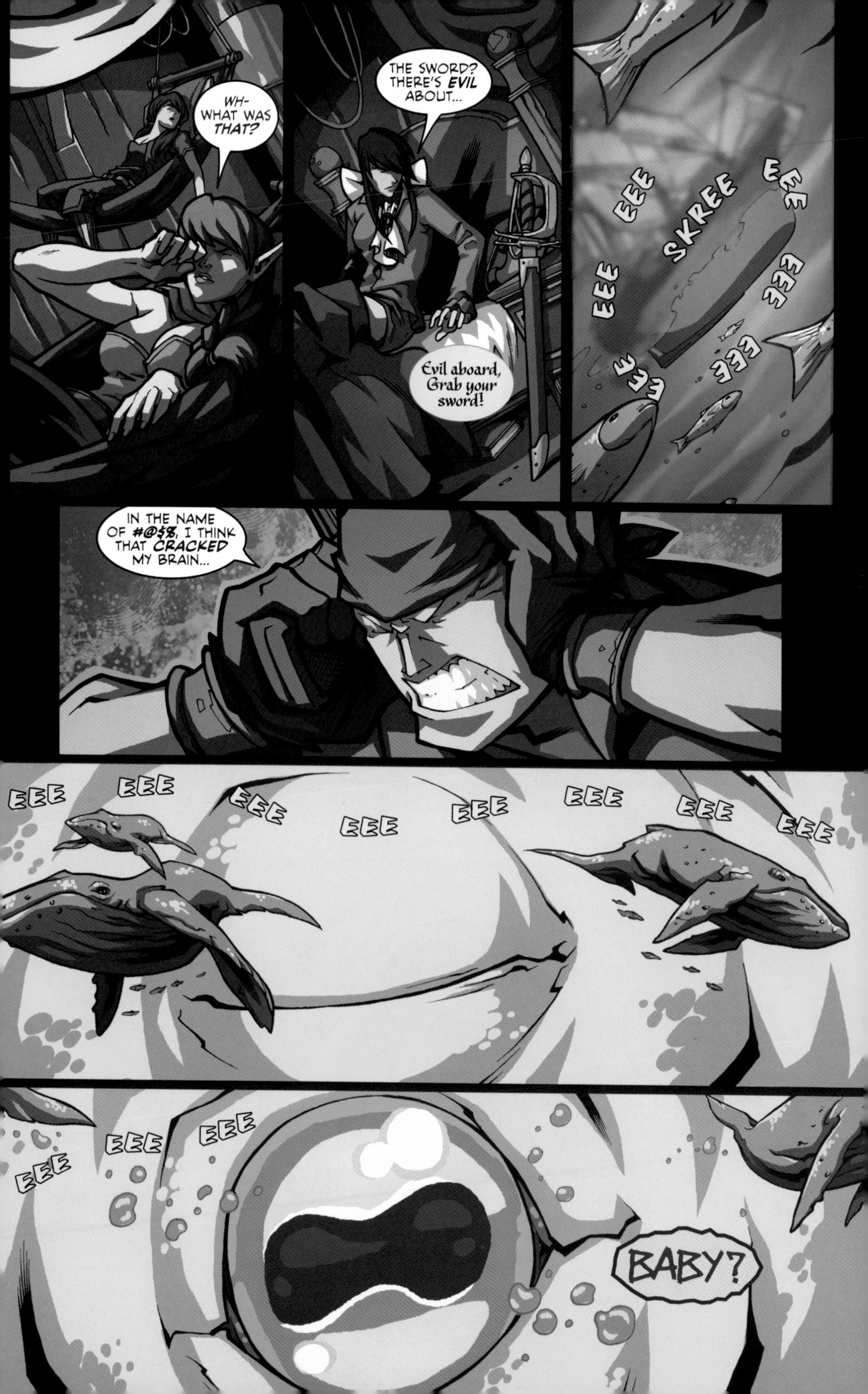
WH- WHAT WAS THAT?
THE SWORD? THERE'S EVIL ABOUT...
Evil aboard, Grab your sword!
EEE EEE SKREE EEE EEE EEE EEE EEE
IN THE NAME OF #@$%, I THINK THAT CRACKED MY BRAIN...
EEE EEE EEE EEE EEE EEE EEE EEE
EEE EEE EEE
BABY?

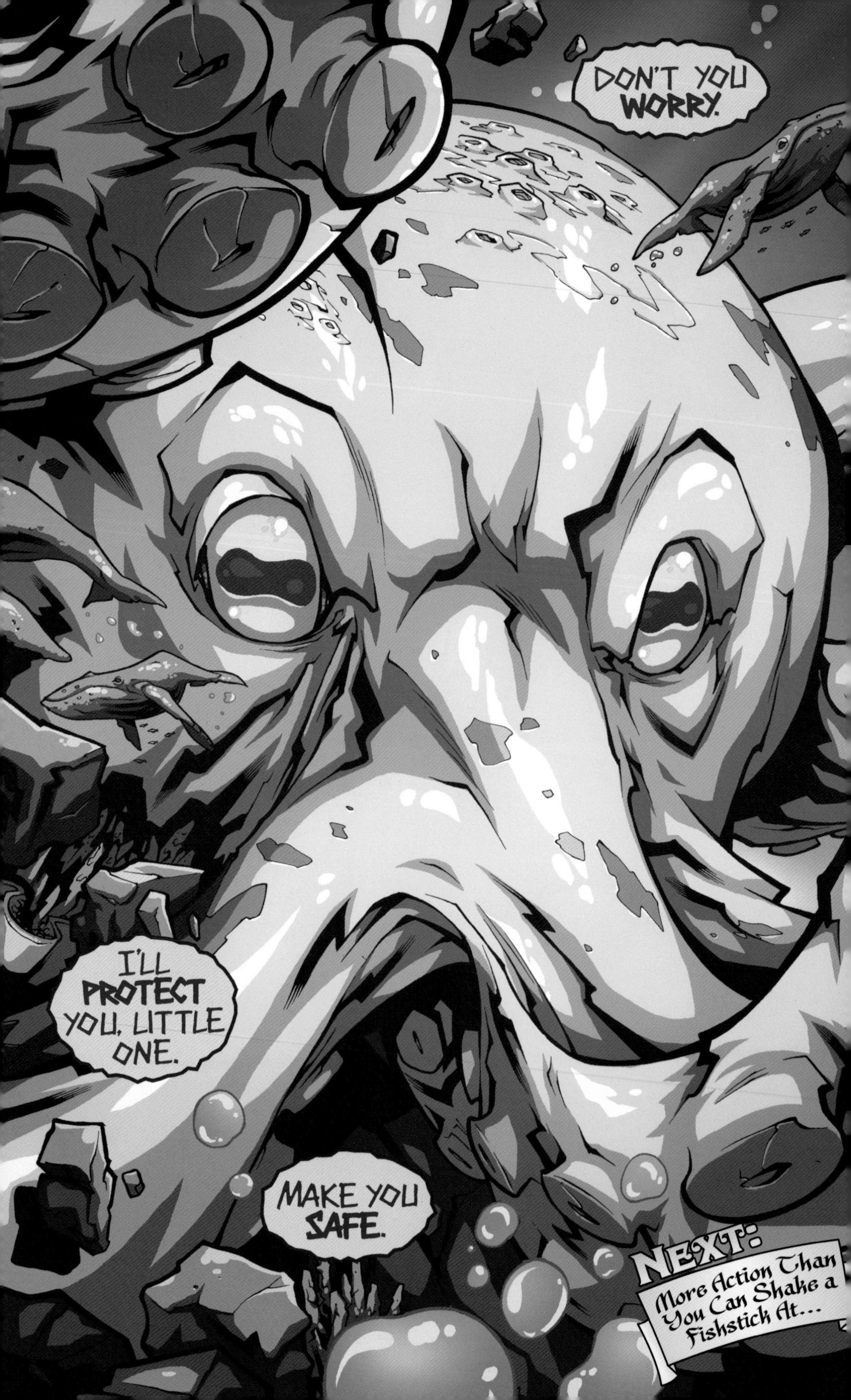
DON'T YOU WORRY.
I'LL PROTECT YOU, LITTLE ONE.
MAKE YOU SAFE.
NEXT:
More Action Than You Can Shake a Fishstick At...

CHAPTER FOUR

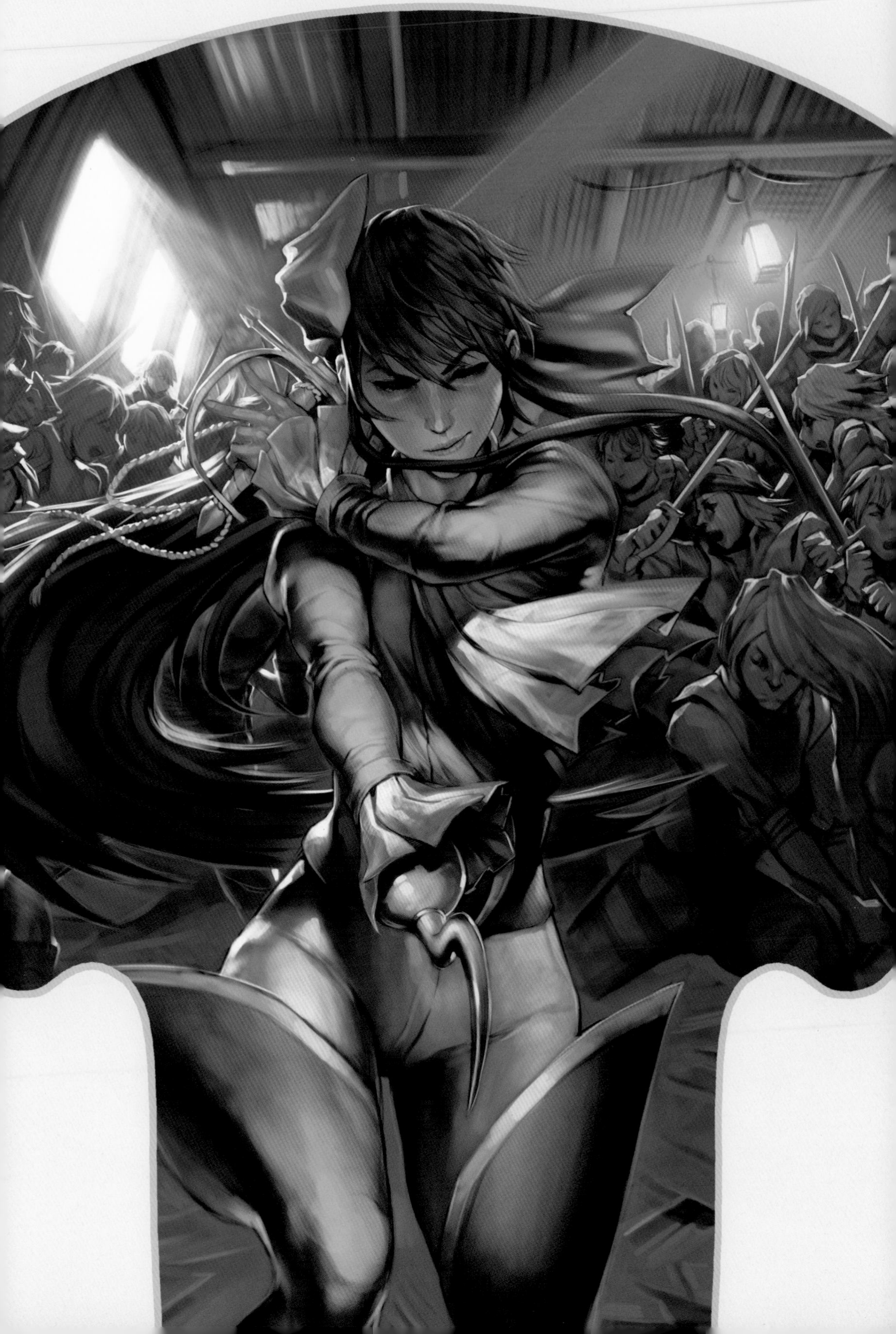

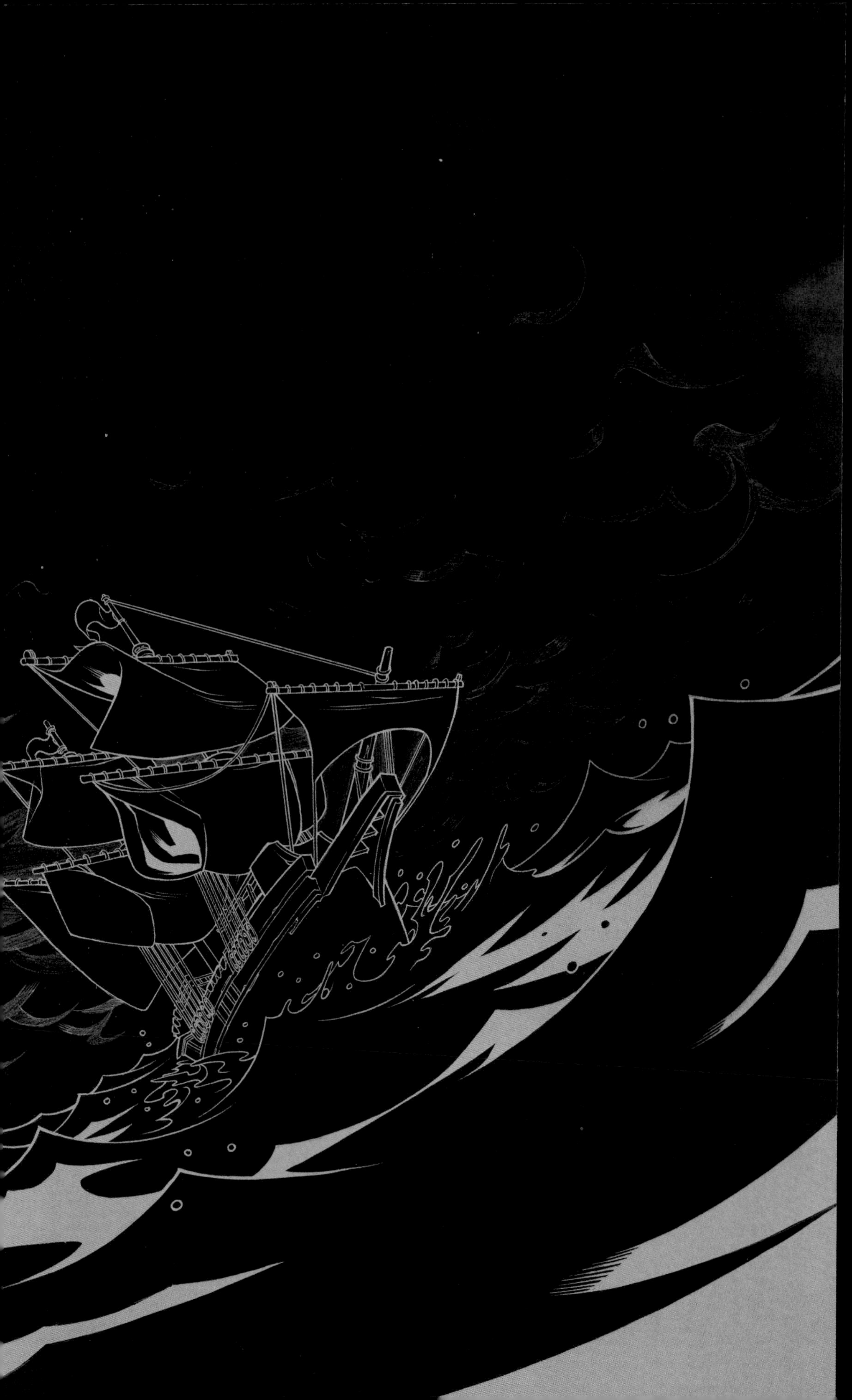

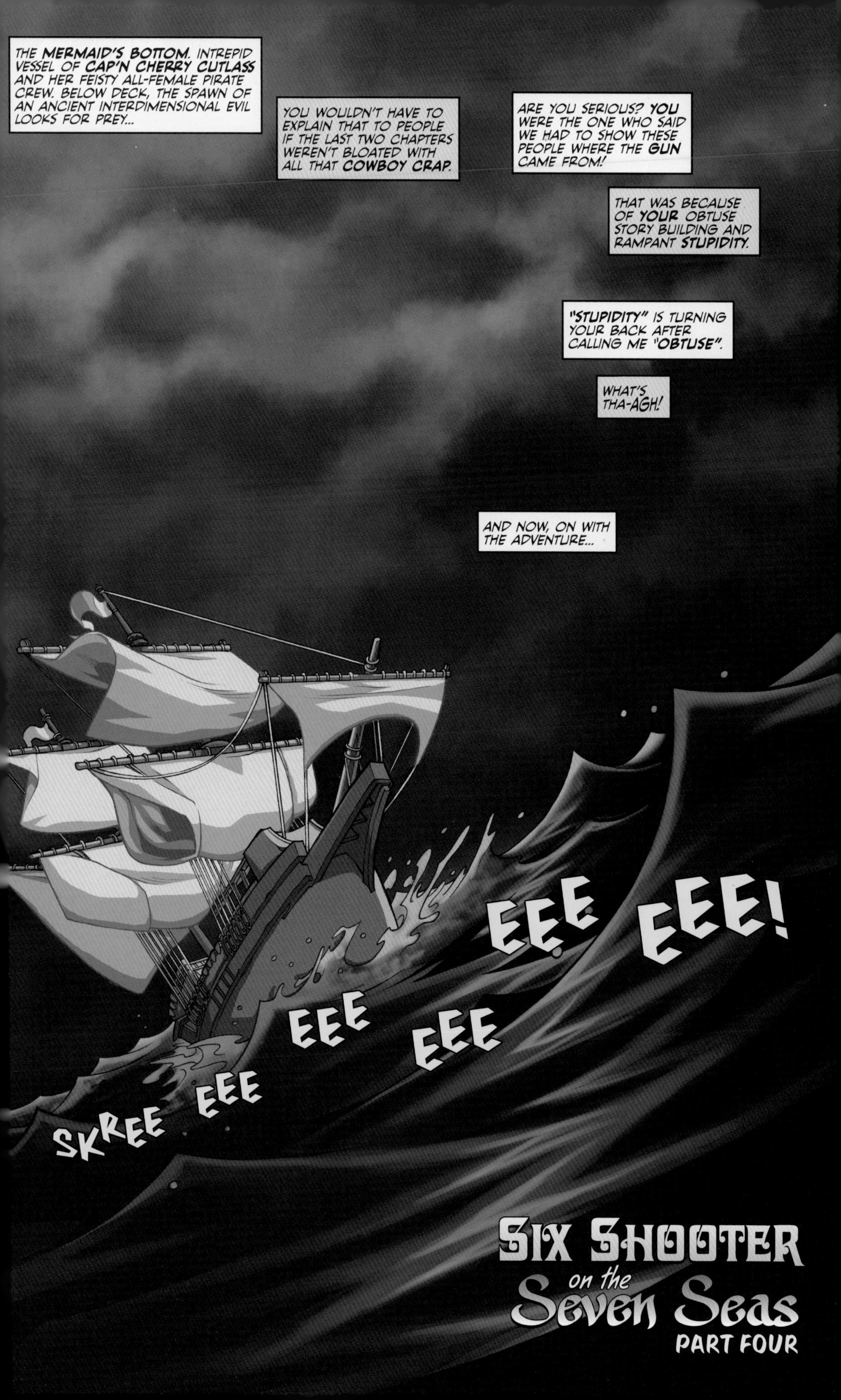

THE MERMAID'S BOTTOM. INTREPID VESSEL OF CAP'N CHERRY CUTLASS AND HER FEISTY ALL-FEMALE PIRATE CREW. BELOW DECK, THE SPAWN OF AN ANCIENT INTERDIMENSIONAL EVIL LOOKS FOR PREY...
YOU WOULDN'T HAVE TO EXPLAIN THAT TO PEOPLE IF THE LAST TWO CHAPTERS WEREN'T BLOATED WITH ALL THAT COWBOY CRAP.
ARE YOU SERIOUS? YOU WERE THE ONE WHO SAID WE HAD TO SHOW THESE PEOPLE WHERE THE GUN CAME FROM!
THAT WAS BECAUSE OF YOUR OBTUSE STORY BUILDING AND RAMPANT STUPIDITY.
"STUPIDITY" IS TURNING YOUR BACK AFTER CALLING ME "OBTUSE".
WHAT'S THA-AGH!
AND NOW, ON WITH THE ADVENTURE...
SKREE EEE EEE EEE EEE EEE!
SIX SHOOTER on the Seven Seas
PART FOUR

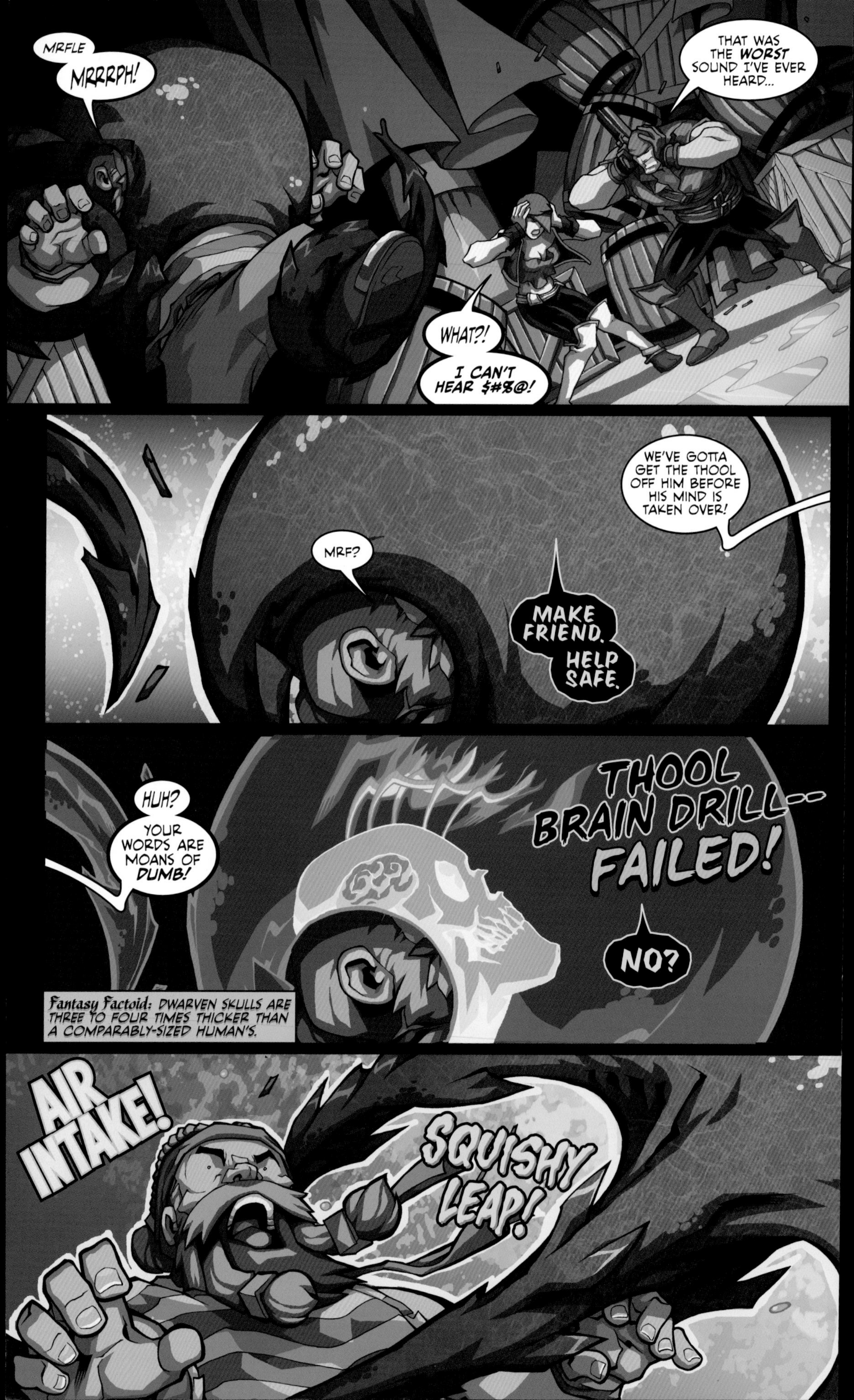
MRFLE
MRRRPH!
THAT WAS THE WORST SOUND I'VE EVER HEARD...
WHAT?!
I CAN'T HEAR $#8@!
WE'VE GOTTA GET THE THOOL OFF HIM BEFORE HIS MIND IS TAKEN OVER!
MRF?
MAKE FRIEND.
HELP SAFE.
HUH?
YOUR WORDS ARE MOANS OF DUMB!
THOOL BRAIN DRILL-- FAILED!
NO?
Fantasy Factoid: DWARVEN SKULLS ARE THREE TO FOUR TIMES THICKER THAN A COMPARABLY-SIZED HUMAN'S.
AIR INTAKE!
SQUISHY LEAP!

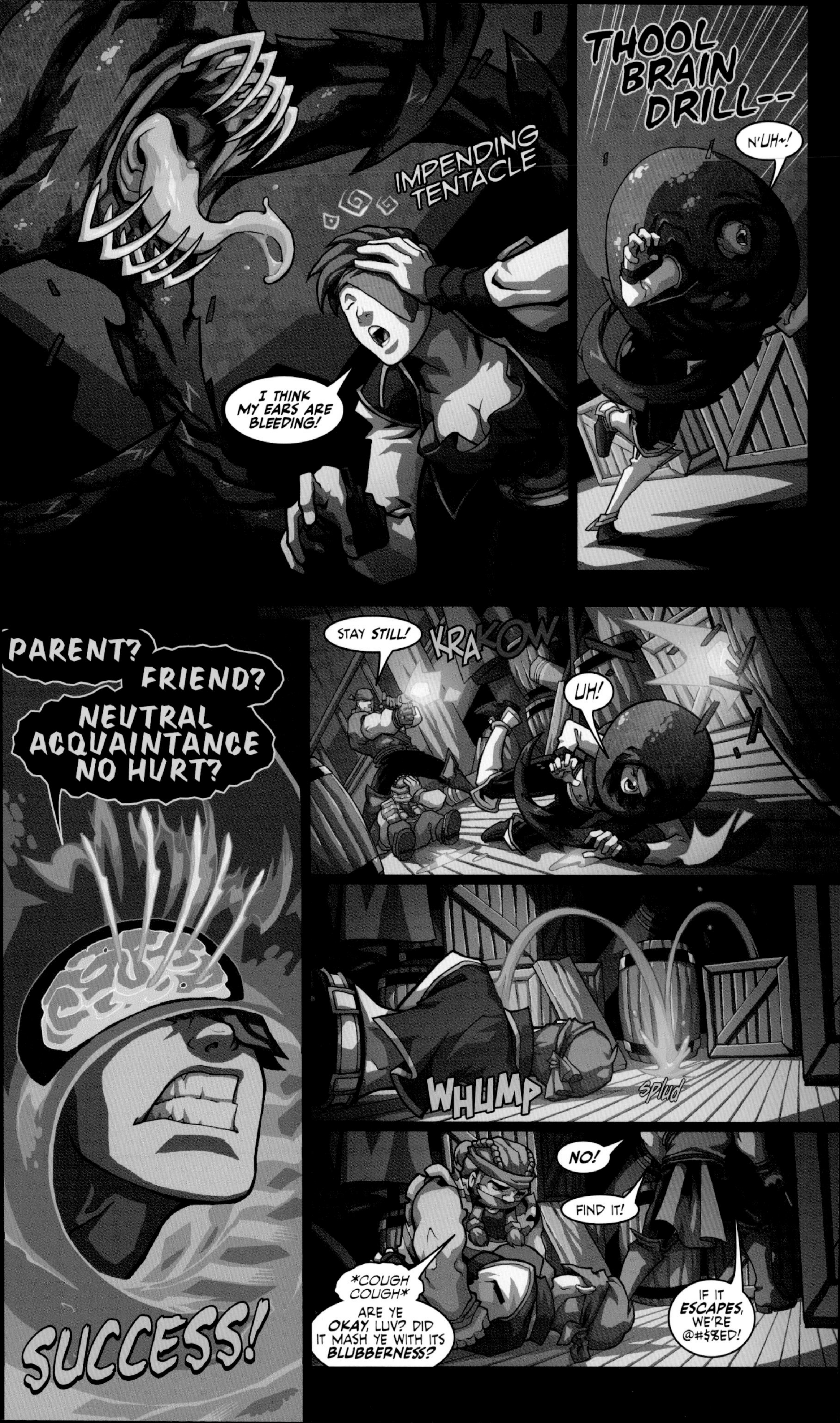

IMPENDING TENTACLE
I THINK MY EARS ARE BLEEDING!
THOOL BRAIN DRILL--
N'UH~!
PARENT?
FRIEND?
NEUTRAL ACQUAINTANCE NO HURT?
SUCCESS!
STAY STILL!
KRAKOW
UH!
WHUMP
splud
NO!
FIND IT!
COUGH COUGH ARE YE OKAY, LUV? DID IT MASH YE WITH ITS BLUBBERNESS?
IF IT ESCAPES, WE'RE @#$%ED!

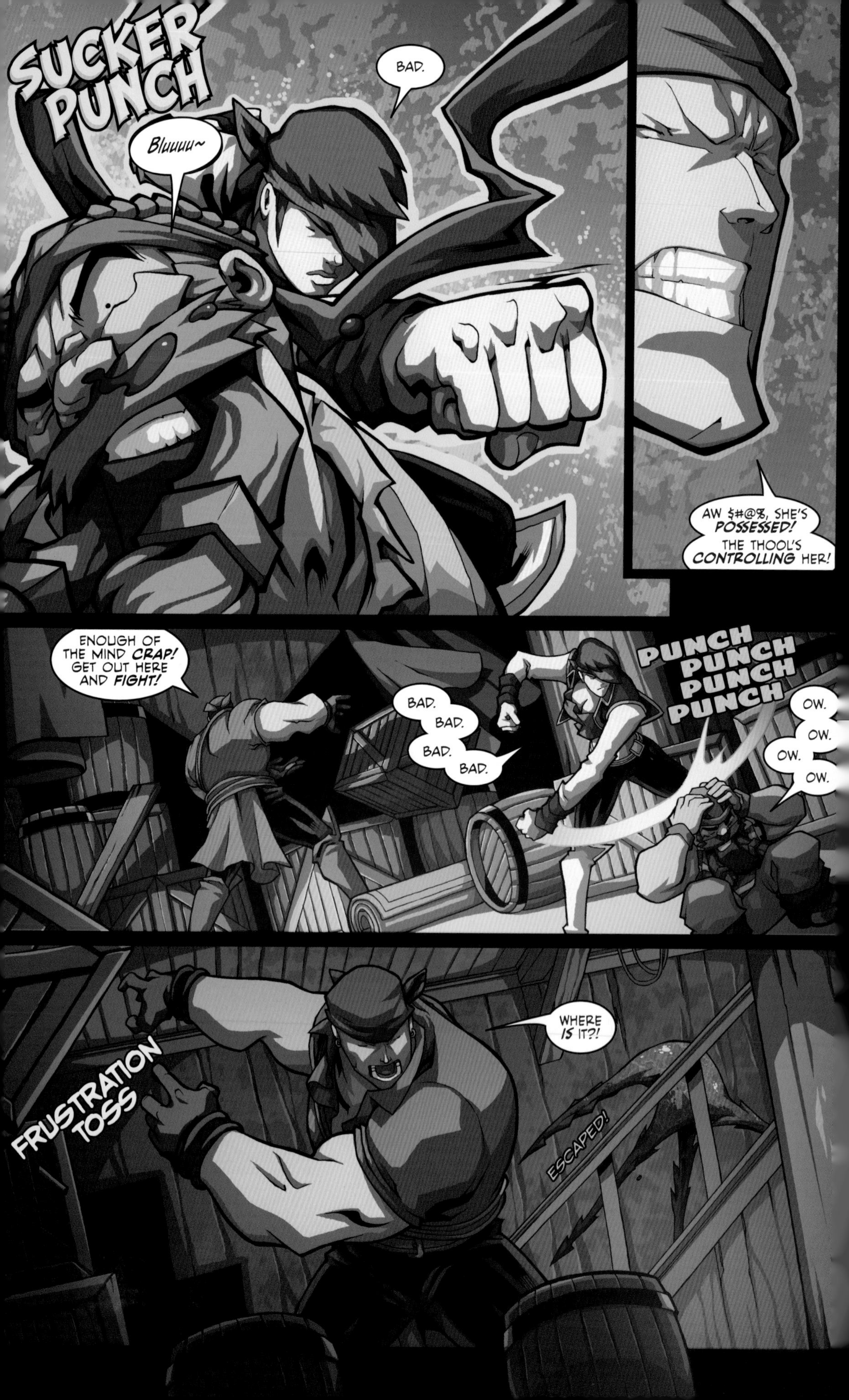
SUCKER PUNCH
BAD.
Bluuuu~
AW $#@%, SHE'S POSSESSED! THE THOOL'S CONTROLLING HER!
ENOUGH OF THE MIND CRAP! GET OUT HERE AND FIGHT!
BAD. BAD. BAD. BAD.
PUNCH PUNCH PUNCH PUNCH
OW. OW. OW. OW.
WHERE IS IT?!
FRUSTRATION TOSS
ESCAPED!

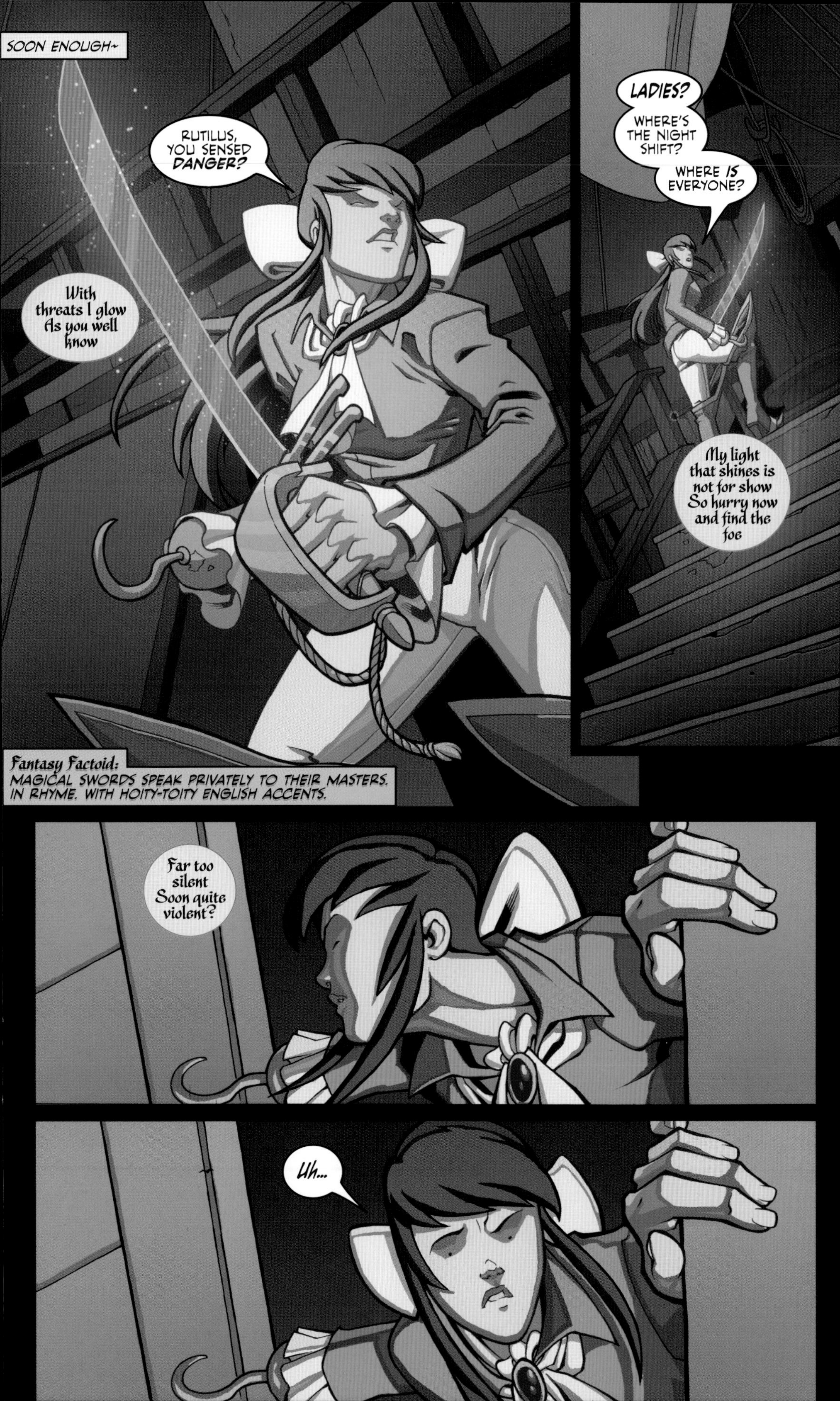
SOON ENOUGH~
RUTILUS, YOU SENSED DANGER?
With threats I glow As you well know
LADIES?
WHERE'S THE NIGHT SHIFT?
WHERE IS EVERYONE?
My light that shines is not for show So hurry now and find the foe
Fantasy Factoid: MAGICAL SWORDS SPEAK PRIVATELY TO THEIR MASTERS. IN RHYME. WITH HOITY-TOITY ENGLISH ACCENTS.
Far too silent Soon quite violent?
Uh...

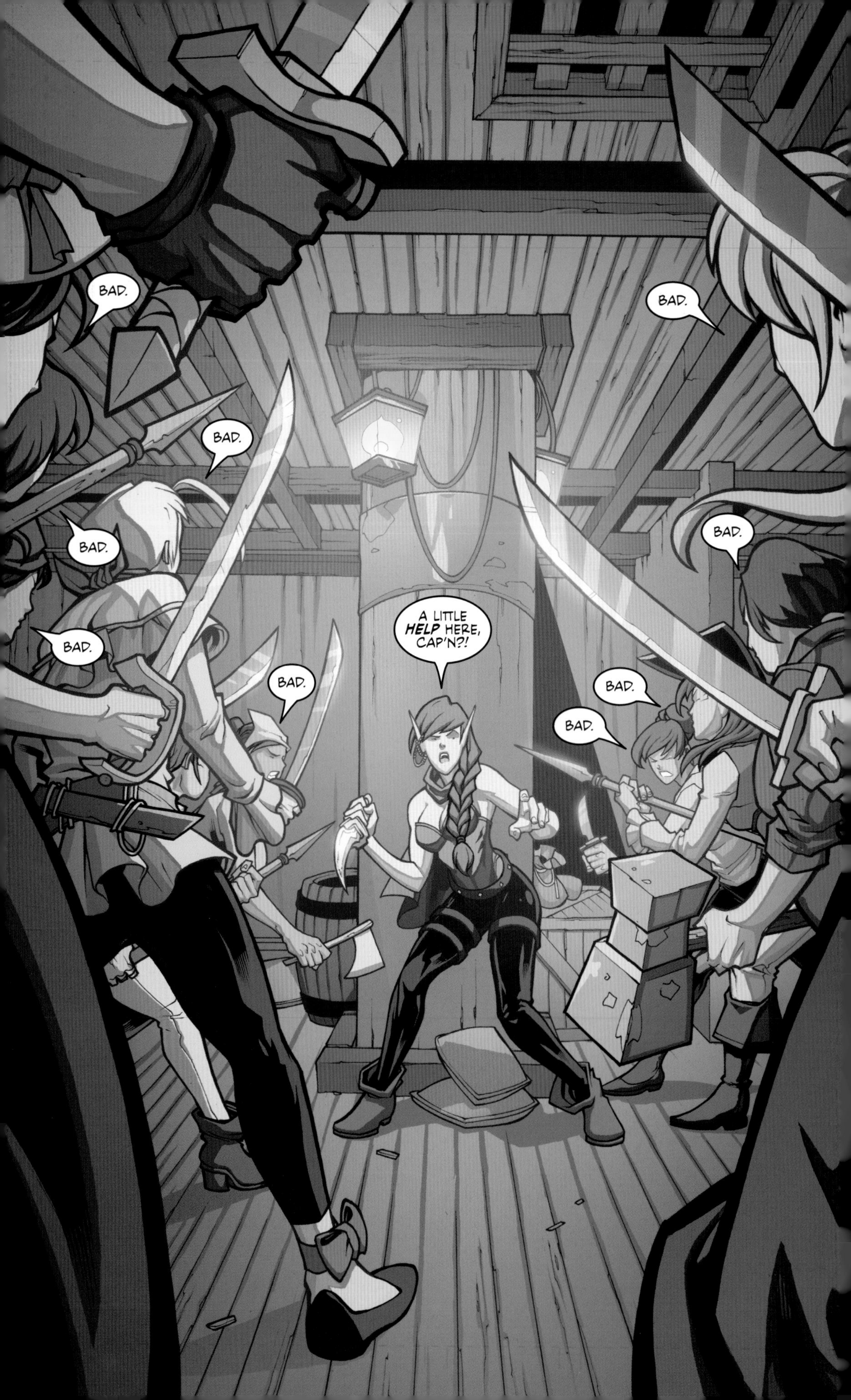
BAD.
BAD.
BAD.
BAD.
BAD.
BAD.
BAD.
A LITTLE HELP HERE, CAP'N?!
BAD.
BAD.

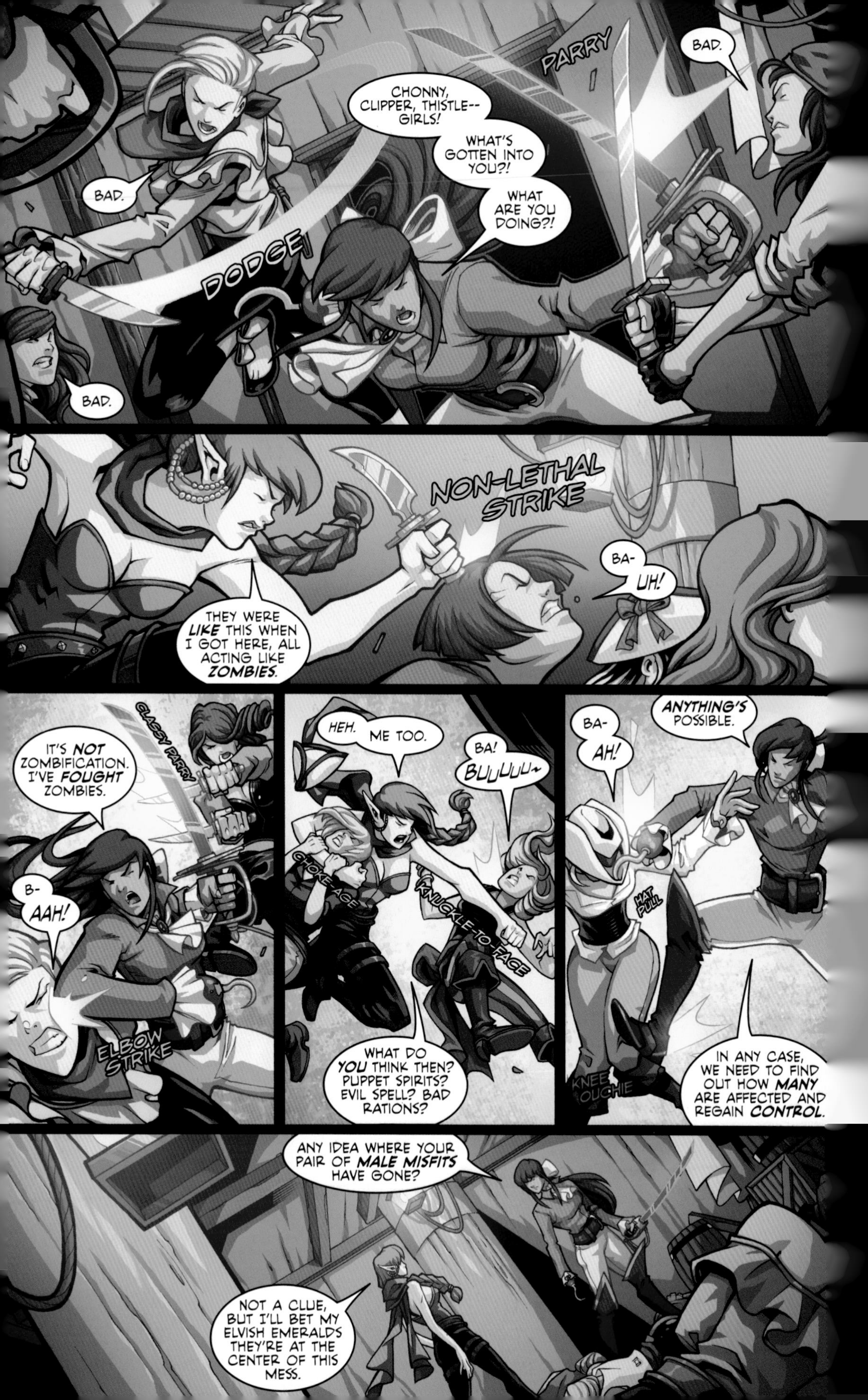
CHONNY, CLIPPER, THISTLE-- GIRLS!
WHAT'S GOTTEN INTO YOU?!
WHAT ARE YOU DOING?!
PARRY
BAD.
BAD.
DODGE
BAD.
NON-LETHAL STRIKE
THEY WERE LIKE THIS WHEN I GOT HERE, ALL ACTING LIKE ZOMBIES.
BA- UH!
IT'S NOT ZOMBIFICATION. I'VE FOUGHT ZOMBIES.
CLASSY PARRY
B- AAH!
ELBOW STRIKE
HEH. ME TOO.
BA! BUUUUU~
CHOKE-AGE
KNUCKLE-TO-FACE
WHAT DO YOU THINK THEN? PUPPET SPIRITS? EVIL SPELL? BAD RATIONS?
BA- AH!
ANYTHING'S POSSIBLE.
HAT PULL
KNEE OUCHIE
IN ANY CASE, WE NEED TO FIND OUT HOW MANY ARE AFFECTED AND REGAIN CONTROL.
ANY IDEA WHERE YOUR PAIR OF MALE MISFITS HAVE GONE?
NOT A CLUE, BUT I'LL BET MY ELVISH EMERALDS THEY'RE AT THE CENTER OF THIS MESS.

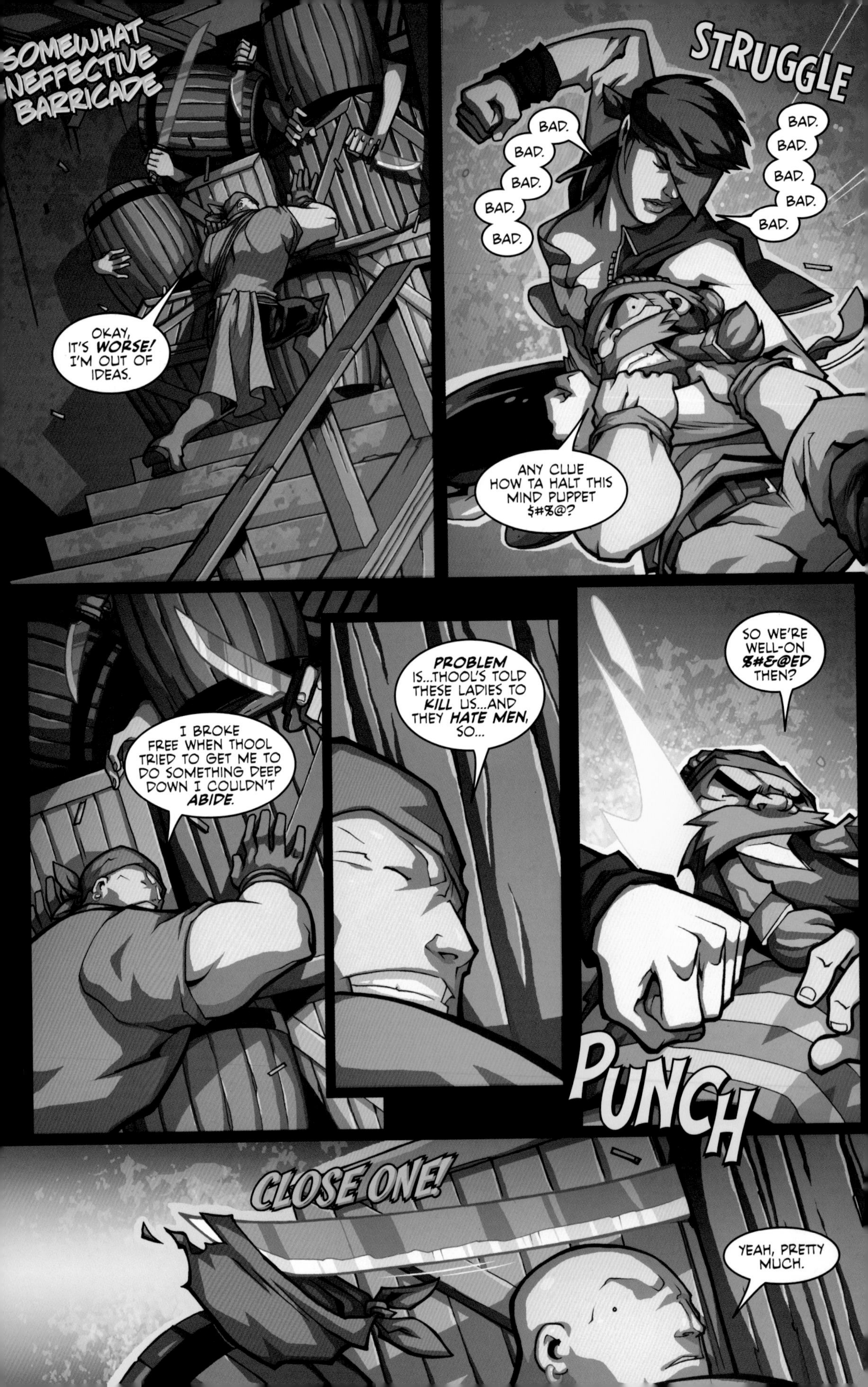
SOMEWHAT INEFFECTIVE BARRICADE
OKAY, IT'S WORSE! I'M OUT OF IDEAS.
STRUGGLE
BAD. BAD. BAD. BAD. BAD.
BAD. BAD. BAD. BAD. BAD.
ANY CLUE HOW TA HALT THIS MIND PUPPET $#%@?
I BROKE FREE WHEN THOOL TRIED TO GET ME TO DO SOMETHING DEEP DOWN I COULDN'T ABIDE.
PROBLEM IS...THOOL'S TOLD THESE LADIES TO KILL US...AND THEY HATE MEN, SO...
SO WE'RE WELL-ON %#&@ED THEN?
PUNCH
CLOSE ONE!
YEAH, PRETTY MUCH.

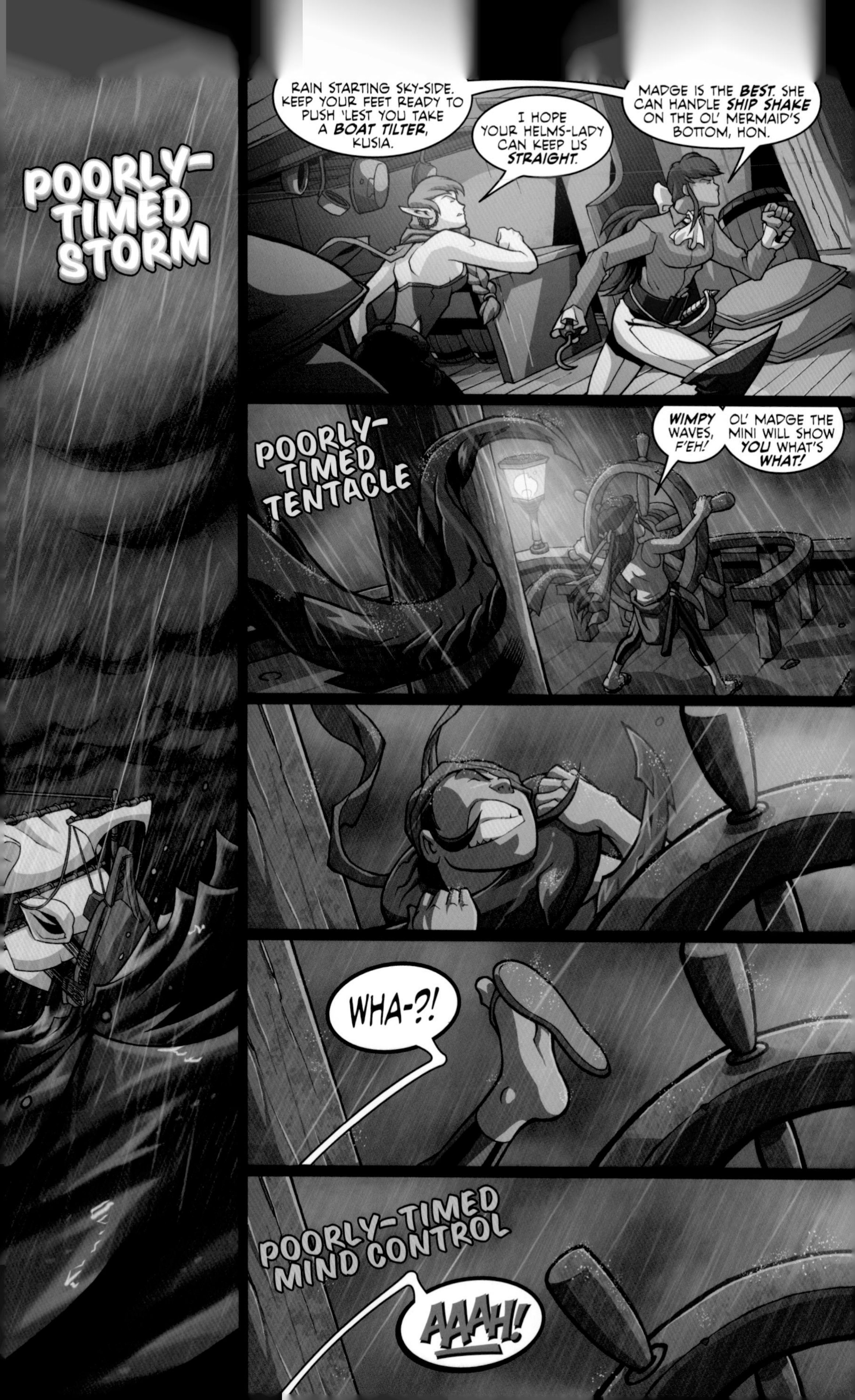
POORLY-TIMED STORM
RAIN STARTING SKY-SIDE. KEEP YOUR FEET READY TO PUSH 'LEST YOU TAKE A BOAT TILTER, KUSIA.
I HOPE YOUR HELMS-LADY CAN KEEP US STRAIGHT.
MADGE IS THE BEST. SHE CAN HANDLE SHIP SHAKE ON THE OL' MERMAID'S BOTTOM, HON.
POORLY-TIMED TENTACLE
WIMPY WAVES, F'EH!
OL' MADGE THE MINI WILL SHOW YOU WHAT'S WHAT!
WHA-?!
POORLY-TIMED MIND CONTROL
AAAH!

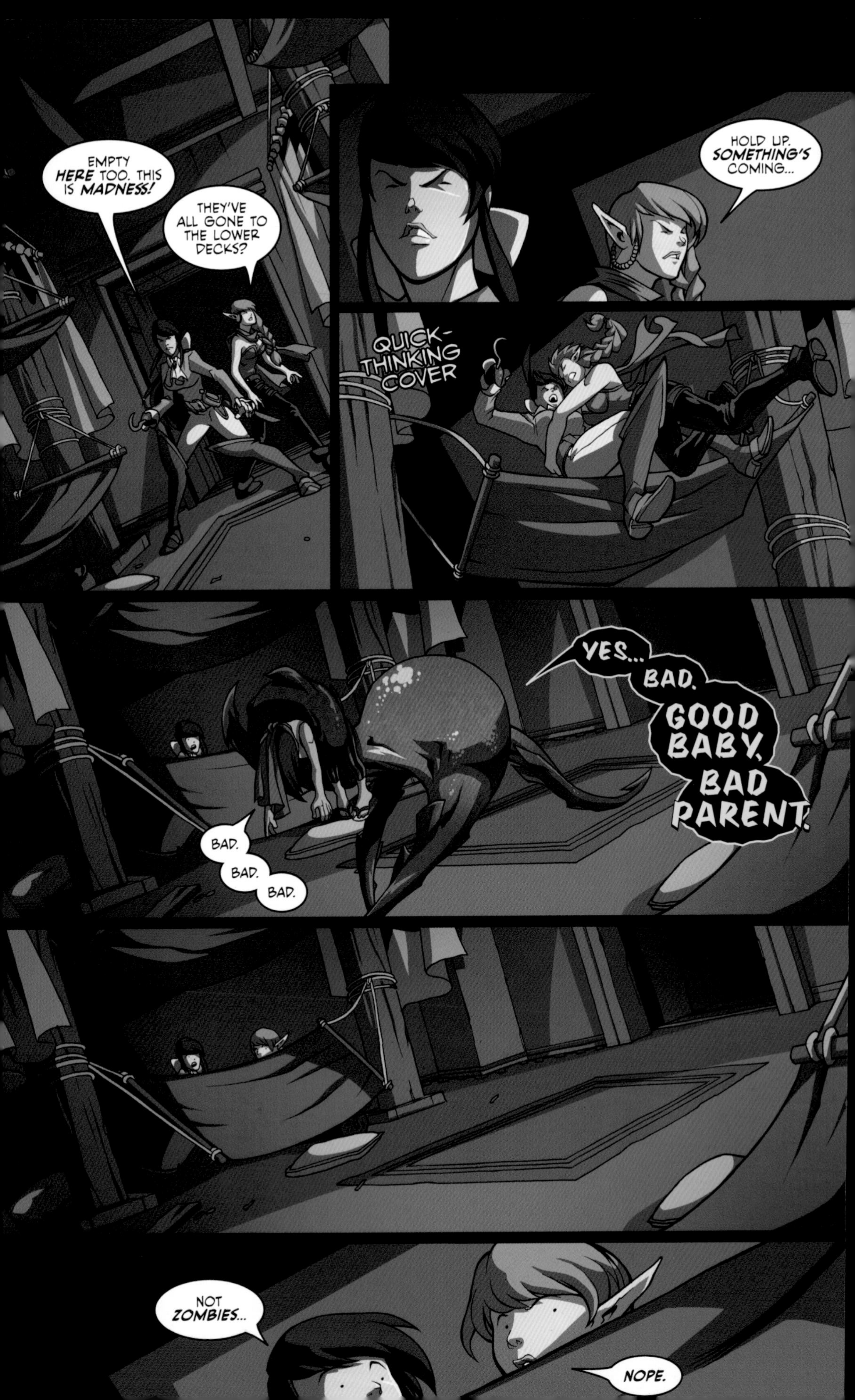
EMPTY HERE TOO. THIS IS MADNESS!
THEY'VE ALL GONE TO THE LOWER DECKS?
HOLD UP. SOMETHING'S COMING...
QUICK-THINKING COVER
YES... BAD.
GOOD BABY, BAD PARENT.
BAD. BAD. BAD.
NOT ZOMBIES...
NOPE.

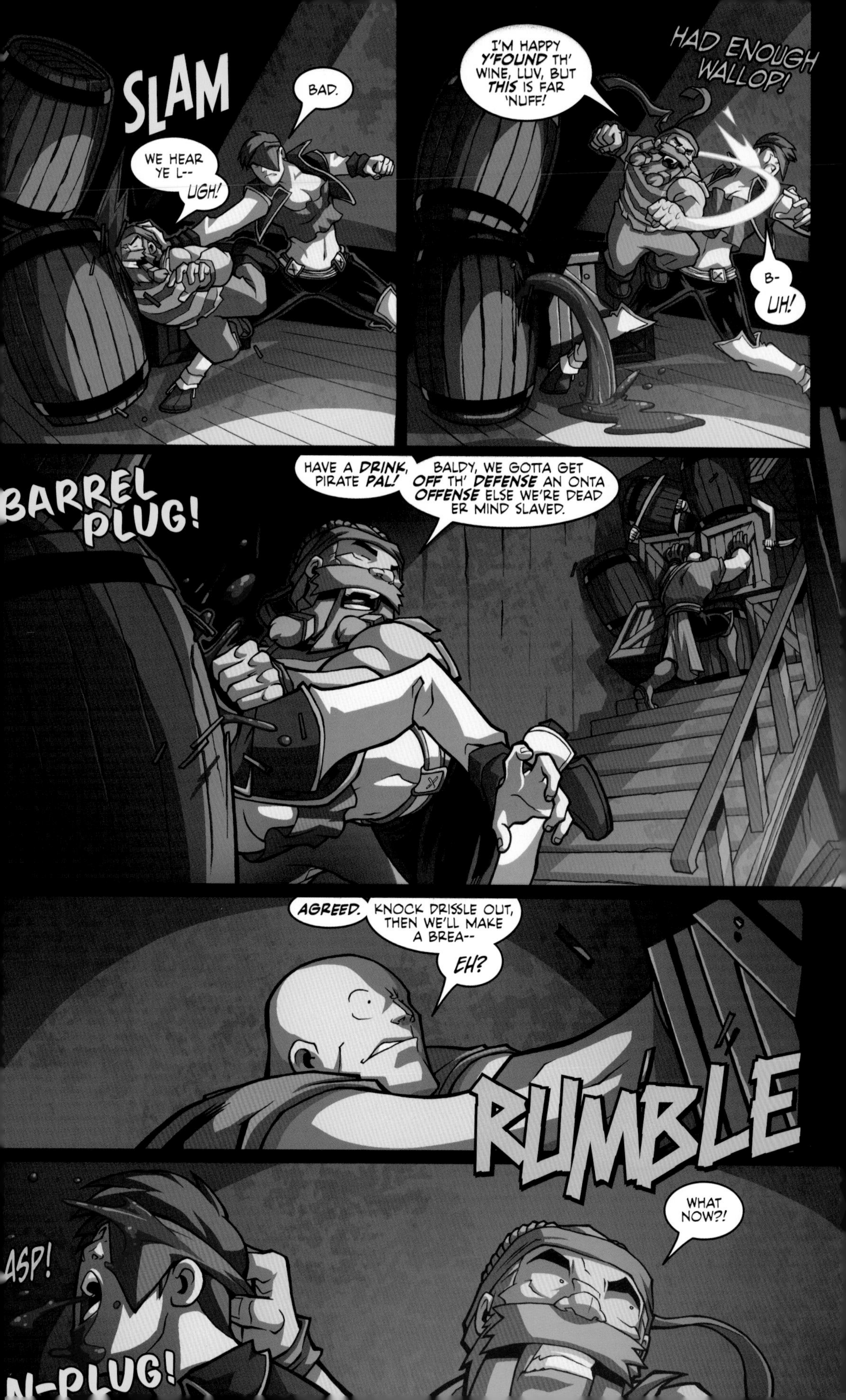
SLAM
BAD.
WE HEAR YE L--
UGH!
I'M HAPPY Y'FOUND TH' WINE, LUV, BUT THIS IS FAR 'NUFF!
HAD ENOUGH WALLOP!
B-
UH!
BARREL PLUG!
HAVE A DRINK, PIRATE PAL!
BALDY, WE GOTTA GET OFF TH' DEFENSE AN ONTA OFFENSE ELSE WE'RE DEAD ER MIND SLAVED.
AGREED.
KNOCK DRISSLE OUT, THEN WE'LL MAKE A BREA--
EH?
RUMBLE
ASP!
N-PLUG!
WHAT NOW?!

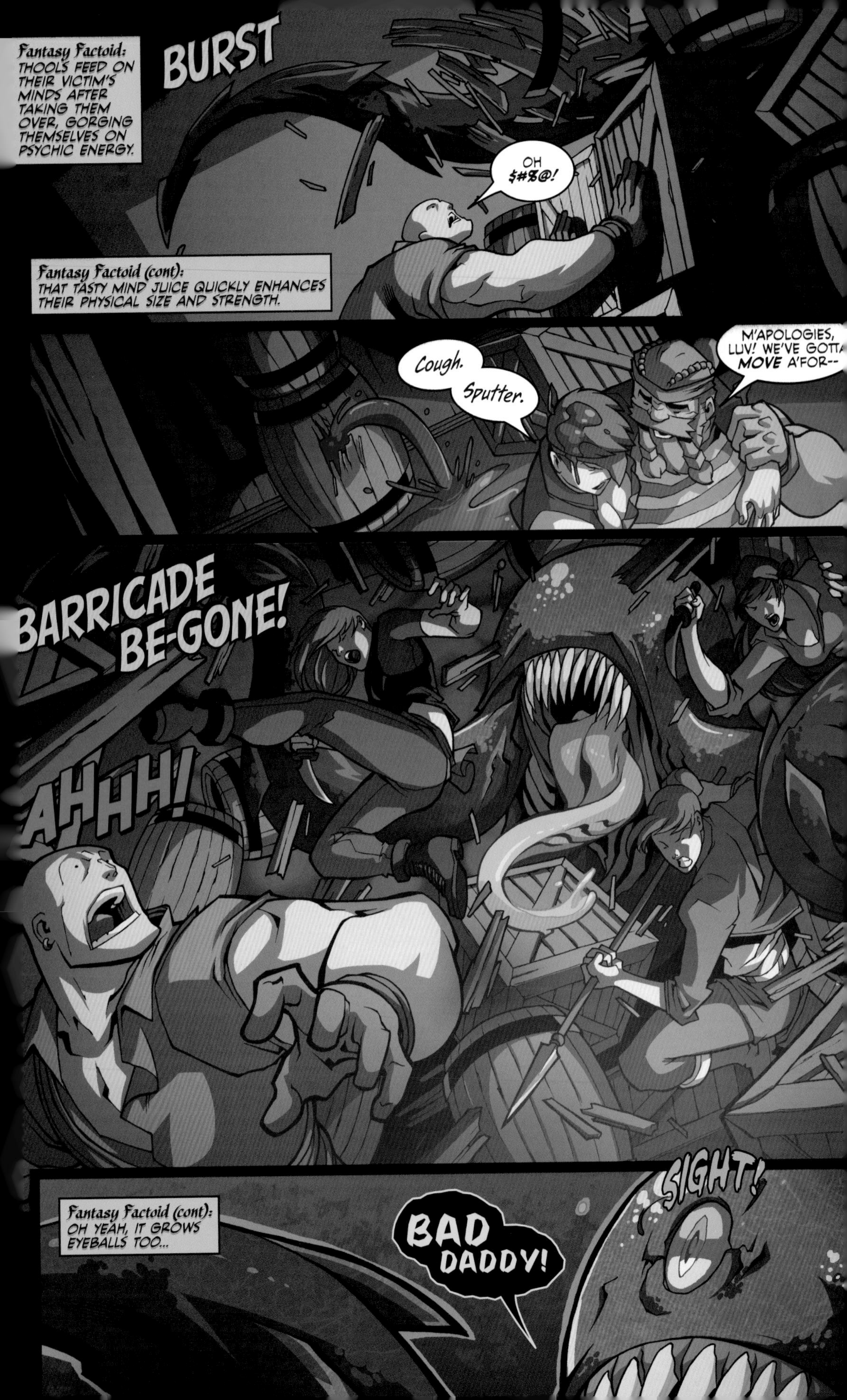

Fantasy Factoid: THOOLS FEED ON THEIR VICTIM'S MINDS AFTER TAKING THEM OVER, GORGING THEMSELVES ON PSYCHIC ENERGY.
BURST
OH $#%@!
Fantasy Factoid (cont): THAT TASTY MIND JUICE QUICKLY ENHANCES THEIR PHYSICAL SIZE AND STRENGTH.
Cough.
Sputter.
M'APOLOGIES, LUV! WE'VE GOTTA MOVE A'FOR--
BARRICADE BE-GONE!
AHHH!
Fantasy Factoid (cont): OH YEAH, IT GROWS EYEBALLS TOO...
BAD DADDY!
SIGHT!

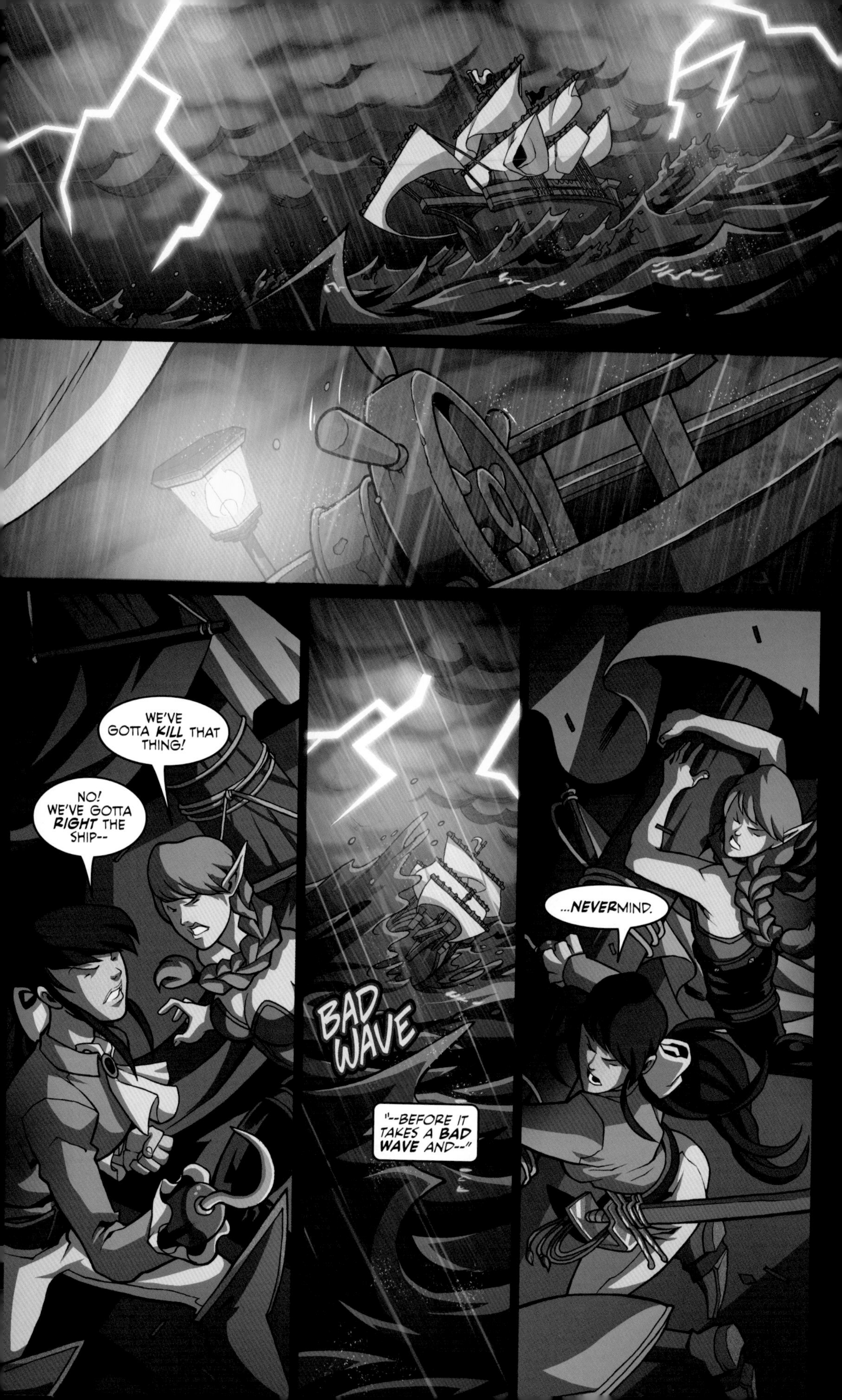
WE'VE GOTTA **KILL** THAT THING!
NO! WE'VE GOTTA **RIGHT** THE SHIP--
BAD WAVE
"--BEFORE IT TAKES A **BAD WAVE** AND--"
...**NEVER**MIND.

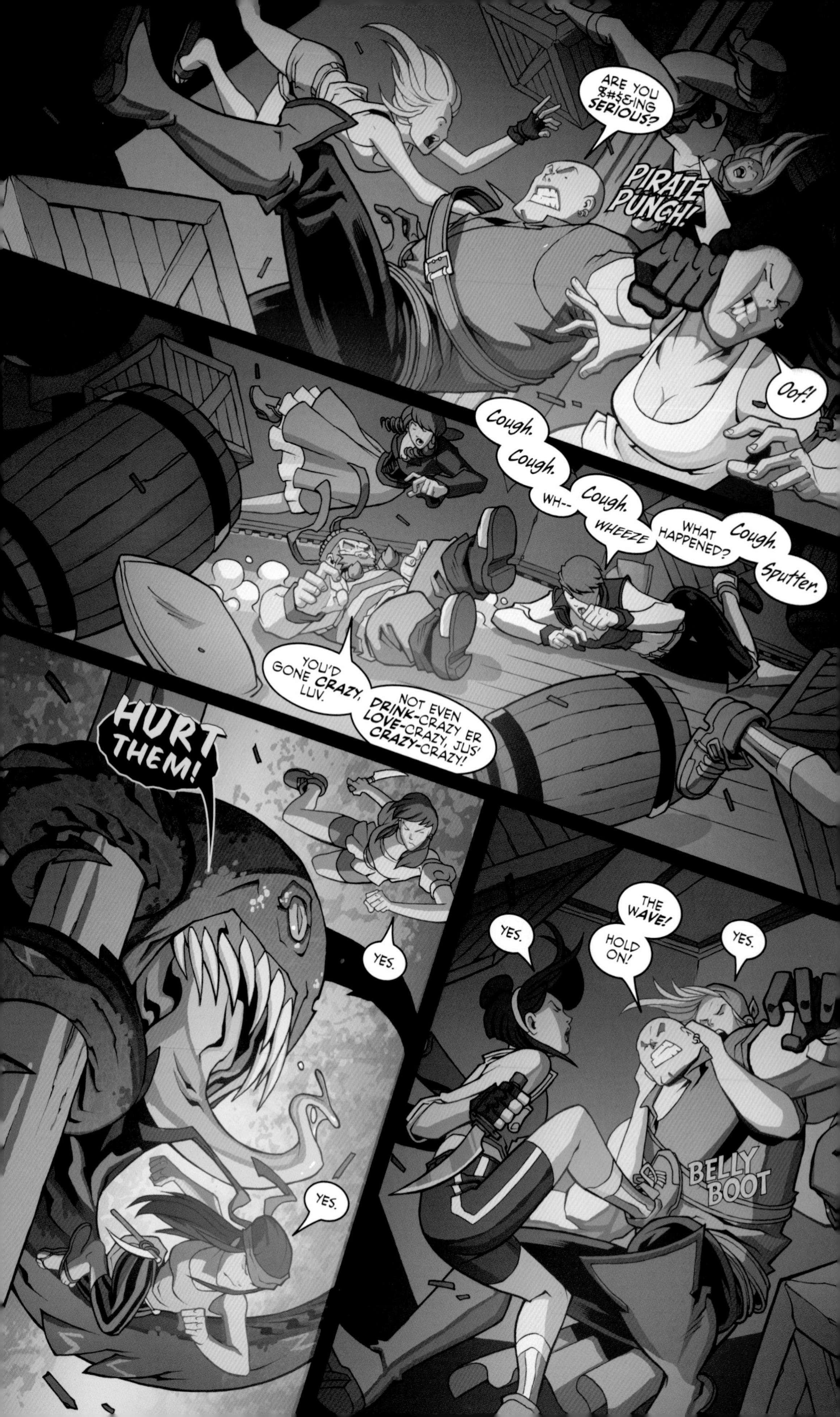
ARE YOU %#$&ING SERIOUS?
PIRATE PUNCH!
Oof!
Cough.
Cough.
WH--
Cough.
WHEEZE
WHAT HAPPENED?
Cough.
Sputter.
YOU'D GONE CRAZY, LUV.
NOT EVEN DRINK-CRAZY ER LOVE-CRAZY, JUS' CRAZY-CRAZY!
HURT THEM!
YES.
YES.
YES.
THE WAVE!
HOLD ON!
YES.
BELLY BOOT

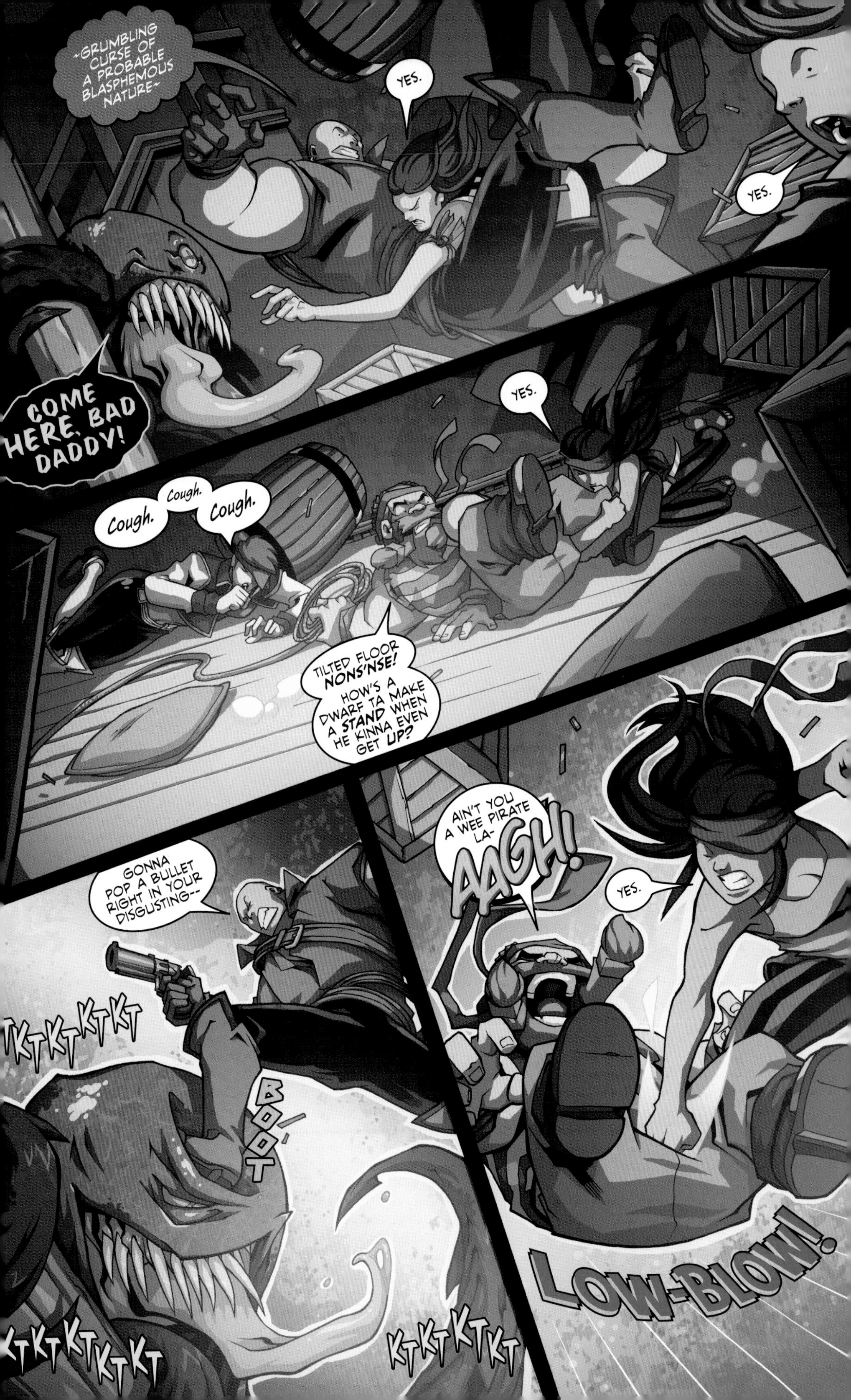
~GRUMBLING CURSE OF A PROBABLE BLASPHEMOUS NATURE~
YES.
YES.
COME HERE, BAD DADDY!
YES.
Cough.
Cough.
Cough.
TILTED FLOOR NONS'NSE! HOW'S A DWARF TA MAKE A STAND WHEN HE KINNA EVEN GET UP?
GONNA POP A BULLET RIGHT IN YOUR DISGUSTING--
KTKTKTKTKT
BOOT
KTKTKTKTKT
AIN'T YOU A WEE PIRATE LA-
AAGH!
YES.
LOW-BLOW!
KTKTKTKT

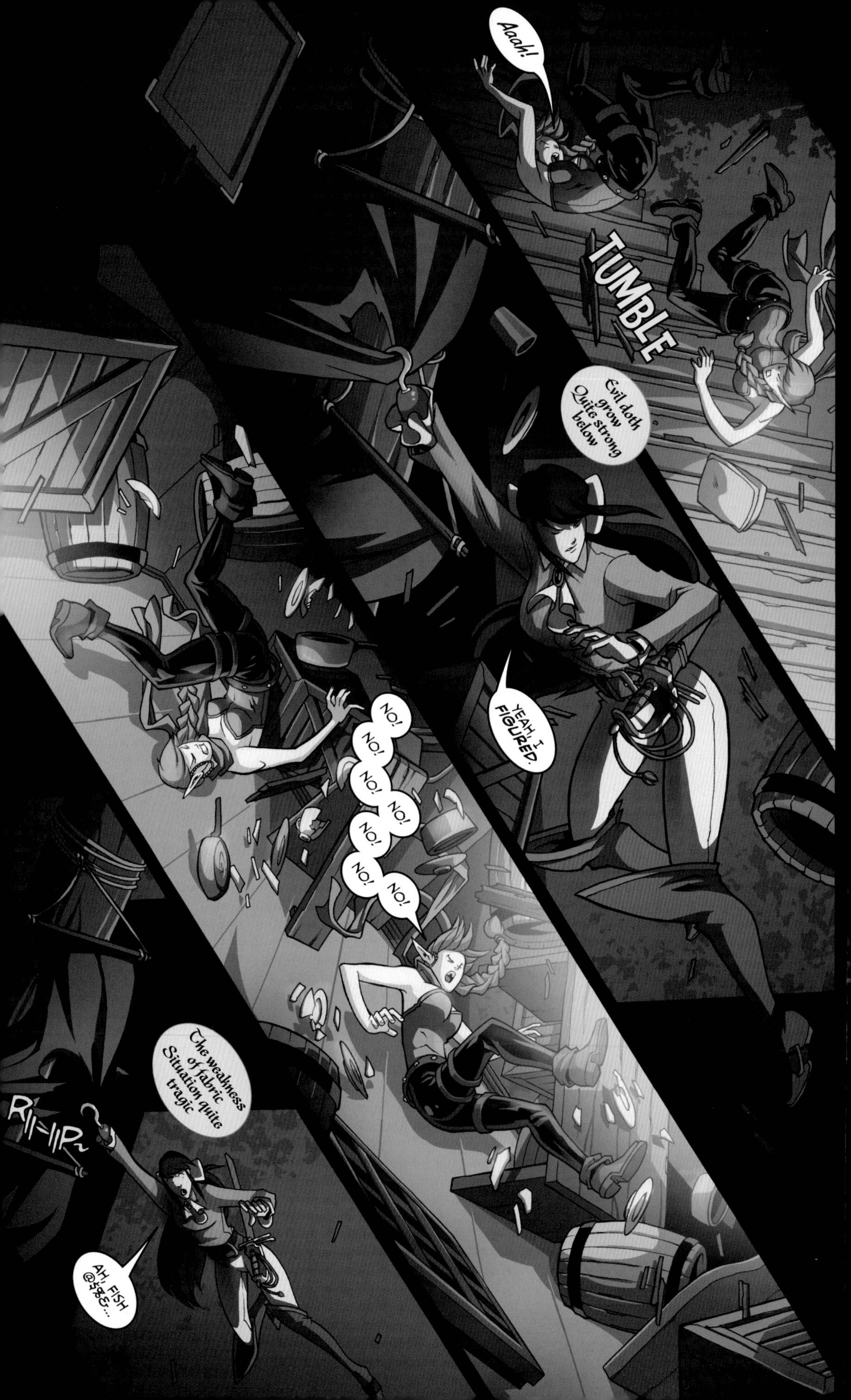
Aaah!
TUMBLE
Evil doth grow
Quite strong below
YEAH, I FIGURED.
NO! NO! NO! NO! NO! NO! NO!
The weakness of fabric
Situation quite tragic
RIIIP
AH, FISH @$%&...

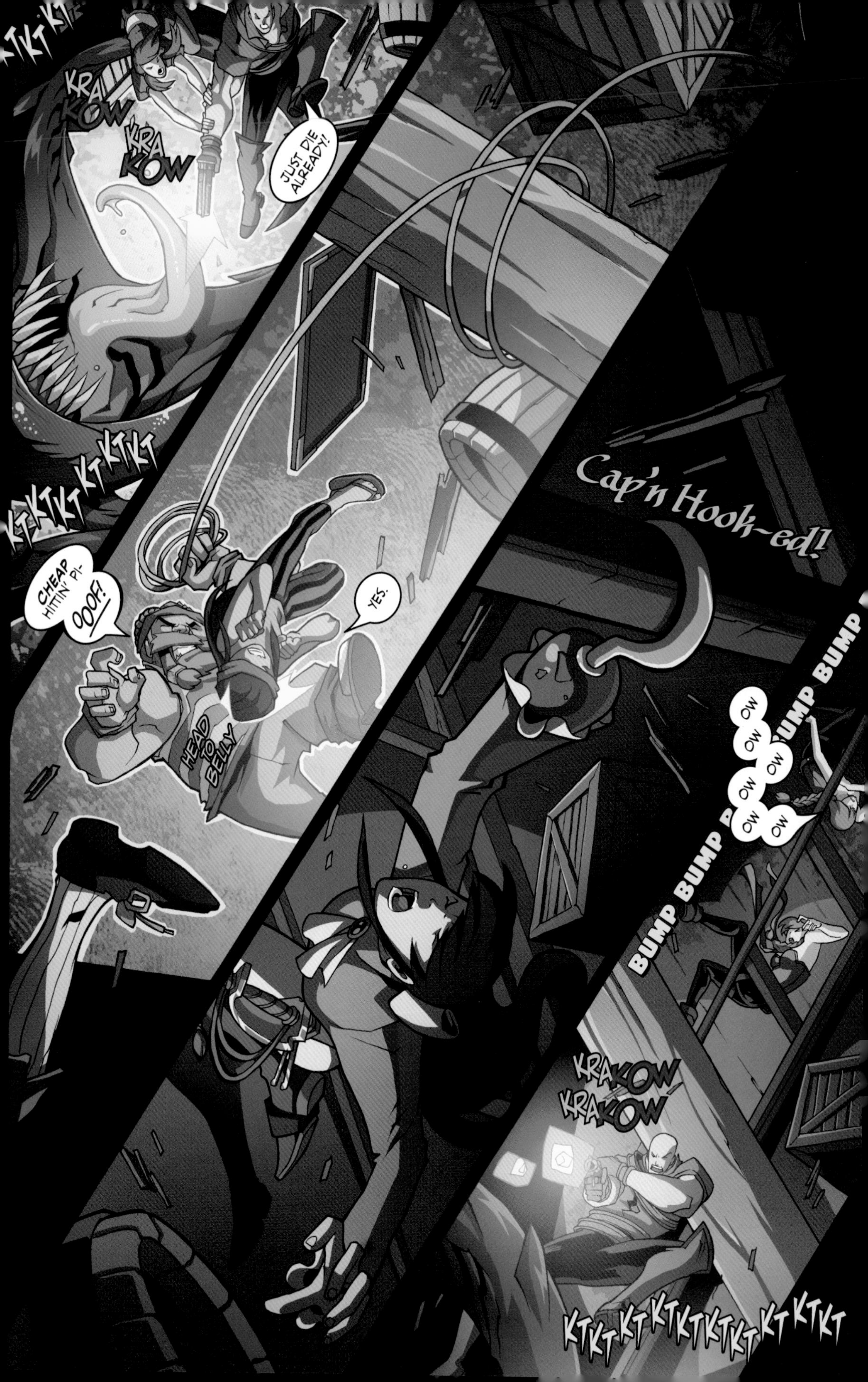
KTKT
KRA KOW
KRA KOW
JUST DIE ALREADY!
KTKTKT KT KTKT
CHEAP HITTIN' PI-
OOOF!
YES.
HEAD TO BELLY
Cap'n Hook-ed!
BUMP BUMP BUMP BUMP BUMP
OW OW OW OW OW OW
KRAKOW
KRAKOW
KTKTKT KTKTKTKT KT KTKT

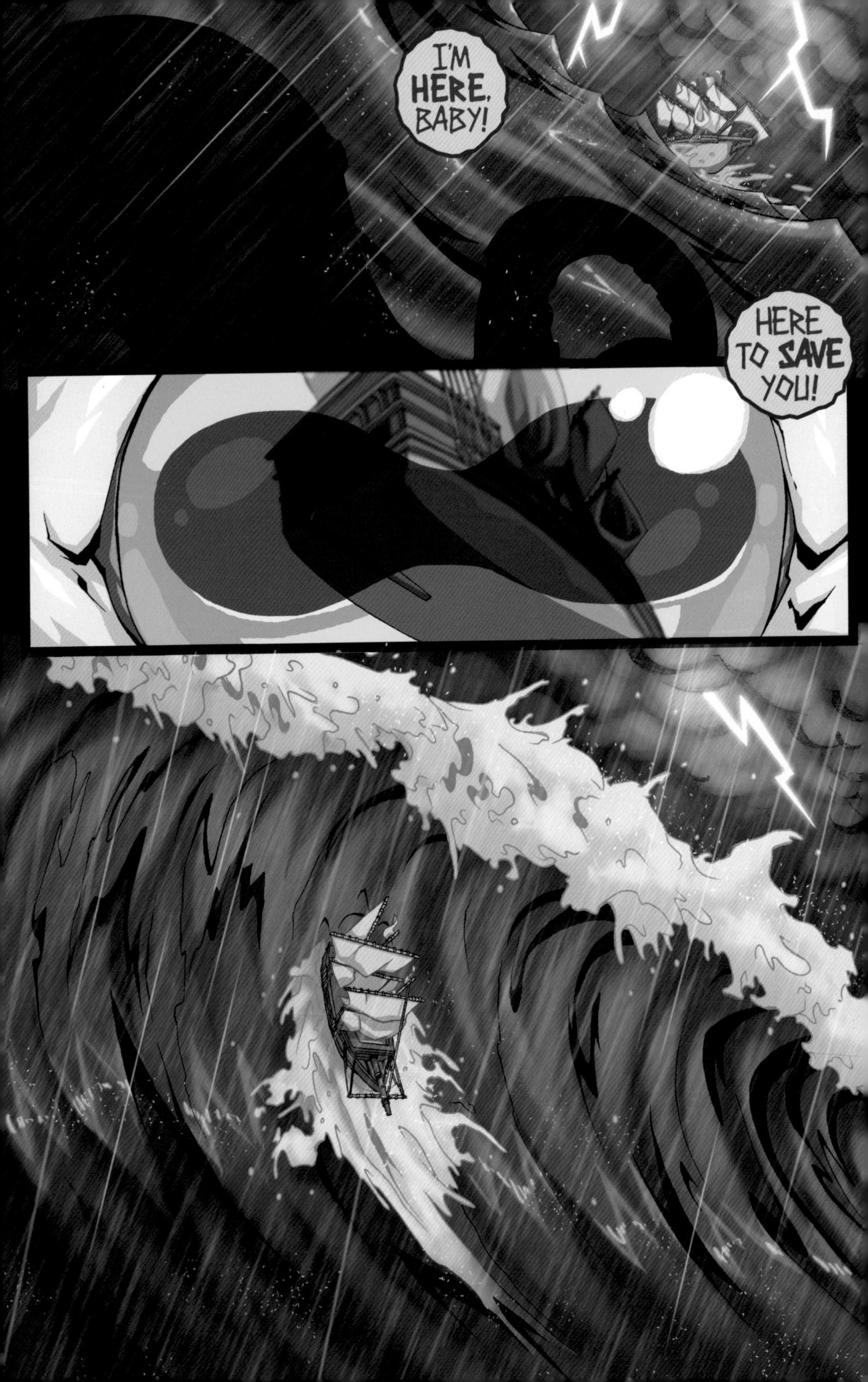
I'M **HERE**, BABY!
HERE TO **SAVE** YOU!

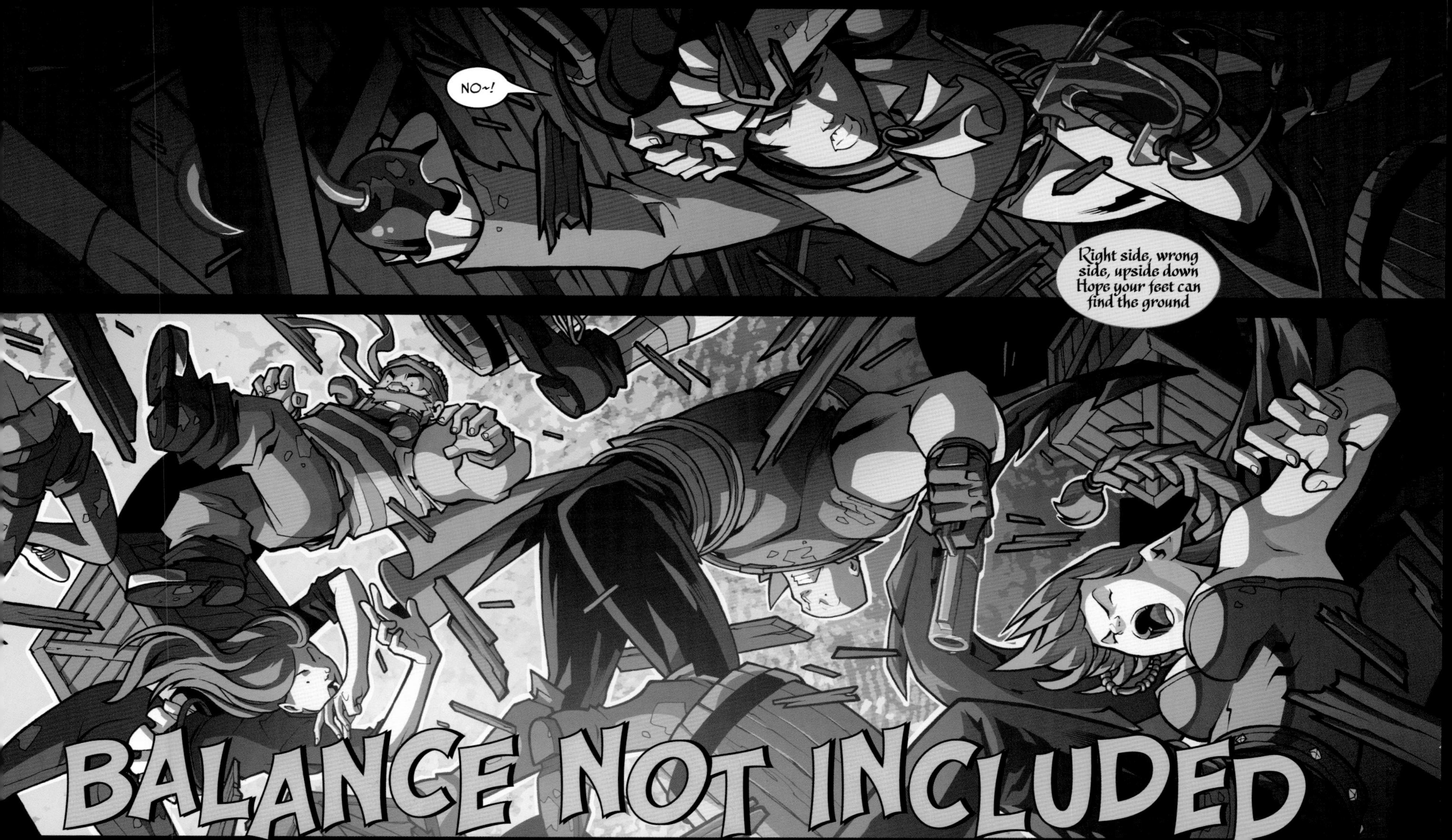
NO~!
Right side, wrong side, upside down Hope your feet can find the ground
BALANCE NOT INCLUDED

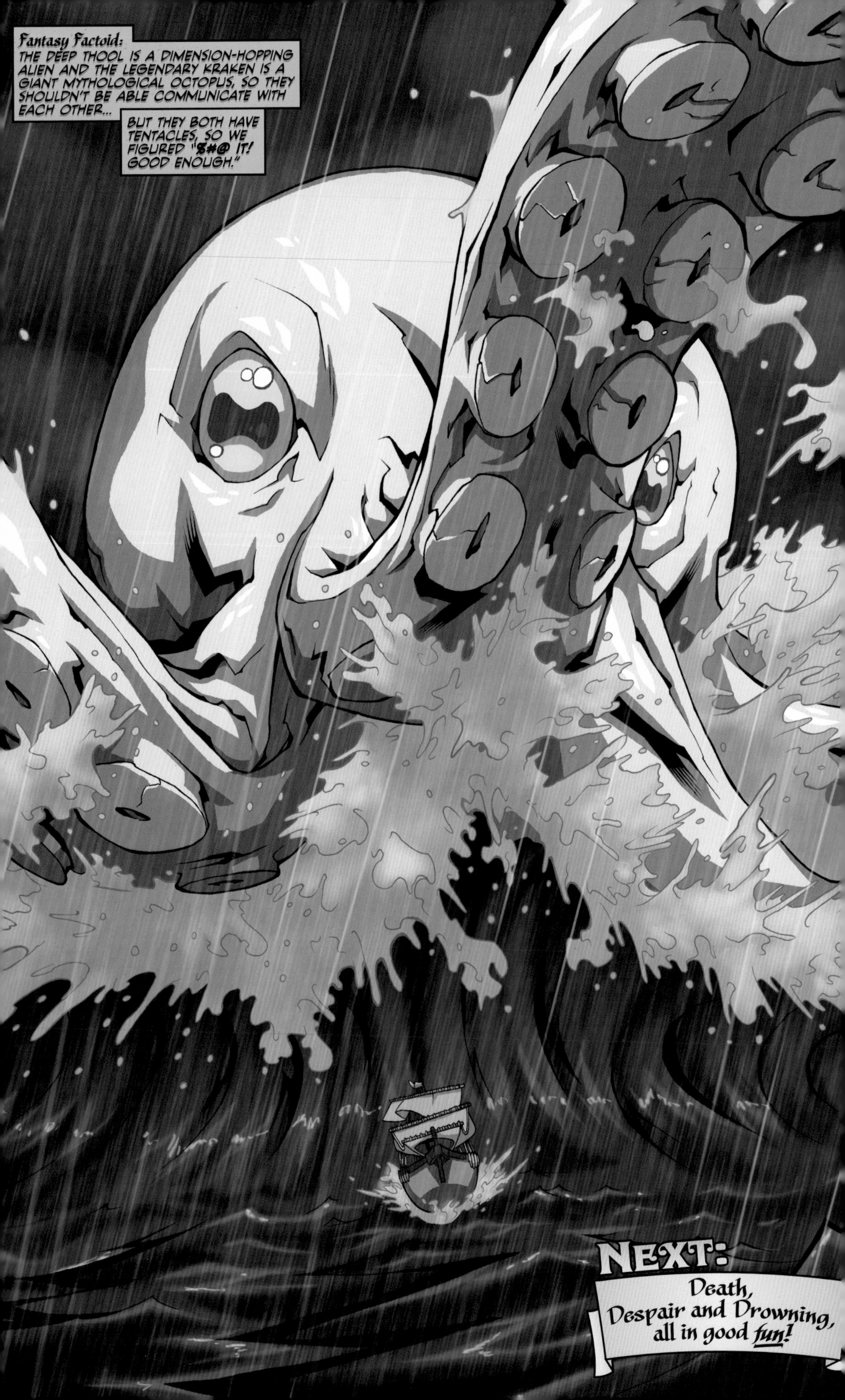
Fantasy Factoid:
THE DEEP THOOL IS A DIMENSION-HOPPING ALIEN AND THE LEGENDARY KRAKEN IS A GIANT MYTHOLOGICAL OCTOPUS, SO THEY SHOULDN'T BE ABLE COMMUNICATE WITH EACH OTHER...
BUT THEY BOTH HAVE TENTACLES, SO WE FIGURED "$#@ IT! GOOD ENOUGH."
NEXT:
Death, Despair and Drowning, all in good fun!

CHAPTER FIVE

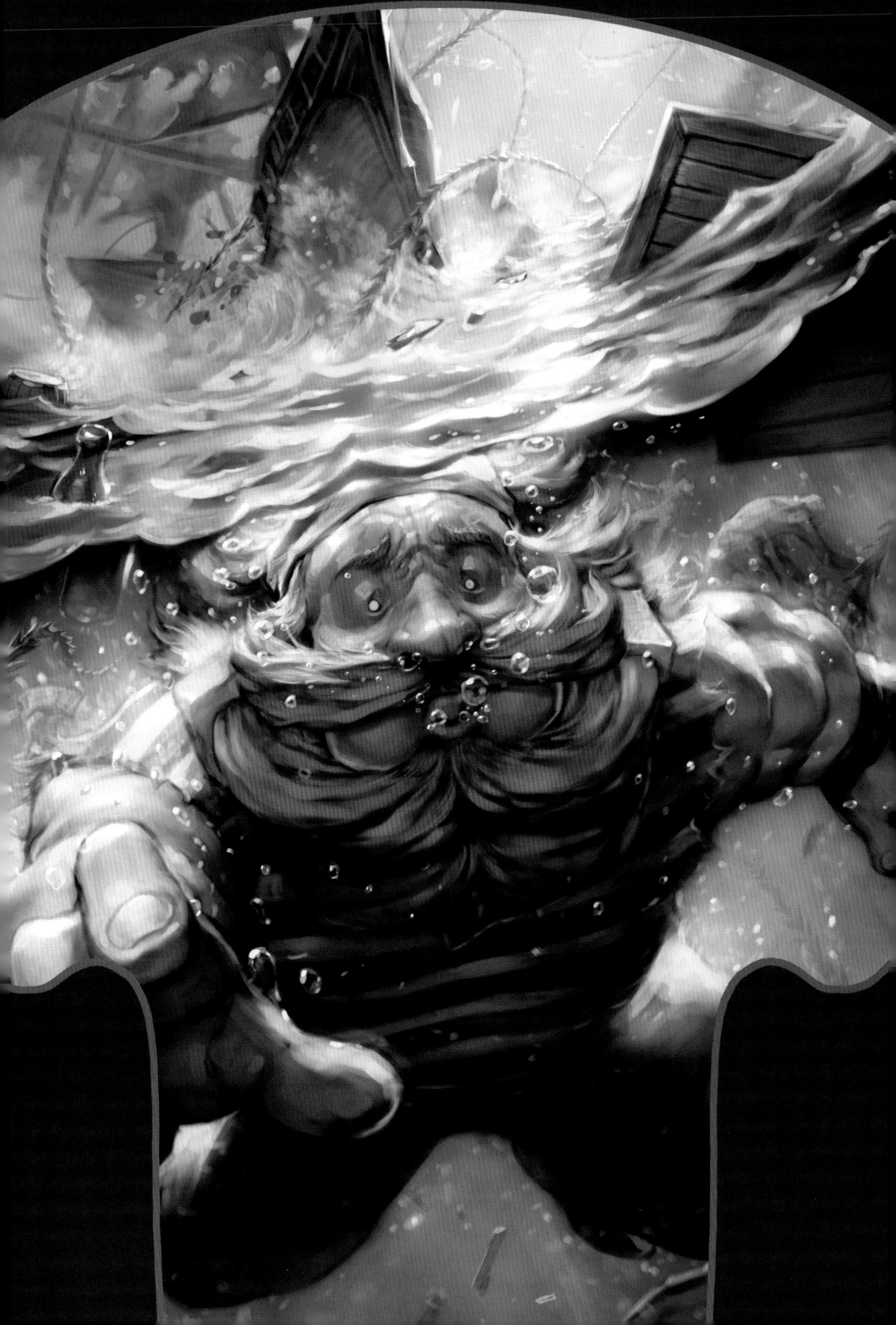

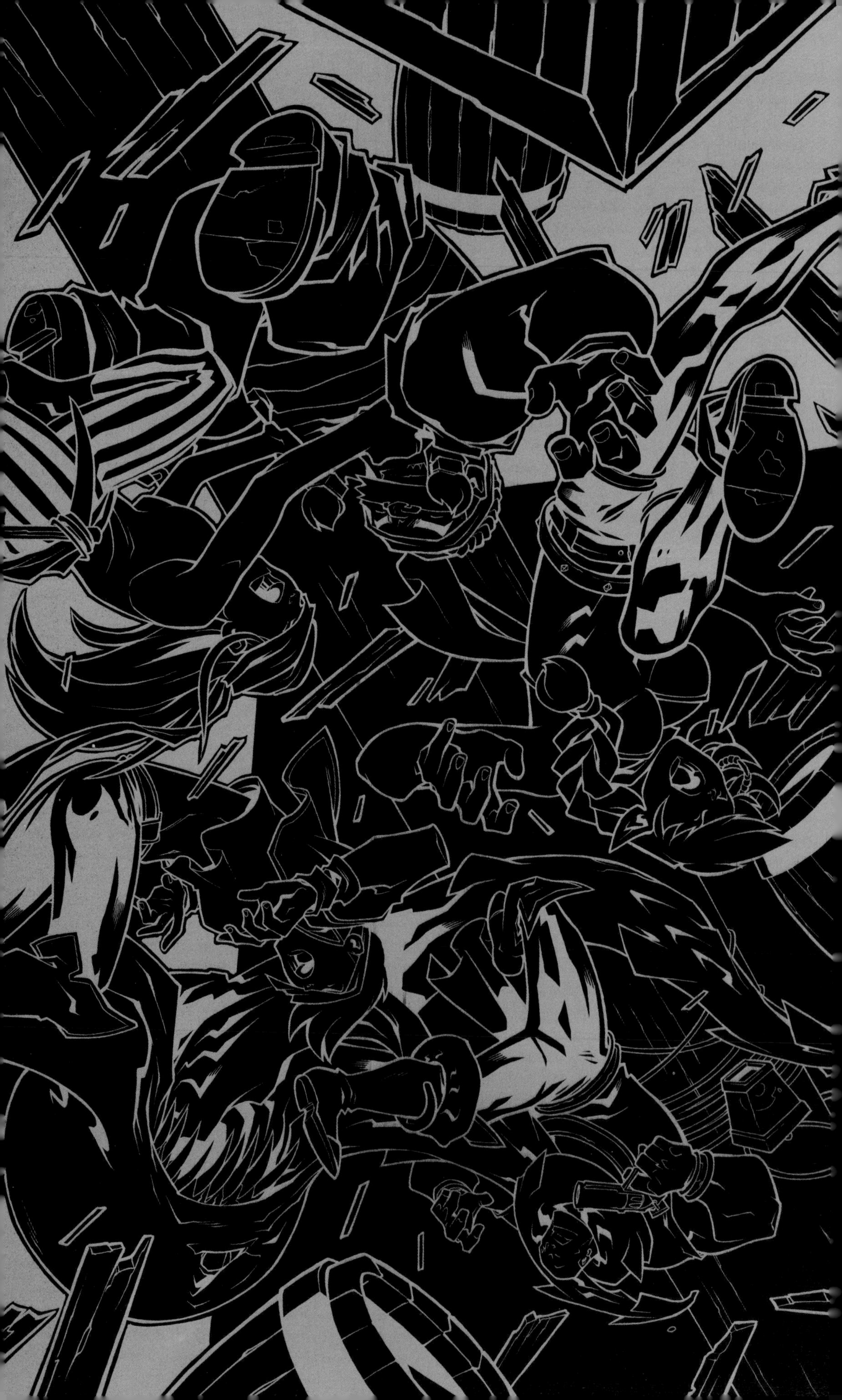

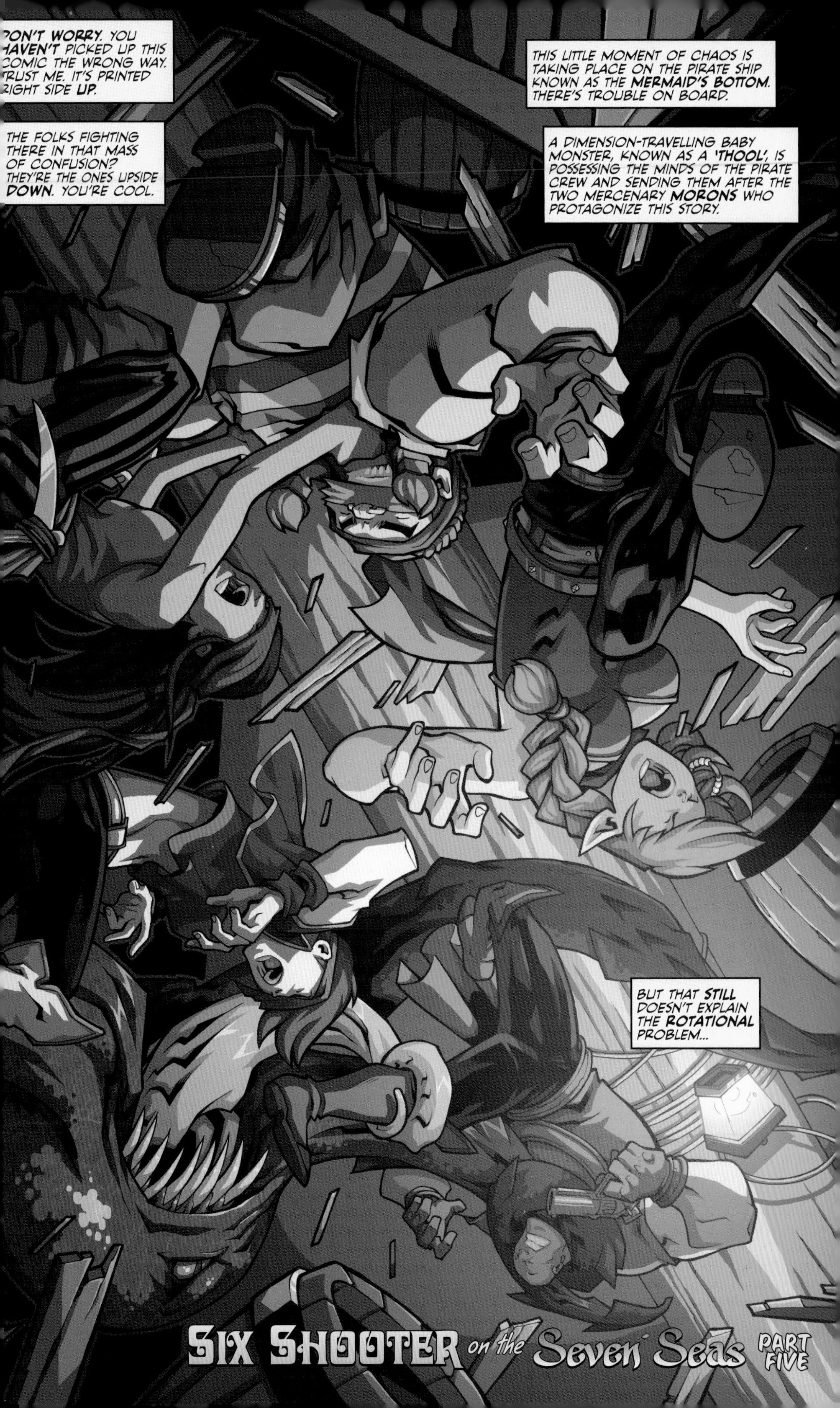

DON'T WORRY. YOU HAVEN'T PICKED UP THIS COMIC THE WRONG WAY. TRUST ME. IT'S PRINTED RIGHT SIDE UP.
THIS LITTLE MOMENT OF CHAOS IS TAKING PLACE ON THE PIRATE SHIP KNOWN AS THE MERMAID'S BOTTOM. THERE'S TROUBLE ON BOARD.
THE FOLKS FIGHTING THERE IN THAT MASS OF CONFUSION? THEY'RE THE ONES UPSIDE DOWN. YOU'RE COOL.
A DIMENSION-TRAVELLING BABY MONSTER, KNOWN AS A 'THOOL', IS POSSESSING THE MINDS OF THE PIRATE CREW AND SENDING THEM AFTER THE TWO MERCENARY MORONS WHO PROTAGONIZE THIS STORY.
BUT THAT STILL DOESN'T EXPLAIN THE ROTATIONAL PROBLEM...
SIX SHOOTER on the Seven Seas PART FIVE

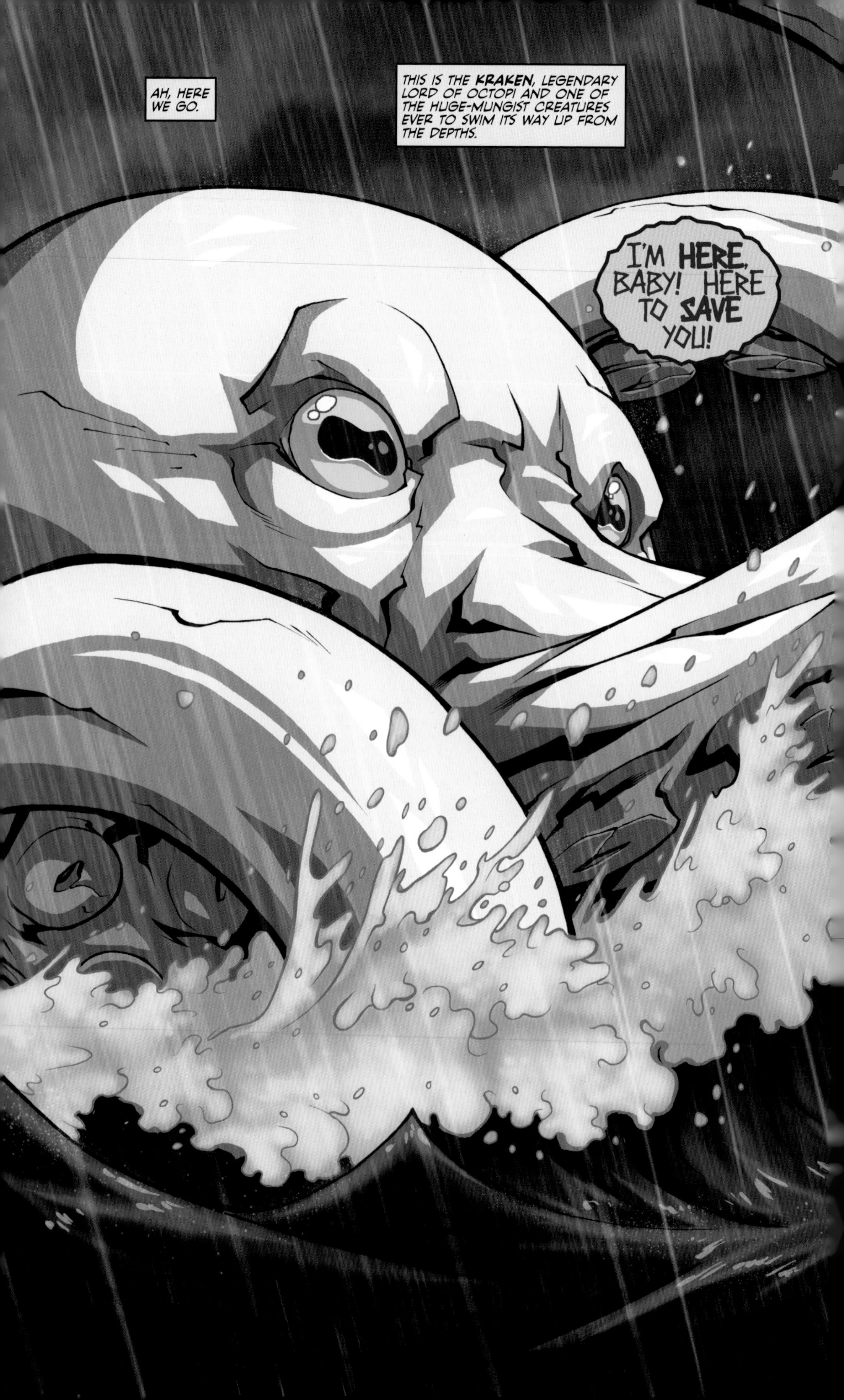
AH, HERE WE GO.
THIS IS THE KRAKEN, LEGENDARY LORD OF OCTOPI AND ONE OF THE HUGE-MUNGIST CREATURES EVER TO SWIM ITS WAY UP FROM THE DEPTHS.
I'M HERE, BABY! HERE TO SAVE YOU!

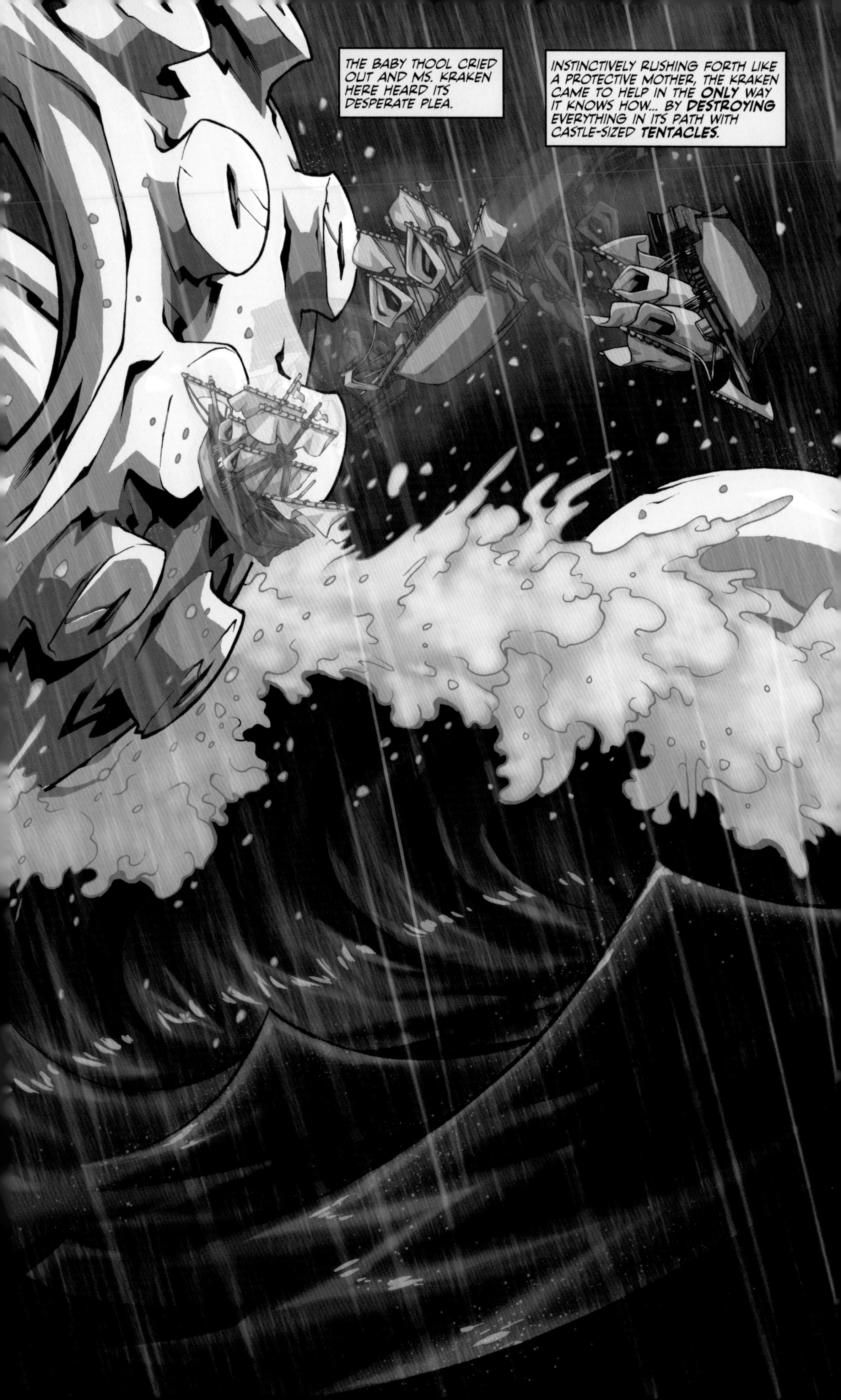
THE BABY THOOL CRIED OUT AND MS. KRAKEN HERE HEARD ITS DESPERATE PLEA.
INSTINCTIVELY RUSHING FORTH LIKE A PROTECTIVE MOTHER, THE KRAKEN CAME TO HELP IN THE ONLY WAY IT KNOWS HOW... BY DESTROYING EVERYTHING IN ITS PATH WITH CASTLE-SIZED TENTACLES.

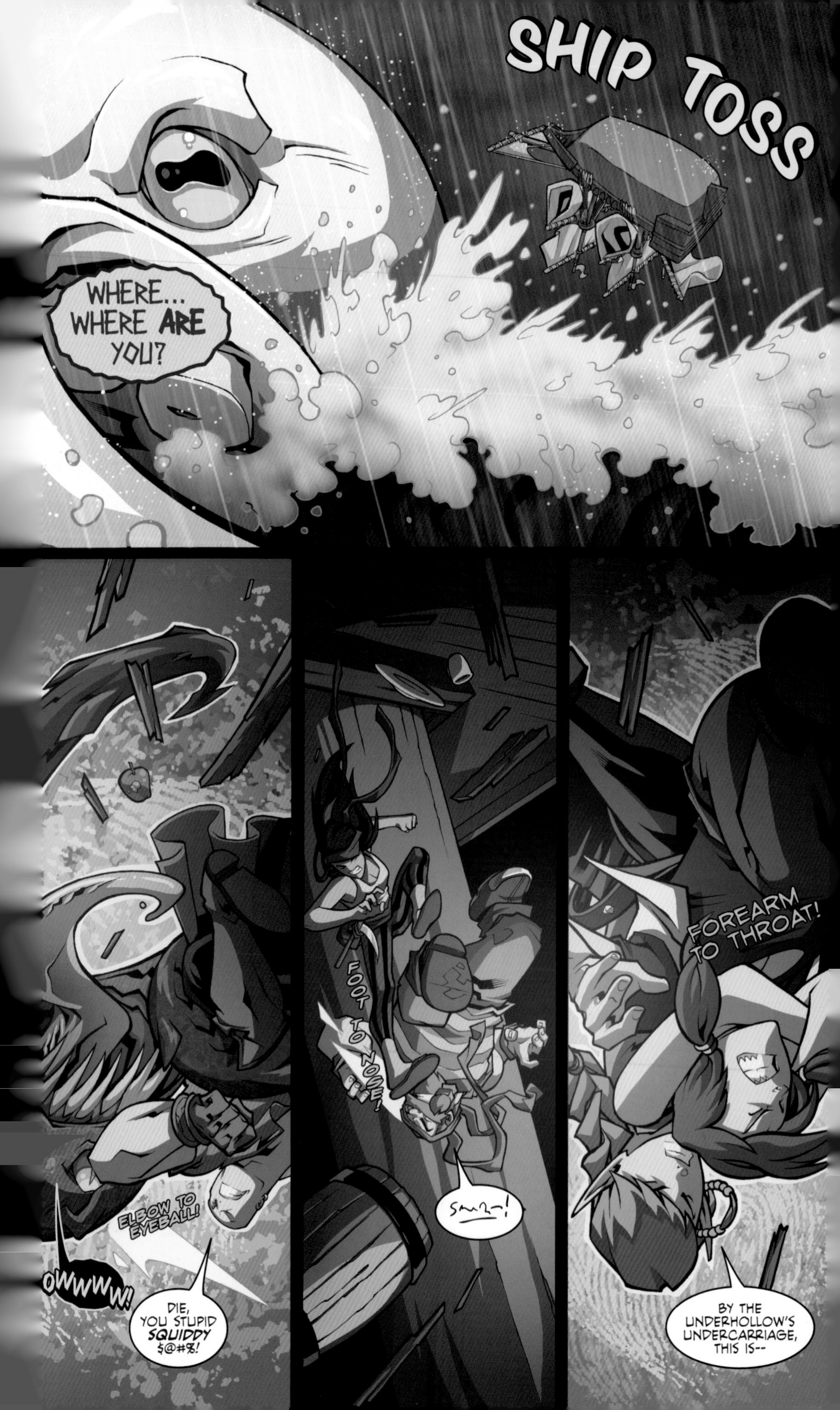

SHIP TOSS
WHERE... WHERE ARE YOU?
ELBOW TO EYEBALL!
OWWWW!
DIE, YOU STUPID SQUIDDY $@#%!
FOOT TO NOSE!
FOREARM TO THROAT!
BY THE UNDERHOLLOW'S UNDERCARRIAGE, THIS IS--

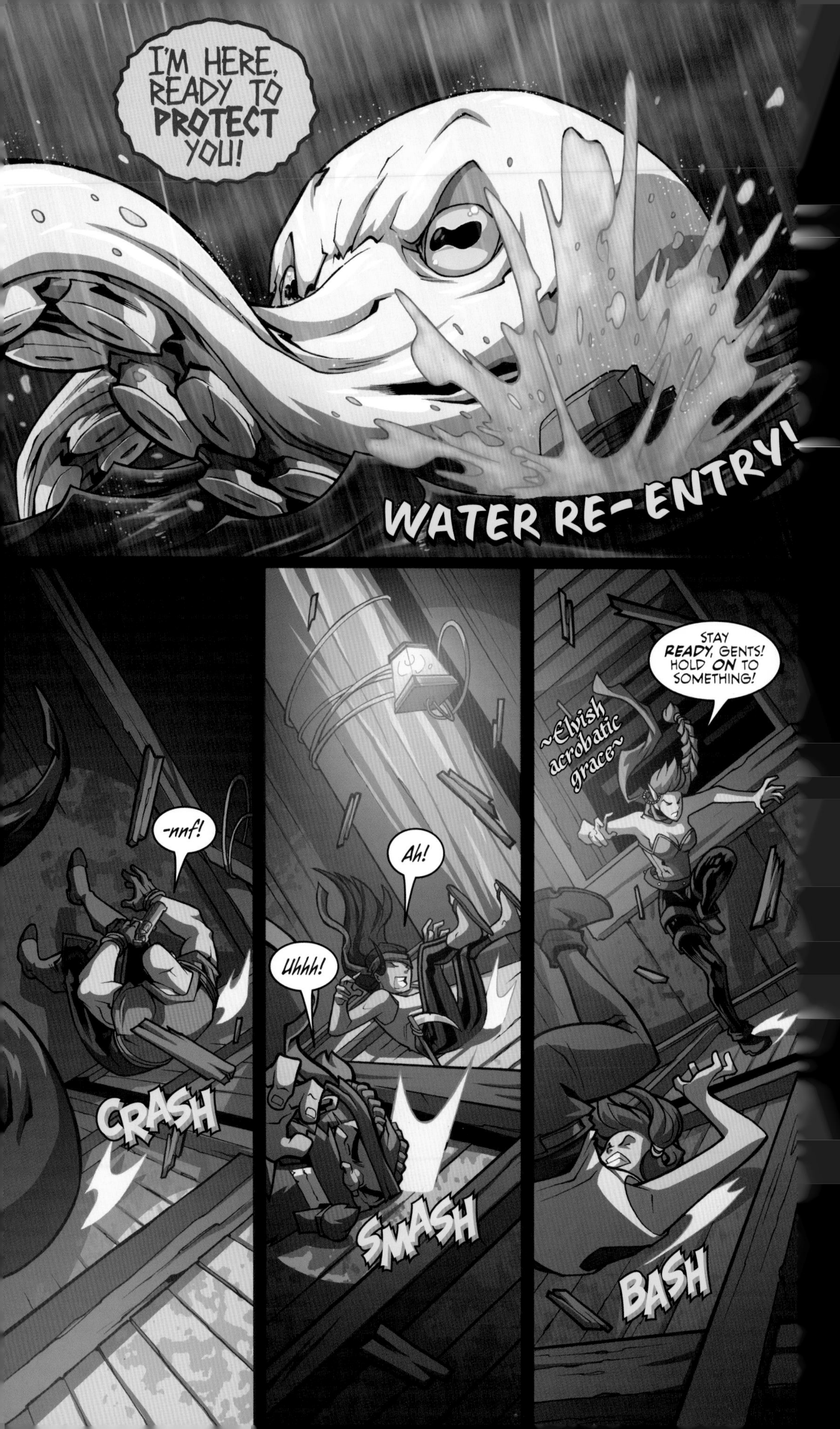
I'M HERE, READY TO PROTECT YOU!
WATER RE-ENTRY!
-nnf!
CRASH
Ah!
Uhhh!
SMASH
STAY READY, GENTS! HOLD ON TO SOMETHING!
~Elvish acrobatic grace~
BASH

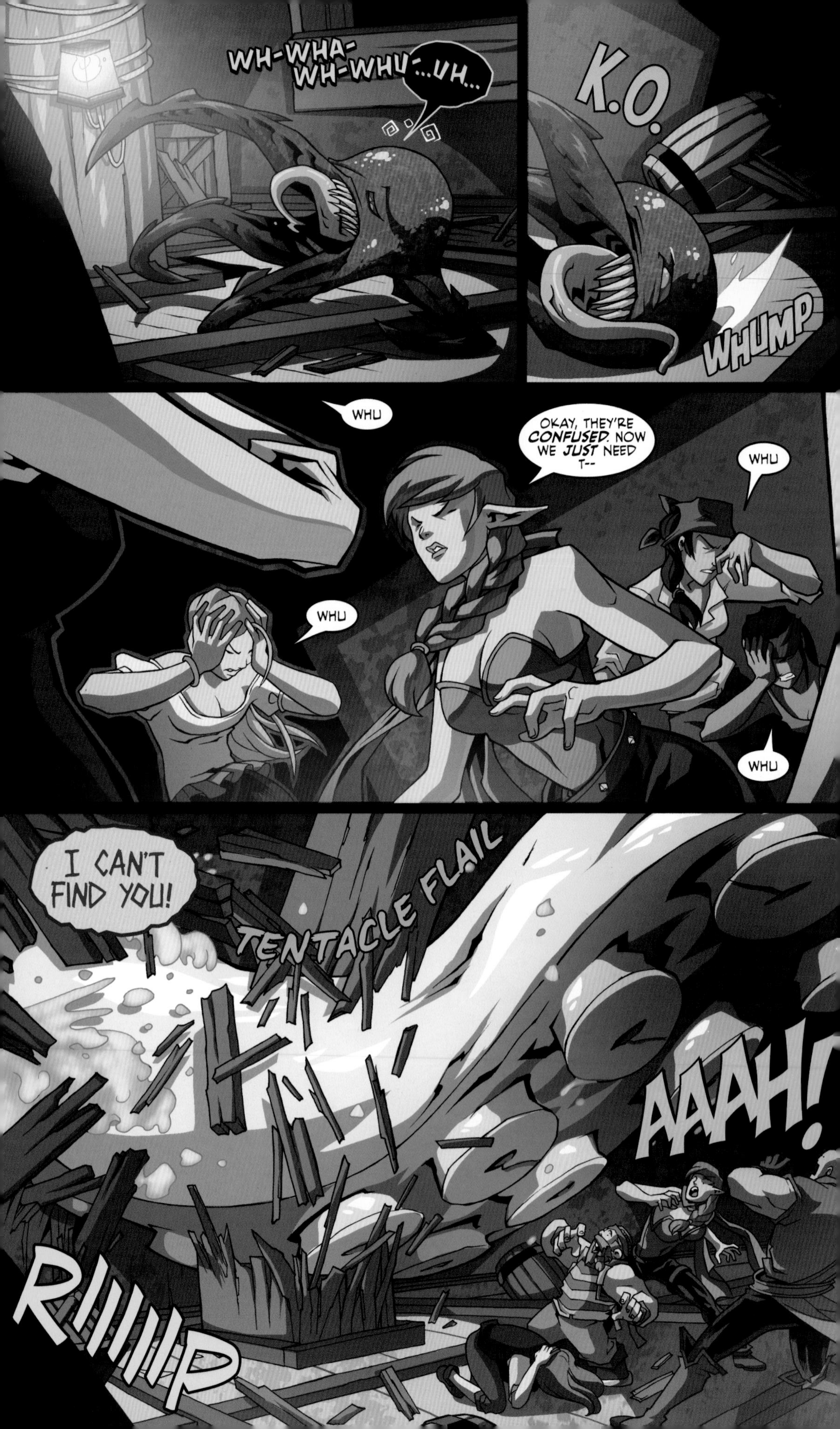
WH-WHA-
WH-WHU-...UH...
K.O.
WHUMP
WHU
OKAY, THEY'RE *CONFUSED*. NOW WE *JUST* NEED T--
WHU
WHU
WHU
I CAN'T FIND YOU!
TENTACLE FLAIL
AAAH!
RIIIIIP

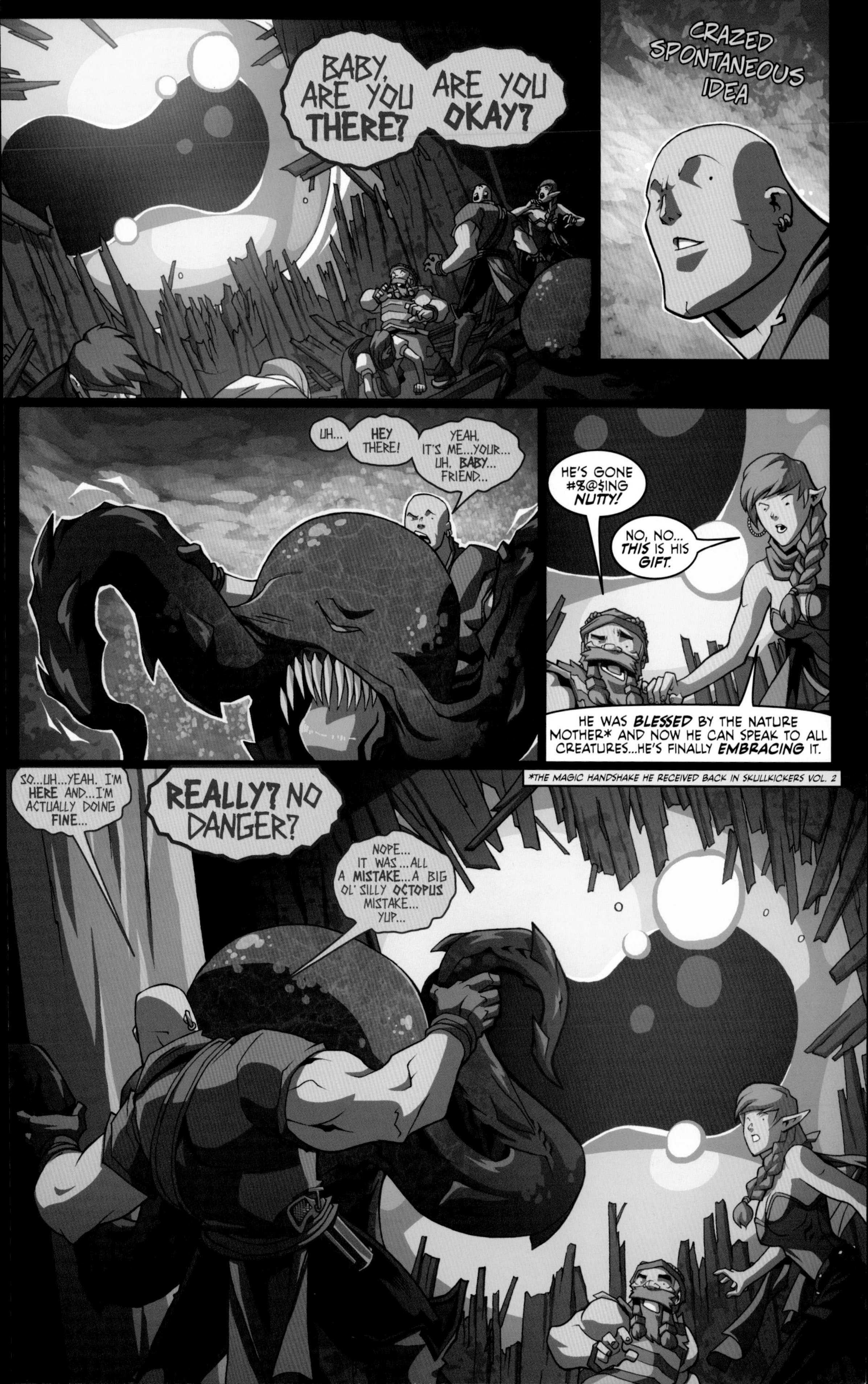
BABY, ARE YOU THERE?
ARE YOU OKAY?
CRAZED SPONTANEOUS IDEA
UH...
HEY THERE!
YEAH, IT'S ME...YOUR... UH, BABY... FRIEND...
HE'S GONE #%@$ING NUTTY!
NO, NO... THIS IS HIS GIFT.
HE WAS BLESSED BY THE NATURE MOTHER* AND NOW HE CAN SPEAK TO ALL CREATURES...HE'S FINALLY EMBRACING IT.
*THE MAGIC HANDSHAKE HE RECEIVED BACK IN SKULLKICKERS VOL. 2
SO...UH...YEAH. I'M HERE AND...I'M ACTUALLY DOING FINE...
REALLY? NO DANGER?
NOPE... IT WAS...ALL A MISTAKE...A BIG OL' SILLY OCTOPUS MISTAKE... YUP...

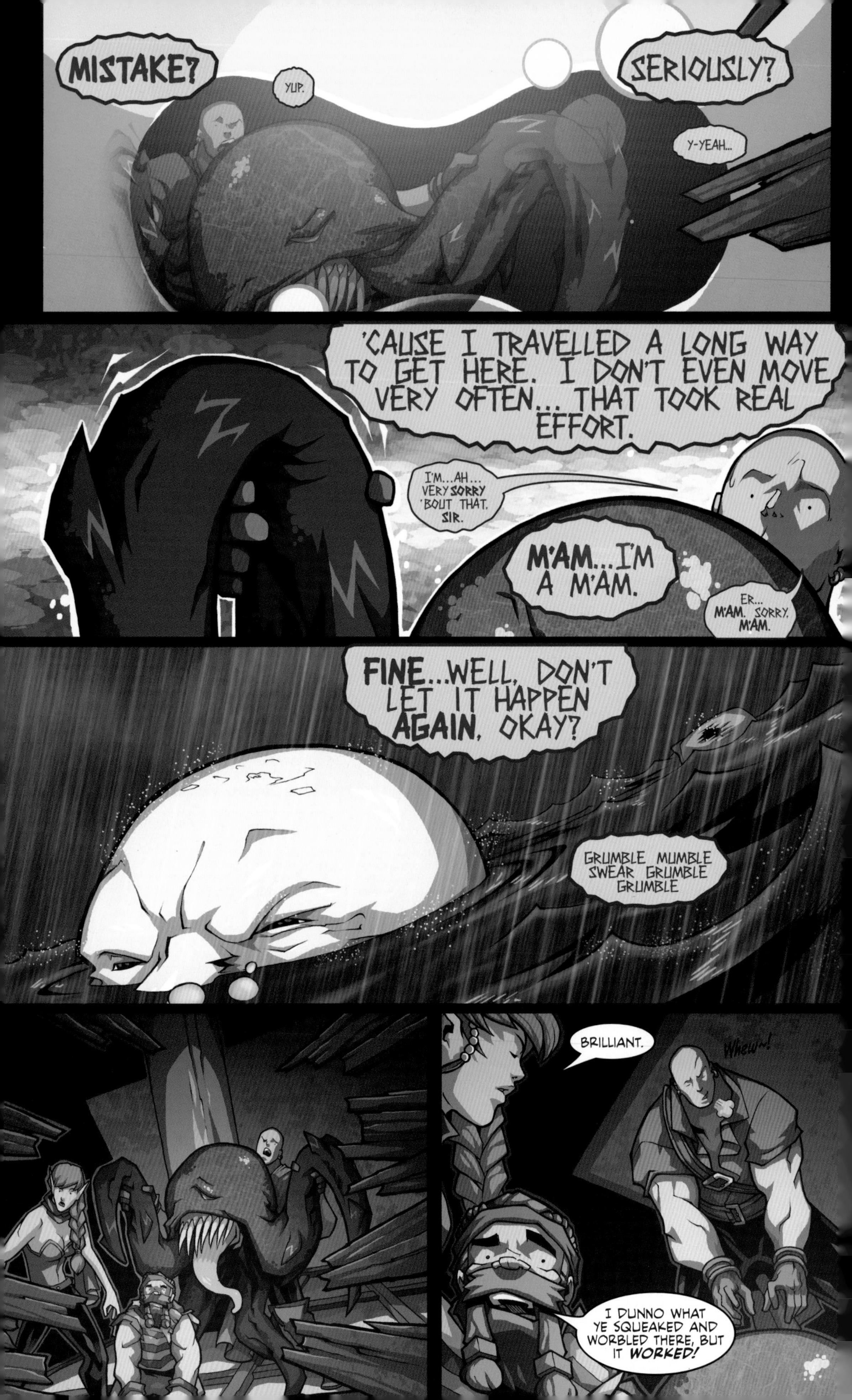
MISTAKE?
YUP.
SERIOUSLY?
Y-YEAH...
'CAUSE I TRAVELLED A LONG WAY TO GET HERE. I DON'T EVEN MOVE VERY OFTEN... THAT TOOK REAL EFFORT.
I'M...AH... VERY SORRY 'BOUT THAT. SIR.
M'AM...I'M A M'AM.
ER... M'AM. SORRY. M'AM.
FINE...WELL, DON'T LET IT HAPPEN AGAIN, OKAY?
GRUMBLE MUMBLE SWEAR GRUMBLE GRUMBLE
BRILLIANT.
Whew~!
I DUNNO WHAT YE SQUEAKED AND WORBLED THERE, BUT IT WORKED!

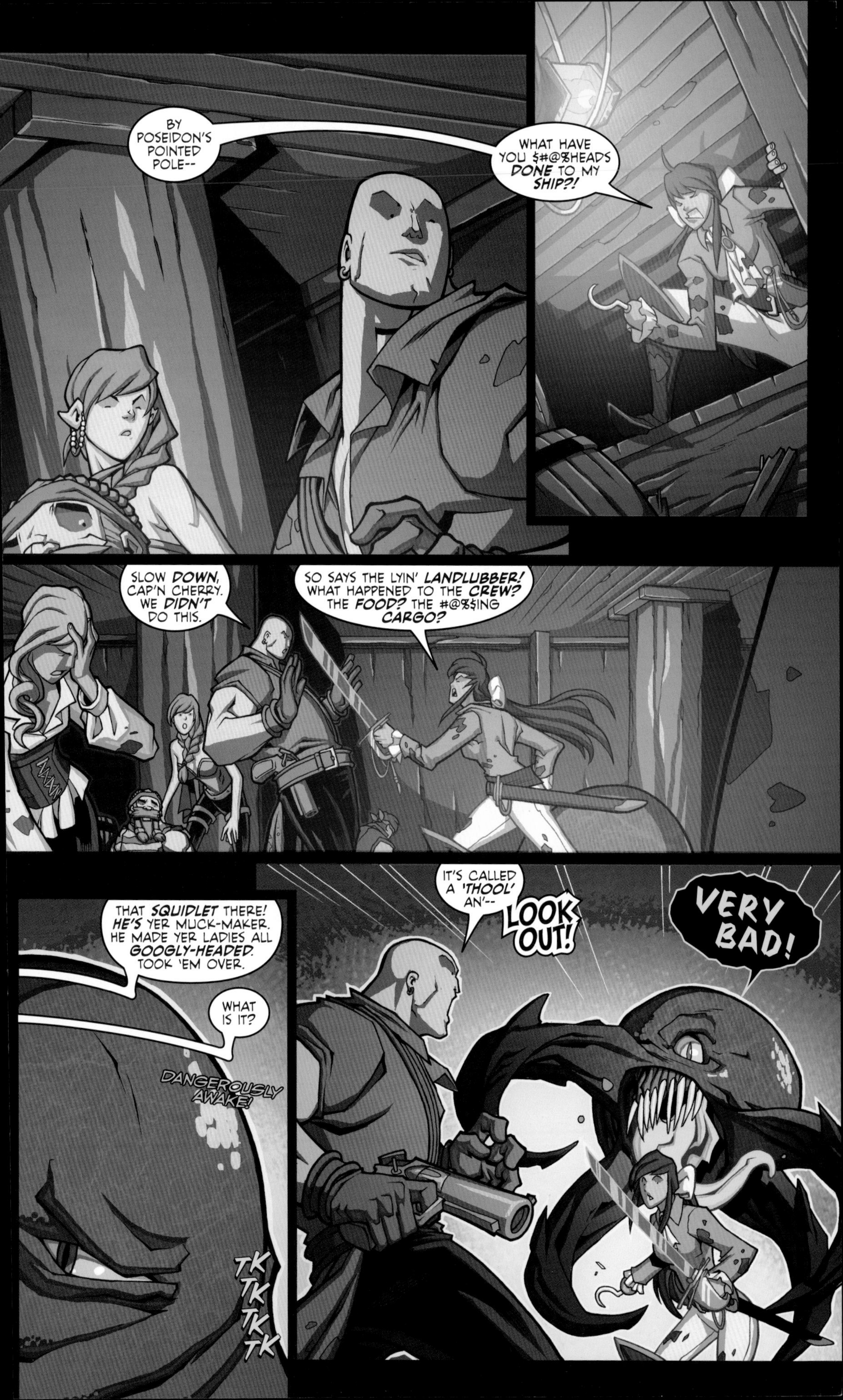
BY POSEIDON'S POINTED POLE--
WHAT HAVE YOU $#@%HEADS DONE TO MY SHIP?!
SLOW DOWN, CAP'N CHERRY. WE DIDN'T DO THIS.
SO SAYS THE LYIN' LANDLUBBER! WHAT HAPPENED TO THE CREW? THE FOOD? THE #@%$ING CARGO?
THAT SQUIDLET THERE! HE'S YER MUCK-MAKER. HE MADE YER LADIES ALL GOOGLY-HEADED. TOOK 'EM OVER.
WHAT IS IT?
DANGEROUSLY AWAKE!
TK TK TK TK TK
IT'S CALLED A 'THOOL' AN'--
LOOK OUT!
VERY BAD!

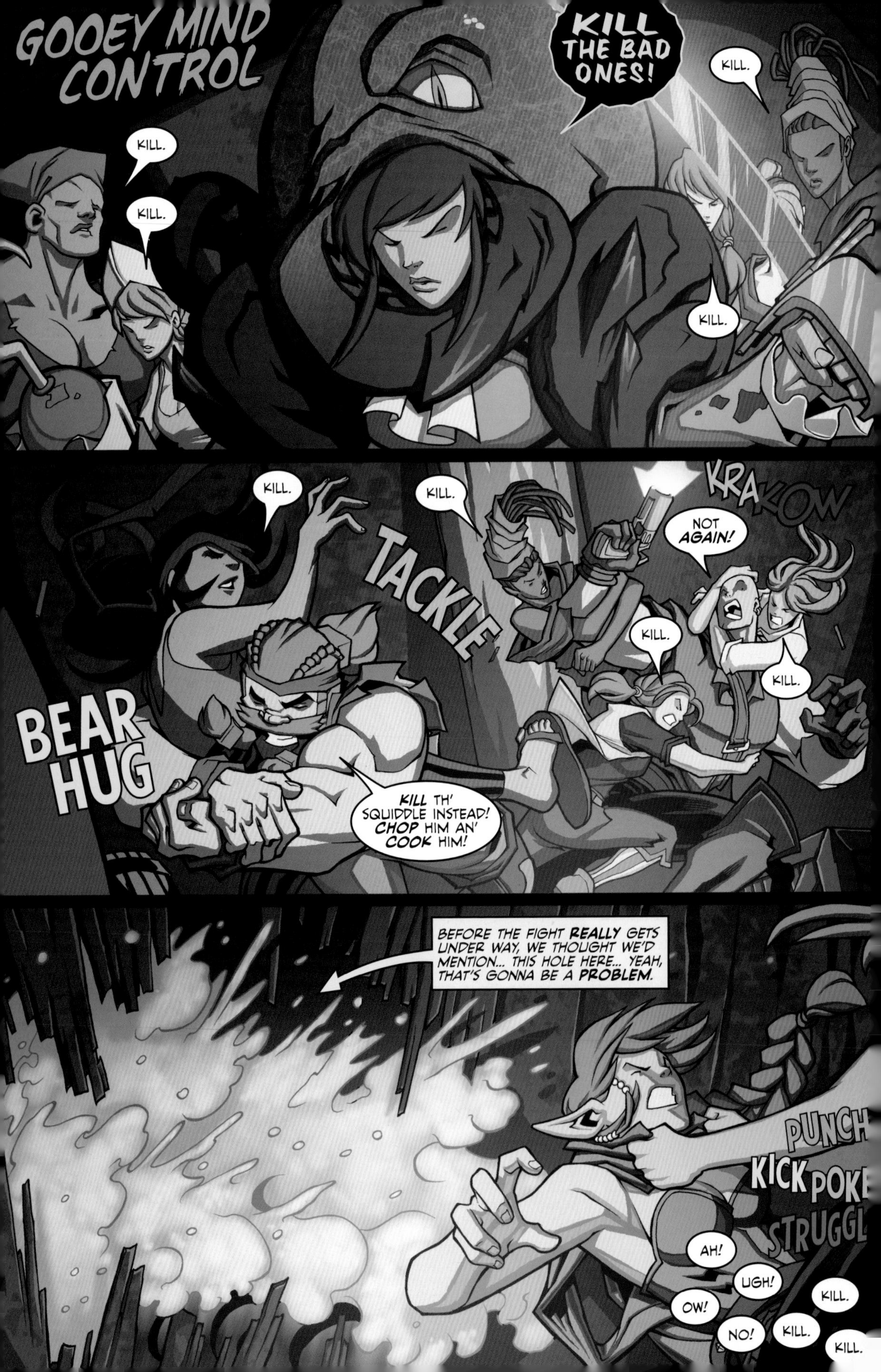
GOOEY MIND CONTROL
KILL THE BAD ONES!
KILL.
KILL.
KILL.
KILL.
KILL.
KILL.
KRAKOW
NOT AGAIN!
TACKLE
KILL.
KILL.
BEAR HUG
KILL TH' SQUIDDLE INSTEAD! CHOP HIM AN' COOK HIM!
BEFORE THE FIGHT REALLY GETS UNDER WAY, WE THOUGHT WE'D MENTION... THIS HOLE HERE... YEAH, THAT'S GONNA BE A PROBLEM.
PUNCH
KICK
POKE
STRUGGL
AH!
UGH!
OW!
NO!
KILL.
KILL.
KILL.

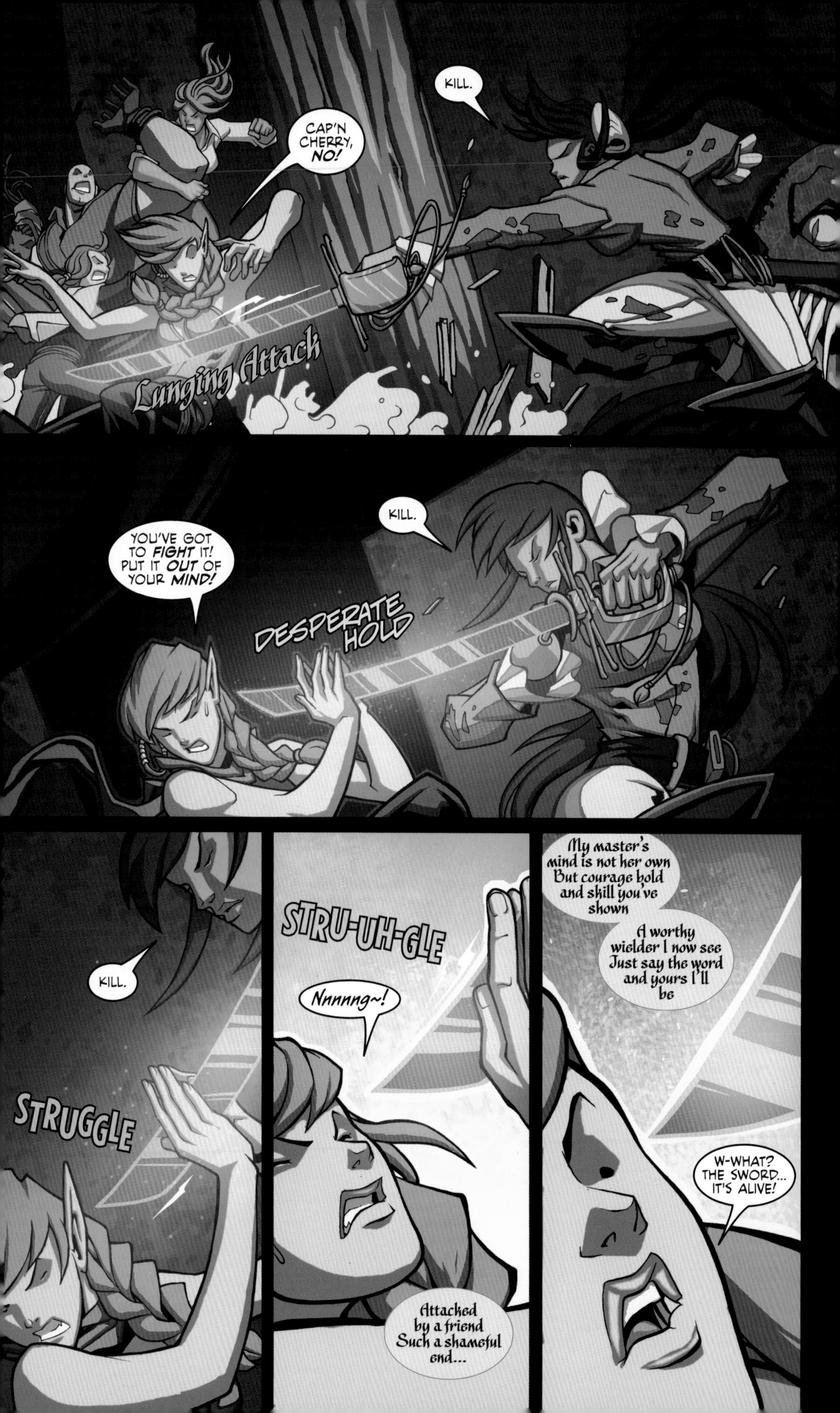
KILL.
CAP'N CHERRY, NO!
Lunging Attack
KILL.
YOU'VE GOT TO FIGHT IT! PUT IT OUT OF YOUR MIND!
DESPERATE HOLD
KILL.
STRUGGLE
STRU-UH-GLE
Nnnnng~!
Attacked by a friend Such a shameful end...
My master's mind is not her own But courage bold and skill you've shown
A worthy wielder I now see Just say the word and yours I'll be
W-WHAT? THE SWORD... IT'S ALIVE!

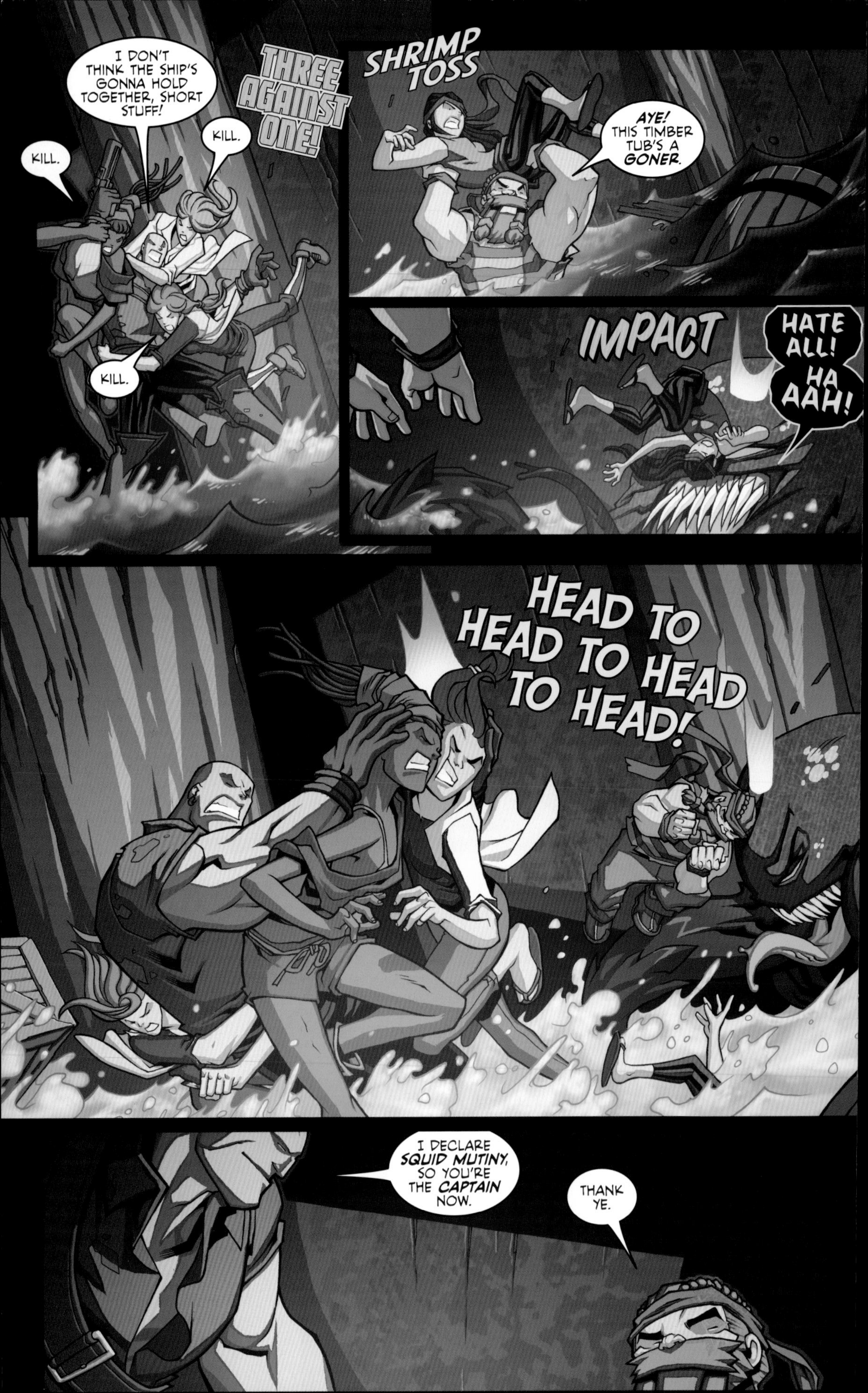
I DON'T THINK THE SHIP'S GONNA HOLD TOGETHER, SHORT STUFF!
THREE AGAINST ONE!
KILL.
KILL.
KILL.
SHRIMP TOSS
AYE! THIS TIMBER TUB'S A GONER.
IMPACT
HATE ALL! HA AAH!
HEAD TO HEAD TO HEAD TO HEAD!
I DECLARE SQUID MUTINY, SO YOU'RE THE CAPTAIN NOW.
THANK YE.

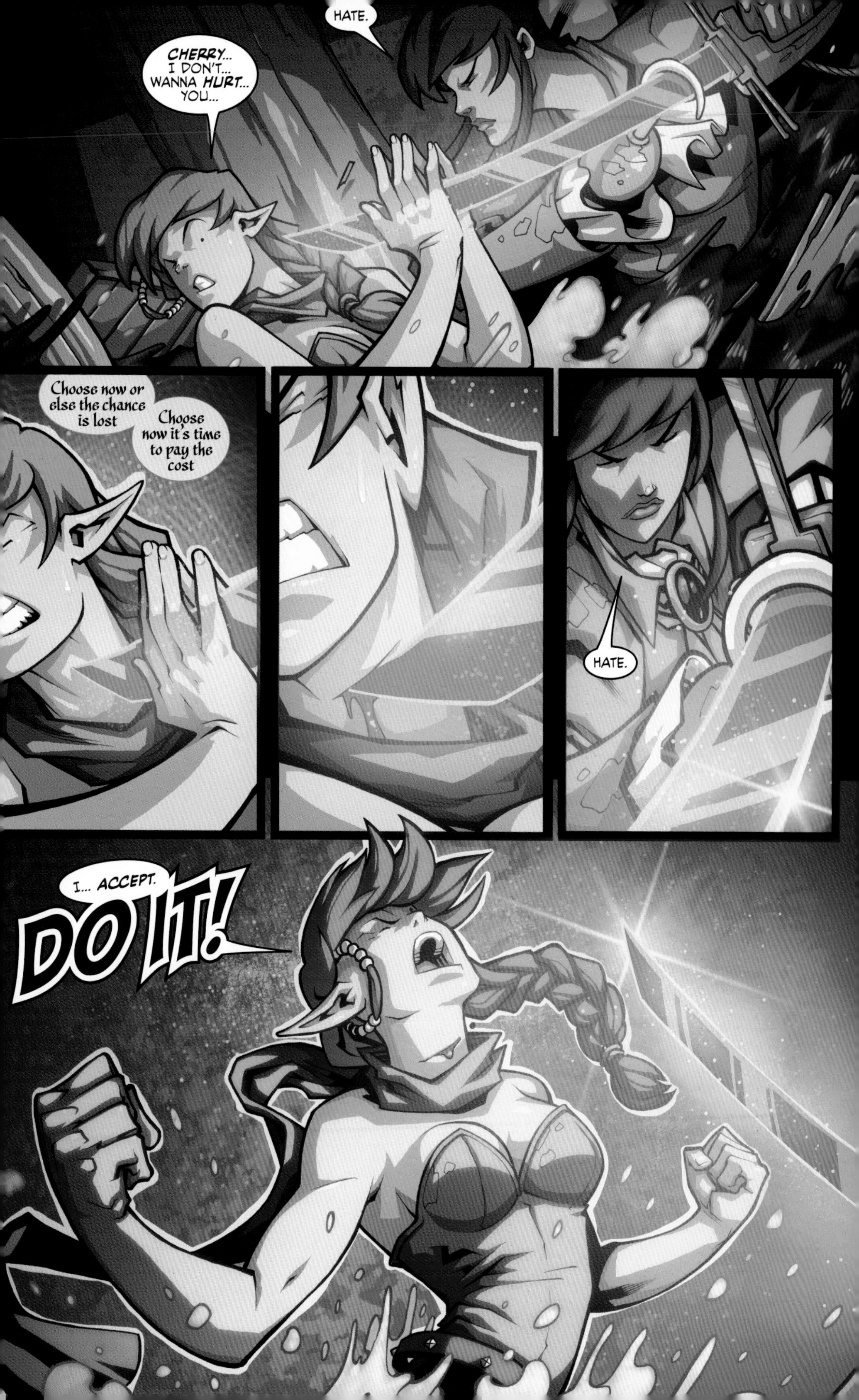
CHERRY... I DON'T... WANNA HURT... YOU...
HATE.
Choose now or else the chance is lost
Choose now it's time to pay the cost
HATE.
I... ACCEPT.
DO IT!

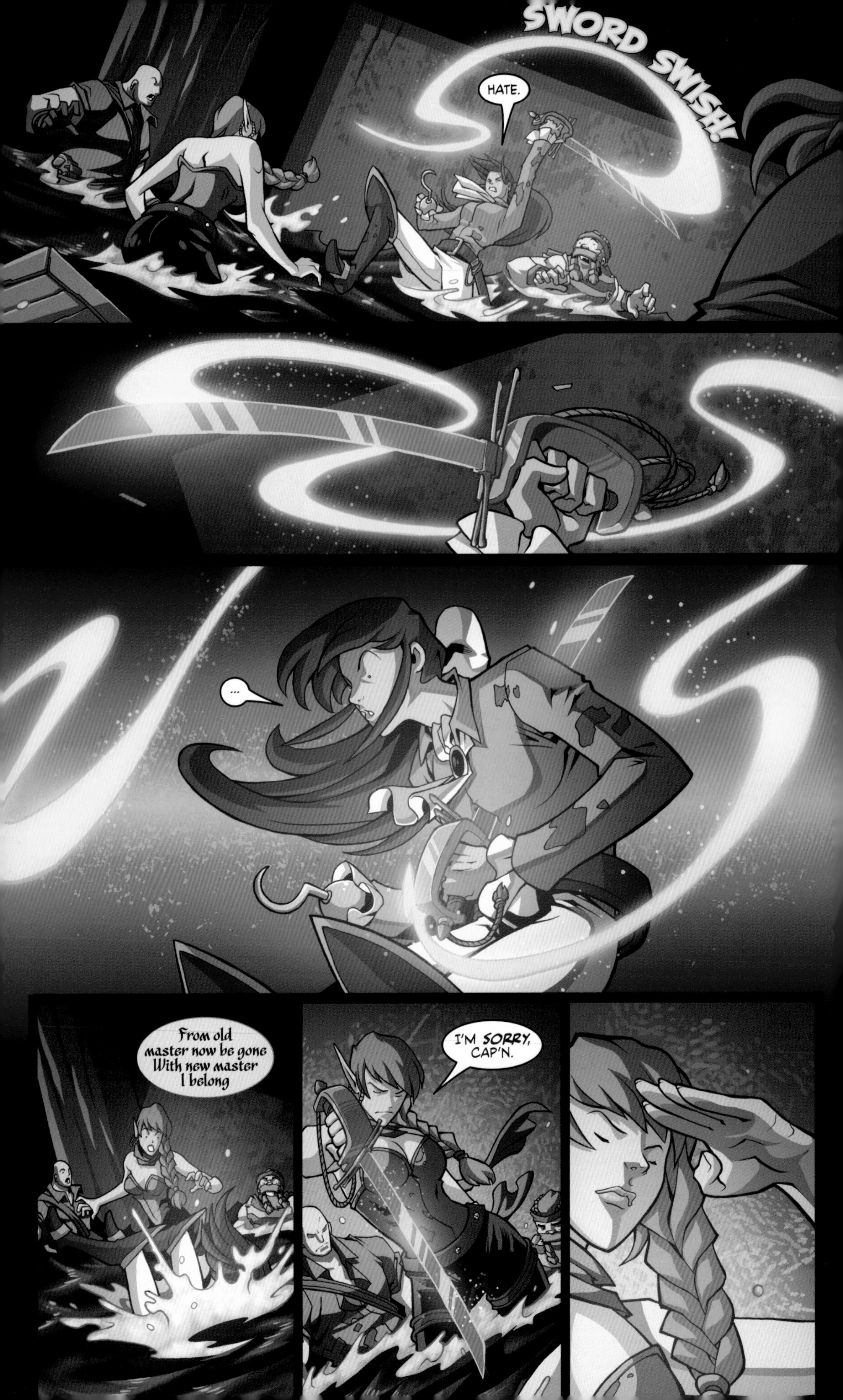
SWORD SWISH!
HATE.
...
From old master now be gone With new master I belong
I'M SORRY, CAP'N.

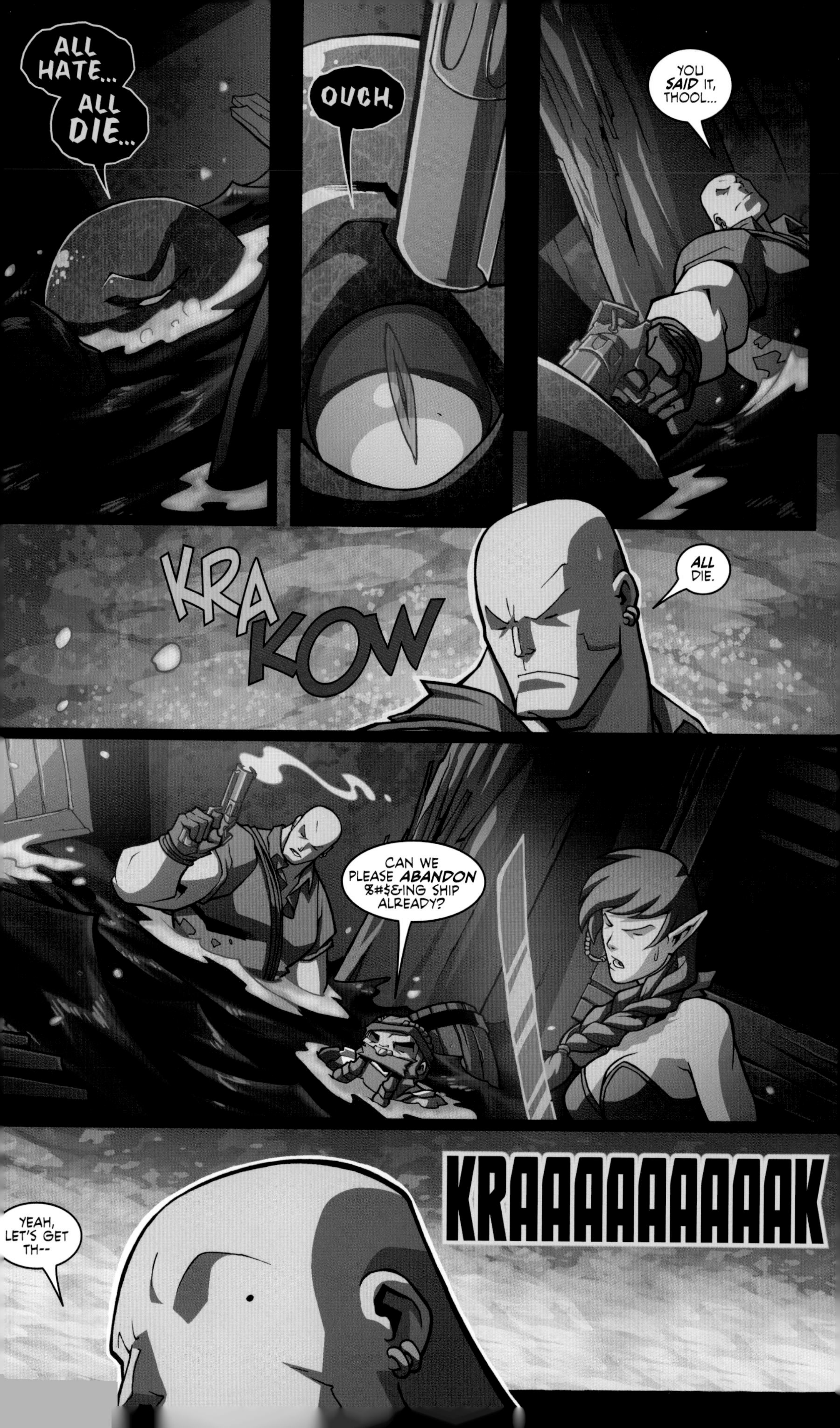

ALL HATE... ALL DIE...
OUCH.
YOU SAID IT, THOOL...
KRA KOW
ALL DIE.
CAN WE PLEASE ABANDON %#$&ING SHIP ALREADY?
YEAH, LET'S GET TH--
KRAAAAAAAAAK

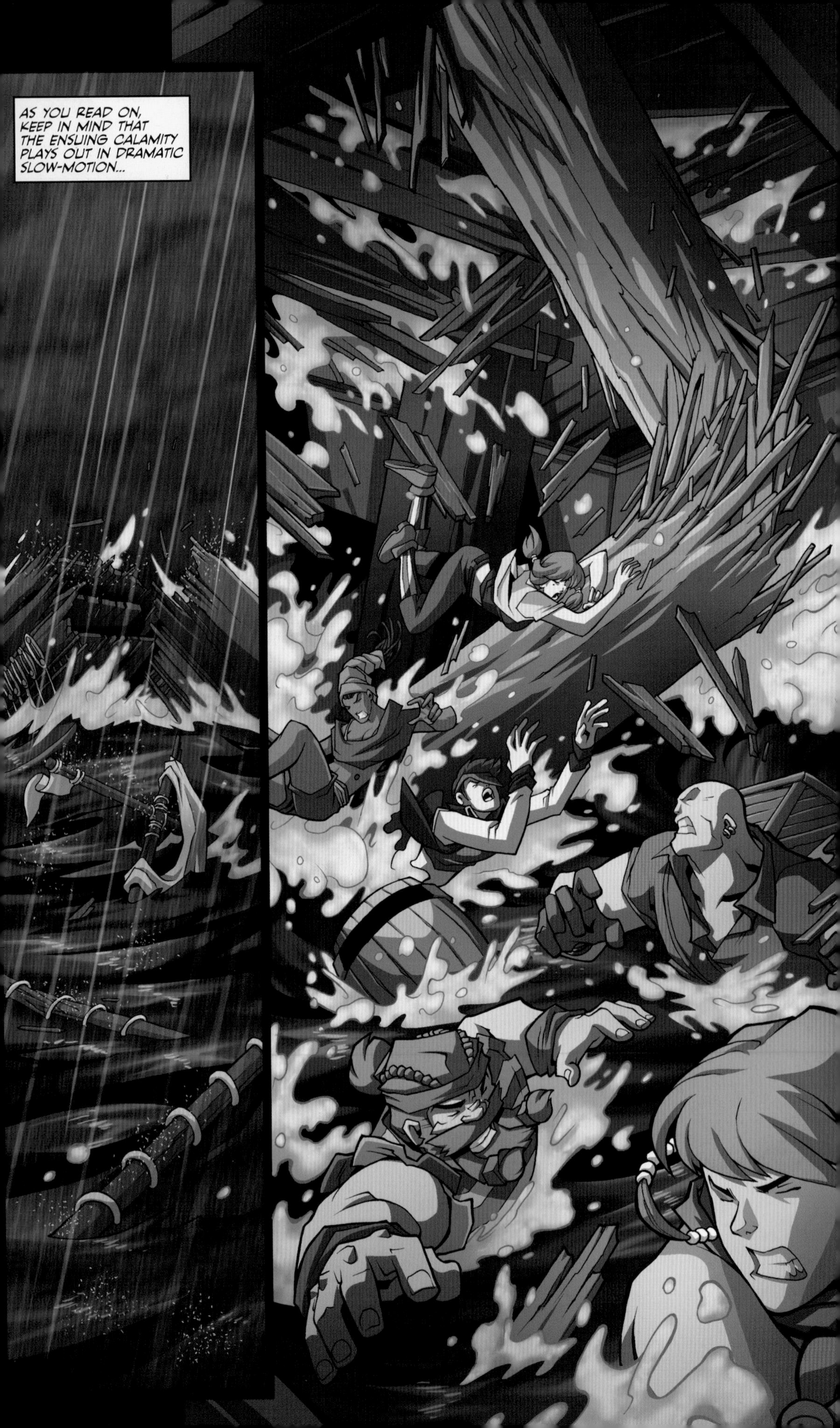
AS YOU READ ON, KEEP IN MIND THAT THE ENSUING CALAMITY PLAYS OUT IN DRAMATIC SLOW-MOTION...

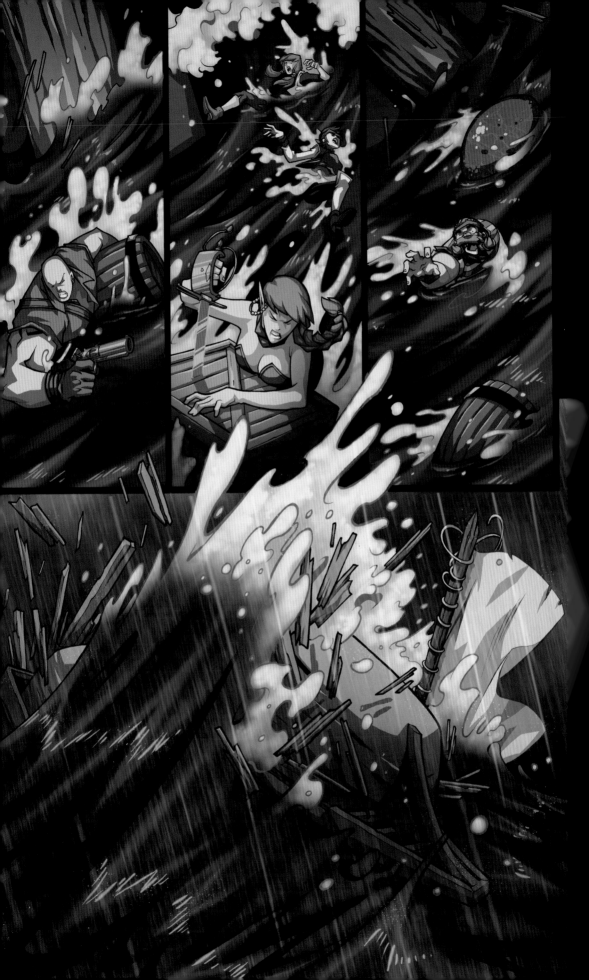

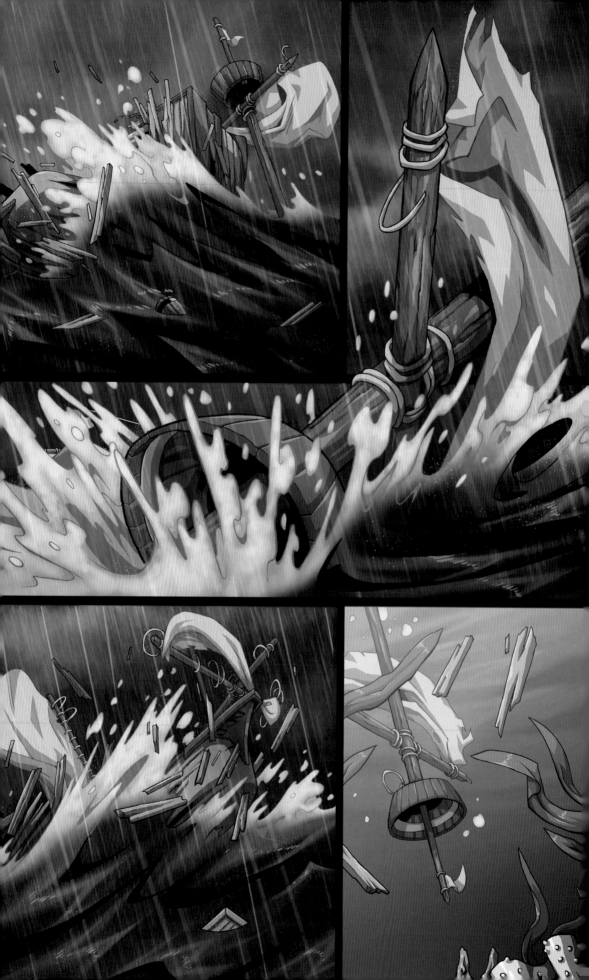

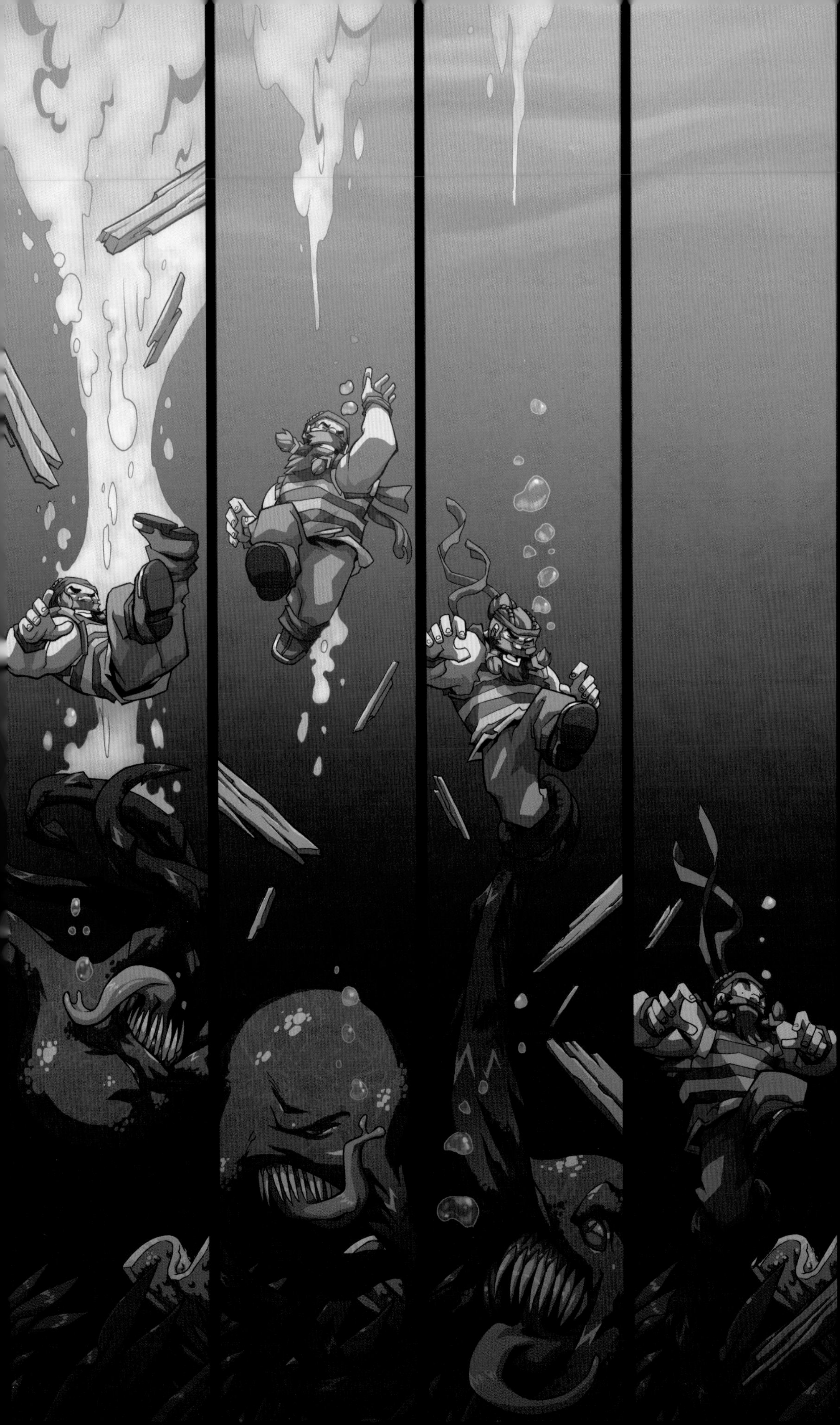

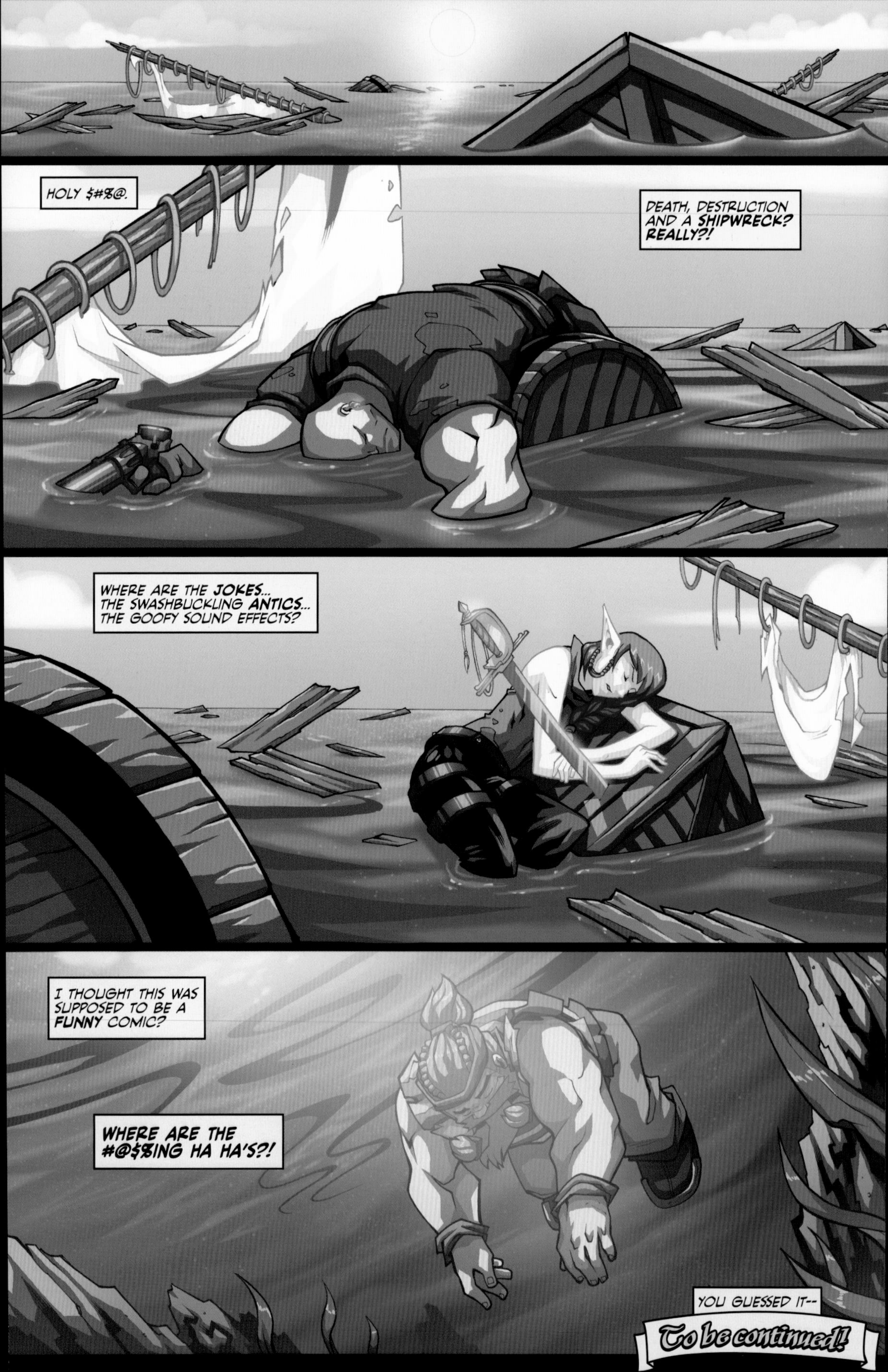
HOLY $#%@.
DEATH, DESTRUCTION AND A SHIPWRECK? REALLY?!
WHERE ARE THE JOKES... THE SWASHBUCKLING ANTICS... THE GOOFY SOUND EFFECTS?
I THOUGHT THIS WAS SUPPOSED TO BE A FUNNY COMIC?
WHERE ARE THE #@$%ING HA HA'S?!
YOU GUESSED IT--
To be continued!

FOUR MORE TAVERN TALES

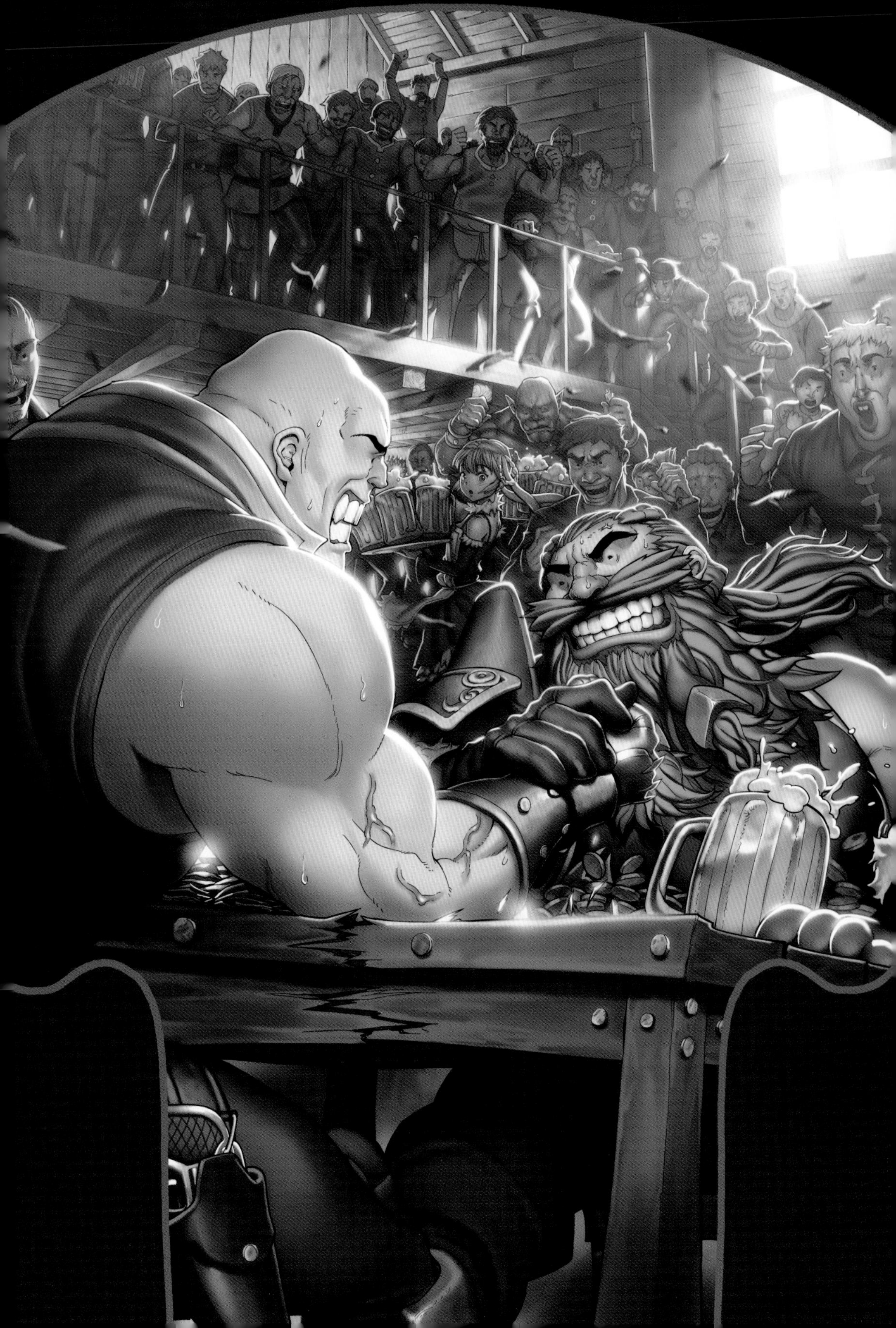

SKULL KICKERS
FOUR MORE TAVERN TALES

The original 'Tavern Tales' issue was supposed to be a one-off way to help keep us on schedule, but it was so much fun that we decided to make it a regular feature, acting as an intermission between each story arc. It was a blast gathering up another crew of creators and letting them go wild with their own Skullkickers short stories.

Band of Bothers is written by Jim Demonakos and Kyle Stevens, also known as the Seattle-based nerd rock band Kirby Krackle. Jim and Kyle brought their musical madness to this bard-bashing epic, with line art by UDON mainstay/Street Fighter artist extraordinaire Joe Ng.

Hornery Horsification is a silent short I put together for cartoonist Joel Carroll. Letting the art do all the 'talking' can be risky, but not with Joel's amazing storytelling and hilarious expressions leading the way. He delivered the goods.

Twang! is written by Hugo-nominated sci-fi webcomic humorist Howard Tayler of Schlock Mercenary fame. This is the first time he's ever written a comic for someone other than himself. I think Mike Luckas, a fantastic artist who's helped keep Skullkickers on schedule with inking and coloring assists, delivered on Howard's potential with this hunting tale of derring-do.

The Beholder is written by another webcomic master, Saturday Morning Breakfast Cereal's Zach Weiner. Zach's sarcastic and disgusting short story was drawn by the incredible Ben McSweeney, a video game concept designer and artist of Joe is Japanese.

Enjoy!

ZUB

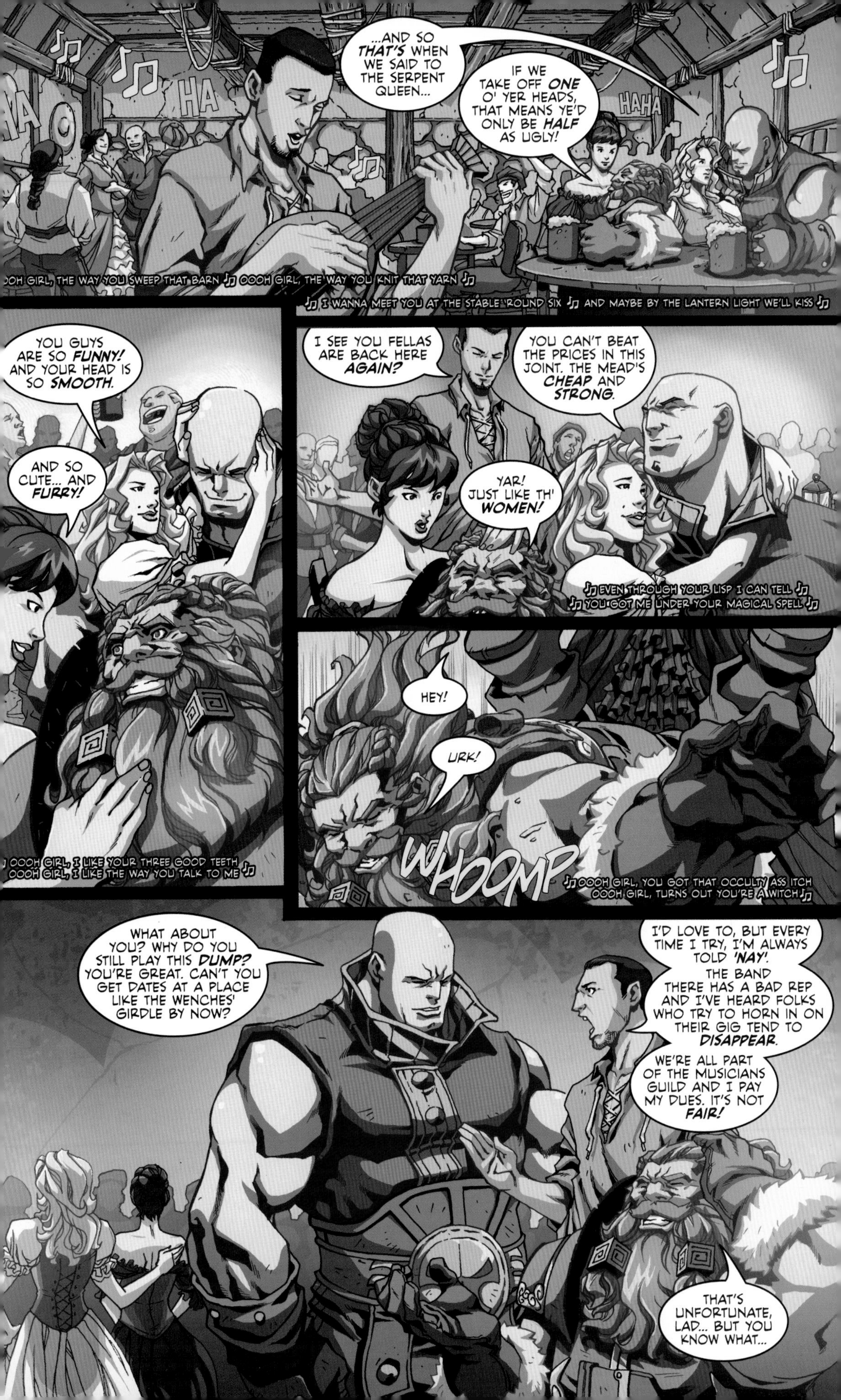

...AND SO THAT'S WHEN WE SAID TO THE SERPENT QUEEN...
IF WE TAKE OFF ONE O' YER HEADS, THAT MEANS YE'D ONLY BE HALF AS UGLY!
HA
HA
HAHA
OOH GIRL, THE WAY YOU SWEEP THAT BARN ♫ OOOH GIRL, THE WAY YOU KNIT THAT YARN ♫
♫ I WANNA MEET YOU AT THE STABLE 'ROUND SIX ♫ AND MAYBE BY THE LANTERN LIGHT WE'LL KISS ♫
YOU GUYS ARE SO FUNNY! AND YOUR HEAD IS SO SMOOTH.
AND SO CUTE... AND FURRY!
OOOH GIRL, I LIKE YOUR THREE GOOD TEETH
OOOH GIRL, I LIKE THE WAY YOU TALK TO ME ♫
I SEE YOU FELLAS ARE BACK HERE AGAIN?
YOU CAN'T BEAT THE PRICES IN THIS JOINT. THE MEAD'S CHEAP AND STRONG.
YAR! JUST LIKE TH' WOMEN!
♫ EVEN THROUGH YOUR LISP I CAN TELL ♫
♫ YOU GOT ME UNDER YOUR MAGICAL SPELL ♫
HEY!
URK!
WHOOMP
♫ OOOH GIRL, YOU GOT THAT OCCULTY ASS ITCH
OOOH GIRL, TURNS OUT YOU'RE A WITCH ♫
WHAT ABOUT YOU? WHY DO YOU STILL PLAY THIS DUMP? YOU'RE GREAT. CAN'T YOU GET DATES AT A PLACE LIKE THE WENCHES' GIRDLE BY NOW?
I'D LOVE TO, BUT EVERY TIME I TRY, I'M ALWAYS TOLD 'NAY'.
THE BAND THERE HAS A BAD REP AND I'VE HEARD FOLKS WHO TRY TO HORN IN ON THEIR GIG TEND TO DISAPPEAR.
WE'RE ALL PART OF THE MUSICIANS GUILD AND I PAY MY DUES. IT'S NOT FAIR!
THAT'S UNFORTUNATE, LAD... BUT YOU KNOW WHAT...

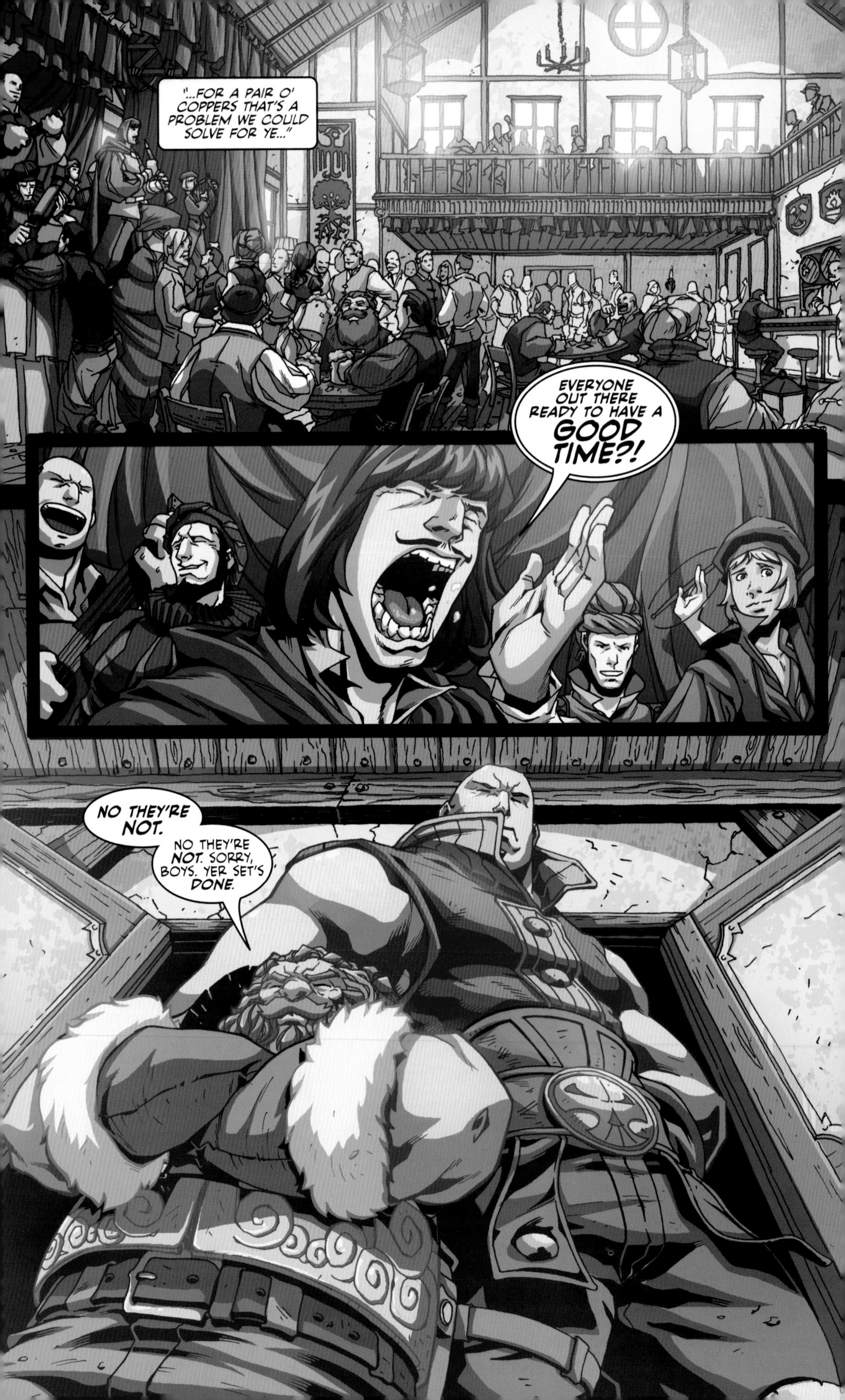
"...FOR A PAIR O' COPPERS THAT'S A PROBLEM WE COULD SOLVE FOR YE..."
EVERYONE OUT THERE READY TO HAVE A GOOD TIME?!
NO THEY'RE NOT.
NO THEY'RE NOT. SORRY, BOYS. YER SET'S DONE.

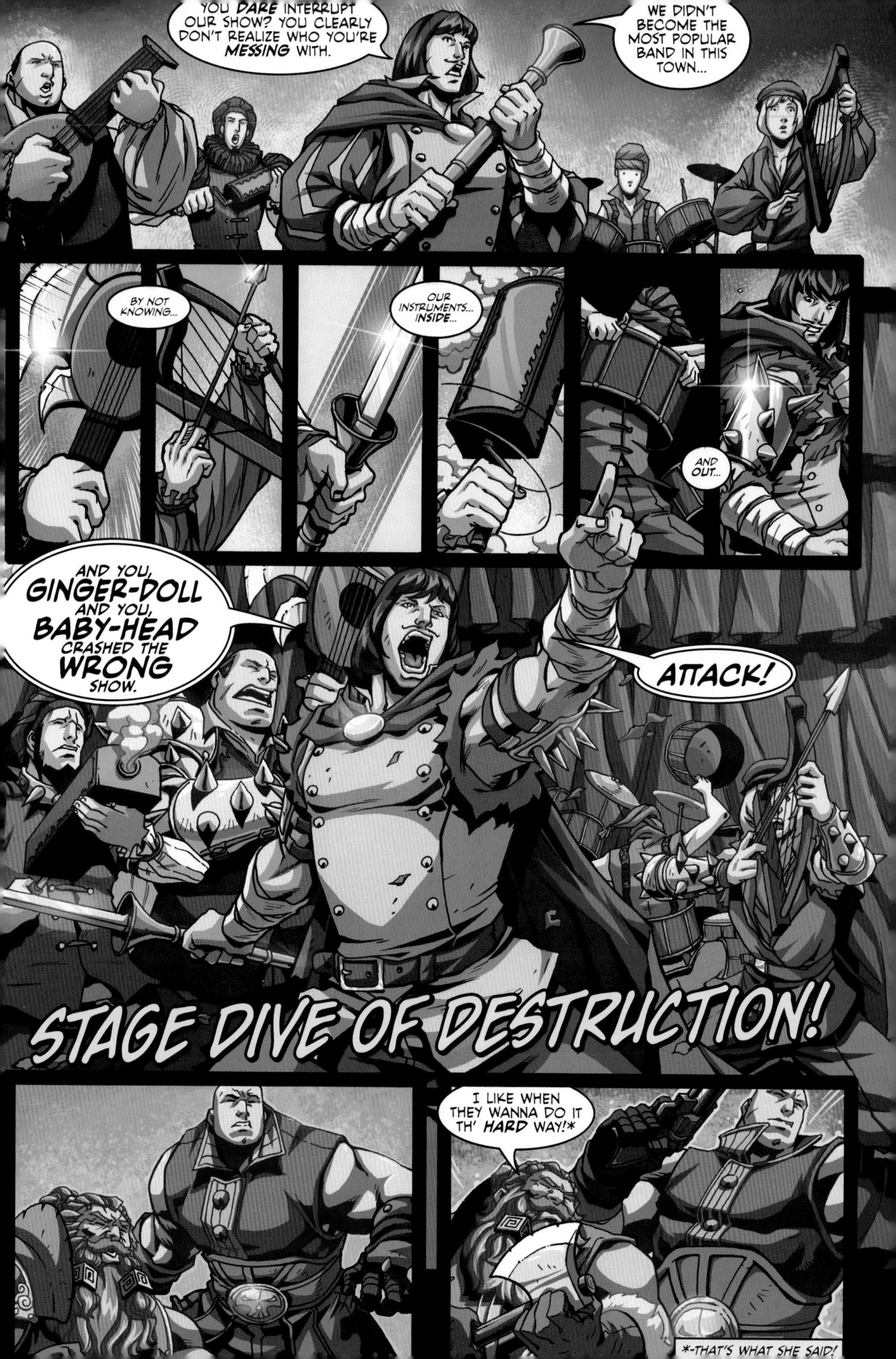
YOU DARE INTERRUPT OUR SHOW? YOU CLEARLY DON'T REALIZE WHO YOU'RE MESSING WITH.
WE DIDN'T BECOME THE MOST POPULAR BAND IN THIS TOWN...
BY NOT KNOWING...
OUR INSTRUMENTS... INSIDE...
AND OUT...
AND YOU, GINGER-DOLL AND YOU, BABY-HEAD CRASHED THE WRONG SHOW.
ATTACK!
STAGE DIVE OF DESTRUCTION!
I LIKE WHEN THEY WANNA DO IT TH' HARD WAY!*
*-THAT'S WHAT SHE SAID!

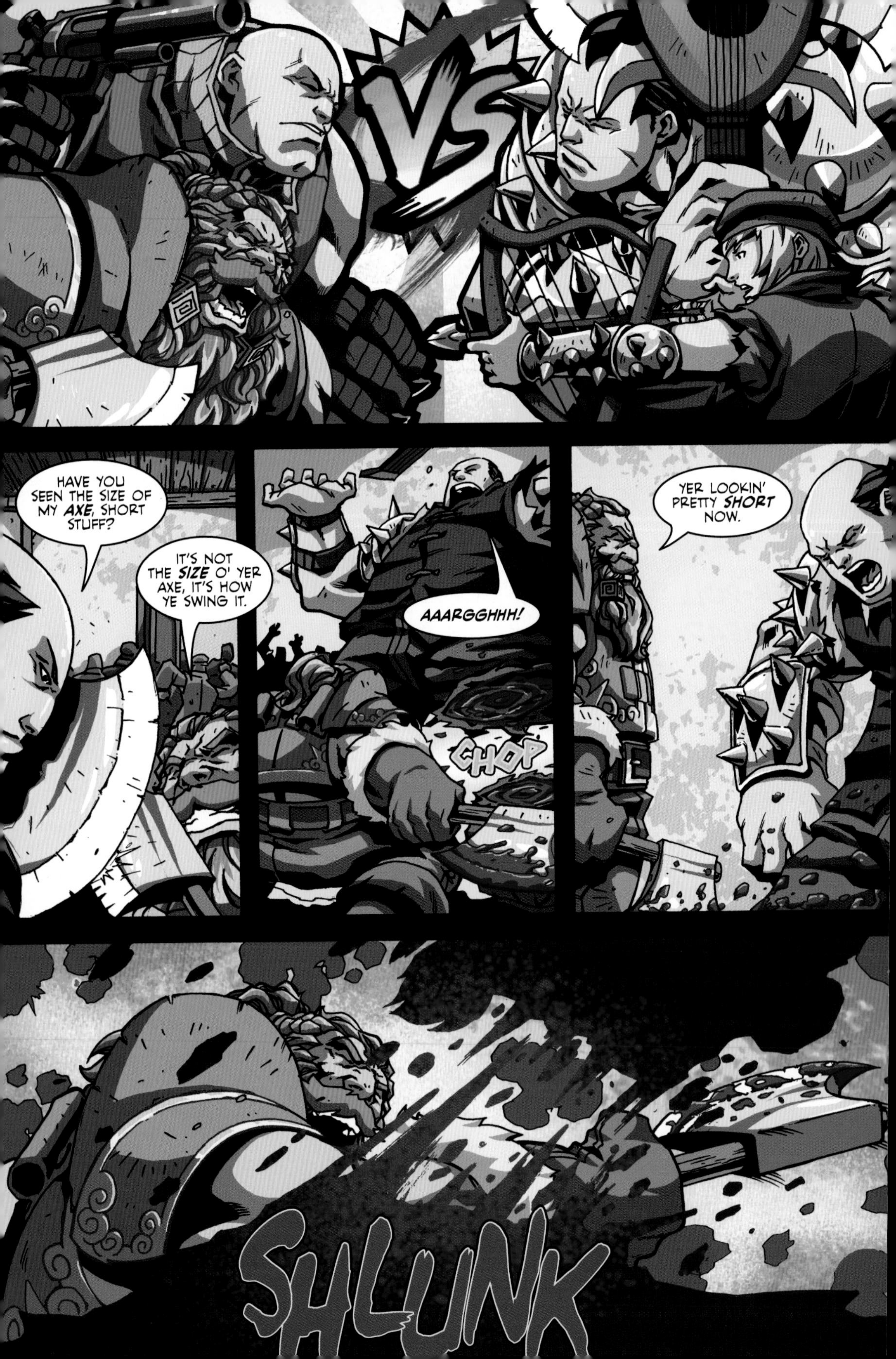
VS
HAVE YOU SEEN THE SIZE OF MY AXE, SHORT STUFF?
IT'S NOT THE SIZE O' YER AXE, IT'S HOW YE SWING IT.
AAARGGHHH!
CHOP
YER LOOKIN' PRETTY SHORT NOW.
SHLUNK

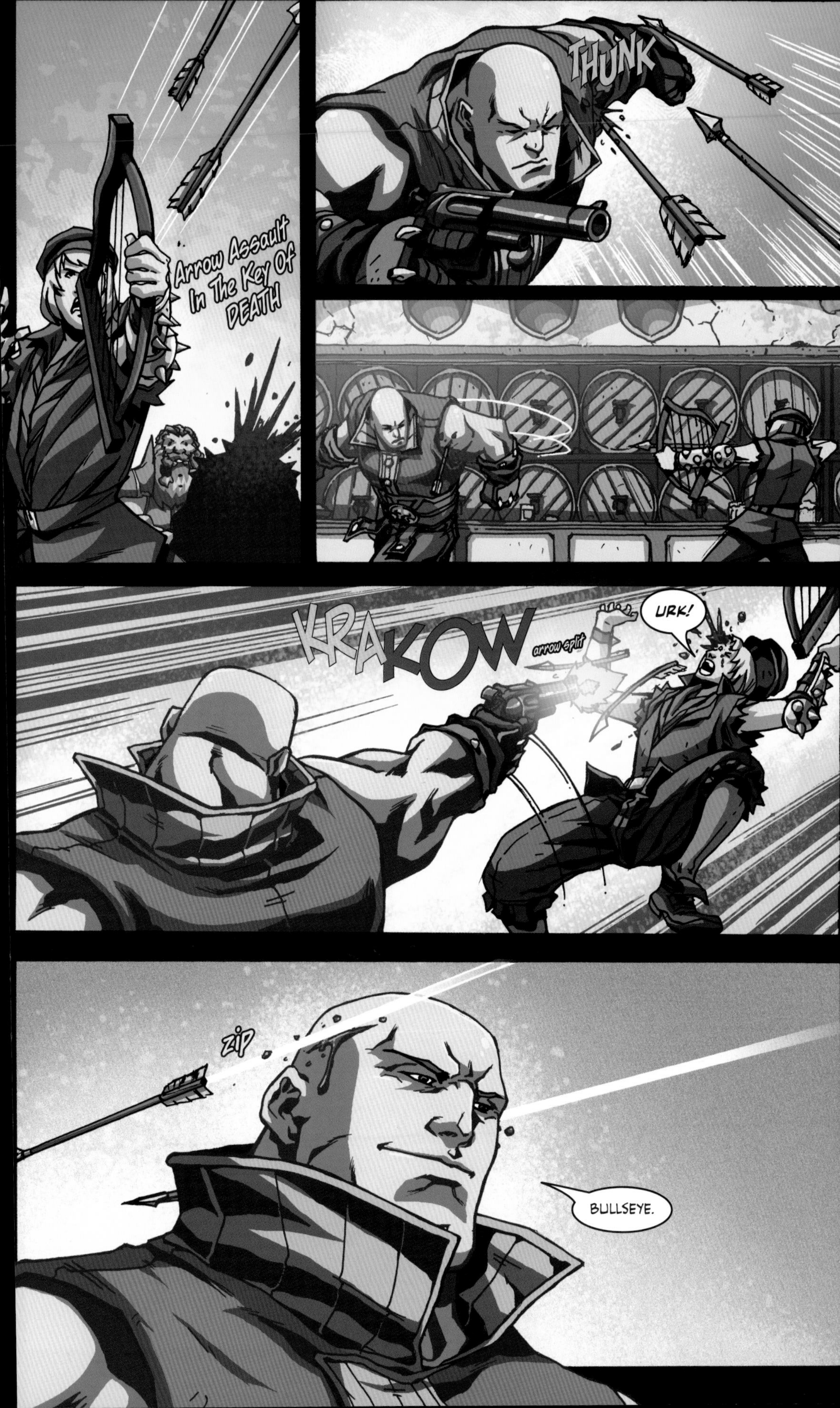
THUNK
Arrow Assault In The Key Of DEATH
KRAKOW
arrow split
URK!
ZIP
BULLSEYE.

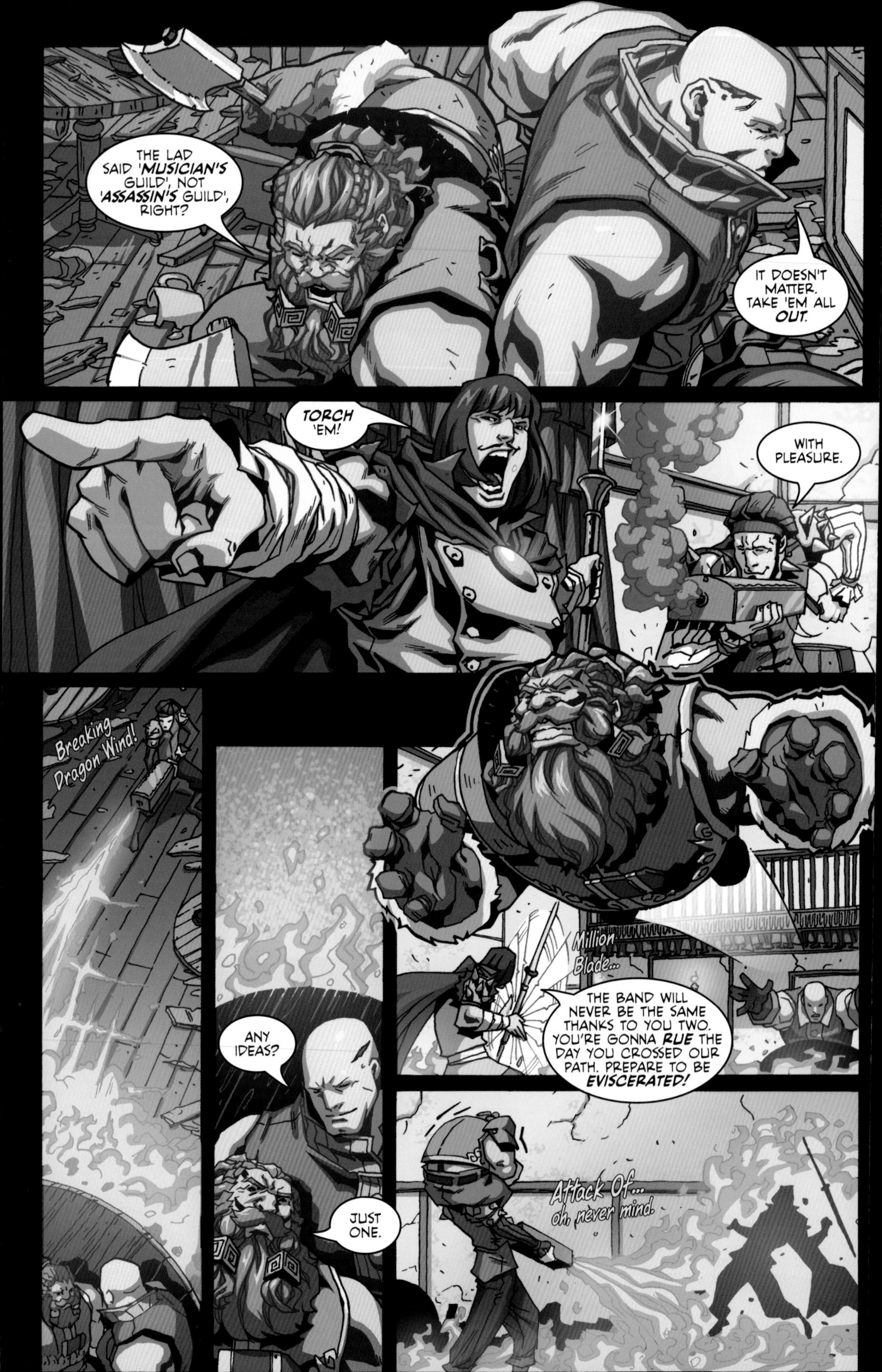
THE LAD SAID 'MUSICIAN'S GUILD', NOT 'ASSASSIN'S GUILD', RIGHT?
IT DOESN'T MATTER. TAKE 'EM ALL OUT.
TORCH 'EM!
WITH PLEASURE.
Breaking Dragon Wind!
Million Blade...
THE BAND WILL NEVER BE THE SAME THANKS TO YOU TWO. YOU'RE GONNA RUE THE DAY YOU CROSSED OUR PATH. PREPARE TO BE EVISCERATED!
ANY IDEAS?
JUST ONE.
Attack Of... oh, never mind.

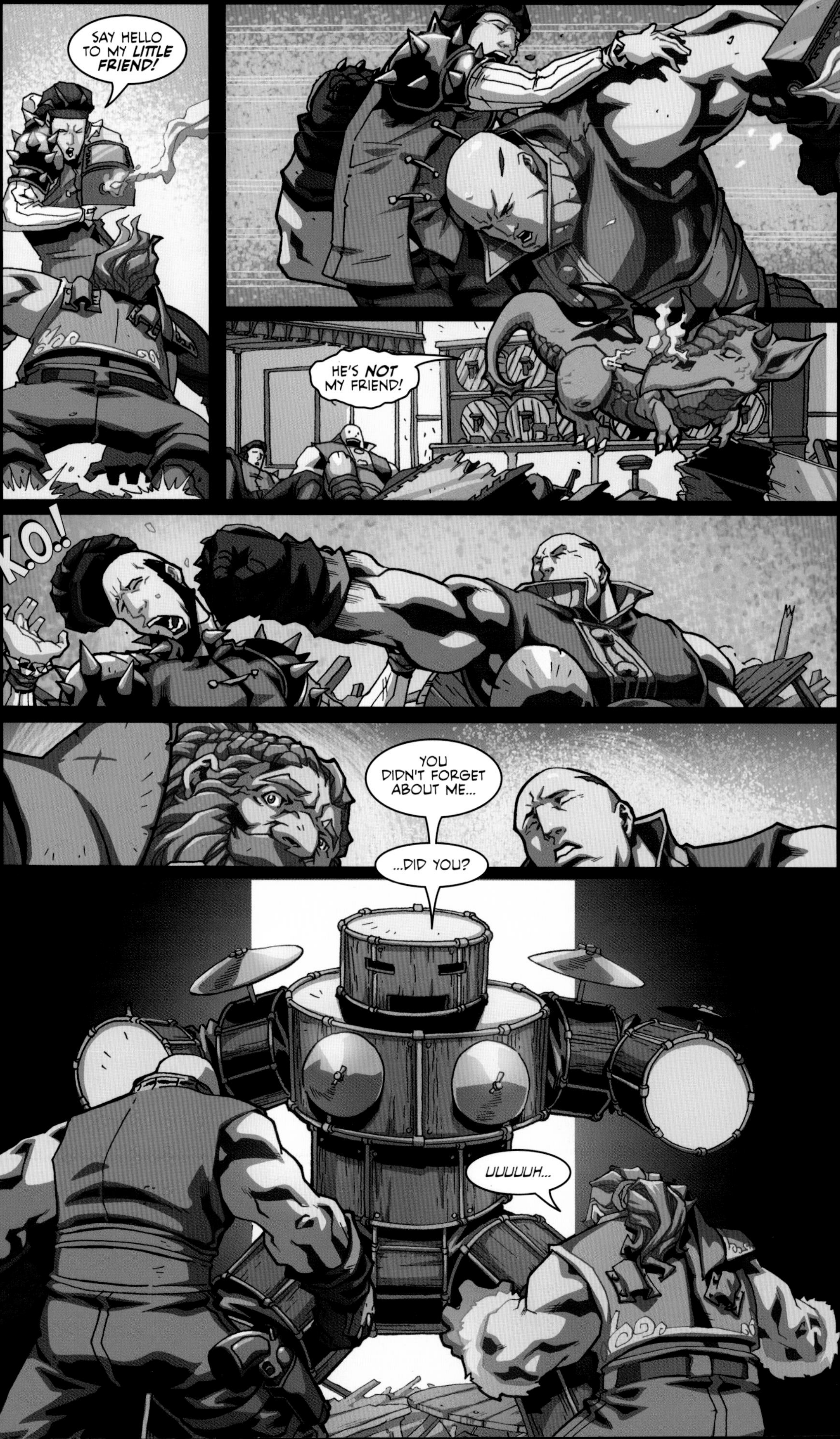
SAY HELLO TO MY LITTLE FRIEND!
HE'S NOT MY FRIEND!
K.O.!
YOU DIDN'T FORGET ABOUT ME...
...DID YOU?
UUUUUH...

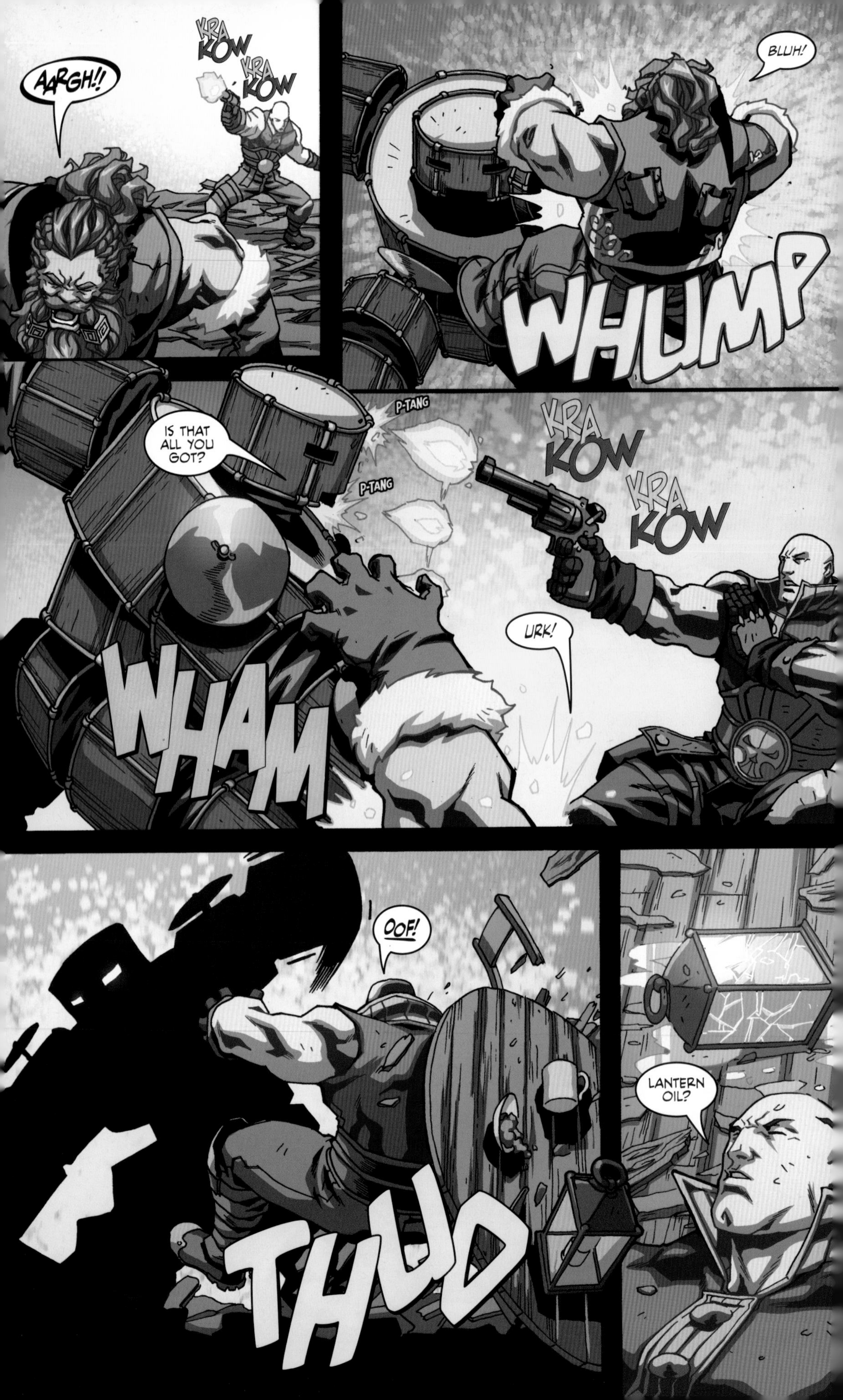
KRA
KOW
KRA
KOW
AARGH!!
BLUH!
WHUMP
IS THAT ALL YOU GOT?
P-TANG
P-TANG
KRA
KOW
KRA
KOW
URK!
WHAM
OOF!
THUD
LANTERN OIL?

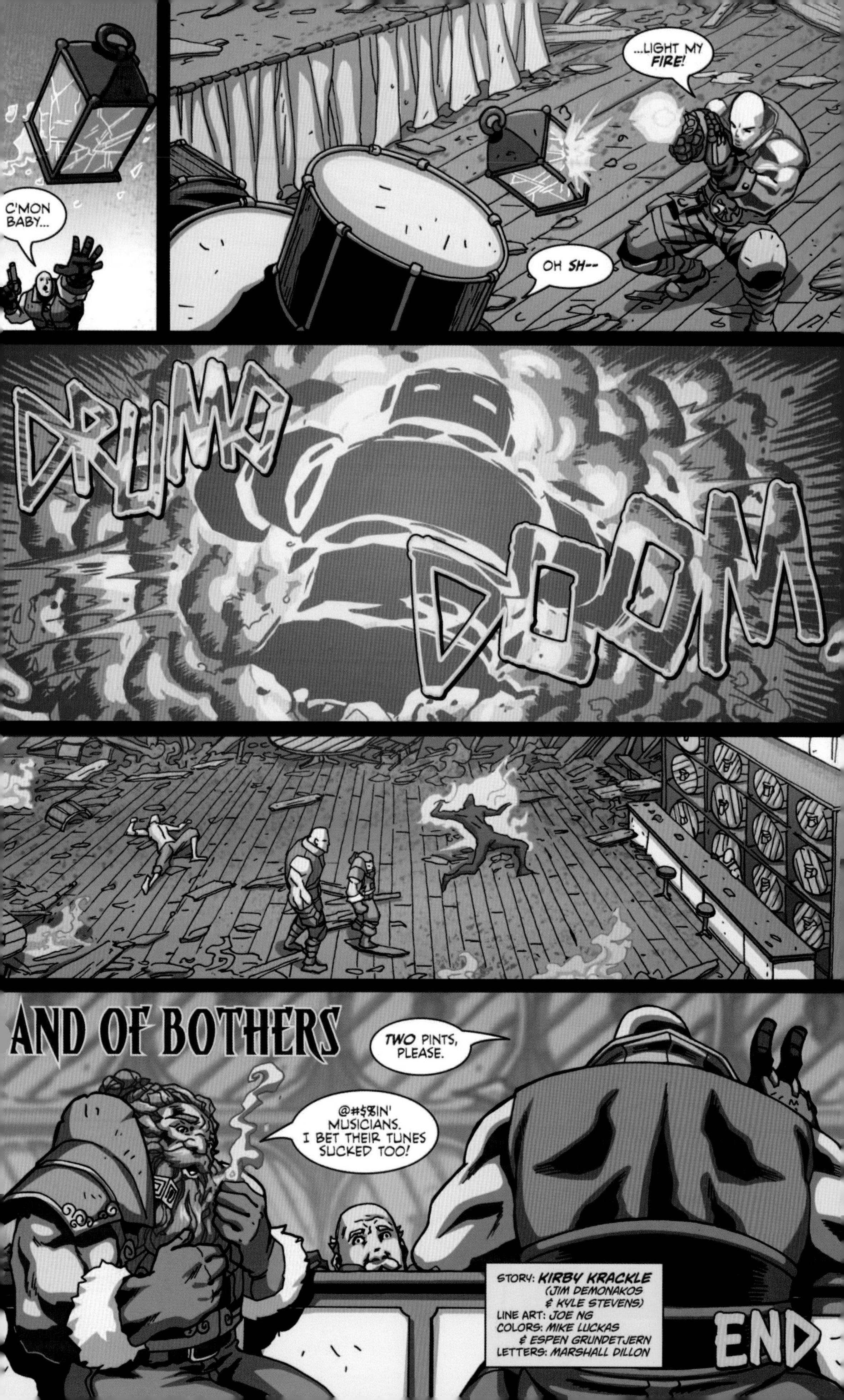
C'MON BABY...
...LIGHT MY FIRE!
OH SH--
DRUMD
DOOM
AND OF BOTHERS
TWO PINTS, PLEASE.
@#$%IN' MUSICIANS. I BET THEIR TUNES SUCKED TOO!
STORY: KIRBY KRACKLE (JIM DEMONAKOS & KYLE STEVENS)
LINE ART: JOE NG
COLORS: MIKE LUCKAS & ESPEN GRUNDETJERN
LETTERS: MARSHALL DILLON
END

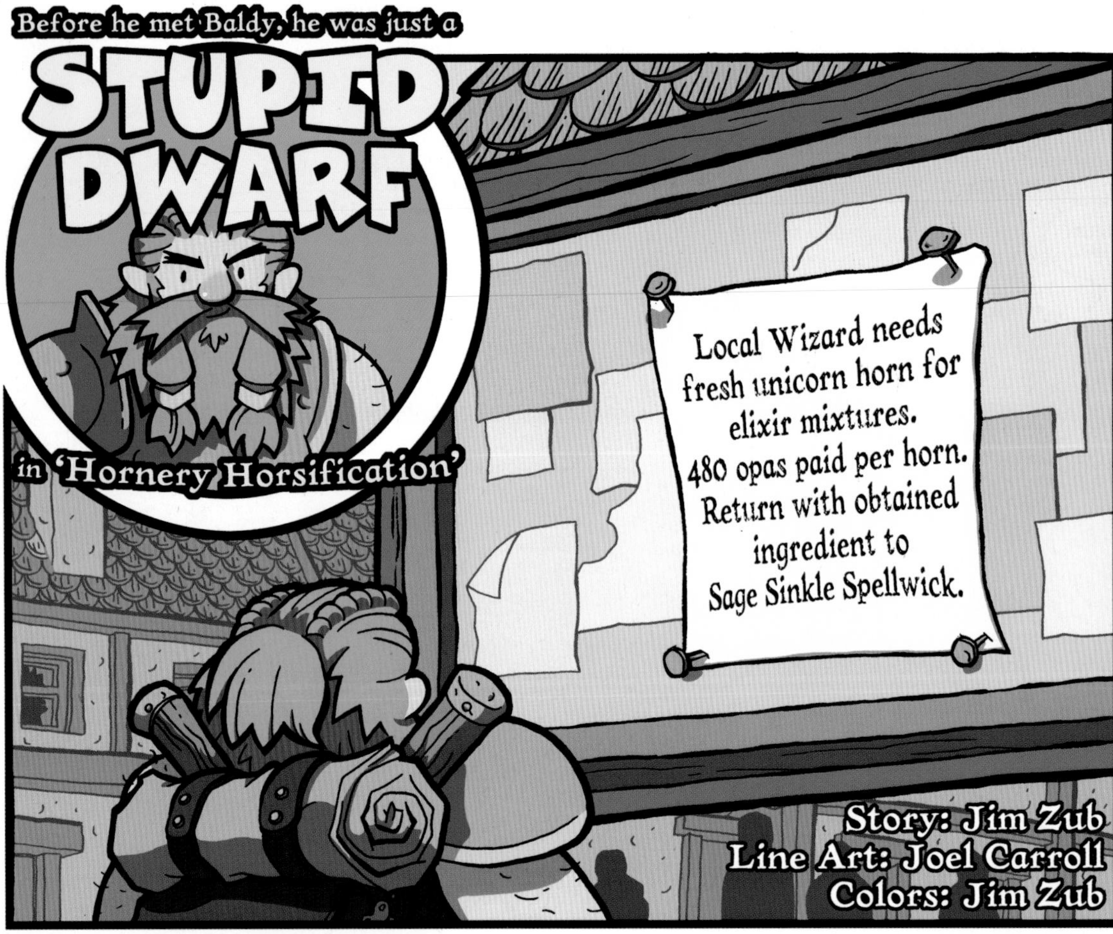
Before he met Baldy, he was just a
STUPID DWARF
in 'Hornery Horsification'
Local Wizard needs fresh unicorn horn for elixir mixtures. 480 opas paid per horn. Return with obtained ingredient to Sage Sinkle Spellwick.
Story: Jim Zub
Line Art: Joel Carroll
Colors: Jim Zub

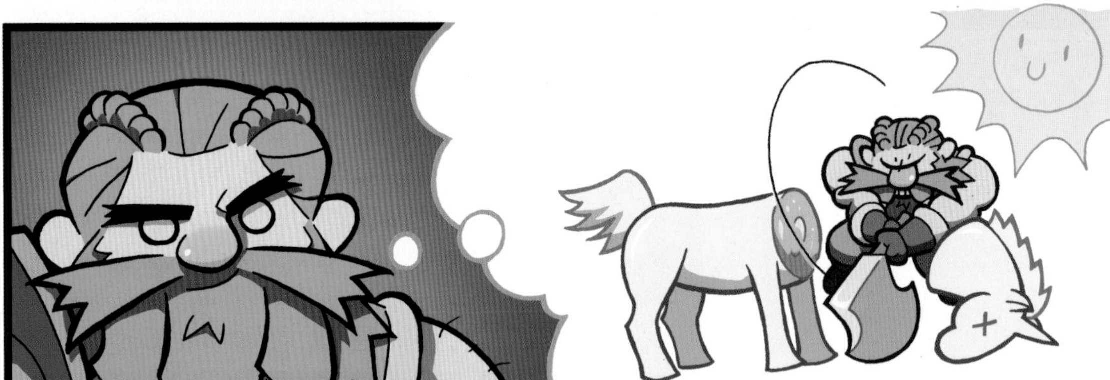

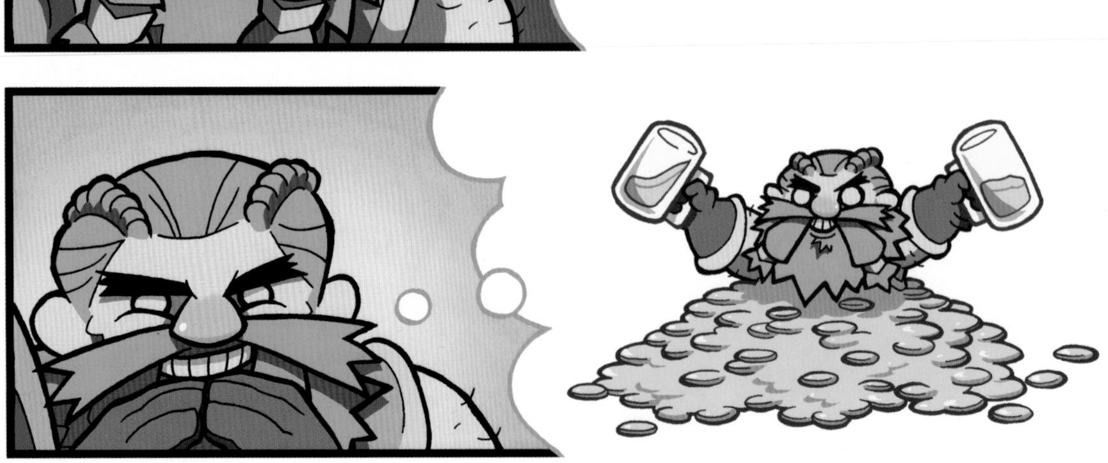

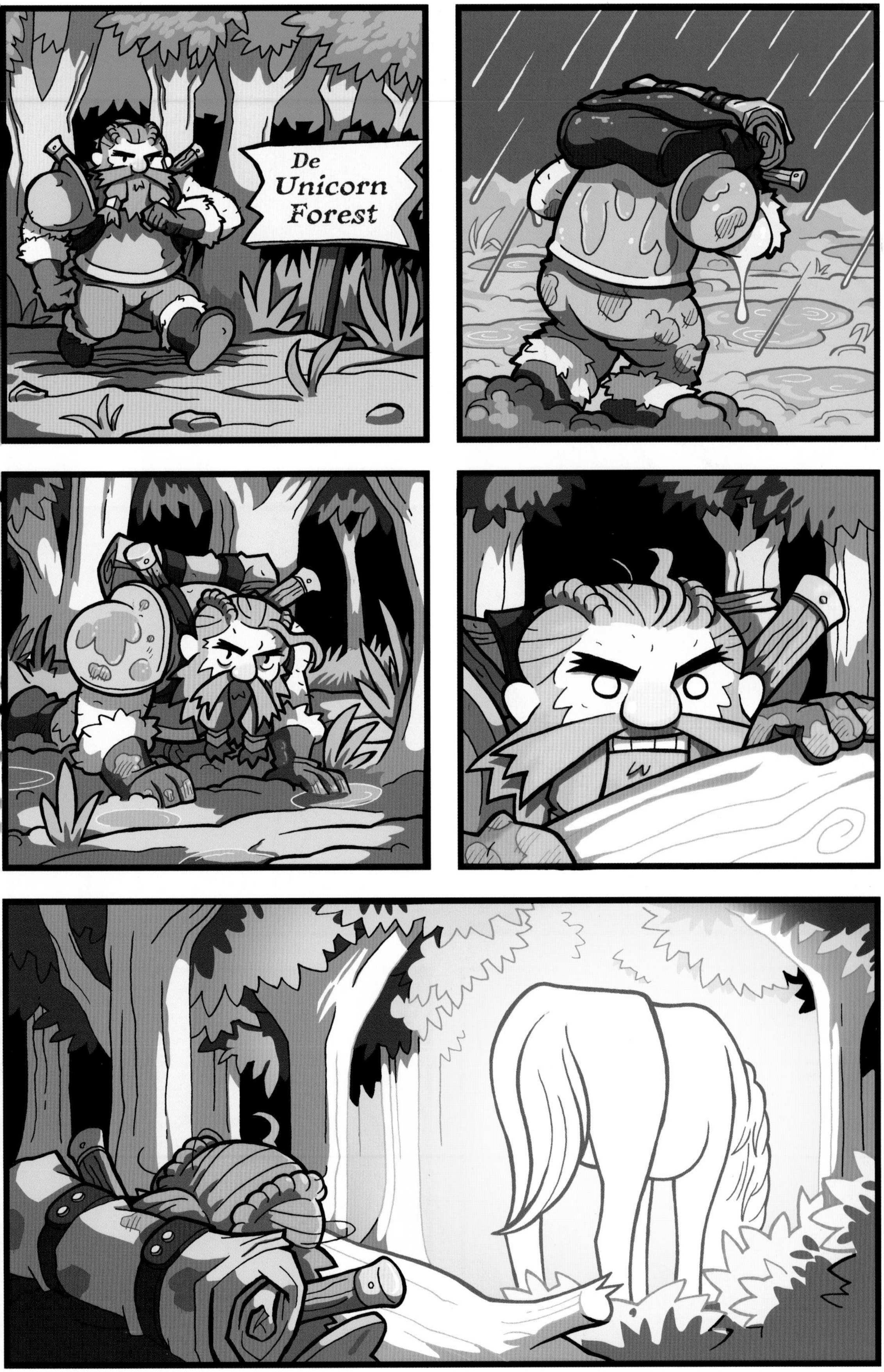
De
Unicorn
Forest

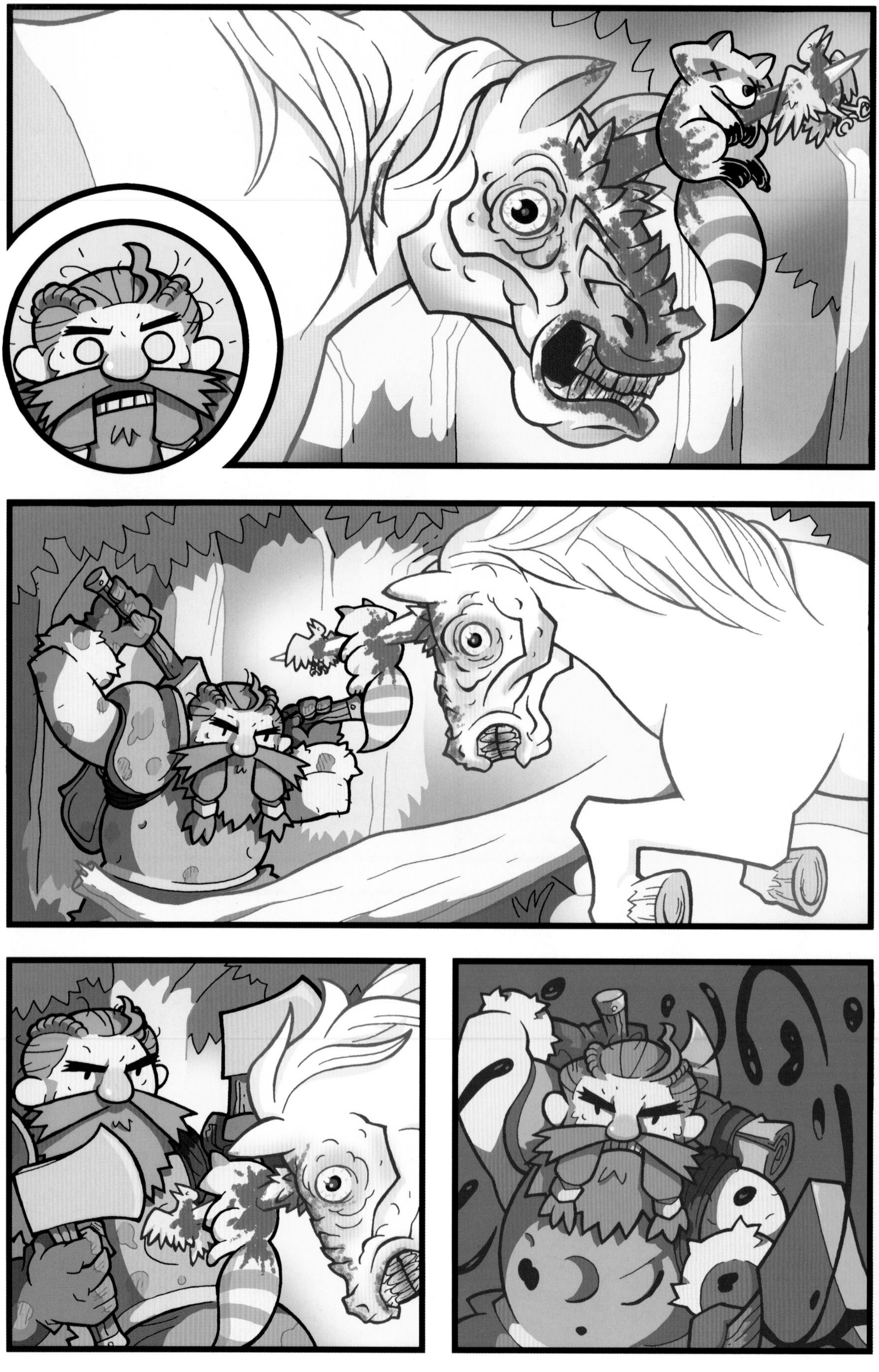

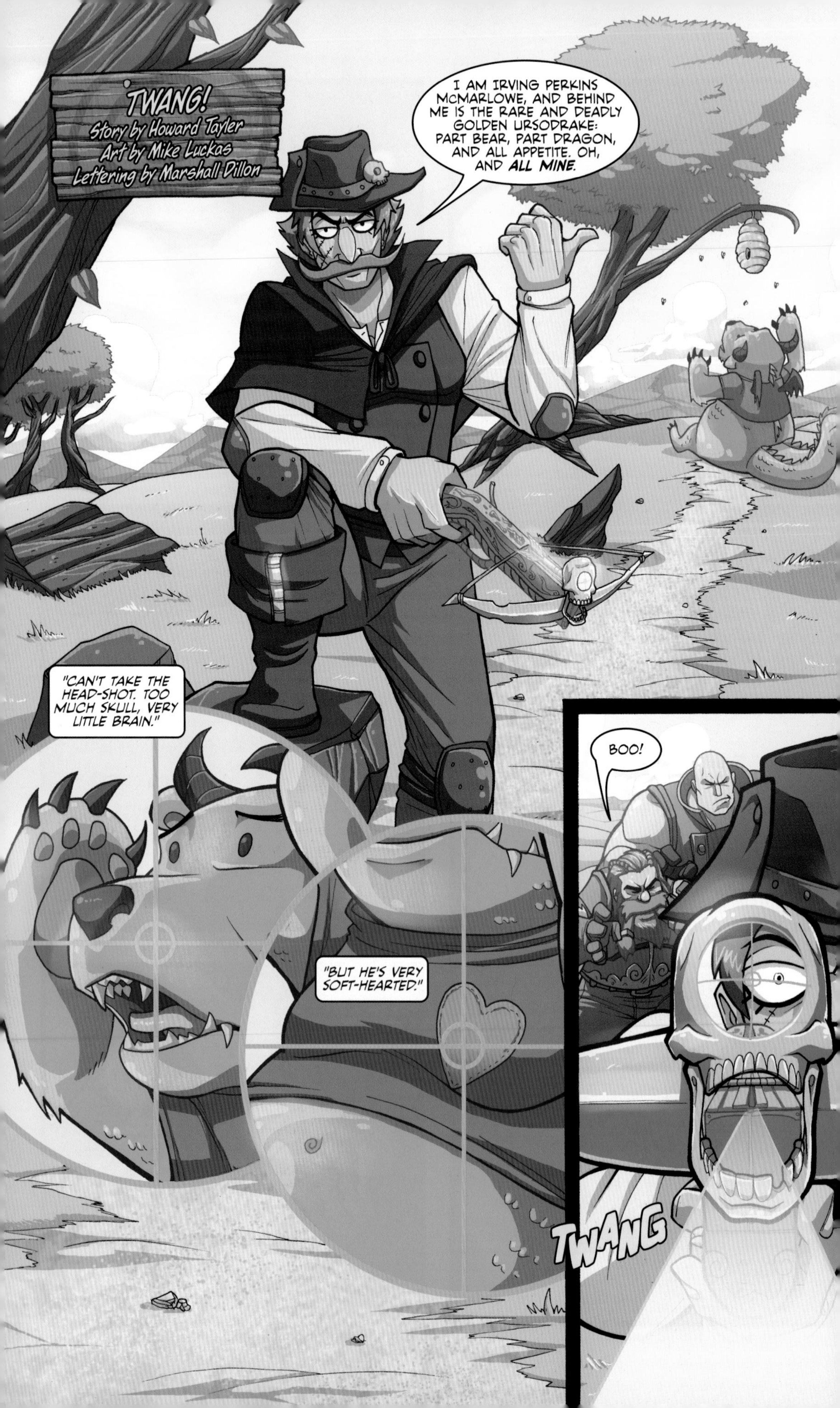
TWANG!
Story by Howard Tayler
Art by Mike Luckas
Lettering by Marshall Dillon
I AM IRVING PERKINS McMARLOWE, AND BEHIND ME IS THE RARE AND DEADLY GOLDEN URSODRAKE: PART BEAR, PART DRAGON, AND ALL APPETITE. OH, AND ALL MINE.
"CAN'T TAKE THE HEAD-SHOT. TOO MUCH SKULL, VERY LITTLE BRAIN."
"BUT HE'S VERY SOFT-HEARTED."
BOO!
TWANG

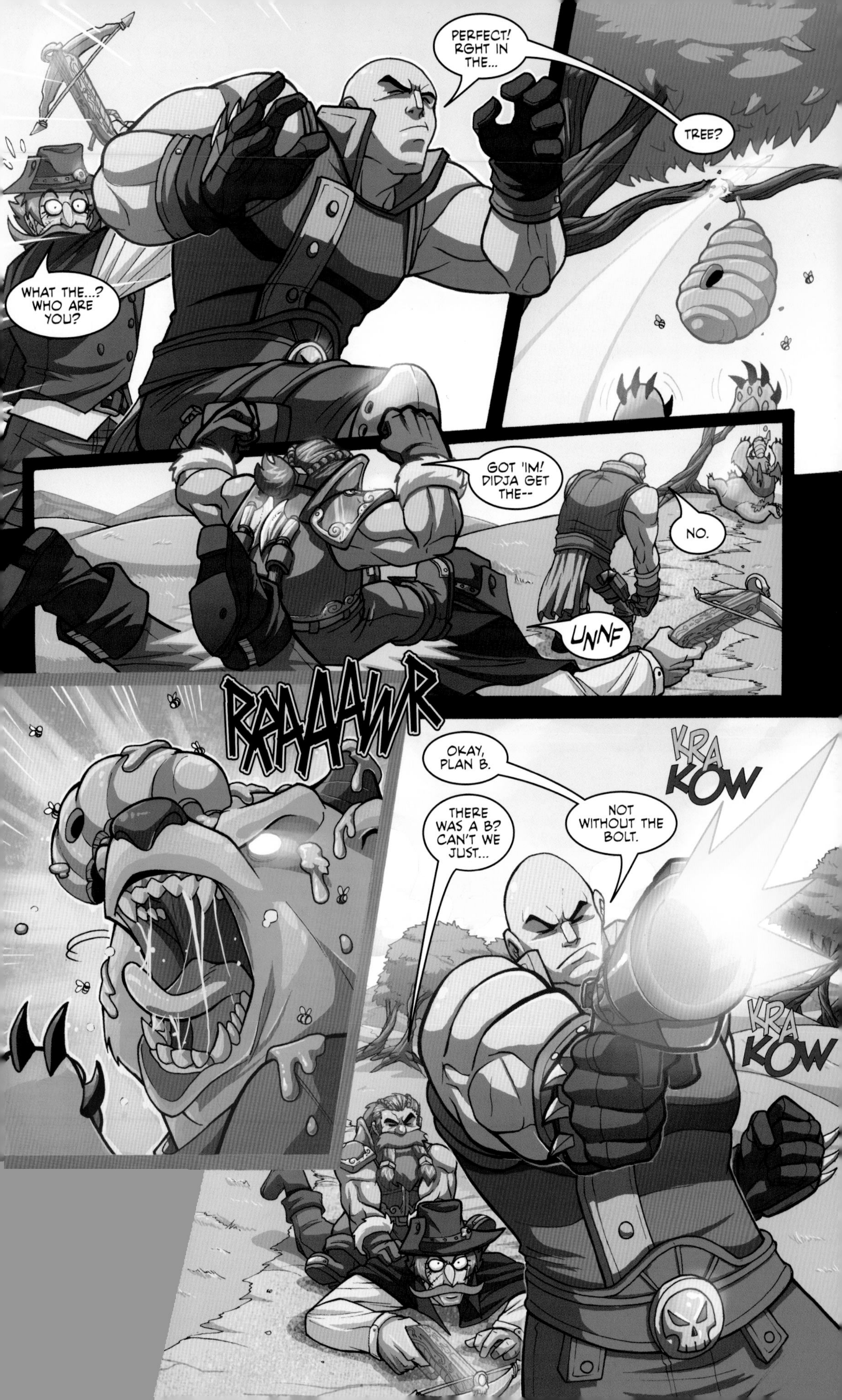
PERFECT! RGHT IN THE...
TREE?
WHAT THE...? WHO ARE YOU?
GOT 'IM! DIDJA GET THE--
NO.
UNNF
RAAAAWR
OKAY, PLAN B.
THERE WAS A B? CAN'T WE JUST...
NOT WITHOUT THE BOLT.
KRA KOW
KRA KOW

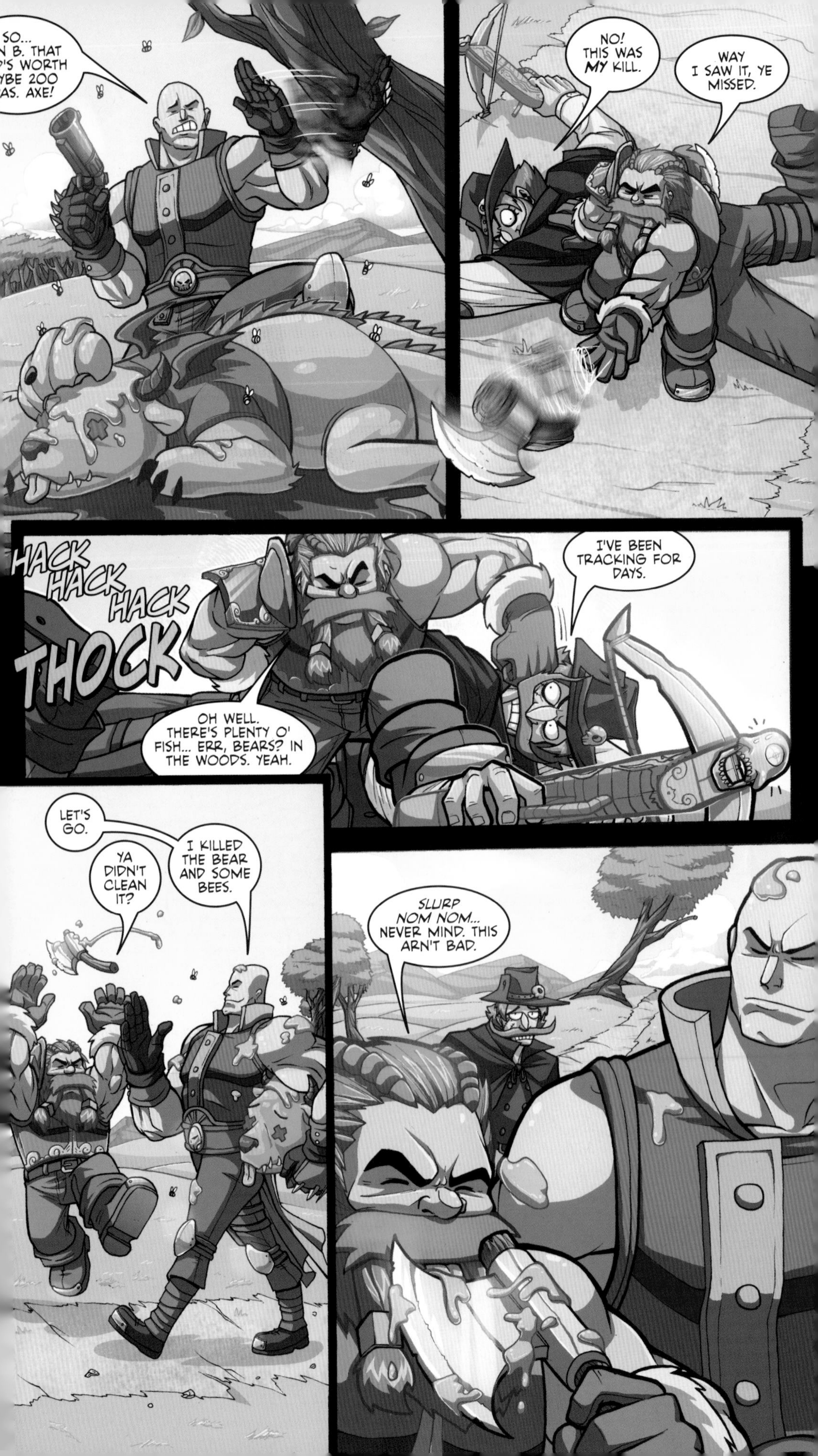
SO... N B. THAT 'S WORTH YBE 200 AS. AXE!
NO! THIS WAS MY KILL.
WAY I SAW IT, YE MISSED.
HACK HACK HACK
THOCK
I'VE BEEN TRACKING FOR DAYS.
OH WELL. THERE'S PLENTY O' FISH... ERR, BEARS? IN THE WOODS. YEAH.
LET'S GO.
I KILLED THE BEAR AND SOME BEES.
YA DIDN'T CLEAN IT?
SLURP NOM NOM... NEVER MIND. THIS ARN'T BAD.

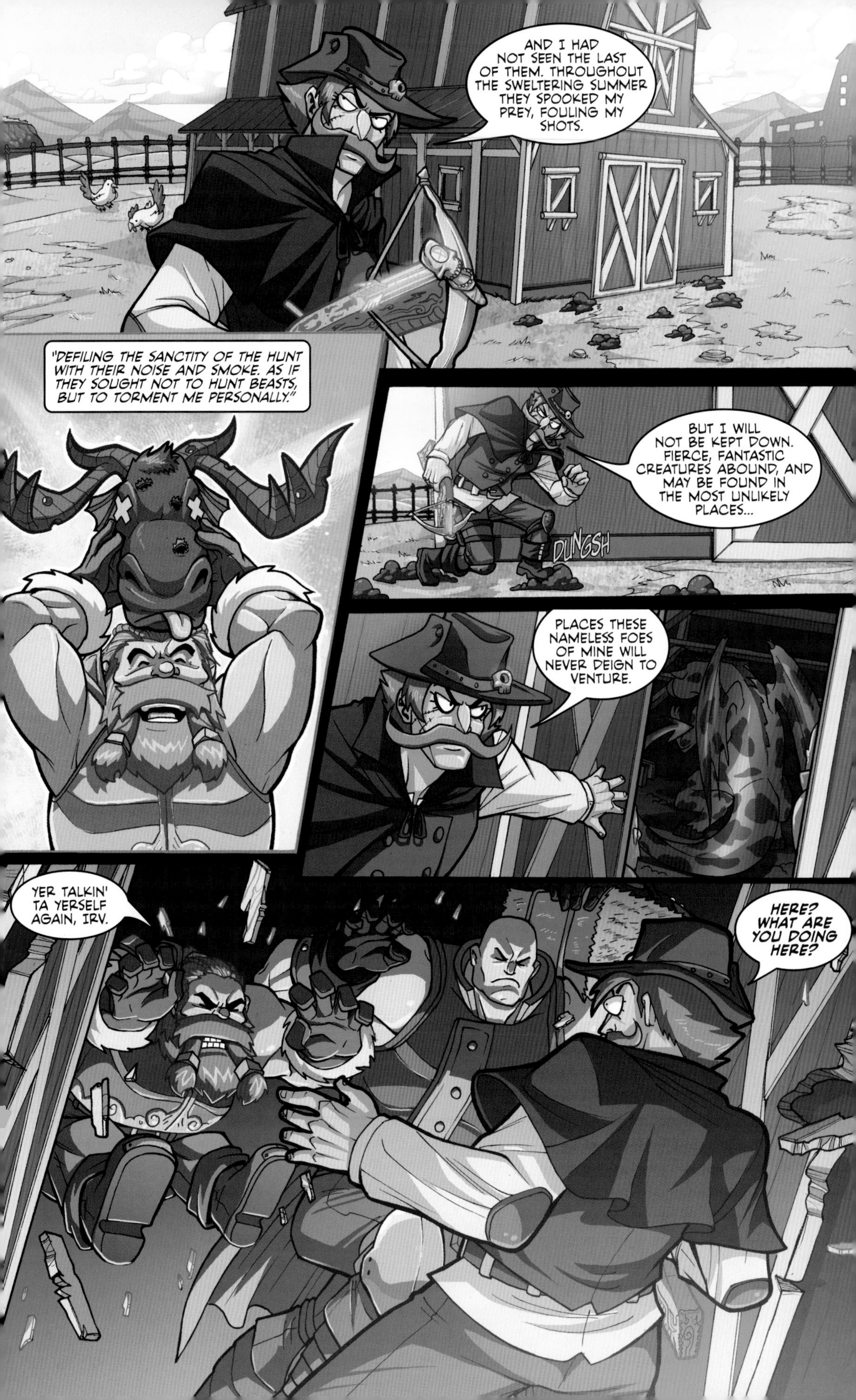
AND I HAD NOT SEEN THE LAST OF THEM. THROUGHOUT THE SWELTERING SUMMER THEY SPOOKED MY PREY, FOULING MY SHOTS.
"DEFILING THE SANCTITY OF THE HUNT WITH THEIR NOISE AND SMOKE. AS IF THEY SOUGHT NOT TO HUNT BEASTS, BUT TO TORMENT ME PERSONALLY."
BUT I WILL NOT BE KEPT DOWN. FIERCE, FANTASTIC CREATURES ABOUND, AND MAY BE FOUND IN THE MOST UNLIKELY PLACES...
DUNGSH
PLACES THESE NAMELESS FOES OF MINE WILL NEVER DEIGN TO VENTURE.
YER TALKIN' TA YERSELF AGAIN, IRV.
HERE? WHAT ARE YOU DOING HERE?

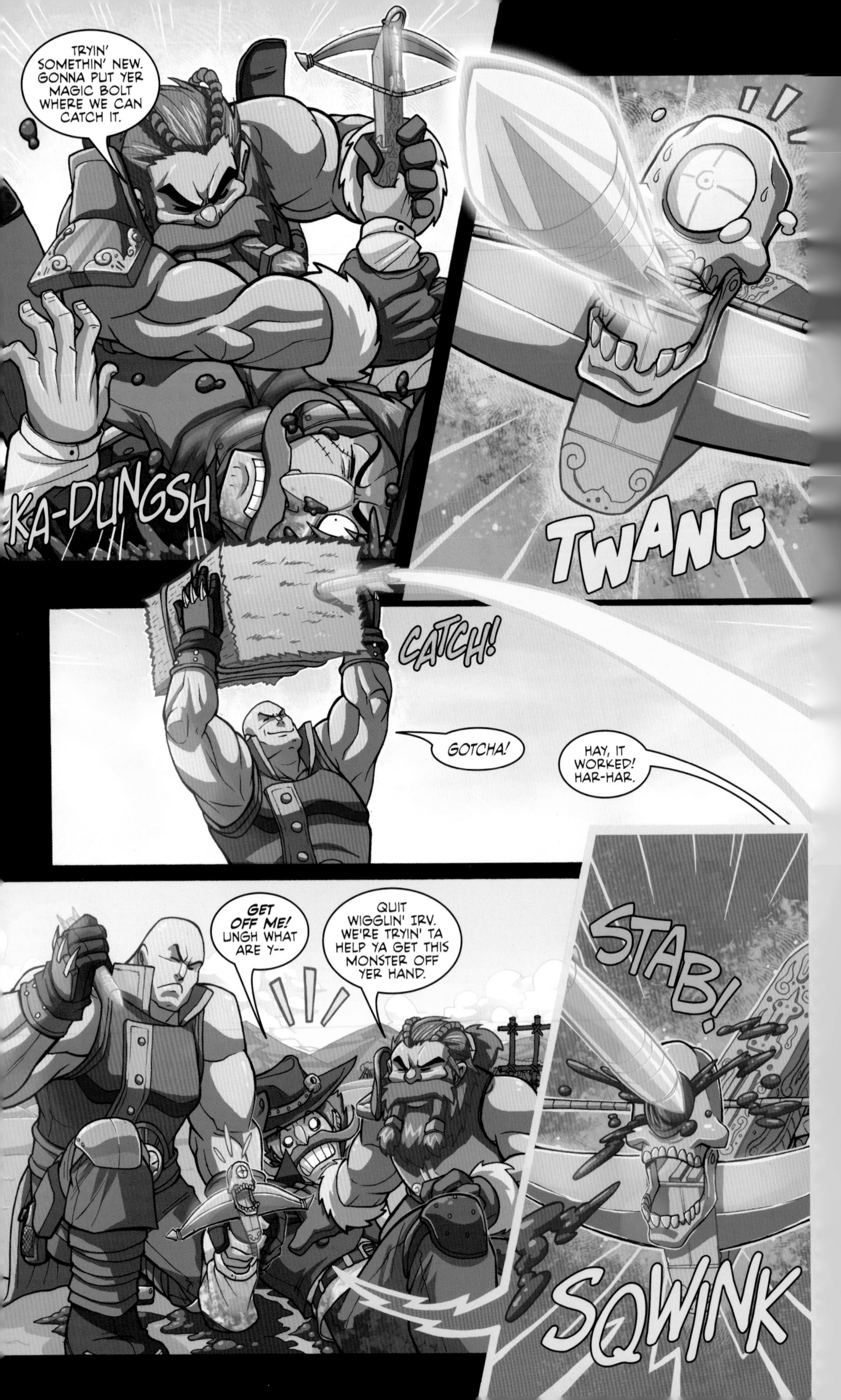

TRYIN' SOMETHIN' NEW. GONNA PUT YER MAGIC BOLT WHERE WE CAN CATCH IT.
KA-DUNGSH
TWANG
CATCH!
GOTCHA!
HAY, IT WORKED! HAR-HAR.
GET OFF ME! UNGH WHAT ARE Y--
QUIT WIGGLIN' IRV. WE'RE TRYIN' TA HELP YA GET THIS MONSTER OFF YER HAND.
STAB!
SQWINK

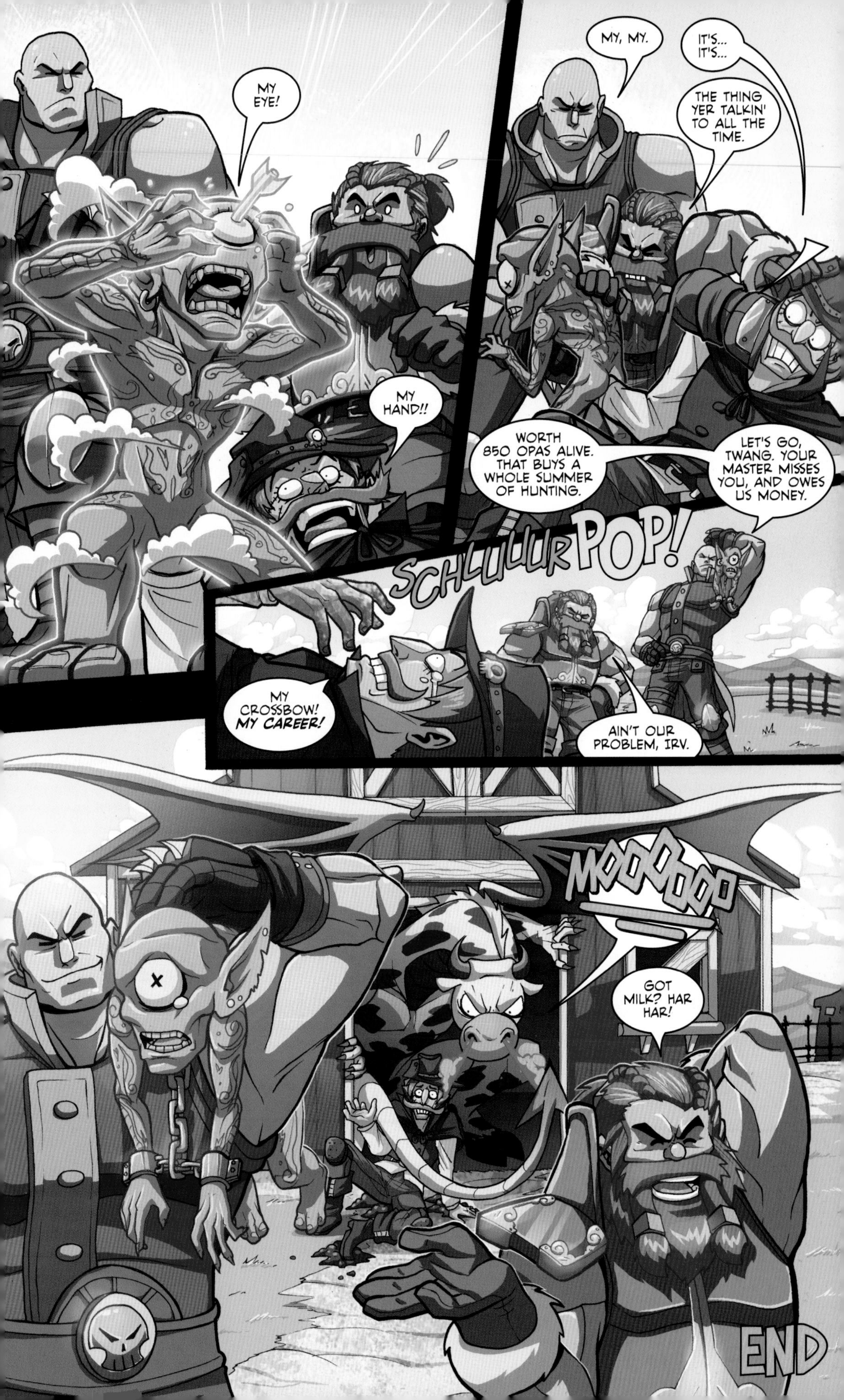
MY EYE!
MY HAND!!
MY, MY.
IT'S... IT'S...
THE THING YER TALKIN' TO ALL THE TIME.
WORTH 850 OPAS ALIVE. THAT BUYS A WHOLE SUMMER OF HUNTING.
LET'S GO, TWANG. YOUR MASTER MISSES YOU, AND OWES US MONEY.
SCHLUUUR POP!
MY CROSSBOW! MY CAREER!
AIN'T OUR PROBLEM, IRV.
MOOOooo
GOT MILK? HAR HAR!
END

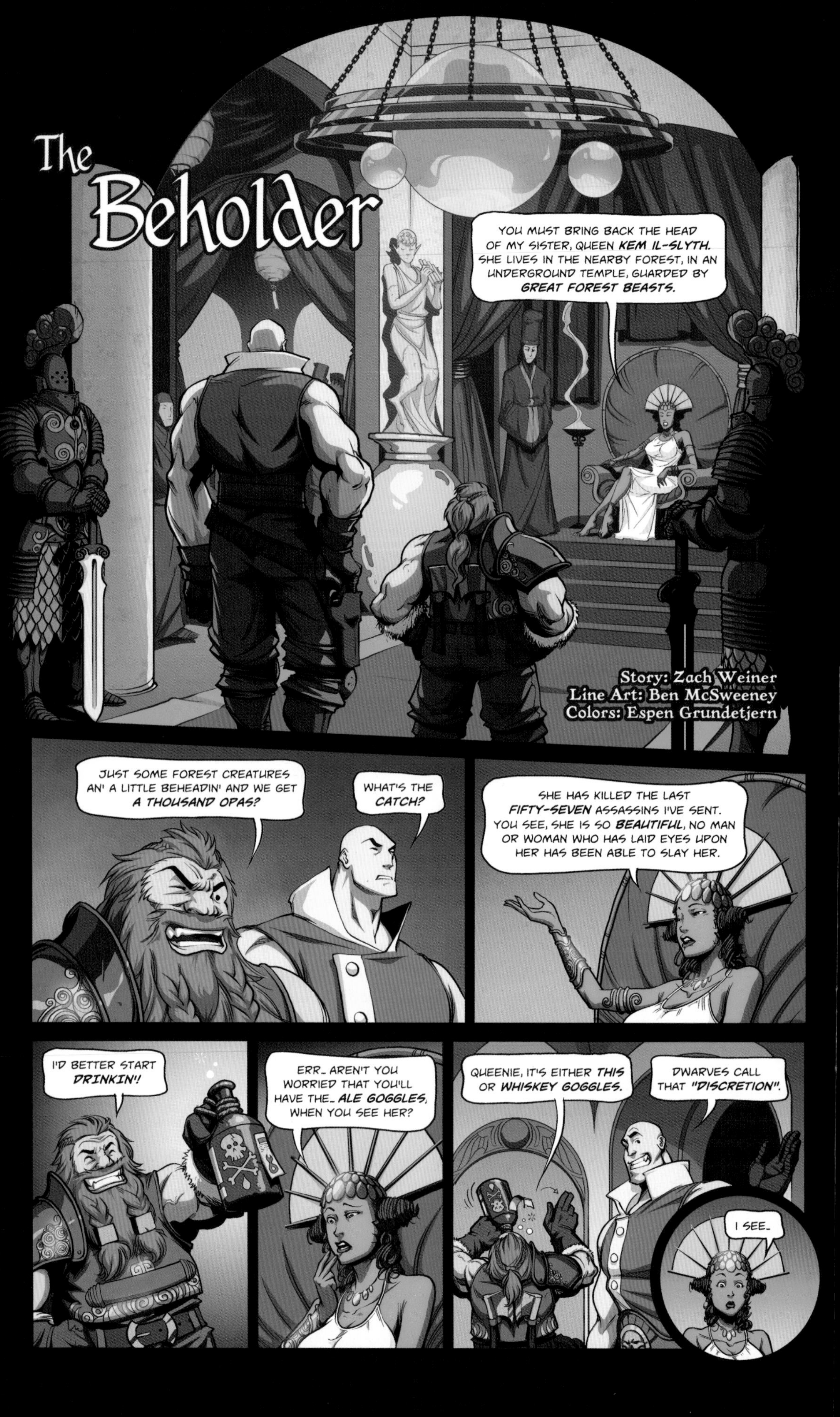
The Beholder
YOU MUST BRING BACK THE HEAD OF MY SISTER, QUEEN KEM IL-SLYTH. SHE LIVES IN THE NEARBY FOREST, IN AN UNDERGROUND TEMPLE, GUARDED BY GREAT FOREST BEASTS.
Story: Zach Weiner
Line Art: Ben McSweeney
Colors: Espen Grundetjern
JUST SOME FOREST CREATURES AN' A LITTLE BEHEADIN' AND WE GET A THOUSAND OPAS?
WHAT'S THE CATCH?
SHE HAS KILLED THE LAST FIFTY-SEVEN ASSASSINS I'VE SENT. YOU SEE, SHE IS SO BEAUTIFUL, NO MAN OR WOMAN WHO HAS LAID EYES UPON HER HAS BEEN ABLE TO SLAY HER.
I'D BETTER START DRINKIN'!
ERR.. AREN'T YOU WORRIED THAT YOU'LL HAVE THE.. ALE GOGGLES, WHEN YOU SEE HER?
QUEENIE, IT'S EITHER THIS OR WHISKEY GOGGLES.
DWARVES CALL THAT "DISCRETION".
I SEE..

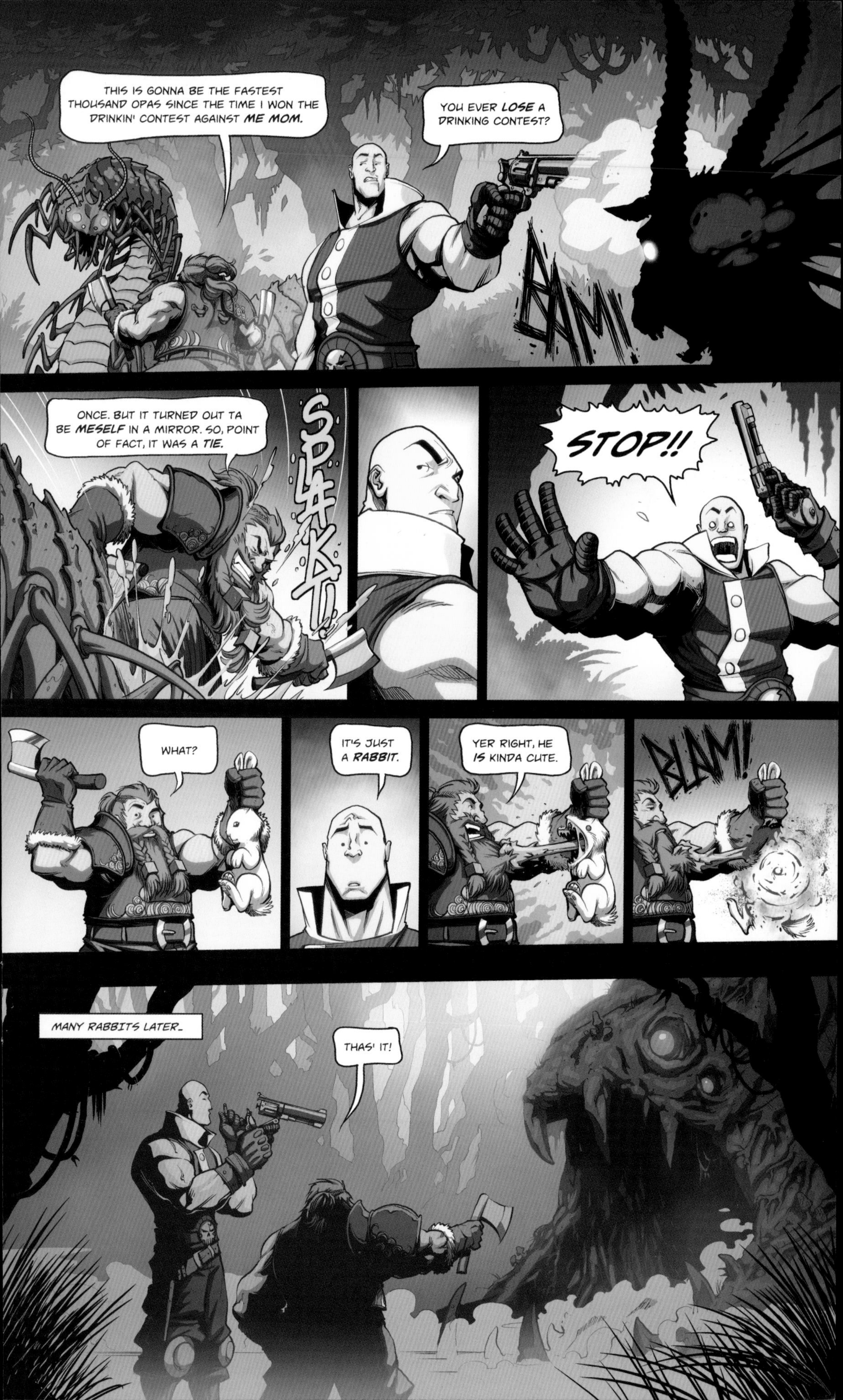
THIS IS GONNA BE THE FASTEST THOUSAND OPAS SINCE THE TIME I WON THE DRINKIN' CONTEST AGAINST ME MOM.
YOU EVER LOSE A DRINKING CONTEST?
BAM!
ONCE. BUT IT TURNED OUT TA BE MESELF IN A MIRROR. SO, POINT OF FACT, IT WAS A TIE.
SPLAK!!
STOP!!
WHAT?
IT'S JUST A RABBIT.
YER RIGHT, HE IS KINDA CUTE.
BLAM!
MANY RABBITS LATER...
THAS' IT!

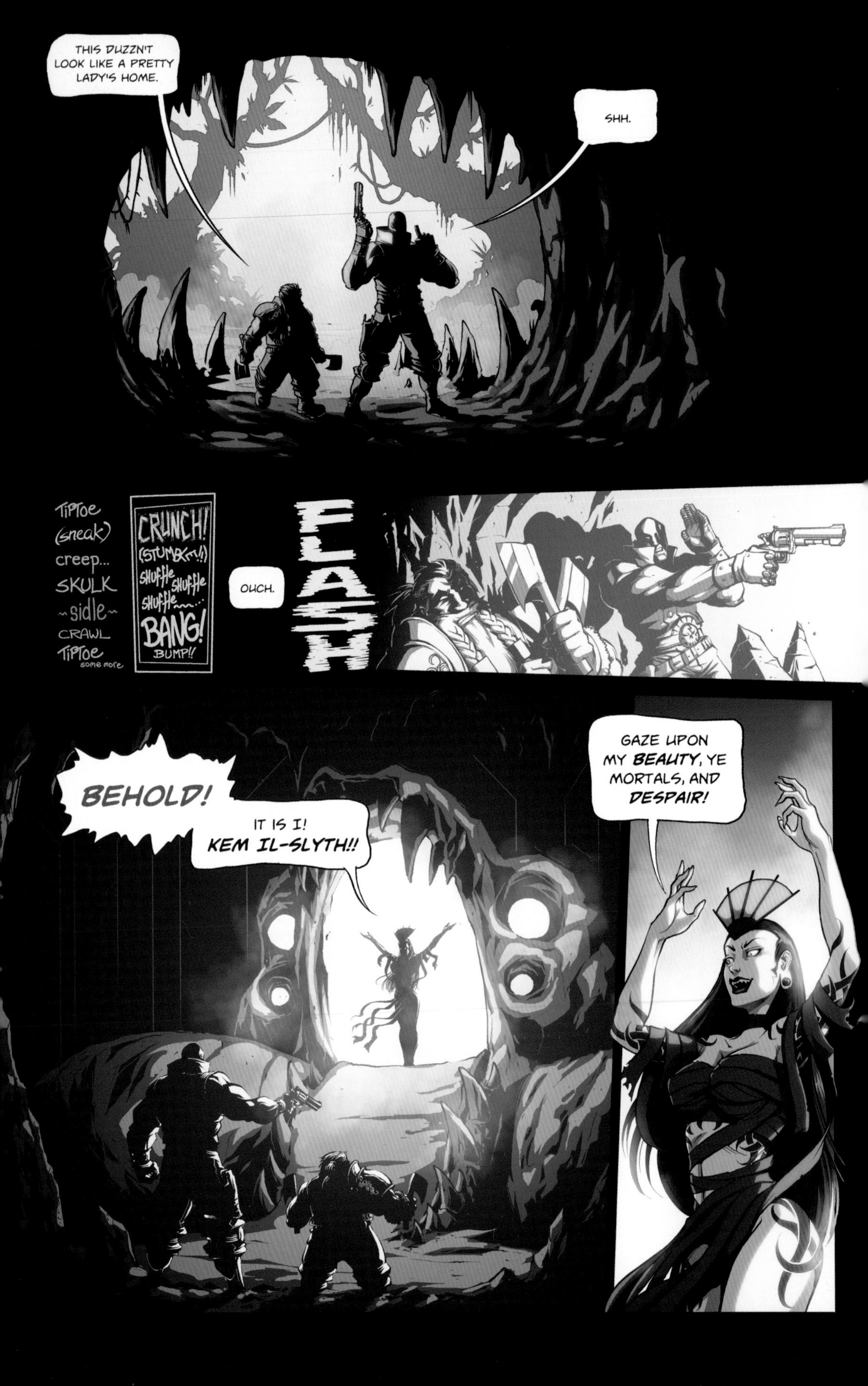

THIS DUZZN'T LOOK LIKE A PRETTY LADY'S HOME.
SHH.
TIPTOE
(sneak)
creep...
SKULK
~sidle~
CRAWL
TIPTOE some more
CRUNCH!
SHUFFLE SHUFFLE SHUFFLE......
BANG!
BUMP!!
OUCH.
FLASH
BEHOLD!
IT IS I! KEM IL-SLYTH!!
GAZE UPON MY BEAUTY, YE MORTALS, AND DESPAIR!

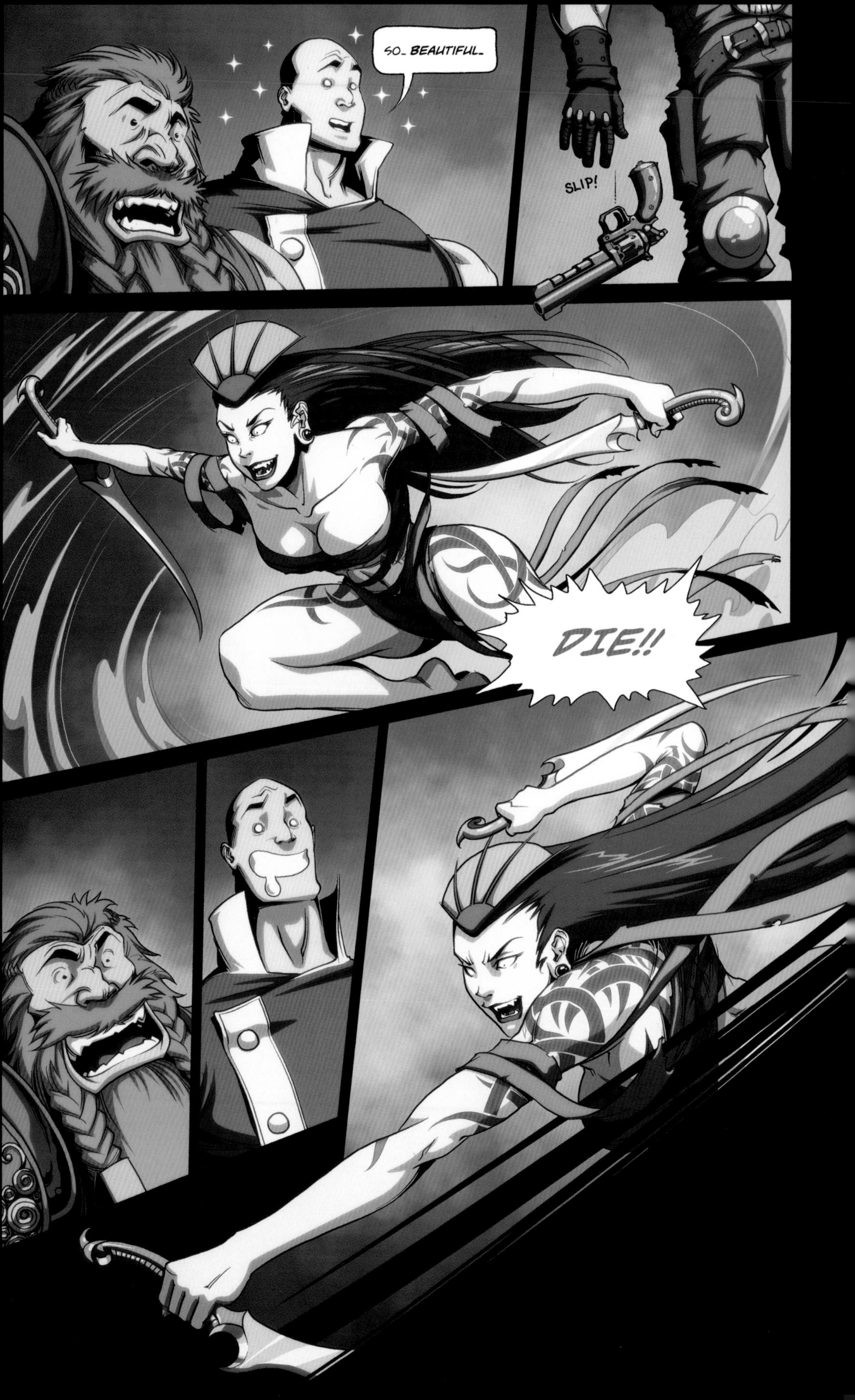
SO… BEAUTIFUL…
SLIP!
DIE!!

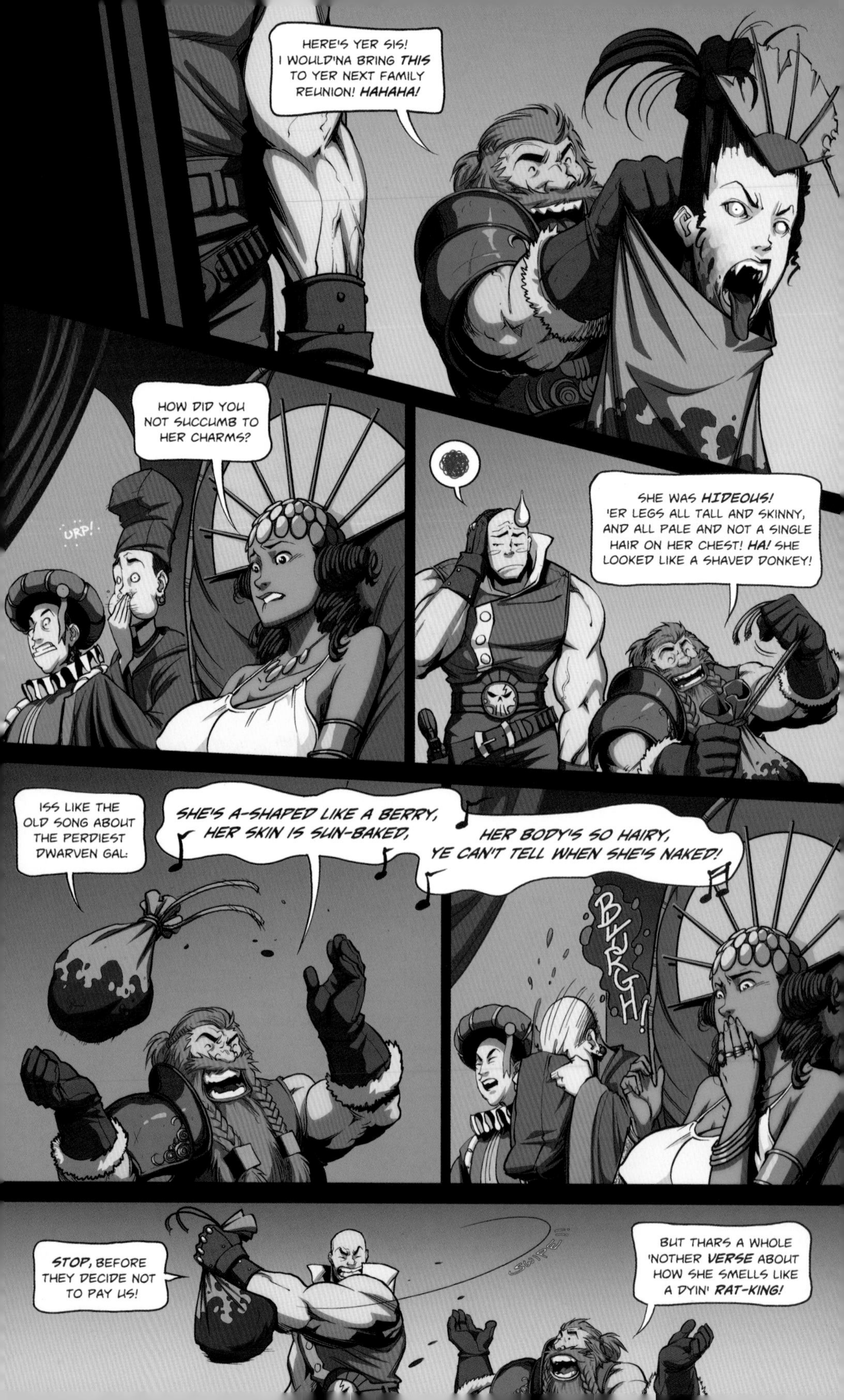
HERE'S YER SIS! I WOULD'NA BRING THIS TO YER NEXT FAMILY REUNION! HAHAHA!
HOW DID YOU NOT SUCCUMB TO HER CHARMS?
URP!
SHE WAS HIDEOUS! 'ER LEGS ALL TALL AND SKINNY, AND ALL PALE AND NOT A SINGLE HAIR ON HER CHEST! HA! SHE LOOKED LIKE A SHAVED DONKEY!
ISS LIKE THE OLD SONG ABOUT THE PERDIEST DWARVEN GAL:
SHE'S A-SHAPED LIKE A BERRY, HER SKIN IS SUN-BAKED,
HER BODY'S SO HAIRY, YE CAN'T TELL WHEN SHE'S NAKED!
BLURGH!
STOP, BEFORE THEY DECIDE NOT TO PAY US!
SWIPE!!
BUT THARS A WHOLE 'NOTHER VERSE ABOUT HOW SHE SMELLS LIKE A DYIN' RAT-KING!

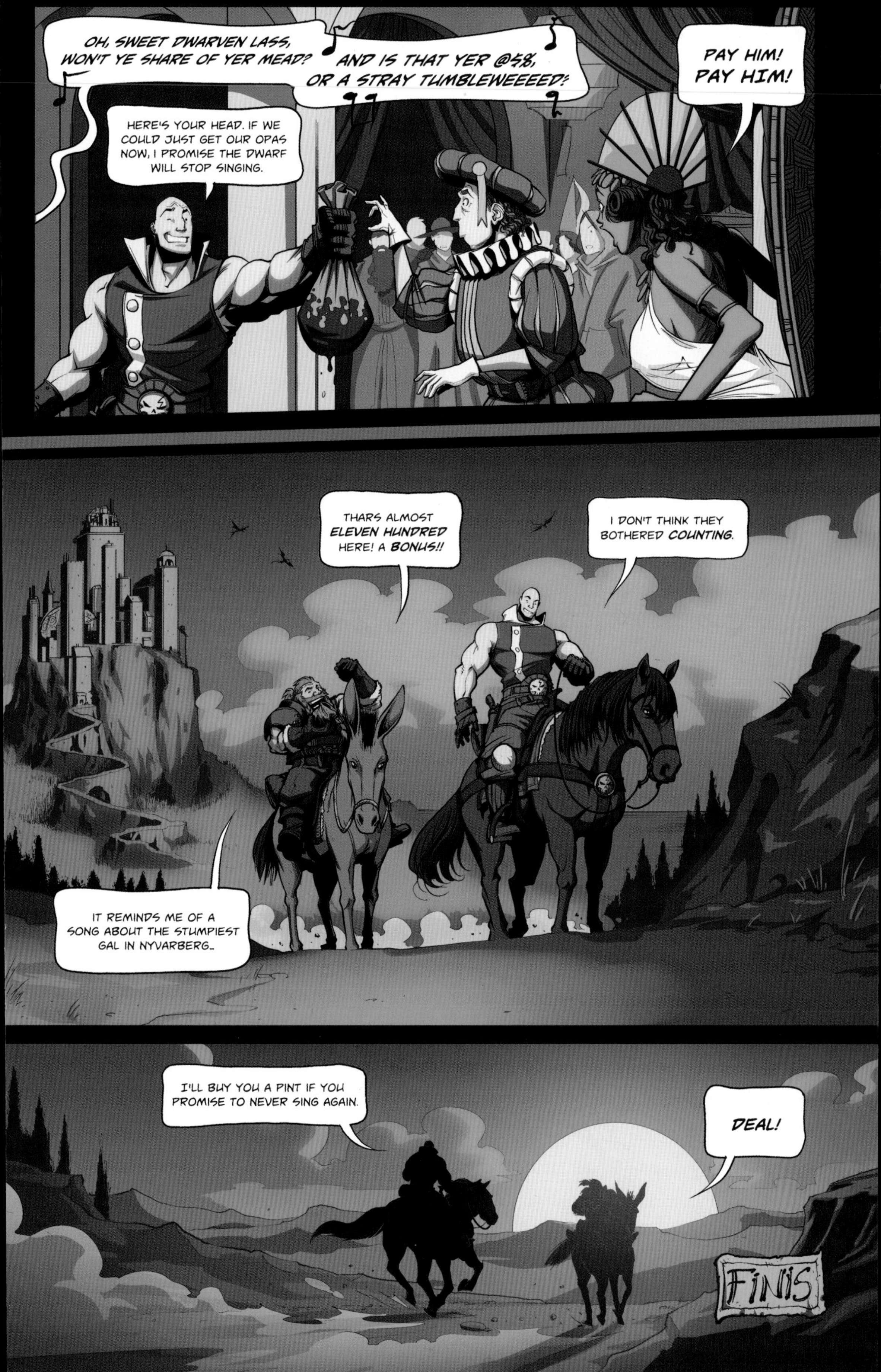
OH, SWEET DWARVEN LASS, WON'T YE SHARE OF YER MEAD?
AND IS THAT YER @$&, OR A STRAY TUMBLEWEEEEED?
HERE'S YOUR HEAD. IF WE COULD JUST GET OUR OPAS NOW, I PROMISE THE DWARF WILL STOP SINGING.
PAY HIM! PAY HIM!
THARS ALMOST ELEVEN HUNDRED HERE! A BONUS!!
I DON'T THINK THEY BOTHERED COUNTING.
IT REMINDS ME OF A SONG ABOUT THE STUMPIEST GAL IN NYVARBERG...
I'LL BUY YOU A PINT IF YOU PROMISE TO NEVER SING AGAIN.
DEAL!
FINIS

SKETCHES

I asked Edwin to sketch up a variety of pirate ladies to crew the Mermaid's Bottom and, as expected, he rocked it. I love the unique shapes and sizes. Even though some of these pirates only had cameos or were never named in the story, it was nice having such a fun and diverse cast of characters to call upon as I was writing.

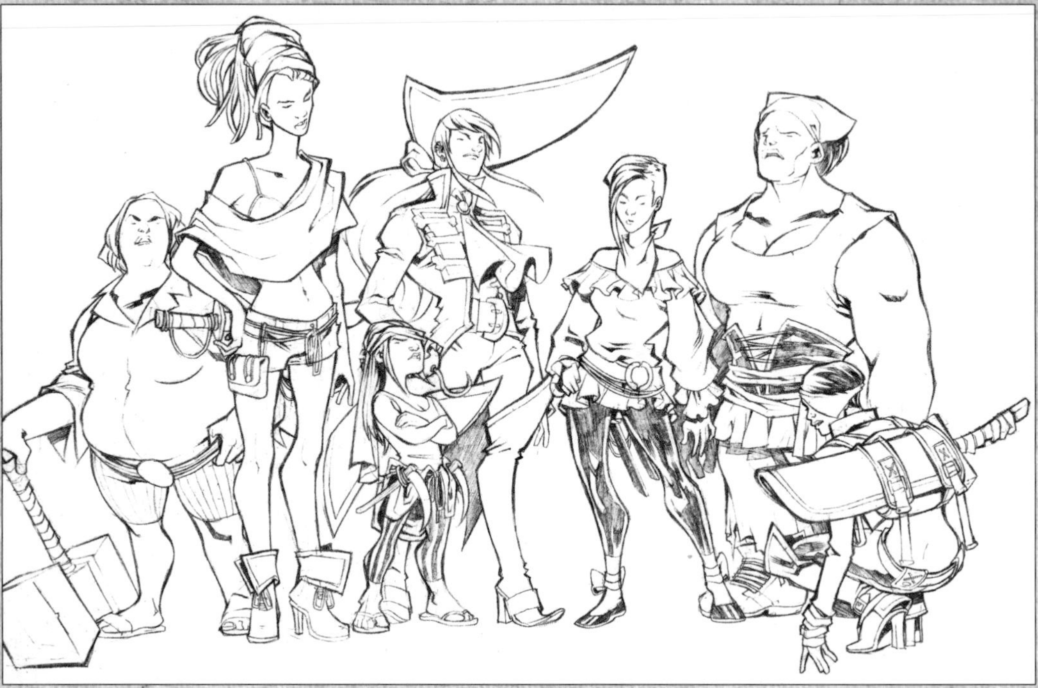

From Left to Right: Chonny the Cook, Lon' Legs, Madge the Mini, Cap'n Cherry Cutlass, Clipper Daile, Thurla, First Mate Drissle.

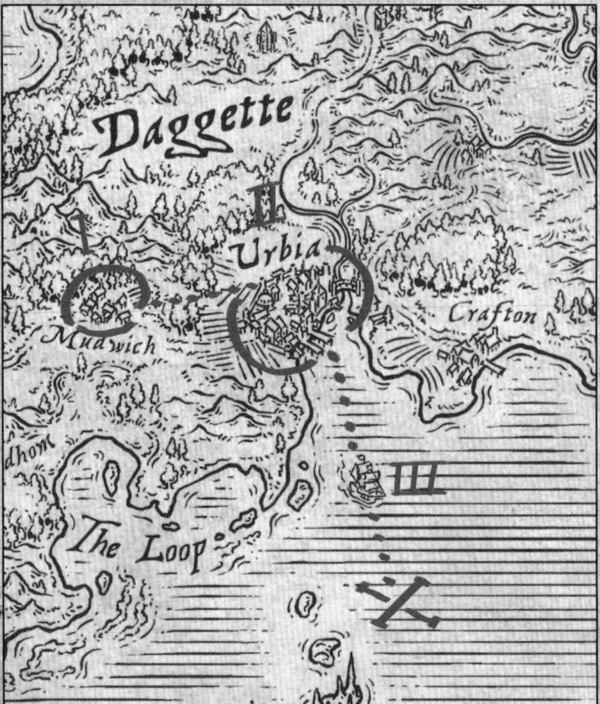
Daggette
I
II
Urbia
Mudwich
Crafton
III
The Loop

Cartographer Mike Schley put together an incredible Skullkickers World Map a few months back and we filled it to the brim with place names and puns aplenty.

To the left is a very small section of that grand map, showing the travel distance covered so far in Skullkickers Volume 1-3.

Needless to say, we have a lot of other great places to explore.

- ZUB